THE GHOSTS OF GUANTANAMO BAY

A MYSTERY NOVEL BY:
K.R. JONES

SEACAY, LLC
STAFFORD, VIRGINIA

The Ghosts of Guantanamo Bay
Copyright © 2006 by K.R. Jones

SEACAY PUBLISHING
Stafford, Virginia 22556

ISBN 13: 978-0-9790973-0-0
ISBN 10: 0-9790973-0-4

Edited by: Robin Smith
Cover design by: Jason Shipley
Interior design by: Bookcovers.com

<u>Dedication</u>

*To my friends and family for their unwavering support
and encouragement*

*And to
C.L.J
for believing in me*

Prologue

HAVANA, CUBA
December 1958

Jose Castagna and Enrique Garza were escorted to the north balcony where Roberto Mercado was waiting. His eyes didn't leave the sea as the two men took their places at the large wrought-iron table behind him. Mercado waited to hear the sound of the men's chairs scraping against the slate patio floor before he turned to face them. Motioning to his *mayordomo* for refreshments, he walked towards his seated guests. The Napoleon brandy swirled into the delicately thin-rimmed crystal glasses, as Mercado placed his hands on the back of his chair and leaned forward slightly towards the men. No pleasantries were exchanged; they were not friends, nor had they ever been. In the cutthroat world of waterfront casinos, the three men were competitors. Their uncompromising spirits and outsized egos made any cooperation between them unlikely and any amity between them impossible. Tonight could be different though; Mercado had invited them over to celebrate and commemorate a day in which they would, collectively, screw Castro. The rising dictator had made it clear that once in power he'd nationalize all property, and the casinos and everything inside them would become government property. Mercado's smug smile and bright eyes made it clear to Garza and Castagna that their host for the evening had come up with a solution to their problem.

"Gentleman, I welcome you," Mercado began. "For many years, we three have shared a common goal, to become the wealthiest man in all Cuba. But tonight, my *compañeros*, we share a different dream."

"Yes, to see that bastard Castro dead!" Garza interjected. The comment brought short-lived and unexpected smiles from all three men, and seemed to crack some of the iciness in the air.

"*¡Sí verdad!* Yes, clearly we all share a certain affinity for wanting him dead," Mercado said, once again taking control of the conversation, "but I think we all know that day will soon come. Castro might be able to grab Cuba, but he can not hold her. I expect his reign will be transitory at best. Obviously, he has seduced the poor and the idealistic, and for a time that may be enough, but soon the people will tire of him and his radical ideas, and there will be yet another change of leadership; more moderate heads will prevail. With any luck, the president who succeeds Castro will be cashing his paychecks in our casinos." The men clinked glasses, toasting Mercado's last statement. "Meanwhile, gentlemen, we need to find a place to hide our fortunes until that day arrives."

Castagna leaned back in his chair. "And how do you plan to do that? I have no doubt Castro and his thugs have already targeted the three of us. They know the money exists. There's no place we could hide it that they wouldn't think to look, and no one could risk being caught hiding it for us."

Garza nodded in agreement, adding, "Only off-island accounts are safe, but what banker could I trust? How do you really know were the money is going? Call me old fashioned, but I've never left Cuba and my money won't either."

Mercado looked confident. "Our money, gentlemen, will never leave Cuba, and the most beautiful part of it is that it will be hidden right under Castro's nose, yet he won't be able to touch it." Castagna and Garza glanced at each other—Mercado definitely had their attention. The two guests followed him with their eyes as he met his *mayordomo* halfway across the patio. Mercado was handed a map and he laid it out across the table for the two others to see. "There, my friends," Mercado said, pointing, "this is where we will hide our money."

Garza sat straight up. "But that's impossible! This must be a joke!"

"I assure you it's most possible," Mercado replied with assurance.

"Señor Mercado, I'm afraid I just lost patience with this game of yours," Castagna spoke slowly, with a hint of the sarcasm for which he was well known. "Guantánamo Bay is an American military installation, but I'm sure that's not a problem. We'll just hand over our money to those Gringos and ask them to watch it for us? ¡No! I don't think so. Thanks for the brandy, and I wish you both the best of luck, but if this is the best that you can come up with," Castagna smiled tactfully and stood up to leave, "then clearly my time is better spent elsewhere."

All smugness vanished from Mercado's face, and he was uncharacteristically diplomatic as he addressed Castagna. "Señor Castagna, please sit down. I think if you'll allow me to explain further, you'll appreciate the thoroughness of my proposal."

Garza, on the other hand, was not diplomatic at all, "Sit your enormous ass down Castagna. Let's hear what the man has to say." After a pause and without further comment, Castagna took his seat, and Mercado resumed.

"As we all know, America leases its base from our government, and has since 1903. According to the language of the contract between our two nations, Cuba cannot dissolve this agreement without consent from the Americans. That means that Castro will never be able to control that part of Cuba, no matter what he demands."

"Continue," Garza said, interested.

"If we hide our money on the base, we don't have to turn it over to Castro."

Castagna leaned heavily on the table with his arms folded. "Assuming we can even get the money that far into rebel-controlled territory, how do we get the money on the base without the Americans knowing it? Where do we hide it, and more importantly, how do we get it back off? I surely hope that you have thought this through."

"Indeed I have, I can assure you." Mercado sat down in his chair and leaned back to a comfortable position. "I know someone who works on the base; a Cuban man who owes me a rather large debt. He lives in Guantanamo City, just outside the Northeast Gate."

"What's the Northeast Gate?" Garza inquired.

"It's the border between the American territory and our sovereign soil. The Americans employ many Cubans to work as housekeepers, waiters and maintenance people. They commute to and from the base each day using this area as their main entrance to the installation."

"Ok, so somehow you'll arrange to get the money on the base, but, again, how do we get it off? What if the Americans terminate their contract and leave? What if Castro tries to invade and recapture the property? Have you thought through all of these variables?" Castagna questioned.

"Indeed," Mercado said seriously. For the next two hours, Mercado explained his plan in great detail. When he was done, the three men once again toasted; Mercado had won them over. Had someone seen them relaxed and smiling on the dimly lit balcony, it would have appeared as though Mercado, Garza and Castagna were old friends; no one would have suspected they hated each other as much as they collectively hated Castro.

"Well, gentlemen, if you'll excuse me for this evening, I have much to prepare," Mercado said with enthusiasm, but also with a hint of gravity. They all shook hands and Garza and Castagna were escorted to the door. Once they were gone, Mercado reached for the phone.

"It's for you," Lupe told her husband, Miguel Herrera.

"Who is it?" Miguel asked.

"It sounds like Señor Mercado. He didn't give his name."

Miguel took the phone from his wife and exchanged few words with the caller. When he put down the receiver, he called to his wife who was washing dishes. "I have to go out for a while, Lupe. Don't wait up for me."

Miguel walked about a mile along an unlit, rutted dirt road to his friend's home. Chico worked with him on the American Naval base, and Miguel was going to need his help. As he hiked, he recounted the advice his father had once given him: Never take a favor from a man who overvalues his own worth. But he had needed his cousin, Roberto Mercado, to make him the man he is today. Now Mercado demanded his benevolence be repaid without questions.

Chico was standing outside his home when Miguel came ambling up the pathway. The house was undersized, little more than a hovel, and many chickens were running wildly around Chico's feet. Miguel pushed them out of his way with the inside of his boot and approached his friend. At first, Chico ignored Miguel, and kept his hands busy with the feed for his fowl. Miguel sensed Chico wasn't pleased he'd stopped by—it was far too late for a social call. At this time of night, Miguel could only be there for one thing.

"So, you got the call tonight?" Chico said, continuing his chores.

Miguel hesitated for a moment and looked off in the direction of the road. "Yes. He called. It's a go. I'm sorry."

"When?" Chico put his feed bucket down and looked directly at Miguel.

"Three weeks," Miguel muttered.

Chico turned away from Miguel and started walking around the back of the house. He called back to Miguel with the hollow optimism of a defeated man, "Then I guess I'll see you in three weeks."

When Chico was out of sight, Miguel sank his hands deep into his pockets and kicked the feed bucket across the yard. He was completely disgusted with himself; it was bad enough he had to be Mercado's string-puppet, but having to bring Chico into this situation made Miguel feel sick inside. As he rambled down the same pothole-ridden street toward home, he tried to figure out a plan that wouldn't include Chico, but he couldn't.

Chico and Miguel had been friends since before grade school, and had always been inseparable. The men, now in their thirties, had even married sisters. A few years earlier, Chico's wife had become gravely ill. In an attempt to save his sister-in-law's life, Miguel had asked Mercado for his help. Mercado responded with the money necessary to obtain proper medical care, but despite his assistance, Chico's wife passed away. Even though Chico had never asked for Mercado's help, he'd accepted the money for his wife's sake. Because of that, he, too, now owed a debt to Mercado. Chico wasn't happy with the situation in which he was thrust, but knew he could either help Mercado or be killed by him. Chico chose to live.

The day they had been dreading came all too soon, and their stomachs were tight with anxiety. While standing in Chico's living room, they went over the plan time and time again so they wouldn't make any mistakes. Miguel looked at the clock on the wall in Chico's living room and let out a terrific sigh.

"What time is it?" asked Chico.

"Almost 5am. The sun will rise soon."

"We should get going now," Chico said, restlessly.

"Yes, but let's go over it one more time."

Chico sat down on his brown tweed couch and took a piece of paper from his coffee table. He picked up a pencil and began to jot notes as he spoke. "At 5:45am, we'll arrive at the Northeast Gate. Instead of walking through to the base, we're going to explain to the Marine guards that we need to drive your truck through because we're carrying building supplies." A thought hit him. "They might ask for papers. Don't we need a manifest or something like that?"

"Yes," said Miguel, "but it won't be the usual Marine guard. Mercado has arranged for one of his people to be there instead."

"That son of a bitch! How the hell does he do it?" Chico exclaimed. "That son of a bitch is everywhere!"

"It doesn't matter how, Chico. We just have to trust that Mercado has made things safe for us. Then, once we're inside, Mercado's contact will escort us to our destination and everything should be pretty normal from there on—just a regular work day."

The two men got into Miguel's truck and made their way southward down the winding, poorly paved road to the Northeast Gate. Miguel paid extra attention to his driving so as not to disturb his cargo, and Chico fidgeted with the door handle to help him ease his nerves. About a mile from the base perimeter, above the scrub and cactus covered ridgeline, the first of the American guard towers came into view through the grime-encrusted windshield. Both men took a deep breath.

The boundary of the naval base was an unimpressive barrier. Its eight-foot chain-link fence could have been scaled at any point, in spite of the three rows of barbwire running along the top. Inside the seventeen mile fence, however, it was a different story. As the political stability of Cuba degraded over the last few years, forty-five watchtowers sprung up inside the border. Well-armed U.S. Marines constantly manned each tower, and the fence-line road between them was traversed by frequent Marine patrols. The intent was obviously to intimidate the hell out of anyone who sought entrance into the base—and it worked.

The road Chico and Miguel were following continued due south until it ran perpendicularly into the unbroken fence-line, at which point it split. The road to the right went westward for about four miles to the port facility at Boquerón, and to the left it paralleled the fence for about half a mile until reaching the northeast corner of the base. As Miguel's truck bounced its way south, the line of guard towers extended beyond the horizon to their right and disappeared behind a ridge to their left. When they took the turn towards the Northeast Gate, the fence was so close Chico could have stuck his hand through the open window and touched it.

The morning sun hung low in the southeast and cast long morning shadows of the taller towers across the road. Even though the morning was still cool, crossing the shadows and seeing the silhouettes of the towers caused both men to sweat. Coming the other way on the dirt road just inside the fence, they passed a short convoy of green two and a half ton trucks led by a white pickup stamped: Property of the US Marine Corps. The convoy paid no attention to the ramshackle three ton truck on the Cuban side, but for some reason, Miguel suddenly felt parched. He didn't know if his dry mouth was due to nerves or the clouds of fine coral dust drifting across his path from the convoy's wake; perhaps it was a little of both.

The gate itself consisted of a simple arrangement of chain-link fencing and metal pipes that divided the entrance into pedestrian and vehicular gates. Between the two was a white masonry guard shack, and above was an arching metal sign: U.S. NAVAL BASE, Guantanamo Bay, Cuba. The large American flag that flew patriotically above the gate, as well as several weapon-carrying Marines, accented this uncomplicated layout.

When Chico and Miguel arrived, they noticed several Cuban commuters already making their way through the metal turnstiles; nothing seemed out of place or unusual. They drove slowly up to the gate, guided by a Marine guard who was waving them forward. He instructed them to stop, and made his way to the driver's side window.

"Identification please," said the Marine. The two men hustled to hand him their pink laminated base IDs. The Marine looked closely at the first ID then compared the photo to Miguel. He moved around the truck to get a better look at Chico. "The two of you aren't authorized to commute with the use of a vehicle. You'll need to park your truck and walk on the base like the others."

"But, sir," Miguel began in passable English, "we were told by our supervisor to bring these supplies on base today. Surely you must have been notified."

"No, sir. We were not," the Marine guard said with finality. "Now, you'll park your truck and walk onto base. Understood?"

Miguel became desperate. "Sir, please look at my papers again. Surely you must've been told I'm coming today with these *special supplies.*"

"Get out of the vehicle!" the Marine ordered flatly. It was at this moment Chico and Miguel realized Mercado must have set them up. "Now, step away from the vehicle." The two men did as they were told and watched helplessly as the Marine walked to the back of the truck to look inside at their cargo. Miguel closed his eyes and prayed silently.

"You! Come unlock your truck!" Miguel fumbled with the keys as he made his way to the Marine. He was nauseous and his vision was beginning to blur; he knew this was his end. As he put the key into the lock, another voice came out of the shadows.

"As you were, Loring. I'll take it from here."

The lance corporal looked confused. "Good morning, Gunny. I was just about—"

"I said I'll take over from here," the gunny continued, friendly but firmly.

"Yes, Gunny. These two Cubans were trying to—"

"I'm well aware of who these men are and of what they're trying to do." Once again the older Marine cut off the younger before he could finish his sentence; this time he was less friendly.

The change in tone did not go unnoticed by the lance corporal. "Aye aye, Gunnery Sergeant," he said crisply and walked away.

The older Marine handed Miguel and Chico their identification and instructed them to follow his Jeep on base. The two men smiled as they drove through the gate; they couldn't believe they'd actually pulled it off. With each mile they drove, their sense of security returned and they began to taste their freedom from Mercado.

The sun had risen well above the horizon and beautifully illuminated the eastern slope of John Paul Jones Hill, which dominated the view ahead of them. As they made their way across base, which occupied over forty-five square miles, they passed numerous little roads leading off to various facilities, training areas and living quarters throughout the military installation. Their guide was leading Miguel and Chico to an area they'd never been before. In fact, they had to pass through several unguarded, yet restricted, areas to arrive at their final destination. When the Jeep stopped, Miguel pulled his truck along side and got out. The Marine and Chico followed his lead.

"Where would you like us to store everything?" Miguel asked the gunnery sergeant.

"Don't worry about that. I'll take care of everything from here," he replied confidently. "You two had better get going before someone notices you're missing."

Chico nodded his head, "Yeah, well, thanks to you we're not missing. We're just late. That was close!" The two friends rewarded their accomplishment with a handshake and began to walk down the road toward mainside.

"No gentlemen, I believe the word I used was *missing*." Seconds later, both men lay dead, each with a gunshot wound to the chest.

The Marine calmly climbed into his Jeep, but sped to the Northeast Gate; he was running terribly late. As he approached the gate, he saw the young lance corporal walking away from his post. He slowed down and came to a stop next to him.

"Yes, Gunny?"

"I need your help on an important matter. Did you just get off duty?" he asked with a sense of urgency and authority.

"Yes, Gunny, about five minutes ago. What do you need me to do?"

"I'll explain when we get there. There's been a terrible accident. Get in." The two men rode the same route the Jeep had traversed a half hour earlier.

Moments before the Jeep reached the place where the men had driven their truck, the gunny inquired of the younger Marine, "Hey, devil dog, did you remember to log-in that blue truck with the two Cubans?"

"N-no, Gunny," the young man stammered. "When you said that 'you had it' I assumed that *you* would."

"Absolutely right," the gunny replied. "Good job."

It was at this point the Jeep's progress was halted by the two bodies lying on the road in a pool of blood.

"Jesus Christ, Gunny! What the hell happened?" The lance corporal was sickened by the sight before him. The gunnery sergeant did not respond as his companion jumped out of the Jeep and raced to the two men. "Oh my God! I think they're dead, Gunny! Here, help me carry this one," he pleaded as he took hold of Chico. "Let's get them to the hospital!"

The other Marine remained seated, completely stoic.

"For Christ Sake, Gunny! Help me!" There was no response. The lance corporal looked at the senior Marine with utter disbelief and stood to engage him. Before he could make the first step, a pistol shot rang out for a third time, the bullet striking the young Marine in the face. The gunny looked around at the carnage he'd created, and stepped over the lance corporal's lifeless body on his way to the Cuban's truck. With the keys he pried from Miguel's dead hand, he opened the lock which protected the cargo. When the gunny swung the back doors open, his eyes grew wide, his jaw hung open. He wasn't as smart as he thought he was.

T here's something incredible about the way the sun sets over Guantanamo Bay. Even though I transferred back to the States some time ago, I often think back to those evenings when I was lucky enough to witness that orange and amethyst sky fuse with the Caribbean Sea. In fact, my wife Audrey and I often visited a place called Phillips Park after dinner because of its unobstructed, one-hundred-and-eighty-degree view of it all. Situated on a rocky cliff, at the mouth of the bay, Phillips Park was also the perfect place to relax after a hard day's work. The rhythmic waves lapping against the rocks and the drone of the naval aircraft flying to and from the Leeward side of base was soothing; it was no wonder I went there on my last day on the island. That time, I not only listened, but watched as a plane flew overhead and touched down on the runway. It made me think back to the day Audrey and I first arrived in Guantanamo Bay; it was July, 1997.

Our plane didn't park at a jetway because the airport wasn't much more than a large hangar and a single runway. When we stepped out onto the mobile stairway, we were struck by a wall of heat that rolled over us. Having grown up in New England, we were unaccustomed to such a climate and beads of sweat formed on our faces. Though there was no relief to be found on the acres of hot asphalt, an almost constant breeze across the island made life on the rest of the base bearable. By the way, I never thought of Cuba as an island until I lived there. I always figured that a country that's as long as the distance from New York is to Florida couldn't be thought of that way. What was even more confusing to me was when I heard others on the base refer to Guantanamo Bay as its own island, because nobody except patrolling Marines could drive more than seven miles in any direction. Talk about Rock fever!

We spent the day before our flight to Cuba at the Norfolk Naval Air Station in Virginia, and we didn't sleep a wink that night. Even though the Marine Corps had moved us five times before, the transfer to Guantanamo Bay felt different. Everything about the place seemed mysterious; we'd never met anyone who had lived there before nor could we find any substantive information about it on the internet. The military website offered us the basic facts, but there were hardly any pictures, so we had to imagine what the beaches and the other parts of the base looked like. Maybe it was that voyage into the unknown that first gave Audrey and me that strange feeling: we instinctively knew that once we boarded that plane, our lives would never be the same again.

Surprisingly, that feeling was reinforced the next day while we were on a short layover at an air station in Florida. We had disembarked to stretch our legs while additional cargo and passengers were manifested for the flight, when a well-dressed woman in her fifties approached my wife in the terminal.

"So you're moving to Guantanamo Bay, are you?" she said smugly.

Audrey was taken by surprise; she didn't know why she'd been singled out from the other military wives for such a comment. "Yes, as a matter of fact we are."

"Do you have any children? I didn't see any when I saw you in Norfolk, so I assume not."

"No, my husband and I don't have any children yet."

"You'll like it there. It gets hot in the summer, but at least we have a lovely breeze on most days."

Audrey was too tired to play games with the woman and decided to cut to the chase. "Excuse me, but do I know you? Have we met?"

"No," the woman snapped back. "You don't know me, but since I already know everyone in Guantanamo Bay, you had to be new. It's my business, after all, to know who's on my husband's island."

I certainly didn't have any questions about who she was after that. I had no idea what her name was then, but it was pretty clear that Mimsey Pickard was the wife of the base commanding officer. In my six years in the military, I'd never seen a woman try to wear her husband's rank like that. Unfortunately, it would be quite common at our new duty station.

As we made our way down the stairs to the blistering tarmac, I found Major Matthew Conway, the Marine I was going to replace, waiting for us. At five foot ten, he was about my height, with reddish brown hair and green eyes, and a build stockier than it was athletic.

"Major Conway?" I asked, reading his name off his uniform.

"Yes. I assume you're Captain Adam Claiborne. It's nice to finally put a face to the voice."

"It's good to meet you too, sir. I'd like for you to meet my wife, Audrey."

Major Conway held out his hand to meet hers. "Although your husband described you as a tall, brown-eyed brunette, his description didn't do you justice."

Audrey immediately fluffed her hair. "Thank you for saying that, but I'm sure I look terrible after five hours of traveling."

After a few more pleasantries, he escorted us to a security-checkpoint just outside the entrance to the airport. When we reached the head of the line, we were greeted by two naval security guards; one checked our orders while the other searched our bags for drugs. We were soon given the go-ahead and Major Conway led us through a set of glass doors and into some well-deserved air conditioning.

The pink terminal building housed a security office, waiting area, ticket counter, restrooms and a restaurant for snacks and sandwiches called the Gitmo Grill. Nobody who lives there calls the base Guantanamo Bay; everyone insists on using its nickname, Gitmo. On the day we arrived, the airport was in absolute shambles due to ongoing renovations. The floor was torn up and numerous ceiling tiles were stained or missing. It looked like an airport one would expect to find in a Third World nation. Audrey actually had the gumption to ask Major Conway where the chickens were. Surprisingly, Major Conway retorted, "Just wait."

Conway wasn't a bad guy at all, but when I first met him, he lacked a little in the personality department and a lot in the hospitality department. Instead of securing a military vehicle to move us and our luggage to the Ferry Landing, he showed up in his own two-seater pickup that had seen better years. Audrey jumped in front with Conway, and I ended up sitting in the scorching metal bed of the truck. You have no idea how thankful I was that the trip to the Ferry Landing took only a few minutes. While we waited for the large gray ferry to carry us across the bay from the Leeward to the Windward side of base, Conway pointed out a seventies era F-4 Phantom fighter plane mounted near the dock. He joked that it was the only air defense left on base.

In a matter of ten minutes or so, the ferry pulled into the pier to first unload passengers and vehicles from Windward, before allowing Leeward passengers to board. Audrey was confused by the whole windward and leeward thing, so I explained it to her this way: Guantanamo Bay is located on the southeastern coast of Cuba. The base itself is almost a rectangle, nine miles by seven miles, with the bottom side running along the Caribbean coastline. The rectangular land area is completely split into two sections by a large bay, separating the base into eastern and western sides. At that latitude, the wind generally comes from the east. Since the naval expression for the side from where the wind comes is called *windward,* so was the eastern side of the base. Leeward basically means the direction to which the wind is blowing. Most of the living areas and base functions were on Windward, while the airport and an abandoned air station were located on Leeward. The ferry was the only thing connecting the two sides.

As Conway drove us aboard for our twenty-minute ride across the bay, Audrey began to glean some interesting tidbits from Major Conway.

"So when do you leave for the States, Matthew?"

"On Friday. I needed a couple of days to review the turn-over file with your husband."

"Are you excited to leave? I bet after two years on this little base, you must be ready to go."

Conway thought about his answer before he spoke. "To tell you the truth, that's a difficult question to answer. Gitmo's been the best tour of duty that I've ever had, but it's also been the worst."

"What do you mean? How could it be both?"

"Well, it was great because I had lots of time with my family. I also got to enjoy the beaches and diving, and we saved a lot of money here."

"So then what made it so bad?"

"It's not what, but who. Colonel Vandermeed, the Marine CO before the one we have now, is the reason I have bad feelings about this place. That asshole arrived in Gitmo just before I did, and what's weird is that we really hit it off. Everyone seemed to like him at first, but after a few months, Vandermeed became more and more irrational and sometimes, well, he acted like he was totally confused. He barked out orders that made no sense, and treated the men under him like crap. He worked all of us so damn hard doing bullshit work, and cared nothing about the morale of our families. If that wasn't bad enough, Vandermeed requested to see me—and get this—in full dress blues, which everyone knows is completely unheard of in any circumstance."

The more Conway talked the more agitated he became. I knew he had to have been really shaken up to use profanity in front of my wife. As he continued his story, I began to feel his humiliation.

"So there I was, dressed up for him like a performing street monkey—and God only knows for what reason—when one of the enlisted Marines—*an enlisted Marine*—tells me to sit on a little red bench outside the prick's office. After seven damn hours of waiting, Vandermeed left for the day without even acknowledging I was ever there."

"But why would he have done that?" I had to ask.

"How the hell should I know? Maybe because he knew he could. Look, the new CO, Colonel Ranagan, isn't perfect, but he's much better than that ass that just left. You have no idea how lucky you are."

"But what would make him change so much?" Audrey asked.

"It beats the shit out of me. I'm done trying to figure that man out."

My head was still swimming from Conway's story when we docked at the Windward Ferry Landing, which was actually just a parking lot, with cliffs on one side and an aqua desalinization plant on the other. The plant, which provided drinking water to the base, was constructed in the early sixties when Castro ordered that the base's water supply be turned off. Until the plant's completion, water had to be shipped in to the base residents by large tankers. Oddly enough, the Ferry Landing, or Fisherman's Point, was not only our disembarkation point, as Conway pointed out, but it was also the place where Christopher Columbus first set foot on the island on April 30, 1494. Looking for gold and fresh water, and finding neither, he left Puerto Grande, as he called it, the next morning. Conway went on to tell us that Guantanamo Bay later became a hide-out for murderous pirates who wished to target merchant ships sailing the body of water between Cuba and the island of Haiti, known as the Windward Passage. However, during the Spanish-American war in 1898, the United States gained control of the region; and in 1903, President Roosevelt signed the initial lease agreement with Cuba. By the way, Conway told me to remember that story because VIPs often visited Gitmo, and when they did, Colonel Ranagan made sure they were kept entertained by the base's fascinating history. Marine officers usually served as their tour guides.

Once we drove off the vessel, Major Conway gave us a tour of the base as we headed to our new home. Our trip took us past an abandoned outdoor movie theatre, run down housing developments and once-upon-a-time charming administrative buildings slated for demolition. There was little color in the landscape; once in a while I'd see a patch of green grass, but mostly everything we saw was brown. At this point, I felt far removed from the tropical paradise Audrey and I'd seen in the base brochures.

"Why is everything so yucky looking?" Audrey asked Conway.

"Because it never rains here. Everything is basically dead."

"But Cuba's supposed to be a lush island. I don't get it," she replied.

"Well, you see, Gitmo is located on the side of the mountain range that doesn't get much rain. Now, if you want to see green, you need to go to the Cuban side, 'cause this is pretty much as good as it gets. Of course, around September, it'll rain more and things will green up for a while, but don't get used to it. The base CO, Captain Pickard, won't allow us to water our lawns to keep them green."

"Well, if he's a captain like my husband, maybe Adam can talk to him about this watering policy."

"Uh, no. Captain Pickard is a Navy captain. That's the same as a Marine colonel. Besides that, Captain Pickard is a jerk. He and his wife Mimsey run this place like absolute tyrants."

"That bad?"

"Well, not exactly—much, much worse!"

"Seriously Matthew, what are they like?"

"Well, I'll start with what I've already said. Captain Pickard is a total dick and his wife is a nosey broad. They walk...no! They promenade around this place like it's their own personal kingdom. Mimsey's into everyone's business and Charlie's trying to kiss the ass of some frickin' bureaucrat in DC because he's been shutting half this base down ever since he got here. He outlawed fireworks, got rid of the horse stables, closed down two restaurants and two swimming pools. Look, it's bad enough that we're all stuck here with hardly anything fun to do for two or three years, but to trash what little we do have is just wrong!"

"Don't hold it in Matthew. Tell us how you really feel," Audrey joked.

Within five minutes, we came to the heart of the base. This area included a working movie theatre, gas station, furniture store, thrift store, base exchange, commissary, and of course, the great American embassy, McDonald's. Conway said that Pickard actually tried to close McDonald's and nearly caused a riot. The Gitmo golden arches was a unique establishment; it was the only one of its kind that would run out of hamburgers and substitute them with unique food items: McBeans and rice, McChicken and rice or the ever popular McSlice of pizza.

Just past the main base area stood an eight-story turquoise building on the left side of the road, overlooking the bay. Since it resembled a hotel, I figured it was the Bachelor Officer Quarters. While I was correct in my thinking, Conway told me with the downsizing of the base, non-commissioned officers (gunnery sergeants and above) were allowed to live there too. I immediately thought Pickard had made the wrong decision;

officers and enlistees living together meant problems, especially in a place the size of Gitmo.

Only a third of a mile further down Sherman Avenue, the only street on the base named for a chief of naval operations, was the place Audrey and I would call home for two years. The road was called Huntington Point, named after a Marine commander who participated in the capture of Guantanamo Bay from the Spanish in 1898, but everyone referred to it as Marine housing. Our new home was the first one on the right. It was a one-level, gray house, with thirty-two picture windows, twelve foot ceilings and a living room you could play basketball in. There were two guest bedrooms, and an oversized master bedroom on the side of the house facing the street. The kitchen and enormous living room faced the fenced backyard, which was filled with banana trees. We could see very little of the bay, but we had an excellent view of my new office building at the Ground Defense/Security Force headquarters, which was known as the White House. It wasn't named for its grand architecture, but rather for the color of its exterior.

A quaint aspect of our home was the unattached garage that, in years past, housed Cuban servants in the upstairs portion. It was a two-story white structure, with orange-clay tile roofing, desperately in need of repair. When I voiced my concern about putting my car in something so unstable, Conway told me the garages had actually been condemned years ago.

"The funny thing here," Conway said, "is that the one frickin' set of structures on this base that are actually a hazard to base residents, aren't the ones Pickard is tearing down!"

"They're charming though," Audrey said with a smile. "They really add a sense of history to the base, and their Spanish architecture makes living in Cuba seem more, I don't know, authentic."

"I'm not really sure what the story is," Conway added. "I think the garages were built sometime in the fifties, but then Hurricane Flora hit the base in 1963, and that's when they started to really deteriorate. I've heard they were actually condemned in 1984, but have yet to be torn down."

"Well, I like them!" she returned. "And I'll enjoy them until they do get torn down. I really think they add to the ambience of the base."

As I reached into the back of Conway's truck, he asked me which bag my Alpha's were in. I knew right away where he was headed with that question. "No way, sir! You can't be serious! I'm not due to check in for another two days!" I was tired, sweaty and hungry. The last thing I wanted to do was put a uniform on—especially that one. It was very hot and besides, it had about a dozen accoutrements that I'd have to measure and rig.

"Colonel Ranagan wants to meet everyone when they first arrive. It's his order, not mine. Sorry."

With great reluctance, I peeled off my traveling clothes and put on my uniform to meet with the Marine CO. I didn't have a problem with checking in early; I just wanted to lay down somewhere and sleep awhile first. A shower would have been nice too. Of course, I realize now no shower in the world would've prepared me for meeting Colonel Ranagan.

2

Major Conway drove me to Marine Hill, the hub of Marine activity, and ushered me into the White House. Although I hadn't wanted to go, I was glad to be settling in a little. We entered the building from the west entrance and walked down a fairly long corridor adorned with old black-and-white photographs of former COs, dating back one hundred years. In short order, we came upon the colonel's office, identified by the words COMMANDING OFFICER engraved in the door. When we were invited to enter, Major Conway smartly introduced me to Colonel Ranagan, dropped my service jacket on his desk, and excused himself for parts unknown. There I was standing before the venerated commanding officer of the Marine Ground Defense/Security Force of Guantanamo Bay, Cuba, and I was struck by how much he looked like Kermit the Frog. I'm not saying I was expecting Jack Nicholson to tell me how I can't handle the truth; all I'm saying is I wasn't expecting the CO to look so much like a Muppet.

"So you're Captain Claiborne, huh?"

"Yes sir, I am."

"You come to us...from...Camp Lejeune...North...Carolina...

isn't that right?" His tone was suspicious, and he talked so slowly I was convinced he had maple syrup for saliva.

"Yes, sir. And actually, I came from the Air Station at New River, just down the road."

"Yes, whatever," he retorted, as he looked through my service jacket. "Same thing. Are you...married, Captain...ah, Claiborne?"

"Yes, sir."

"Did your wife accompany you?"

"Yes, sir."

"My wife's here with me too. God, I love that woman. Her name is Lois and I tell you what, no man has ever had a finer woman as his wife and life partner."

I didn't know what to say. Eventually, "She sounds lovely, sir," sprang from my lips.

"You're damn right she's lovely," he said, slapping his hand against his desk. "You'll get to meet her this Saturday night at the Hail and Farewell."

"Looking forward to it. sir," I said out loud. Inside, I was thinking this guy was too much, and his strangeness only continued. Ranagan stared at me like he was in a trance. After about a minute, I almost waved my hand in front of his face. Thank goodness I didn't have to. He snapped out of his Lois-induced state of unconsciousness all on his own.

"Dismissed."

Major Conway was waiting for me outside of Ranagan's office with a smirk on his face; he'd obviously overheard my conversation with the CO. We continued down the hallway to my new office, but we didn't start to speak until we were safely behind closed doors.

"Mind telling me what that was all about?" I asked Conway.

Conway burst out laughing. "How the hell should I know? None of us have been able to figure that man out."

"So you overheard the speech about his wife?"

"Claiborne, we all get the speech about the marvelous Mrs. Ranagan."

"Why? Is she hot or something?"

Conway giggled like a school girl. "I'll let you be the judge of that. All I'll say is that she's something else and I'd give anything in the world to be there when you meet her."

"What's that supposed to mean?"

"It means that I almost want to change my flight to see the look on your face when you see her!"

AFTER A WHIRLWIND TOUR of Marine Hill, which is where the Marine administrative offices, barracks, base convenience store, and a restaurant called Post 46 were located, Conway dropped me off at home, where Audrey had been waiting. She'd been bored while I was gone since she had no car, and all of our personal effects were on a barge headed to the island. The base had loaned us some temporary furnishings, affectionately known as Flintstone furniture, but all of it was rather worn and not terribly comfortable. Everyone wondered where that Flintstone term came from, but no one knew for sure. Some people said it was because the furniture was hard as a rock.

"So how'd it go?" Audrey asked excitedly.

"To tell you the truth Audrey, I have no idea," I replied as I got ready for a nice cool shower.

Audrey followed me into the bathroom. "What do you mean you don't know? You chose not to keep your head and body together again, didn't you?"

"Look, I walked in, told him who I was—or rather—he told me who I was, and then he went off about his awesome wife."

"Then what?"

"Then he glazed over like a Krispy Kreme donut. I swear—he was totally weird."

"That does sound weird."

I prepared to feel the cool shower water run down my body. Unfortunately, it didn't take too long for my little fantasy to fade. "Audrey, there isn't any cold water! I have this piece of crap faucet on Cold and all that comes out is warm water."

"Well, try it on Hot, maybe it's backwards!"

I tried her suggestion and just about received third-degree burns. I guess I learned the hard way that warm is as cold as the water gets in Gitmo. Some genius, many years ago, decided to put the water pipe above ground and paint it black. As the months went on, Audrey and I got used to this little Gitmo quirk, but at that moment, it sealed my affection for that first day. And, my pain wasn't over yet.

"Adam, I can't sleep in this bed."

"And why not?" I asked as I made myself comfortable, pretending not to know what was coming next.

"Because I don't know who's slept in this bed before."

"Well, I'll fill that blank in for you Audrey...people. Lots of strange, unclean, people." I was way too tired to be diplomatic.

"That's it. I'm totally grossed out."

I held my tongue because I love my wife and after the exhausting day I had, I knew anything I'd say would turn into a fight. "What would you like me to do, honey? Would you like me to go fetch some palm branches and weave you a new bed, huh?"

"Don't be like that. I just want a couple of extra sheets in between me and—"

"I know Audrey—between you and the sweaty, naked man who slept on this bed before you, right?"

She smiled brightly and gave me an angelic look. "Exactly." My wife is a freak about public cleanliness. She can go a week without doing the dishes, but take her to a hotel room, and if she sees just one hair on the bathroom floor, she's hotwired into the manager's office demanding the room be sterilized. I personally don't care what's on the floor as long as I have a bed to sleep in. Once, when Audrey saw a long hair on her hotel room floor, I said, "Look honey, the previous guests left you some floss!" Audrey wasn't amused.

As far as that "sweaty, naked man" comment, whenever we go into a hotel room, the first thing she does is take off the bedspread. God help me if I sit down on it first because all hell breaks loose if I do. Who am I kidding? It's not if I do, but when I do, because there is a certain joy I get at watching her freak out.

"Oh my God!" she always begins. "How do you know a sweaty, naked man didn't lay on that spread before you?"

My comeback is always the same; I pretend to lick the bedspread. The look on her face is priceless.

As I was finding my way to the hospitality basket to get more sheets for Princess Audrey, I felt something under my feet go crunch. I flipped the light on in the kitchen to see three dozen or so Jurassic-sized cockroaches running around. Even I was utterly disgusted, but my first reaction was, "Must hide from Audrey!" I begged God to be on my side for this one, but learned that He was missing in action. She'd followed me to the kitchen.

"Oh my God, Adam! You have to get them out—now!"

She looked like she was going to cry so I grabbed the roaches bare-handed and flushed them down the toilet. I walked back to her as a super hero, giving her a reassuring hug. Audrey whispered in my ear, "Did you wash your hands?"

⤝⤝ ⤝⤝ ⤝⤝

Day two began early. Major Conway gave me a call and told me that while I had not officially checked in, he wanted to show me the ropes of my new job since he was leaving in a couple of days. I agreed to meet him at the White House at 7:30am. Audrey wasn't excited to hear I was going to leave her alone, so she decided to venture out on her own using the base transportation system she'd read about in the welcome pamphlet. However, the pamphlet had neglected to tell her that the transportation system was a decrepit Jamaican man named Cornelius driving a white, seventies era school bus at twenty-five mph.

As the new Air Officer, my job—in the case of a Cuban assault— was to call for fire and coordinate air strikes. In such a role, I was assigned to the Operations Office, or S-3, of the Ground Defense Force. My immediate supervisor was a major by the name of Dan McCarran. Major McCarran was a tall man with a decent physique. Despite his thinning sandy-blonde hair and big ears, he was also absolutely in love with himself. When I walked into his office, he was giving dating advice to one of the single officers.

"Maybe I have less hair on my head, and more on my back now, but once upon a time, I was a babe magnet. Women loved me, so I want you to know that I know what you need to do here," McCarran preached shamelessly.

Conway knocked on the partially opened door. "Pardon me, but I have my replacement here to meet you."

"Yes, come on in." He waved the single officer off and told him they would continue the conversation in the gym later.

"This is Captain Claiborne," Conway said and I greeted him respectfully.

"So when did you get here?" he asked me.

"Just yesterday, sir."

"So what do you think of our little prison colony, Captain?"

"Excuse me, sir?"

"Gitmo. It's a prison. Hell, if you don't know that now, you will in a week. Right Conway?"

Conway responded by rolling his eyes in agreement with McCarran.

"Well, actually, sir, my wife and I think it's kind of cool here—like an adventure."

"Yeah, you say that now Claiborne, but just you wait. After a few weeks of living next to the people you work with, sitting beside them in one of the three restaurants, standing behind them in line at the store and bathing with them on the beach each weekend, you're gonna want to get the hell out of Dodge. Shit—only being able to drive in your car for ten minutes in any direction will want to make you slit your throat."

"Major McCarran, I'm not really sure that Adam's ready to hear so many negatives. After all, he hasn't been here twenty-four hours yet. I think he needs to be broken in slowly."

"Understood," McCarran called back. "By the way, Conway, what's the troll up to today?"

"Haven't seen him yet. I'm not really sure. Why?"

"No reason. I'm just trying to keep up my situational awareness."

"The troll?" I asked.

Conway turned to me. "That's our little nickname for Colonel Ranagan."

"That little piece-of-shit-troll," McCarran added. "Look, I'm a really squared-away Marine, and I know I shouldn't be making fun of our CO to you on your first day, but, well, to put it frankly, I just can't help it. He's a joke, but that's for me to worry about. Listen Claiborne, just do as I tell you to do and you'll be fine here. Got it?"

"Yes, sir."

⁂ ⁂ ⁂

After spending the morning going through my new daily routine with Conway, I strolled to my house to have lunch with Audrey. It took less than ten minutes since it was located on the next peninsula over; I had a clear view of my house the whole time. I could even see Audrey sitting on the picnic table in our backyard.

"Hello, beautiful. How was your day?"

"I met a couple of people," she said happily. "One's name is Rhonda Romero. Her husband is the CO of one of the rifle companies here. I think she said his name was Manny."

"What did you think of her? Is she nice?"

"I'm not sure. I mean, she was pleasant, but she seemed a little full of herself. But who knows? You can't always go by first impressions."

"Yeah, I know what you mean. I met Major McCarran today and talk about full of yourself! But, in the end, I think he's going to be a really cool guy to work for."

"That's funny because I met McCarran's wife too. She stopped by to say hello. Her name is Regina, and she's really attractive."

"Really? Well, based on what I heard McCarran say about himself, I'd expect nothing less. What does she look like?"

"She's almost six feet tall, with a small frame, very slender. She has black hair and the bluest eyes you've ever seen in your life. And on top of it all, she's as nice a person as you want to meet."

"Sounds like you have a couple of new friends. Not bad for twenty-four hours." We dug into lunch, and in between bites of my ham sandwich, I asked, "So where did you go today?"

"Well, let's see. I walked to the bus stop at the end of the street and that's where I met Rhonda. Then when the bus came, I took my seat among a plethora of young, tight-bodied Marines and enjoyed the view all the way to the exchange."

"I'm sure you did. I bet you also felt old, considering that most of those Marines are eighteen."

"Pretty much, especially when I heard a couple of them talking about who had the better senior prom. That's when this twenty-nine year-old decided to admire the landscape instead."

"Good idea. So, what did you think of the exchange? Did it have the same stuff that Walmart has?"

"You mean the exchange slash commissary? It's one store! And on top of it, the grocery store part looks like a large convenience store and I didn't see any Twinkies. How in the world can I live on this island without Twinkies?"

"I'll take that up with Colonel Ranagan at the next meeting. They can't expect my wife to live without her Twinkies!"

Audrey leaned over and slapped my leg. "Oh you laugh now, but haven't you noticed something about the bread on your sandwich? It's not squishy bread—it's stale. All the bread here is stale. Also, there was hardly any fresh produce because they don't get produce except once a week, and then it's like this mad frenzy to stock up."

"I feel you have more to tell me."

"And the clothes! Oh my God! It's like so last season. Catalog shopping, here I come! And the milk is weird."

"Weird how?"

"Correct me if I'm wrong, but this is the month of July and the milk I bought is good through October. Tell me that doesn't seem strange somehow."

"That's because it's radiated milk. It lasts longer."

"What do you mean, radiated?"

"It means you won't have trouble finding me in the dark because I'll be glowing. Of course we can always experiment on whether or not I'll last longer too."

Audrey rolled her eyes at me and laughed. Gitmo was different, but we were both still happy to be there.

"Do you have to go back to work today?" Audrey asked sadly.

"I'm afraid so, but only for a couple of more hours. I should be home by three. What are your plans?"

"Actually Regina McCarran asked me to go with her to Dermo, whatever that is. What is it?"

"That's D-R-M-O—the Defense Reutilization Management Office. It's a place that takes old military office furniture and supplies and sells them to the public. It's basically a military garage sale."

"So it's used stuff?"

"Yup. Not your kind of place, huh?"

"Well, I'll go for the company, but that's all."

"Have a good time. I have to get back to the White House now." I gave Audrey a kiss.

As I strolled along Sherman Avenue, I was taken in by the raw beauty of the land. The bay was an amazing fusion of azure and aqua greens, the palms were drooping lazily with ripened coconuts, and the fire-orange blooms of the mimosa tree lit up the landscape like a lightening bolt in a stark western meadow. Gitmo didn't have the lush scenery one would expect from a tropical paradise, but to me, it was a paradise none-the-less.

3

About a half hour later, Regina McCarran arrived to pick up Audrey in her white, convertible Le Barron. Regina had four boys, all elementary school age, which allowed her the freedom to come and go as she pleased during the day. Major McCarran didn't want her to work, as he prided himself on being the breadwinner.

"Ready to go?" Regina said as she polished her sunglasses.

"Sure. Is it far?"

"Nothing is far on this base. It's near the turn off for the Ferry Landing, about five minutes away."

"How long have you guys been in Gitmo?"

Regina stopped to think. "We got here about a month before you. How do you like it so far?"

"To be honest, I haven't seen too much of it yet, but I think Adam and I are going to like it. What about you?"

"I hate it here."

"Really? Why?"

"I don't know. It's just not what I thought it would be. Everything's so brown and phone calls home are expensive. Captain Pickard, our wonderful base CO, is tearing down all the neat historical buildings, taking away recreational things, the roads are in disrepair—I could go on and on."

"Is there anything you do like about this place?" Audrey asked in an upbeat voice.

"I like the outdoor movie theatre. There's nothing like watching a movie under the Caribbean stars. I also love Kittery Beach and climbing up the sides of the rock cliffs. The boys and I go hiking most every weekend. Once we found a boa's skin just laying there!"

"And this excited you?"

"Absolutely! One of my boys found a tarantula by the slide in the park and now we have him in a jar!"

"For what?"

"To watch. He's a very clever spider."

"Look Regina, I don't mean this in a bad way, but your body sure doesn't match your manly disposition. You look like you'd be a girly girl."

"No way! I love communing with nature and messing around with critters."

"And where is your husband when you head out on these safaris of yours?"

Regina's smile faded. "Who knows? The gym, work, McDonald's? Who cares? All I know is that he isn't with us and I have no idea why."

Audrey's attention was suddenly diverted by a herd of small goats. "Hey—what's with the goats I see all over the place?"

"In the early nineties, there was an insurgence of Haitian refugees that came here. Most of them brought chickens and goats."

"Yeah! That's right. I saw a lot of chickens by my house today!"

"When people were taken back to Haiti, the Coast Guard wouldn't allow the animals to travel on the ship. They were abandoned here, and now, the CO let's them roam freely.

The DRMO warehouse came upon them quickly. Audrey and Regina were surrounded by everything from canteens to rucksacks to couches. Audrey was turned off right away by the musty smell accompanying the items. She followed Regina, but had absolutely no intention of buying anything for herself. They'd not been there long before Audrey spied Mimsey Pickard, the base CO's wife. Audrey attempted to shield herself from Mimsey's view, and for a while she was successful.

"How much is this desk?" Audrey asked the DRMO manager as Mimsey came up along side of her.

"That's funny, dear, I was just about to ask the same question." Mimsey turned to the salesman. "Yes, how much is it? Actually, I don't need to ask. I'll just take it."

Audrey became enraged. "Excuse me, but I was here first."

"Were you, dear? Because I really don't remember who was here first. Who was it?" Mimsey asked the manager, "This lady or me, the wife of the base CO?"

Audrey and Regina couldn't believe how Mimsey was trying to intimidate the DRMO manager. "Well, uh, ladies, I'm not really sure who was here first."

Audrey's eyes grew as large as saucers. "I'll tell you who was here first! Me!" Audrey said as she pointed to herself. "And when I know how much this desk is, I'll make an educated decision on whether or not I'd like to buy it." She stopped to take a breath. "Now, sir, how much is this desk?"

The manager looked at Mimsey, who was smirking like the Cheshire cat. "It's twenty-five dollars," he said, avoiding eye contact with Mimsey.

"Sold!" said Audrey, as she gave a hard stare to the base CO's wife.

Mimsey returned the look. "We'll see about that, dear." Mimsey sauntered out of the building.

Regina couldn't help but laugh. "Do you have any idea who that was?"

"Mimsey Pickard—the base CO's wife."

"Do you have any idea what you did?" Regina continued.

"Yes, I know exactly what I did. I refused to let that bitch bully me. She might be the CO's wife, but she's still a wife, just like me. She has no authority over me, or anyone else for that matter!"

Regina shook her head and continued to smile. "You obviously haven't met Colonel Ranagan's wife yet, have you?"

"No, why?"

"Just asking."

❧ ❧ ❧

It was after dinner when Audrey's purchase arrived at the house. I looked across the room at her, wondering what was so special about that desk which made it worth jeopardizing my military career. The Jamaican delivery men put it in the middle of the living room and then left promptly. Audrey was standing there, biting her nails and avoiding eye contact with me.

"So—this is the magical desk," I said as I looked at it closely. It was large and wooden, and had obviously been well used over the years. There were coffee ring stains on it and scratches galore. Nothing about that desk seemed attractive to me, and I couldn't imagine why Audrey would have wanted it so badly. "Mind telling me what really happened today?"

"Adam, you don't understand! I was there first and she raced over there like she owned the place."

"Well, she kinda does, Audrey. I mean not really, but come on—we've only been here two days. Isn't this a little early to be making enemies?"

"So you're on her side?"

"No Audrey, of course I'm not on her side. I just don't think this desk was worth the fallout that's bound to take place. We have two years here. Let's try and play nicely with the others, ok?"

I knew my last comment belittled her feelings and put distance between us, but I felt I was right. Like it or not, there are many military wives who wear their husband's rank and I was sure Mimsey Pickard wouldn't be the last one my wife would encounter. But since I knew the move to Gitmo was a big deal for her too, I offered her a white flag.

"Come on Audrey—let's just forget about this, ok? I love you, and well, that raggedy old hag got what she deserved."

That made Audrey smile and the two of us sat on the desk together and she rested her head on my shoulder. I cannot and will not ever try to control my wife. I had to accept that Audrey was going to do what she was going to do. I only asked that she run her ideas by me first. She agreed and I let out a long sigh of relief as we made our way to bed.

ॐ ॐ ॐ

On our third day, Audrey decided to go to one of the beaches with Regina McCarran and I was going to spend my last day with Major Conway. While I'd only known him a short while, I had begun to really like him.

"Good morning, Adam. Ready for your final day of Gitmo Air Officer 101?"

"Absolutely." After the first day, he told me not to call him sir anymore since he was only a year or so senior to me. This allowed us to talk more frankly. "What have you got for me today?"

"Well, to be honest, a lot—but there are some things I want to talk to you about first that have nothing to do with your job."

I looked at him enthusiastically, thinking that I was ready to hear anything. "Sure—fire away!"

"I heard about your wife's altercation with Mimsey Pickard yesterday at DRMO."

"Well, I'd hardly call it an altercation, but what about it? And how in the world would you know what happened?"

"That's what I want to talk to you about. Look Adam, you and your wife are two of five hundred military people on this base. There's nothing you can do or say without everyone knowing exactly what's going on in your life. And what's worse, when everyone around you can't figure out the truth, they just fill in the blanks however they want."

I was stunned. "Come on, Conway, you can't be serious! So my wife wanted the same desk that Mimsey Pickard wanted—so what? I'm sure she'll find another one."

Conway rolled his eyes. "Now, see. That's not what I heard happened. I heard your wife called her some colorful names and shoved her."

"No way! That's not what happened at all."

Conway moved closer to me. "That's what I'm talking about! No one here cares what's right. Well, some people do, but Gitmo does strange things to people and I have no idea why."

"What are you talking about? Come on—that makes no sense."

"Adam—I can't explain it, but remember Colonel Vandermeed— the one who had it in for me? When he first got here, we saw eye to eye on everything, and then he just changed out of the blue. Look at Colonel Ranagan—he was cool too and now he's beginning to act really weird. People who you think are your friends will turn on you in a New York minute to protect themselves. Watch your back Adam—I mean it."

"Ok, let's play it your way for a second. You're telling me that normally good people come to Gitmo and then become possessed or something? That's ridiculous!"

"No, Adam. I'm just saying that being isolated here—it does something strange to some people—not everyone, but some, and I just wanted you to know. And by the way, if you don't believe me, one of your collateral jobs here is to be the Barracks historian." Conway reached into the file cabinet drawer and pulled out a huge stack of journals, logs, books and photographs. He dropped them down on his desk with a thud.

"What's all that?" I said as I moved closer to examine them.

"This is ninety years of strange shit. Some of this will amuse you, and some of it will scare the hell out of you."

I reached into the pile and pulled out a stack of thirty neatly stapled, white pages with edges that had begun to yellow. The title on the front sheet read: *Book of the Dead.* The hair on the back of my neck stood on end. I held it up so Conway could read the cover too. "What's this?"

"More strange shit. Adam—the best advice I could give you is to tell you to make only one or two good friends, and trust only them. That way, you can't go wrong."

"Roger." I acted calmly, but I was having a hard time taking in everything he told me.

"Oh—and if I may add one more thing, tell your wife to stay the hell away from the Marine Wives Association."

"I don't have to worry about that. Audrey hates those wives' groups. She's never been in one before, and I fully expect her to avoid it like the plague. But of course I have to ask, why the warning?"

"Because I want you to be happy here, that's why."

Conway began to go over my duties with me. I listened closely to what he was saying, but I kept replaying our earlier conversation in my mind. I wasn't sorry we'd moved to Gitmo, but I was beginning to embrace it less. If Conway was right, our tour wouldn't be the expedition to Margaritaville we'd thought it would be.

I'd seen a T-shirt on some sailor the day before that said, "Gitmo...a strange little place." I didn't think much about it then, but now my mind was racing.

Audrey was pouring on the aloe vera as I walked through the door at dinner time. I don't think I'd ever seen anyone so red in my life. Lecturing her on the effects of a tropical sun on fair skin was in the front of my mind, but I decided to be sympathetic instead. I helped her rub the after-sun gel on all those hard-to-reach places and was amazed at how hot her skin felt.

"You know, Audrey, if you wanted to have a barbecue, you could have invited me. Of course, I would've suggested using steaks or ribs—not your body, but then again who am I to second guess?"

She looked at me with misery engraved in her face. "Very funny."

"Well, besides the third degree burns, how was your day?"

"Actually it was nice," she replied as she slowly made her way to the Flintstone couch. "Regina McCarran's a lot of fun, and she laughs a lot, but I don't think she's that happy. I mean, she loves to be around people, so that makes her smile, but I think her life in general isn't that great."

I joined Audrey on the couch and lifted her legs onto my lap. "What makes you think she's not happy? Did she tell you that?"

"I know she hates Gitmo, and, she's insinuated that things aren't so great with Major McCarran."

"Maybe she just needs a friend, and you'd probably be a good one for her."

"Yeah maybe...but all I can really think about is me right now. I can hardly feel my face...it's like numb or something."

"Do you think you'll be okay to go down to the Ferry Landing tomorrow to say goodbye to Major Conway?"

"Yeah sure, but what's that all about?"

I shrugged my shoulders. "I'm not sure, I was just told to be there at 10am sharp to say good bye."

All of all sudden Audrey's eyes lit up. "Adam—I forgot to tell you! The lady from personal property called...our stuff will be here next week and our car will be here tomorrow!!!!"

I was very excited to hear such news. I'd protected Audrey from the reality of Gitmo. Most everyone I'd met thus far had nothing but horror stories to tell me about their personal goods. One officer had to wait five months for his family's belongings, and he wasn't alone. I knew the sooner we had our own things, the sooner Audrey would settle down and be happy. And although I wanted to shield her from as much as I could, there was something I had to tell her.

"Audrey, have you made many calls on the portable phone since we've been here?"

She thought for a moment. "Yes, since it's the only phone we have. I called Regina a couple of times and my parents—why?"

I took a deep breath. "There's a Marine signal intelligence company here in Gitmo, and, well, their job is to monitor Cuban communications."

"So?"

"Well, I was told that sometimes they get bored listening to the Cubans, and they listen to our phone calls too."

Audrey's faced got even redder. "What in the world, Adam? Are you telling me that a bunch of yahoo Marines have been listening in to my private conversations ever since we got here?"

I looked at her, scared to tell her the truth. "I'm not saying they have been, but they've been known to do it, and, yeah, it's possible."

Audrey marched around the living room. "Oh my God! I have no idea what I've been saying! I've no idea what they might have heard! I have to live with these jerk-offs for two years and they can just listen in to whatever they want? Can they do that? Can they? God! I feel so humiliated!"

"No! They're not supposed to, but they do when no one's around, and all I'm saying is that we need to use the landline phone and then we'll be ok."

"For heavens sake, Adam! That's not right. We shouldn't have to buy another phone to protect our privacy. What side of the border do we live on?"

At ten o'clock Friday morning, I went to the auto warehouse to take possession of my car and drove back to our home to find a very happy Audrey. She was standing outside in the driveway, next to the dilapidated white garages with the orange-tile roof, looking like a million bucks in her white sundress. The rays outlined her curves and the light picked out the red hues in her brunette hair. The sky was exceptionally blue that day and there wasn't a cloud for a hundred miles.

The ride to the landing was short, less than ten minutes in all. By the time we arrived, there were quite a few people standing around the parking lot, waiting to say goodbye to their friends and co-workers. This tradition was one of the best things about life in Gitmo. Because there was little to do, and because the base was so isolated, the people who shared your life with you while you were there made all the difference in the world. The pilgrimage to the Ferry Landing each Tuesday and Friday offered us our last chance to thank those leaving for their friendship and to let them all know how much they'd be missed.

About five minutes before the ferry actually pulled away, those traveling to the Leeward for their flight got on-board while everyone else continued to wave and dry their eyes. With the sounding of the ferry's horn, it left the dock amidst a roar of shouts ringing out from the shoreline to those departing. On that day, not only was Major Conway leaving, but a fireman and a doctor as well. As a tribute, an ambulance and a fire engine pulled along the shore with sirens blasting out across the bay. In a complete surprise to Audrey and me, a number of military personnel from both the Marine Corps and Navy jumped into the water, fully clad in uniform. The ritual had gotten a little out of hand over the years, since only the next person slated to leave the island was supposed to jump. However, depending on a person's popularity and the sense of humor of those jumping, it had more or less become a free for all.

That morning at the Ferry Landing was filled with unreserved sadness and good old fashioned fun. I'd never experienced such a combination of tears and laughter in all my life. On my drive home, I thought about the day I'd leave Gitmo and what it would feel like. Although I was excited about the next two years, I didn't feel any connection to the island yet, or to the people there. It was hard for me to believe Audrey and I would be missed when it was our time to go, or that we'd even be sad to leave. But seeing all those people that day made me want to feel more plugged in to that place. When we got back to the house, Audrey and I agreed to spend the next few weeks submerging ourselves in the history and the community of Guantanamo Bay.

4

The big day had finally arrived; we were to meet Lois Ranagan that evening and I was totally unsure of what to expect. I still wasn't certain if I should tell Audrey what Conway had told me about her. After Audrey's run-in with Mimsey Pickard, I thought I probably shouldn't put any preconceived notions about Mrs. Ranagan into my wife's head. One power struggle with a CO's wife was all I could handle.

Audrey and I decided to spend the morning driving around base, so we packed ourselves a picnic lunch and headed to the farthest point we were allowed to drive, Cable Beach. The ride took us through the main shopping area of base, past DRMO and up a short hill to our first stop. At one time, Phillips Park—named after Rear Admiral W.K. Philips, a former base commander—had been a race track. As the years passed, it became a nucleus of activity for the base with ball fields, outdoor movie theatres, picnic shelters, and an extended fishing pier. Regrettably, it had become an overrun ghost town, whose glory years had long since faded. A hurricane in the early nineties had almost completely destroyed the pier, and the ball fields had become overgrown. The drive-in movie screens, which once brought the residents of Gitmo action and adventure underneath the Caribbean sky, had been torn down. A handful of picnic shelters, desperately in need of repair, were among the bits and pieces left to remind us of Guantanamo Bay's more prosperous past.

The seemingly abandoned park sat upon a large rocky cliff, and a rickety stairwell, concealed by an abundance of leafy trees, led us to the old pier. All that remained was a landing mounted above the stirring salt water surf, and at the far end, a diving platform utilized by scuba aficionados. As we walked down the few remaining steps towards the divers, Audrey noticed a small cave underneath the stairwell. I followed closely behind her, awed of the rock formations, local plant life and the echoing sea against the coral cliffs. Crevices along the way allowed light to pave our way, and eventually we arrived at the bottom of the highest precipice. Waiting for us was an interesting creature, who Audrey named Iggie. He was a three-foot long rock iguana, indigenous to Cuba, and spectacular to observe. After our encounter with the reptile, we took special note of all the Iguana Crossing signs throughout the base. The rock iguana was a protected species on our oasis and automobiles were a constant threat.

When we returned to the car, we continued to drive along the cliff towards Cable Beach, passing an old lighthouse—the keeper's house still in its shadow. Stationed like a protective mother who once guided her children home, it had been long vacant and neglected. So charming and full of character, I didn't have to close my eyes to imagine the light keeper climbing the stairs through the rain and fog, nor to picture his children running around its base. When we were almost completely past it, I caught a glimpse of a sign: MUSEUM. Audrey and I knew we'd have to visit one day.

After a steep section of road, we rounded a turn and saw a miniature tropical nirvana. The first thing that struck us about Cable Beach was its austere setting. The small lagoon was complemented by numerous palm trees and petite desert-like mountains to every side but the one facing the sea. What made it even better was that we had it all to ourselves as we walked along the rocky beach. The color of the water was a striking cerulean and cobalt blend, with a hint of indigo along its edges. Audrey and I looked at one another and ran down the beach, jumping into the waves. We splashed and played like children, totally unaware others had joined us. As we emerged from the water, a child—around ten—approached us. I smiled at him and knelt down to meet his eyes.

"Boy! You guys are sure brave!" the child announced loudly.

"What do you mean?" I said, still smiling.

"You're swimming," he replied.

"The water is wonderful today!"

"Don't you care about the hydroids?"

I looked at Audrey, then back to the boy. "What are hydroids?"

"Oh...you guys must be new. Hey Dad! These new people are swimming and they don't know what hydroids are!"

I refused to look at Audrey because I already knew she'd begun to panic. I followed the boy to his father and inquired further.

"Hi, my name is Adam Claiborne, and like your son's already told you, we're new to Gitmo. What's this about hydroids?"

"Hydroids are, well, bottom line is that from March until September, they float in our waters and give you one hell of a skin rash. As you can see, that's why no one's swimming." I could've sworn he ended his sentence with "Dumb-ass".

Later that afternoon, I was diagnosed with the worst outbreak of a hydroid-induced rash in recent Gitmo history. Audrey didn't seem to be affected much, but I broke-out in places people don't like to talk about at parties. Audrey and I sure made a couple; between her sunburn and my rash, we looked like the founders of a leper colony. And of course, that night was the evening of the Hail-and-Farewell party, where we'd meet all of the other officers and Mrs. Ranagan.

With a little help from Audrey's cosmetics, and with a lot of help from the prescription steroids the dispensary gave me, she and I were able to keep our date with the rest of the Marine gang. As we walked down our street toward the colonel's house, we read the name-signs posted in front of everyone's home, acquainting ourselves with some of our neighbors. Across the street from us were Master Sergeant Nelson Moser and his wife Phyllis. He was tall and lanky, while she was short and round. While they smiled at us pleasantly, they had an oddness about them I couldn't put my finger on. Right next door to us was Captain Ryan and Arlene Hill; they were from West Virginia and quite outgoing. They ran ahead of us to help set up the party, but assured us they'd make time for us when we got there. To the right of the Mosers were Lieutenant and Mrs. Ken Bradshaw. His wife, Rosie, was the base gossip.

Further on down, the street became a small traffic circle divided around a modest playground. On one side of the park were Major McCarran and his wife Regina, and on the other side of the park were Rhonda and Manny Romero. As we passed the park area, we came upon the home of Captain Evan Geller and his wife Maura, who was busy breaking Pickard's rule about watering her lawn.

Next door to the Gellars was the home of the new executive officer, Lt Colonel Henry Ray and his wife, Drew. I'd not yet met Lt Col Ray since he'd only arrived on that morning's flight. Lastly, across the street from the Rays lived Warrant Officer Tony Razor and his wife Jackie. They were just ahead of us as we walked.

At the end of our street sat the U-shaped home belonging to Colonel and Lois Ranagan. The residence was a large, one level home. The pathway to the front door had been adorned with a garden, cared for with great attention by Mrs. Ranagan herself. As the Ranagan's lawn was a particularly striking shade of green, it was clear the watering law didn't apply to them, or at least she didn't think it did.

As we knocked on the door, I couldn't help but notice the unusual architectural style of the home. Later that evening, I found out the house had once been a barracks, which explained its industrial design. The left side of the U accommodated the garage and kitchen, while the right side housed the bedrooms. The middle section was home to the public rooms, where Lois and the colonel did their entertaining.

When the door opened, we were surprised to see Arlene Hill, our next-door neighbor, standing in the doorway.

"Glad to see ya'll didn't get lost!" she said with her West Virginia drawl. "Come on in!"

Audrey and I stepped into the house and were immediately struck by the size of the room. We weren't sure whether it was the sprawling floor plan, the immaculately polished salmon-tinted tile, or the magnificent stone veranda which gave the room so much character.

"Good evening, Arlene," I said.   Audrey also exchanged pleasantries.

"Good evening to you, too. Do you know many people here tonight?" she asked my wife.

"No. We've waved at a few of our neighbors, but we really don't know anybody yet." Audrey caught sight of Regina and excused herself.

"So where's your husband tonight?" I asked Arlene, but just as the words came out of my mouth, Ryan came up behind me and handed me a beer.

"Flirtin' with my wife, are ya? Here. Drink up. It's the only way you're gonna make it through the Hail and Bail."

Arlene was a petite woman and a lady in every sense of the word. She had a warm smile and tons of freckles; her beauty was simple, but magnified by her sweetness. Ryan, on the other hand, was a man's man. He was laid back, talkative, rowdy and funny as hell. Ryan Hill also had nuts of steel since he was the minefield maintenance officer. He became one of my favorite people on the island.

"I could try to steal her away, but it looks like she's only got eyes for you," I said, grinning.

"Well then, we'll let my little woman return to the kitchen where she belongs," Ryan said as he winked at Arlene, "and I'll introduce you to the other guys."

I followed Ryan to the other side of the room, but the whole time I was hoping to get a glimpse of Lois Ranagan. I saw several women about my age and one lady who reminded me of Barbara Bush, but no Lois Ranagan. As I was about to ask Ryan to point her out to me, I heard him introducing me to Evan Gellar.

"Evan, this is our new Air Officer, Adam Claiborne."

I reached out to shake his hand. "Hey. It's nice to meet you."

Evan Gellar was a Marine captain stationed there as the logistics officer. He was a short man, with the reddest hair I've ever seen. Gellar seemed to have a great personality and never minded being the butt of a joke.

Next I was introduced to a few of the single officers. To my left was an intelligence captain named Gordie Shaw. He appeared quiet, but friendly. To his right was Lieutenant Guy Armstrong, a communications officer. And lastly, the most conceited Marine I've ever met in my life, First Lieutenant Chester Dingle, who liked to be called Chet.

Chet Dingle considered himself to be quite a prize for the ladies, despite the fact he had a fiancé back in the states. He'd appointed himself the leader of the bachelor Marines, but I had no idea how he obtained his status; he didn't impress me, and I had a hard time buying the gigolo thing. He also had really weird lips; they were almost too big for his face.

After a few moments of conversing with the single officers, I heard Colonel Ranagan call for our attention. I joined Audrey, who was standing beside the entrance to the veranda, and waited to hear the colonel's speech.

"I want to thank you all for coming here this evening," Ranagan began slowly. "Tonight we unfortunately have to say goodbye to a few of our fellow Marines, but we also have the privilege of welcoming a few new faces to our family here at the Barracks." Ranagan told the three rotating Marines to stand, said a few words about each one, and presented them with a small plaque to commemorate their time in Gitmo. After a modest round of applause for each, Ranagan turned his attention toward me and Lt Colonel Ray. "We have two new families joining us on Marine Hill now: Lt Colonel Ray, who will be the new executive officer and Captain Adam Claiborne, our new air officer." He instructed Lt Colonel Ray to join him up front, and, after a few comments, Lt Colonel Ray made some jokes at the colonel's expense. When Ray sat down, the CO turned toward me. "Now, Captain Claiborne and his wife, Audrey, come to us all the way from Camp Pendleton, California."

"Actually, sir, it was Camp Lejeune, North Carolina," I said, interrupting the colonel respectfully.

Ranagan froze like a statue. He stood there, just staring at me for what seemed like hours. His eyes glazed and he didn't even blink. I looked behind me to see if there was something going on outside my line of sight, but, in the end, I realized he was just staring at me. Everyone looked around uncomfortably, not knowing what to do. As I was about to do something to break the awkward silence, he snapped out of his daze and spoke brusquely.

"Then who the hell gave me this card with the wrong information on it?"

Gordie Shaw stepped forward. He was a stand-up kind of guy and I really respected that. "Sir, I wrote the card. I guess I made an error. It won't happen again."

Ranagan composed himself, made a cruel comment about Gordie's ineptitude, and continued to introduce me to the group. Later that night, when Ranagan discarded the note card, I took a look. Gordie had—in fact—written Camp Lejeune, North Carolina, so it hadn't been his mistake; it had been the colonel's. I wondered why Gordie had taken the heat for something he hadn't done. I'm not saying I would've been belligerent about it, but I might've at least joked with the colonel.

Finally, the moment I'd waited for. Colonel Ranagan announced that his wife wanted to say a few words to the ladies. I cricked my neck as I looked around the room with anticipation, however, the only lady I saw coming towards the front of the room was Barbara Bush. My brow notably wrinkled as her mouth opened.

"I want to welcome the new wives to our group and let you know that I'm looking forward to getting to know each of you as the months go on. Hopefully you'll join the Marine Wives Association, as it's a wonderful way in which to share each other's company while doing charitable work for those less fortunate on base. Please enjoy yourselves tonight and let me know if there's anything I can do to make your time here more comfortable and pleasant. Remember, we're one big family here, and my home is always open to you all."

I couldn't believe it. The celebrated Lois Ranagan—the woman the colonel couldn't live without—looked like his mother. I was stunned because after the way the colonel spoke about her, I thought she was going to be buxom and beautiful. The only thing I could honestly give her was that she seemed exceedingly kind and caring about the other wives and families. I expected Lois Ranagan would prove the old axiom that you can't judge a book by its cover. Audrey and I took a liking to her instantly and welcomed the chance to become better acquainted.

When Lois finished speaking, everyone began milling about, so Audrey and I went out onto the veranda and stared with envy. The porch was roughly forty feet long and semi-circular. There was attractive white patio furniture neatly situated around the terrace, and many potted plants carefully positioned along the wall to create the perfect tropical ambiance. The balcony itself overhung a small cliff, which allowed for a panoramic view of the bay, the mountains on Leeward, and the Cuban city of Caimanera.

As we took a seat to watch the sunset, we were joined by Evan Gellar's wife, Maura, and Rhonda Romero. Maura was a slender woman in her mid-twenties with sandy blonde hair and brown eyes. She'd been an interior designer before moving to Guantanamo and she and Evan were expecting their first baby in January. Rhonda wasn't as slender as Maura, nor was she as well educated. She came across as being snobbish—there was very little one could tell Rhonda that she didn't already know. Every time Audrey or I made a comment, Rhonda was quick to let us know we were misinformed. The one thing I did like about Rhonda was her smile. She also liked to laugh and, despite her shortcomings, we enjoyed her company.

After an hour or so of people stopping by our table to introduce themselves, Audrey and I decided to call it a night. As we walked to the door, Mrs. Ranagan greeted us.

"So how are thing's going for you so far? Are you settled yet?"

"Hardly," Audrey shot back. "Our stuff doesn't arrive until next week. I'm getting tired of the Flintstone furniture."

"Well, we've all been there. I think we had to use the Flintstone stuff for four months because we'd come from Yuma. The base CO offered to loan us higher quality furniture with Frank being the Marine Commanding Officer and all, but we declined. If the other Marines had to use the uncomfortable stuff, then we wanted to as well. We didn't want any special treatment."

"I might have taken Captain Pickard up on his offer!" Audrey joked.

"Are you planning to get a job while you're here?"

"I'm not sure yet. I—"

"Good," Lois interrupted. "I think an officer's wife has a duty to her husband and home. That's career enough! Lord knows this household would fall apart if I wasn't here to constantly be on top of things."

Audrey didn't know what to say. It was obvious that while Lois was only in her early fifties, there was a huge generation gap between them. "Well, I guess I'll just have to wait and see. Adam is pretty good about pitching in around the house, so I don't know how useful I'd be as a stay-at-home wife."

Lois put her arm around Audrey's shoulder. "Now don't you ever underestimate your worth to your husband." Lois cupped her hand around her mouth and whispered. "Behind every successful man is a strong woman. Don't ever forget it."

Audrey nodded. "I'll sure try."

The walk back to our home was much different than the walk had been to the Ranagans. With the absence of light, the neighborhood took on a different personality. The long-standing banyan trees covered in Spanish moss, with there expansive branches and deeply rooted trunks, became characters rather than scenery. Bats were gliding trough the air like seagulls riding the windy surf, and the night sky enveloped the viewer in a starry heaven. While we were only a few hundred miles from America, we felt like we'd been sent back in time to a faraway place. As we strolled, we felt we were now a part of something extraordinary, witnesses to living, breathing history.

5

On Sunday morning, we decided to continue our sight-seeing tour. We drove in the direction of Phillips Park, but before the incline which led us there, we took a right onto a less traveled road. Audrey and I made our way up a fairly steady hill until we came upon an abandoned air field. The runway was decayed and useless, with grass blades standing tall in the myriad of cracks and crevices which criss-crossed the pavement. The dilapidated chain-link fence surrounding the field offered little protection, as many sections were being held together with make-shift connectors. In the middle of the area was a hangar with broken windows and a roof that was on the verge of caving in. The old control tower stood sadly as a relic of a by-gone era.

"What is this place?" Audrey asked me as we pulled over to the side of the road near the hangar.

"This is McCalla Field, named after Rear Admiral B.H. McCalla. He commanded the forces that captured Guantanamo Bay in 1898. Back in the early years of the base, this was the airport."

"Why don't they still use it? I mean, after all, it's a lot more convenient than having to ferry over to Leeward to catch the plane."

"They decided in the fifties that they needed a longer runway and Leeward offered the only solution."

Audrey walked over to the fence and put her fingers through the chain link. "This is really sad. I bet at one time that this was a hoppin' place to work. Now, the hangar's falling apart, the tower looks so lonely."

"Yeah, I agree. At one time, this was the base's lifeline to the rest of the world, and now, it's like nobody cares about it." I looked across the runway to its far side. "You want to know what's even worse? Come on."

Audrey and I drove to the end of the street, and, as we made a left at the stop sign, we saw a marker: OCEAN VIEW HOUSING. In an instant, we were transported back fifty years. Small white cottages, with large louvered windows and enormous breezeways adorned this tiny section of base. Magnificent old trees encircled the homes in the same way as ashen picket fences bordered the yards. Remnants of play equipment littered the landscape and long forgotten clothes-lines dangled in the current of the Caribbean wind.

We came across an abandoned tree house—whose owners had once taken great pride in their creation—and discovered a child's shoe wedged in one of the rungs of the wooden ladder. Several names had been inscribed in the bark, along with these words:

GOODBYE TREE HOUSE, WE'LL MISS YOU
October 1962   PS: Castro Keep out!!!

"October 1962? Adam, that was the time of the Cuban missile crisis! These kids must have been evacuated." Audrey reached out and ran her hand along their words. "They must've been so scared. They were told to leave and they didn't know if they'd ever come back. Is there any way we can find out what happened back then? Learn more about these people?"

I recalled Conway speech about me being the new Marine historian and remembered all the documents he'd shown me in the file cabinet. "Yeah, I know exactly how to find out." I didn't have the heart to tell her Captain Pickard had chosen Ocean View Housing as his next demolition project.

On our way to Marine Hill, Audrey and I decided to make a spur-of-the-moment detour and drive to the peak of John Paul

Jones Hill. The ride to the highest point on base was curvy and somewhat intimidating to those who had a fear of heights—like my wife—but, even so, the trip was completely worthwhile. At one time, a modest weekend home for the base CO had been there, but had been long since torn down. All that remained were the office spaces of the Marine signal intelligence company.

From the summit, the entire naval station, along with the Cuban cities of Caimanera and Guantanamo City, were visible to the naked eye. The airport on Leeward, the palm trees of Cable Beach, the housing areas and hospital, were all there in one inclusive frame. In the same way a member of a monarchy would admire his kingdom from the highest tower, I too, looked with a sense of ownership and inspiration. At that moment, I became a part of Gitmo.

After pulling ourselves away from JPJ Hill, we drove past Cooper Field, which sat catty-cornered to McDonald's, and noticed a soccer game between the Jamaican and Philippine workers. Since there were only about five hundred military members on the base, the maintenance people, store workers, restaurant help and all other domestic jobs had been contracted to a few large companies who employed foreigners to fulfill the contracts.

Just as I made the right off Sherman Avenue onto Marine Hill, my beeper went off. On my first day, like everyone else, I was issued a beeper so the CO could have constant communication with his officers and staff NCOs. I never understood the whole beeper thing; Gitmo was the first place I'd ever had to wear one while in the Corps, and Gitmo was so small that if I was urgently needed, I could be in only one of seven places. Seriously. No one ever really had a day off since we'd been instructed to wear the beeper everywhere, every day. Since it had been my first beeper incident, I assumed the Cubans had begun their attack and raced to my office. In my excitement, I even told Audrey to walk home from the White House in case I needed the car.

Upon my arrival there, I questioned the Marine on duty who paged me. "Lance Corporal...I received your page. What's the situation?"

"CME, sir."

For a moment, I must've looked like Ranagan—completely static—as I racked my brain trying to remember that particular acronym. The military is full of them, so much so, one would swear we had our own language. Then it hit me. "Where was the location of the Cuban minefield explosion?"

"About a quarter mile from the Northeast Gate, sir."

"Any casualties?"

"Yes, sir." My stomach sank. "A cow."

I furrowed my brow and bit my lower lip. "A cow, Lance Corporal? You did just say a cow, right?"

"Yes, sir, a cow."

So it wasn't the invasion of Castro's Communist armed forces I secretly hoped it had been, but I still had to pass this information on to Major McCarran, and, he in turn, would tell it to Lt Colonel Ray, who, as the XO, would tell Ranagan.

Redundancy meant nothing to these people. In the real Marine Corps, the CO is shielded from the minutia to free his time for more pressing issues, but not there. The CO wanted to know everything that occurred on every square inch of the base, every time. The enlisted Marines who monitored the fence-line activities could've saved a lot of time by just calling the CO directly, but Ranagan wouldn't hear of it. He prized the chain of command and wanted it utilized one hundred percent of the time. To me, the whole cow thing wasn't worth mentioning: nothing needed to be done, nobody had to go out and inspect anything. It was totally inconsequential. Why the colonel, or anyone besides me, had to know was beyond reason.

After I paged Major McCarran, who informed me my "fucking cow story" had interrupted something erotic between him and his wife Regina, I made my way to my office to grab a few of the folders, old newspaper clippings, and log books for Audrey and me to go through. On the top of the pile was the mysterious *Book of the Dead*, which I planned to scrutinize first.

"AUDREY," I CALLED OUT, "I'm home!"

"We're in here, Adam!" My wife answered.

I walked into the living room to see Audrey and Regina McCarran sitting on top of the desk for which Audrey had battled Mimsey Pickard. "So how do you like our be-yoo-tee-ful antique?" I asked Regina.

"I'd call it shabby-antique. Come on, we both know your wife wanted to pick a fight with Mimsey. How else could you explain her wanting this...this...well, we can all use our imagination on which word, or series of words, I could use to describe it."

"Thanks a lot, friend! You guys are so bad!" Audrey chimed in playfully. "So maybe I don't know why I wanted it exactly, but something about it called out to me."

Regina stood up and began to act out a dramatic scene. "Audrey...yes, you! Come to me...feel me...take me home. Don't let Mimsey Pickard have me. It's you that I want." Regina finished her performance by lying across the top of the desk.

"Very funny," Audrey said, as she jumped up on the desk, pushing Regina's legs off to the side.

"So what brings you down here, Regina?" I asked her. "Tired of the good major?"

Regina sat up. "Actually, after my husband got that call from the White House, he dashed off like a bat out of hell. He said something serious had happened that needed his immediate attention. Hey, aren't you supposed to be there too?"

I thought about what to say. "Yes, I just wanted to grab a sandwich. I have to go right back. It's a pretty important matter, but I can't tell you the details."

"I understand. Dan gets those calls all the time, even in the middle of the night, but he can't ever tell me any of it. Well, I'll let you guys have some time alone. Call me later, Audrey."

When the door closed behind Regina, I looked at Audrey with a puzzled look.

"What is it?" Audrey asked.

"There's no problem at the White House. Some stupid cow got blown up in the minefield, and I'm the one who called McCarran. There's no reason in the world for him to have left Regina. Shoot, as a matter of fact, he berated me about having called him at all."

"What do you think it means, Adam?"

"I think it means Major McCarran isn't where he's supposed to be. He obviously used my phone call as an excuse to get away from Regina, but I have no idea why."

"Regina told me that he often leaves home, and she has no idea where he goes."

"Well, I think I can safely say that it's none of my business. It's all too strange. Speaking of strange, look what I brought home." I held up the *Book of the Dead* for Audrey to see. Her eyes widened as she reached for it, but I pulled it back.

"Not so fast!"

"Why?"

"I want to know why you really bought that ugly desk."

"It's not ugly!"

"Ok, I take that back. It's hideous."

"Adam! You're *sooo* not nice!"

"And you're *sooo* not telling me the truth!"

"The truth is I saw the desk and something about it made me want it. That's all!"

"So it had nothing to do with Mrs. Pickard wanting it too?"

"Absolutely not. Believe what you want, Adam. I just liked it."

"Okay, I believe you."

I handed her the *Book of the Dead* and she raced over to the kitchen table and began to thumb through the pages. I soon took a seat next to her and we didn't stop reading until it was time for bed.

🙟🙟 🙟🙟 🙟🙟

Although I read it in stories and had seen it in a thousand movies, I never really knew that roosters went "cockadoodle-doo" in real life at the crack of dawn. I also had no idea how incredibly maddening roosters are. I now understand why farmers keep firearms along their bedside; clearly the guns are for some basic doodle-doo management. In all honesty, had I slept the night before, I probably wouldn't have heard that stinkin' bird at all. However, Audrey and I had spooked ourselves pretty good the previous evening reading about dead people, and well, we tossed and turned quite a bit.

"What did you dream last night?" Audrey asked me as I was about to put my pillow over my head. Audrey dreams every night, and always remembers her dreams. I never remember mine. If it hadn't been scientifically proven that we all dream, I'd swear on a bible that I don't.

"I don't remember. What was yours?" I asked, knowing full and well that I was going to hear her dissertation at any moment.

"I dreamed I decided to fix up the desk, but I did it really wild. I painted it pink and yellow, and then I sprinkled glitter everywhere. It was weird."

"But colorful," I said, as I tried to drift back off to sleep.

"No, I mean the dream was weird. When I was done, I put it out on the lawn and everyone on base wanted it."

"So how much did you sell it for?" I asked, pretending to be interested, otherwise I get the you-don't-care-about-anything-I-say speech.

"I didn't. Every time someone would shout out a bid, someone else would raise the bid. It never stopped, and then I woke up."

"Bizarre," I said, like I say every morning. Then I actually mouthed the words she spoke next.

"What do you think it means?"

She always wants an answer so I always come up with something. "You're feeling guilty because you bought that desk to make a point, and so, in your dream, you made it all pretty so that it wasn't junk anymore."

"You think so?"

I was spared further questions by the ringing of the phone. It was Regina calling Audrey to ask when I'd be home. As it turned out, McCarran eventually went home and then left again in the middle of the night, telling Regina I'd called him. Audrey played dumb and told her I'd just walked through the door. Before Regina hung up, McCarran returned home. Audrey and I had no idea what to think. We were very uncomfortable covering for Major McCarran, but we didn't know what else to do.

6

Our first two months in Gitmo flew by. We could hardly believe it when we woke up one morning to find an invitation to a neighborhood Labor Day picnic taped to our door. It seemed as though we had just celebrated the Fourth of July and now it was September. The summer had been spent getting settled, so we hadn't interacted much socially with the other couples. The picnic afforded us the opportunity to relax and get to know everyone.

On our way down to the small park, which was located in the middle of our small traffic circle, I passed Master Sergeant Nelson and Phyllis Moser. They were sitting on lawn chairs facing the park, but, oddly, they seemed to go out of their way to pretend not to notice us. I waved anyway, but they continued to ignore us. As we continued down the road, we met up with Lieutenant Bradshaw and his wife, Rosie. His hands were full of sand toys for their children and her hands held a platter of a wonderful-smelling appetizer. We didn't engage in conversation as we walked, but we did exchange pleasantries.

When we arrived at the park, the women were gathered around the small, brown gazebo that served as a picnic area, arranging the foods that each brought to share. The men were busy setting up the volleyball net. Audrey and Regina had become the best of friends, and she'd also become friendly with Arlene Hill and Maura Gellar. She didn't hesitate to join the ladies around the goodies, and, having worked with all of the Marines daily, I was quite comfortable spending time with them. Just as I reached the corner of the volleyball court, I felt a hand on my shoulder.

"Adam!" Audrey said in a breathless whisper. "She's here!"

"Who's here?"

"The lady I had it out with at the exchange! She's over there by Arlene. I think they're friends."

A couple of weeks earlier, my wife had been in the parking lot at the exchange. While she was walking to her car, another car came flying into a parking space and almost hit her. Audrey watched the lady go into the employee entrance and decided to march back into the store. In a matter of moments, my wife had her second confrontation since arriving on the island. At the Labor Day picnic, we learned the employee she chose to confront was the wife of the sergeant major of the Barracks, the most senior enlisted Marine on base.

"So what do I do?" she asked me.

"What do you mean, 'what do I do?' Go over there and talk to her."

"No! She was the wrong one. God, this is so uncomfortable! What do I do?"

"Look, Audrey, if you're gonna have a confrontation with someone, you have to be willing to take the discomfort that comes with it. I'm sorry, but that's the truth of the matter. Listen, if you're not going to talk with her then just relax and hang out with the other ladies."

Audrey walked away from me, completely upset at my lack of sympathy for her. My wife is a lady of principle, and at times, she forgets she doesn't have to fight every battle that falls in her lap. Watching Audrey try and evade the sergeant major's wife made me feel good. I truly believed Audrey was learning an important lesson. Living in such close proximity to everyone on that little island made it wise to keep one's opinions to one's self, and keep confrontations to a minimum.

After a while, I had the opportunity to ask Warrant Officer Razor about Master Sergeant Moser. Audrey and I thought they were trying to ignore us.

"Hey, Tony, why isn't Master Sergeant Moser down here? He's just sitting on his lawn with his wife, staring at all of us."

Tony glanced down the street towards the Mosers, and in his thick New York accent said, "Fuck 'em."

"Okay, I can do that, but what's with them?"

"They're just pissed 'cause they didn't get a paper invitation. My wife ran out and had to call 'em instead. They think that they gotta call 'cause they're enlisted. Fuck 'em."

"Let me get this straight. They're mad at you because your wife ran out of invitations so she had called to invite them instead?"

"Yeah, they took it as an insult that they didn't get no formal invite. By the way, they ain't mad at only us. They're mad at everyone at the picnic, and they probably think it's some friggin' officer conspiracy."

I still didn't get it. "Why are they mad at everyone?"

"They think that we like you more than them 'cause you guys are officers."

"That's so stupid!"

"Tell me about it."

In spite of the Moser's private feel-sorry-for-us lawn party, and my wife's efforts to avoid all contact with the sergeant major's wife, I'd say we actually had a great time. There were conversations about base politics and upcoming events, parenting tips, and a whole lot of delicious food. At one point, Maura Geller and Rhonda Romero faced off in a cold pasta competition, since each lady claimed to be the better chef, but it was all in good fun. The volleyball game was especially entertaining with Ranagan and the new XO, Lt Colonel Ray, heading up the two teams. Mrs. Ranagan and Mrs. Ray pulled lawn chairs alongside their husbands' court, and rooted noisily. Out of six games, Colonel Ranagan's team won five. After the sixth game, when Ranagan's team lost, Lois promptly folded her chair, waved good-bye to everyone and walked home. Colonel Ranagan was close behind her.

On the way back to our house, Audrey told me she had a meeting to attend the following night.

"What meeting do you have to go to?"

"The Marine Wives Association, tomorrow at 6 pm."

I stopped dead in my tracks. Conway told me to keep Audrey away from that association. "What do you mean? You hate those kinds of clubs."

"You're right, I usually do, but Gitmo's different. Lois Ranagan told me about all of the wonderful things that the MWA does with their money, and besides, Maura, Jackie, Arlene, Rosie, Regina, Drew and Rhonda are all in it too. I'd feel left out if I didn't join."

I waited to continue the discussion at home. We were approaching the Moser's house, and they were still out on their lawn with scowls on their faces.

"Audrey, please don't join this group. Conway told me to have you stay away from it."

"Why would he have said that?"

"I'm actually not sure, but he said it, and something's telling me to listen to him."

Audrey broke into a smile. "Ah, come on, Adam, don't be like that. There's nothing wrong with that group or with any of the ladies. I had a great time with all of them tonight. I even think I misjudged Rhonda. She's actually really friendly."

I shook my head, knowing I'd been defeated. "Whatever Audrey. I just hope you know what you're getting into."

Two days later, the morning *after* the MWA meeting, I was standing outside Colonel Ranagan's office with Evan Geller in front of me and Ryan Hill behind me. We'd been instructed to report promptly at 0830.

"What's this all about?" I asked the other guys. Both men shrugged. When the door to Ranagan's office opened, Major McCarran stormed out without looking at any of us. We were soon gestured in.

"Gentlemen," the colonel began firmly, "I'm absolutely shocked and appalled right now. Do any of you know why I might be feeling this way?"

"No, sir," we said in unison.

"Last night, my wife—who gives her heart and soul to the Marine families here—was insulted, berated, criticized, and quite honestly, deeply offended. She cried her eyes out all night long. Do you know who made her feel this way?" the colonel barked.

"No, sir."

"Your wives! That's who!" The colonel paced around the room, muttering to himself. "I never thought the day would come when

I'd...see...something like this! Ungrateful wenches...that's what they are...ungrateful wenches!"

The three of us just stood there clenching our fists. We wanted to lash out, but we knew we wouldn't survive the aftermath.

"You Marines had better go home now and teach your wives some damn manners! Am I understood? Why such a lovely woman is treated so poorly is beyond me. Dismissed."

"Yes, sir," we answered, and each of us raced home to find out what the hell had happened at the Marine Wives Association meeting the night before. I bumped into Major McCarran in the parking lot; he was on his way home too. It turned out that anyone who had a wife at that meeting had been called in on the carpet and scolded by the colonel. I even saw Lt Colonel Ray heading home. Word had it that he'd gotten the brunt of the colonel's anger.

⩘⩘ ⩘⩘ ⩘⩘

The first meeting of the year for the Marine Wives Association came into session in the break room in the White House at 6pm sharp. The XO's wife, Drew Ray, had been voted in as president and she called the meeting to order. Curiously, Lois Ranagan didn't take a seat among the other wives, but instead chose to stand at a lectern, which was located behind Drew. Drew asked Lois if she wanted to sit around the table, but she told the ladies she was serving only as an advisor for the club. This unsettled Audrey because the last club advisor she remembered having was in high school.

Drew announced the first order of business—to vote in the new board members. Audrey was voted in as children's activities, Arlene as hospitality, Rhonda as fund raising, Regina as secretary, Maura as Newsletter Editor, and Jackie as Vice President. There were two other offices left to be filled.

"Is there anyone who wishes to be nominated for healthcare rep or exchange rep? These two jobs require the individuals to attend monthly meetings with these organizations, and to represent all concerns of the Marine families," Drew announced.

Rosie put her hand up immediately, but Lois calmly called out, "Actually, those jobs are no longer on the table."

Drew Ray, the XO's wife, turned around to look at Lois. "And why not?"

"Those are my responsibilities."

Drew looked down at her notes. "No, I don't see that written anywhere here. I think we need to have a vote."

"No. I can assure you that it's my responsibility, as the colonel's wife, to represent the Marine families on this base. There will be no need for a vote. Enough said," Lois said sternly.

Rhonda chimed in. "But, Lois, these are positions to be held by board members, and you said that you aren't a board member. You said you were only an advisor. I mean really, you don't even sit at our table—you stand behind us."

Lois Ranagan's face turned red. "Let's move on to the next order of business."

Drew reluctantly went down the list of items that were up for discussion. Most of them were inconsequential, except for the last one. "Okay, ladies, one more thing. We need to decide on whether or not to have a Fall Festival for the Marine families here in Gitmo."

After some dialogue, Drew took the vote and everyone agreed to have one.

"But what about the single Marines?" Arlene asked. "We really need to do something for the Marines who guard the fence-line and who have no families here."

"What were you thinking?" Maura asked Arlene.

"Well, since most of them will be on duty, what if we make little goodie bags and drop them off at the Barracks. We can decorate the packages and stuff them with candy and home-baked goods. I think it would be a great morale booster for these guys!"

Everyone agreed and seemed quite enthusiastic about Arlene's idea. Drew took it up for a vote and it was unanimous—there would be goodie bags for all of the single Marines.

"I'm sorry," Lois interrupted, "but I can't allow that."

Drew spun around to look at Lois again. "What do you mean 'you can't allow that'? We voted on it as board members."

"You heard what I said. I won't allow Marine Wives Association money to be spent that way."

"I guess you're not hearing me, Lois, but you don't have the authority to make any decision," Drew insisted.

Lois clinched her jaw tightly and stared angrily at Drew Ray. "Drew, I'm the advisor here and I believe I've made myself clear."

Rhonda was biting her lip to keep from shouting. "Lois, could you please show me *where* in the by-laws it says that the advisor can veto the board?"

"Yes," said Audrey calmly. "I'd like to see the by-laws too."

Lois stood still, unable to comprehend the insubordination. "You'll all receive copies tomorrow, although it hardly seems necessary."

"Well, actually, Lois," Drew replied, "I think that it's very necessary. If you don't have a vote at the board-member table, but you can veto our decisions at any time, what we really have here is a modified dictatorship, not a club!"

"Why don't we table the decision to make goodie bags for our next meeting in October?" Regina offered politely to ease the tension. Everyone agreed. When the meeting was over, the CO's wife walked out of the room without talking to anyone.

～❧ ～❧ ～❧

"And that's all that was said?" I asked, unconvinced.

"Yes Adam, that's all, everything! The whole shebang!"

"Then who was the one that berated her and made her cry?"

"Listen to me, Adam, no one was rude to her. Perhaps, at times, we challenged her opinion, but no one called her any names, no one raised their voice, and no one was mean to her. The worst thing we did was to politely tell her she wasn't queen bee."

"But I don't get it. Ranagan flipped out! He made it sound like you guys were horrible."

"Well, maybe the story I told you wasn't the same story he heard. Maybe she made up a whole bunch of other stuff so that he'd feel sorry for her."

"No way. Ya think?"

"Look, she basically stood over us and said, 'No matter what you say, do, or think, the only decisions you can make are the ones I like.' Now what the hell kind of association is that?"

"Sounds more like the *Cuban* Marine Wives Association, huh?"

"No kidding. It's actually kind of scary. By the way, there's something I want to tell you about," she said, changing the subject.

"What is it?"

"I got a job today. I saw it on the roller last week and applied for it."

The roller was the base TV news station where all of our current events and weather are posted. "Fantastic! What's your job gonna be?"

"I'm going to be the new Spanish translator at the Cuban migrant camp."

My smile fell quickly. Once or twice a week, Cubans would try to seek asylum on our base and were invariably caught by the Marines. Other times, Cubans built boats and sailed to America, only to be caught by the Coast Guard and shipped back to Gitmo to a immigrant camp to await repatriation to Cuba. These people braved shark infested waters, minefields, Cuban gunboats and possibly retribution from Castro upon their return, but they still tried to flee anyway. All in all, most refugees were decent people, but sometimes there were criminals, and there were occasionally riots in the camp.

"I'm not going to say no, but I'm not really excited about this."

"I know, but I need to do this. Besides," Audrey said with a wink, "it will keep me away from the CO's wife for eight hours a day."

She had a point.

7

I returned to the White House after talking to Audrey, feeling like the day would never end. After the tongue lashing we'd all received earlier that morning, I wasn't motivated to do much work. Morale among most of the married Marines was low. We all loved our wives and wanted to believe their story, but the colonel was so adamant about the way his wife had been treated, it was hard to believe nothing more had occurred that night. In any event, close-of-business eventually arrived, and we were all thankful to go home and put the Wives Association incident into the past.

When I got home, I fully expected Audrey to be waiting for me on the lawn to discuss the day's events, but she wasn't. She was in the back guest bedroom, sitting on the hard green tile, papers and books littered about.

"What ya doing, honey?" She didn't answer me. "Sweetheart? What are you looking at?"

"Oh, hi," she said as she continued reading.

"*Oh, hi*? How about an 'I'm glad your home' or 'God! I missed you'?" I joked.

Audrey put down her papers and smiled at me. "I'm sorry,

Adam, but I'm just so absorbed in all of this right now." She cleared a spot for me to sit next to her. "Come here. I want to show you something."

I sat beside her on the floor. "What have you got there?"

"Well, when you left today, after telling me about that freak Colonel Ranagan and his tirade, I was so furious that I had to do something to get my mind off of what he said. Anyway, I decided to look over the *Book of the Dead* again and I found some of the stuff Conway told you about."

"What did you find, and what does Conway have to do with it?"

"You told me he'd said strange things happen in Gitmo, and now I've found some of them!"

"Like what?"

"Like this," she said, consulting some notes scribbled on a legal pad. "When we first looked at the *Book of the Dead*, we looked at it at face value, meaning we read it as a death log—written by the hospital staff over the years—which listed the hows, whats and whos of those who have died here in Guantanamo Bay over the past one-hundred years."

"Well, that's because it's a death log. There's nothing strange about that." I was unimpressed.

"No, you don't get it! If you look at it line by line, you see dates, but when you do it like this," she said pointing to her notes again, "you see *patterns*."

"Bring it home Audrey. I'm lost."

She let out a big sigh and took her papers back. "From 1930 to 1939, seven babies were born dead. From 1940-1949, 18 babies were born dead. Now get this, from 1950-1959, when the base female population was virtually the same as it was in the forties, 124 babies died at birth or shortly there after."

"Wow, that sounds like a lot of deaths."

"Yeah, too many. But wait, from 1960-1969, when the base female population was almost doubled, there were only twenty babies born dead."

"What else did you find?" I asked, now giving Audrey one hundred percent of my attention.

"There have been numerous drowning deaths over the years, but if you look closely, three people drown every eight and a half years—exactly. You gotta admit that's strange. And what's more, each of the deaths happen in the same bodies of water."

"Are you sure about that?"

"Positive. From 1908 until 1979, it happened in threes, every eight and a half years."

"Ok. I'm spooked. Anything else?"

"In each decade, exactly eleven people die from the same disease. For instance, in the twenties, eleven people died of malaria. In the thirties, eleven people died of pneumonia. In the forties, eleven people died of small pox. And in the fifties eleven women died..."

I interrupted her before she could say the words. "Eleven women died in childbirth."

"No, cancer, but you get the idea."

"Did you learn anything else besides stuff about dead people?"

"Ah...yeah," she said as she looked down her list. "In the seventies, a Cuban worker mysteriously took out a hatchet and chased a sailor around Cooper Field until he was all chopped up. They never found a motivation for the murder. And another weird thing: in the fifties, a Marine corporal was presumed dead when his uniform and ID were found at one of the beaches, but they never found a body or anything."

"This is some strange stuff," I said shaking my head.

"You ain't kidding! But also in the fifties, I think about the same time, two Cubans reported to work on base, but they never signed back out. No bodies were every found nor any signs of foul play, and the truck that they drove on base has never turned up. Bizarre, huh?"

"You can say that again. Hey, did you find out anything about our Ocean View residents?"

"Not really. But I got lots more for ya!"

Audrey and I spent the rest of the night talking about the things she'd uncovered about our sleepy little town. In 1962, during the Cuban missile crisis, all the women and children had been given fifteen minutes to pack a bag and wait out front of their homes for a bus to the airport or dock. Some had to leave their dinners cooking on the stove. They'd been instructed to lay their house keys on the dining room table and shut off the lights. In the late seventies, a Marine captain and his family were whisked away by the Naval Criminal Investigative Service and flown off the island to protect their lives. It turned out that the Marine

CO at the time had been smuggling weapons out of Gitmo and the captain blew the whistle. NCIS had uncovered a plan by the colonel to have the captain killed in an military mishap. In the fifties, when servicemen could take liberty in some of the local Cuban cities, twenty-six Marines and sailors were kidnapped while out in town. Once they had returned, four of them had been diagnosed with a form of Stockholm Syndrome, a disorder which makes the captured sympathize with his or her abductors.

The creepiest tale of all came from the chaplain's report to the base CO in the early nineties. Marines who stood guard at Post 13 on Leeward would often describe hearing and seeing events of the supernatural. In some cases, Marines saw the decapitated body of a Marine sergeant, killed in a land-mine explosion many years earlier, warning the men to stay alert. In other instances, numerous Marines reported hearing the cry of a woman who had drowned with her children in the Gitmo River while trying to escape Communist Cuba. Her screams were always the same: "Help us Marines...please help us."

❧ ❧ ❧

At six in the morning, my alarm rang to welcome me to another sunny day in beautiful Guantanamo Bay. If you've ever seen the movie *Ground Hog Day* with Bill Murray, where a man is force to relive the same day over and over again for years, you'll understand life on our island. Even the five-day weather planner on the TV always looked the same. In all five boxes, each representing a day, there sat an enormous yellow circle forecasting unremitting sunshine and cloudless blue skies. From September to March, the high is eighty-six degrees and the low is seventy-six. In the months of April to August, the high is always ninety-six and the low is always eighty-six. I think once, no, maybe twice, there was a yellow circle with half a cloud through it. You can't imagine how much chatter was generated from half a cloud.

Audrey was up early too—she was starting her new job at the migrant camp. After reading the article about the crazed Cuban hatchet man, she was understandably more cautious, which made me happy.

"Well, wish me luck!" she said as she hugged me goodbye.

"Good Luck. I know you'll do great!"

"Thanks, but I feel bad that I'm taking our only car. We should really think about getting a second one."

"Yeah," I said disappointedly, "but I guess that'll have to wait for now." But I was way ahead of her. As a matter of fact, Guy Armstrong—the Communications Officer—was about to swing by and take me car shopping as a surprise for Audrey. We'd brought our five-year-old Jeep with us to Gitmo, but I wanted to buy something nicer for Audrey to drive.

I kissed her goodbye and watched her leave. Not five minutes later, Guy pulled up in the ugliest car I've ever seen in my life. It was a 1976 orange Pacer, or fishbowl car; I wasn't sure whether I should get in or grab a plastic castle to stick in the window. The unattractive nature of his Pacer was further accentuated by high tech aerials mounted on the hood and mega speakers installed in back. Yup, he was a total geek, but in Gitmo, that made him kind of cool.

"What the hell is this, Mr. Armstrong? Has there been a pay decrease for Comm O's?" I snickered.

"I'm here to tell you I have one of the finer Gitmo specials on base and I resent your last comment!"

"Gitmo Special...what's up with that?"

"Oh Adam. Poor, ignorant, Adam. You've no idea what you're in for today, do you?" he said, putting his arm around my shoulders. "I have five cars lined up for you to see. Mind you, these are the only five cars on the island for sale, so you'll be bringing one of them home, unless, of course, you want to walk everywhere."

That sounded easy enough until we actually saw the automobiles. To put this car shopping experience in perspective, I ended up buying the nicest looking, best running car in all of Gitmo. Audrey was soon to be treated to the sight of our classic 1975 Purple Gremlin with flames painted down the side. The car cost me $1250 cash-on-the-barrel head. Truthfully, that was more than it was worth when it was new, and it didn't even have a radio or AC.

To top it all off, the gentleman I bought it from—a Jamaican — had long since lost the title, so we used a Gitmo title. A Gitmo title was a 4x8 inch piece of paper printed at the base print shop, and no joke, it read like this:

I, _____ declare that this _____ is owned by
STATE YOUR NAME   YEAR, MAKE, AND MODEL
me.

On the reverse side it stated that:

On this date of, ____, I am selling this car to, _____.
DATE   BUYER'S NAME

SELLER SIGNATURE   WITNESS SIGNATURE

We didn't have to have it notarized or have it checked over by
base security; he just signed the bottom and had a passerby in
the parking lot witness it. Then, the Gremlin was mine—all
mine! The informality was unreal—not that I would've ever
shipped that jalopy back to the States. But if I had, just imagine
the reaction of the DMV lady when I presented my Gitmo title.
I can't imagine it going well for me. It would look as credible
as taking a piece of paper and writing a random date on it in
crayon, and telling her it was my birth certificate.

Well, at least I had a car to drive, no matter how embarrassing
it was. Guy told me later that he was a little jealous of my
purchase, which worried me until he clarified himself. It seems
that everyone has one nice car and one Gitmo Special in their
driveway. Because of this, coolness was based on how crappy
your second car was. And, in that case, I guess I was pretty
damn cool.

〜〜 〜〜 〜〜

Due to a last minute meeting, I was late coming home that
evening. By the time I'd gotten to the house, Audrey had dinner
prepared and we sat down to eat as soon as I walked through
the door. I apologized for being late, but Audrey hadn't even
noticed—she had something else on her mind. It was also clear
she hadn't seen me drive up in my purple babe magnet.

"Is something wrong?" I asked. "Did something happen at work
today? You look sad or upset."

Audrey tossed around her food before answering. "Work was
great. I really think I'm going to love it there. Right now there
are only five families and a few single men, so the group is pretty
small. I actually only translate for the women."

"Was it exciting?"

"Yeah, it's nice being able to use a skill I've spent years and
years perfecting."

"Then what's with the long face?"

"When I got home, the phone was ringing and I thought it was you, but it was Lois Ranagan."

I put my fork down and wiped my face with the napkin. "So what did she want?"

I sat back and she recited the whole conversation to me.

"Hello?"

"Audrey?"

"Yes?"

"This is Lois Ranagan. How are you today?"

"I'm fine. How are you?"

"I'm doing just grrreat! Are you all settled in and enjoying your new job at the camp?"

Audrey wondered how Lois found out about her job, but didn't want to ask. "Yes, everything's really homey for us now and I think my job's going to really work out nicely."

"That's super! Listen, the reason I'm calling is because I wanted to ask if you'll be coming to my tea next weekend. As you know, I'm going to have some wonderful guest speakers flown all the way from Quantico. It would be a shame if you weren't there."

"Well, actually, while it sounds lovely, next weekend is our sixth wedding anniversary and Adam said he's made some romantic plans for us. But I do want to thank you for inviting me. That was very thoughtful of you."

"Oh really? Well, I know my husband has told your husband how important this event is, so if your husband planned something on a day he knows he's not supposed to, then I don't think my husband would understand. Do you understand what I'm saying?"

Audrey was speechless. For all intents and purposes, Lois had just threatened my wife. It was clear that if Audrey didn't go to Lois Ranagan's Tea, then I was going to have to have another lashing from the colonel. "Yes, Lois, I'll be there."

"Wonderful! Remember to dress appropriately—sharp and snappy! See you next weekend!"

I SAT BACK IN MY KITCHEN CHAIR, absolutely dumbfounded. Lois Ranagan had no right to say what she had to my wife, and I told Audrey not to go to the tea. I forbade her to go. After much discussion, Audrey said she wanted to. I didn't understand her thinking until she explained she'd felt guilty for the run-in with Mimsey Pickard, and for getting me in trouble with the colonel for the whole Wives Association mess. If she went to the tea, it's true it would be uncomfortable, but she felt it was a better option than getting me flogged again by Ranagan.

"Changing the subject, what did you do today?" she asked me.

"Funny you should ask, honey."

"Oh, why's that?"

"Well, I'd like to tell you the truth, but you'll probably revoke all purchasing privileges for the rest of my life"

She rolled her eyes. "What did you buy, Adam?"

My mind was racing. She was going to absolutely hate my new car. The only thing that could possibly redeem it was if I'd bought her some amazing diamond ring and placed it on the front seat. "I bought a car."

"A car? You bought a car without including me in the decision?"

"Yeah, but it's only because it was going to be for you. I wanted it to be this huge surprise." Which was kind of true; she'd definitely be surprised.

"What kind of car is it?"

"Close your eyes and imagine the car you've always dreamed of: sporty, trendy, eye-catching—a true American classic!"

"Is it here?" I just pointed to the driveway and got ready to duck and cover.

"Ho-lee, Adam! Tell me we don't own that...that...thing out there!"

I met her in the driveway and threw in some humor before I showed her the title. "Well, actually, no, Audrey, it doesn't belong to us. But after fort-eight payments, this baby's gonna be all ours!" That was the point where she started to shake "Come on, Audrey. This is the best I could find, and just to show you that I'm a good sport, I'll even let you drive it every other day. Look at it this way, you always wanted to be the center of attention, and in this fine automobile, you'll be the center of attention, even when you don't want to be!"

Audrey just looked at the car with the violet flames running down the side, and at about the time I thought she was going to ask for a divorce, she began to laugh. After a few moments, I started to laugh, too.

She opened the car door, settled into the fuzzy purple seat cover, and gave me a very seductive look. "Hey," she called out, "how 'bout we go and christen this thing?"

8

The day before Lois Ranagan's tea, I had my first flight aboard one of the Naval Station's two Search and Rescue helicopters, the HH-1N—or Huey. It was sitting outside the pink hangar on Leeward, festooned in shiny orange and white paint. All the other Hueys I'd flown in the Marine Corps were the utility variant and had been painted a flat battleship-gray, so this was a little bit of a change for me. Once inside the cockpit, however, she looked like every one I'd ever flown, and I was excited to get her airborne.

The Huey is not a high-tech, high performance bird by any means. In the sixties and seventies, it was the military's workhorse, seeing action from the Mekong Delta all the way to the DMZ. When I was at flight school, a Marine colonel on the brink of retirement asked me which aircraft I would fly. When I told him the Huey, he shouted back, "That's God's machine!" I didn't quite know what generated that response, but after 1000 hours or so flying it, I came to share the sentiment.

Because the Navy no longer used Hueys except in a few isolated locations, I was the only pilot on the island who was actually a Huey pilot by trade. The other two Navy pilots in Gitmo normally flew other aircraft and had been given a three-month transition course in Hueys prior to arriving at Gitmo. Though they both had more flying experience than I did, neither of them had much time in Hueys; this caused some initial contention between us.

I think most pilots would agree that the twin-engine Huey is probably one of the hardest helicopters in the US inventory to fly. It doesn't have any real type of stabilization system and it's relatively easy to damage both the engines and rotor because it doesn't have effective systems to prevent them from over-speeding or over-torqueing. To put it simply, without a lot of experience piloting them, Hueys are relatively hard to fly and easy to break. My confidence was high due to the relatively large number of Huey hours in my logbook and the demanding tactical flights we Marines conducted in them. On the other hand, neither of the Navy pilots had many Huey hours at all, nor had they flown them in anything other than the benign, controlled environment of Gitmo.

They were the station pilots, however, and even if they hadn't outranked me, I would still have tried to fly the bird at their comfort level. Though I saw nothing wrong with some controlled aggressiveness behind the stick, I truly had the best of intentions to tone it down. It didn't work out so well.

As it turned out, their comfort level was so insufferably low— as was their impression of Marine pilots—it would probably have been impossible to satisfy them. Though I didn't try anything remotely interesting, let alone risky, I did fly that helicopter like it was meant to be flown, and, that scared them a little. While I might admit I should have flown less assertively the first time around, there was absolutely no justification for the spaz attack Captain Pickard had in back.

On the day in question, Navy Commander Tom Stanford, Navy Commander Bruce Cleary, the base CO Captain Pickard, and a Navy photographer were all on board for my first flight: ferrying the CO from Windward to Leeward, then flying a routine intelligence-gathering flight around the base perimeter. We loaded up our passengers in a large clearing on Radio Point before I pulled in some power for a smooth no-hover takeoff. Per the manual, I simultaneously lowered the nose and we crossed the edge of the cliffs and dipped momentarily to the rocks below. As I transitioned the bird into level flight for the short two-mile trip to the other side, my comfort level was high and my only concern was that I might mistakenly fly into Cuban airspace. I had no idea I'd already confirmed their worst opinions of "those reckless Marine pilots". The CO was most upset by the "unnecessary maneuver"— apparently, he'd have preferred a vertical takeoff to a hover instead of me dipping the nose like I did.

The base CO promptly disembarked on Leeward Airfield and the rest of us continued with the intel-gathering portion of the flight. Having no idea of the ruckus my takeoff had created in the back of the helicopter, I was able to enjoy the remainder of the flight. From the air, Gitmo had an extraordinary affect on me and all the people who got to see it from a bird's-eye view. The contrasts between the modest-sized base against the magnitude of its host-nation, the jagged cliffs rising from the foamy sea, the picturesque waters of a hundred shades of blue all stir an emotion which is unparalleled.

Taking off again from Leeward Point, we climbed across the mouth of the bay to Windward point and set up for a counterclockwise circuit of the fence-line. We climbed along the coast until we reached the cooler air at about 1500 feet and I edged to the right and headed out to sea about a half a mile. As we leveled off, I banked left and headed east, paralleling the rocky shoreline. The whole Windward side of the base looked like a small movie set. What would take an hour or more by car took seconds by air and the whole coast was visible in a single frame: Cable Beach, Cuzco Wells, the magazine area, a small cemetery, and Windmill and Kittery Beaches, were all laid out neatly in a row. At Kittery Beach, I made a hard left so I didn't cross the fence-line into Cuban territory, and we began the circuit. We paralleled the fence-line road and crossed over some of our minefields, as the intel photographer took telephoto shots of all of the Cuban guard posts and any traffic along the Castro Barrier Road or CBR. A short eight miles later, we were hovering over the Northeast Gate and its companion Marine Observation Post (or MOP) 34. Originally, there had been forty-five MOPs along the fence-line, but as the towers grew taller, the smaller ones in between were abandoned, but the remaining towers still kept their original number designation.

We next turned west towards the water gate and MOP-21. The water gate was the narrowest point of Guantanamo Bay: it was only about 150 yards wide and the closest point to any Cuban cities. The steel tower of MOP-21 stood next to the water gate and it was like having a window into Guantanamo City and Caimanera. From there, the Marine sentry could also see sharks swimming, as well as the Cubans' swimmer-nets and light towers that hampered attempts by Cuban nationals to swim to the naval base. Although the view from MOP-21 was one of my favorites on the base, it couldn't compete with the view we had from up above.

I finished the circuit on the Leeward side before starting the whole trip over again at a lower altitude. Though it was tempting to take her down low along the cliffs of the bay or blow right by the colonel's office at the White House, I had no such fun. We finished the flight uneventfully before returning to Leeward to photograph a few of the minefields for Ryan Hill. Prior to bringing her back to the airport, I cruised slowly over the Gitmo River at a few hundred feet to search for an alligator one of the crew chiefs claimed to have seen before setting her back down at the airfield.

Everything was so uneventful, it wasn't until the next day that I caught the rumor that Captain Pickard was pissed. I never really figured that one out. The thing was, I hadn't done anything that aircraft wasn't designed to do, nor had I done anything illegal or even very interesting. I was just the only pilot on the island who wasn't timid with the aircraft. Although no one actually told me I was in the doghouse, the absence of my name on the flight schedule for the next few months told me exactly what had happened. Captain Pickard had spoken. Could I've been showing off a little? Sure. But it still stung that the most enjoyable part of my duties at Gitmo had been striped away, if only temporarily.

Although Audrey was supposed to get home long before me, she wasn't there when I got back. I took a shower, grabbed the *Gitmo Gazette*, and stretched out on the bed waiting for her to come home. Since Audrey usually reads the *Gazette* and tells me about it, it had been my first real look at our base paper. At only eight pages, it was more like a newsletter, but it's all we had. The front cover had a story about a Cuban worker who was celebrating his ninetieth birthday, a story about conserving water, and a blurb about the completion of the Ocean View Housing demolition project. Fifty or more years of memories were gone with the push of a bulldozer.

When Audrey got home, she had her hands full of shopping bags. Feeling sorry for the Cubans she worked with, she decided to swing by the base thrift store to pick up some clothing for them, which is why she was late. At the bottom of one of the bags, she had a special surprise for me.

"Adam, I found this in one of the old boxes in the back of their storeroom." With that, she pulled a set of fifties-era Marine cammies out of the sack. "Being a history buff and all, I thought that you might want this old uniform."

"Yeah, thanks. This is really great," I said as I looked over the uniform carefully. "I can't believe how different they are from the ones we wear today."

"I wonder who used to own this and why it's been sitting in the thrift store so long? I'd think that a lot of people would want it."

"Who knows? You said that it was well hidden—maybe it's just gotten overlooked over the years." I began to search through the pockets and came up with something really neat. "Hey look, honey. This was stuck in one of the back pockets."

"What is it?"

"I can't believe it! It's a Gitmo car title and it looks almost exactly like the one I have for the Gremlin. I guess that things never change."

"Who owned it?"

"I can't really read all the writing, but the kind of car is very clear. It was a 1950 Chevy Bel Air—with turquoise and white paint."

"That's really exciting. That guy stuck that in his pants pocket, dropped his uniform off at the Thrift store and now we have his car title in our hands almost fifty years later. That's kinda cool."

I hated to ruin the moment, but I knew that I had to tell Audrey about what Pickard had done to Ocean View. We took a drive down there after a while and looked around. The foundations were still there, as were the paths that lead to the front doorways, but no other signs of life. Even the tree house had been destroyed.

Ryan Hill, the minefield maintenance officer and my next-door neighbor, had told me the next time I was down in that area, to drive to the end of the development to an old chain-link fence. Once there, I was to pass through the opening and follow the worn-out road to its end. The road ran along the cliff's edge, overlooking the mouth of the bay.

We came upon a long-abandoned fortification. It was a two-gun shore battery from long ago that once held soldiers, cannons and ammunition. Audrey and I climbed on it with the vigor of kids pretending to be on the look-out for pirate ships entering the bay. As it turns out, way back when, Guantanamo Bay was a famous stopping ground for pirates. They often used the protected waters of the bay to ride out storms, abandon their sick or to re-stock their supplies. And, though Audrey and I enjoyed our brief pirate fantasy, the fort and its companion, Hicacal Fort on Leeward, were actually used to guard the mouth of the bay in World War I, long after buccaneers had faded into lore.

Since we could see the end of the road from the fort, Audrey and I decided to walk the rest of the way. All along, we kept seeing tons of little rodent droppings which looked exactly like the droppings on our back walkway, in the picnic areas, and on the streets. We knew it had to be from the legendary banana rats. As they were nocturnal, neither of us had ever actually seen one in real life, but we'd heard a lot about them. They looked a lot like a possum/rat and were about the size of a raccoon. They loved to get under cars and chew the wires, eat decorative plants in gardens and lay their droppings everywhere. Despite the fact the base had become over-run with them, despite the sanitation risk they posed to school children on the playground, and that they'd caused thousands of dollars in damages to our cars, Pickard wouldn't allow anyone to kill them. In Cuban territory, they had been hunted and eaten to near extinction, so Pickard said they could swarm our base freely.

About the time we had grown tired of dodging rodent feces, we came to the end of the road. To the right of us was a very steep stairway down along a rocky cliff. We started down the stairs, keeping a tight grip on the railing, and when we reached the bottom, we felt as though we'd discovered a private seashore all our own. Glass Beach, as we later learned it was called, was merely a small strip of sand among boulders and coastline. There was barely enough room to put your towel down without getting it wet. As we strolled along, we noticed the inordinate amount of broken, polished glass lying on the sand. The shades of the smoothened shards were unlike any I'd ever seen. Of course there were greens and browns, but also pinks, turquoise, aqua, lavender, lilacs, yellows and sapphire. We couldn't come up with any reasonable explanation as to why all that glass was there, but we didn't care. We collected as much as we could carry and headed back for the car.

On our way back to the house, we decided to go out to dinner, even though on our small base, the choices were limited. At one time, Guantanamo Bay had numerous places to gather and eat, but during our tour, we only had the Jerk House, a Jamaican-style outdoor grill; the Windjammer, which was also the enlisted club/multi-purpose building; the Navy Exchange Sandwich Shop; Post 46, which served hot poppers, onion rings and fried chicken; The Cuba Club, featuring Cuban foods; McDonald's; or the Bayview, which was the officer's club.

The Bayview, which was located in Captain Pickard's neighborhood, Deer Point, wasn't just for officers; because of the downsizing of the base, the club was opened for all base residents to dine. Attached to the restaurant was a decent sized bar called Rick's Lounge. On certain days and special occasions, Rick's became an officer only establishment. I've never been one to affix my rank to my ego, but I soon realized the officers and enlistees were much more familiar with each other in Gitmo than in any other place that I'd ever been stationed. We lived in the same neighborhoods, worked in the same spaces, shared walls in the BOQ, ate at all the same places. Work was never separated from home life and more importantly, home life was never separated from work. And as the base population continued to decrease, the officers and enlistees became that much closer. Although there never came a time when giving an order to a Marine was difficult, many good friendships did develop across ranks. Work occasionally got done slower, and feelings were easier to offend.

When we walked through the Bayview doors, the first thing that Audrey noticed was the new XO, Lt Colonel Ray and his wife motioning to us. While Audrey and I were hoping to have a quiet dinner alone, we could hardly ignore the XO.

"Good evening!" Drew called out. "Why don't you both take a seat with us?"

"That would be very nice," Audrey said. "Thank you for the invitation."

"How are you doing tonight, sir?" There's nothing like sitting down to eat and having to mind your P's and Q's throughout the meal.

"I'm doing well. You better dig in! This is some pretty good chow."

"So, how do you like it here Drew?" Audrey asked. "We arrived the same week, but I've hardly had any time to talk to you."

Drew Ray wiped her mouth before answering. "I like it here, I do. Of course, there are a few people that I could do without." She looked at Audrey like Audrey knew who she was talking about.

"How about you, sir? Do you like it here?"

"Yes and no. I think this island is great and the scuba diving is awesome, but administratively, I have some problems with the way things are run here."

"How's that, sir?" I said, not believing I'd asked that question. He obviously had problems with Ranagan's management style and I had no business asking for details.

"He could answer that," Drew cut in, "but then his meal would get too cold to eat."

Lt Col Ray laughed as he sipped his drink. "You can say that again!"

"I have to know, Audrey, what you thought of the Wives Association meeting this week?" Drew asked.

"What do you mean?" Audrey didn't want to touch that question with a ten foot pole.

"I mean, didn't you think that Lois was out of line?"

Audrey looked at me, hoping I could dig her out of that one, but I was at a loss for words myself. "I think...I think that Lois has a different idea about the association's direction than the board members do."

"So you agree that she was out of line?" Drew probed.

"Ah...out of line? Maybe...but then again, it was our first meeting and we all just kinda need to get to know each other I think."

"Well, I certainly think that she was totally out of line! She wants to meet with me after the tea tomorrow. Are you going?"

Audrey would've loved nothing more than to spill her guts about her real feelings for Lois Ranagan, but the Rays were new to us too. We had no idea who we could trust yet. "Yes, I am."

"Did she tell you to dress 'sharp and snappy', too? I've been a Marine wife for a very long time and no one has ever told me how to dress, much less at my age."

"How about me?" Lt Col Ray added. "I'm a Lt Colonel with umpteen years in the Corps and I had to get counseled on how my wife needs to treat the CO's wife! For goodness sakes. I've already been a CO elsewhere—I think I know a little about how to treat a CO's wife!"

Audrey and I kept as quiet as we could. We really started to like the Rays. They seemed to be friendly, warm people, but while we shared their frustration, anything we said to them could—and probably would—come back to haunt us later. Instead, we told them about Glass Beach.

🙢🙢 🙢🙢 🙢🙢

It was still pretty light out when we finished dinner, and we thought about going to Rick's for a drink, but decided to drive around instead. After only a few minutes, we passed an automobile junkyard that had the most amazing cars in it. We decided to go back for a better look, and we were lucky enough to find the gate unlocked. As we walked around, it felt like we had just entered a time warp.

The cars were some of the greatest American classics of all time: Mustangs, Thunderbirds, El Dorados, Fairlanes—they were all there. The newest model parked was from around 1968, and the oldest dated back to the forties. Of course they were all in desperate need of total restoration, but that didn't matter to us. We just wanted to get up close and take a look for ourselves. While I was busy checking out a '67 Bug, Audrey had inexplicably wandered to the far side of the yard toward a 1950 Chevy Bel Air with turquoise and white paint. She walked all the way around it and managed to pull open the driver's side door. I watched her climb inside and take hold of the wheel. Her interest in the run-down car puzzled me since she'd never been much of a car enthusiast. Then it hit me! She'd found a car that matched the description on the title we'd found in the uniform.

"Hey, did you find one that you want to take home?" She acted as if she didn't hear me and continued to crawl around the front seat of the car. "Audrey...did you hear me? I asked if you want that one instead of the Gremlin," but no answer.

She turned every switch she could, felt underneath the seats, jimmied the lock on the glove compartment open and rummaged through it. I finally stuck my head into the car to get her attention. "Audrey, what's going on? Why are you ignoring me?"

She sat up and looked at me. "There's something about this car Adam. I think this is the one that we read about."

"There's no way that this is *the* car. I admit that it looks just like the one on the title, but this was an extremely popular car back then and these were extremely poplar colors." Audrey jumped into the back seat and continued her examination. "Don't suppose you want some company back there, do you?" I asked her in my extra sexy voice, but she ignored me again. "What are you doing Audrey? Are you looking for something specific? Maybe I can help you look."

She sat back up and looked straight out the windshield. "I'm not looking for anything, but all of a sudden I'm very intrigued about the owner of this car."

I decided to play along with her. "Ok, I'll go look in the trunk." I walked around the car to the back and fidgeted with the lock, until it sprang open. Fifty years of rust really ran in my favor. When I looked inside, I saw the metal frame of the car, pieces of worn carpeting, a tire iron, banana rat poop, and what looked like a small tool kit. I decided to show it to Audrey, holding it out for her to see. "Is this what you're looking for?"

"I said I'm not looking for anything in particular. I guess I'm just looking for clues to the owner's identity. Let me see what you found."

I opened the door and slid in next to her across the deteriorated fabric. I gave it to her to open, and, after a moment, she lifted the top off. There was nothing inside.

"Adam, where did you find the tool kit...*exactly?*"

I walked to the back of the car. "Right here, next to this tire iron."

Audrey lifted what remained of the trunk carpet from the place where I'd found the tool kit. Lying there was a set of dog tags, encrusted with what looked like dried blood or old paint. She put it in my hand. I scraped away some of the dried substance, and I made out the name engraved in the metal. With a quickened pace, I walked towards our car.

"What are you doing, Adam? Where are you going?"

"You know exactly where I'm going!"

"Adam! Come back."

I stopped and headed back to the car. "What is it?"

"Look at this," Audrey said, pulling back all of the trunk flooring, exposing an incomprehensible sight. "I think that it's blood too. The trunk's just covered in it." The sun had begun to set and we were losing light, so we weren't sure about anything. But I caught a glimpse of something tucked in the wheel well.

"Audrey, this just got even stranger." I reached into the wheel well and pulled out a set of fifties-era Marine cammies, which reminded us of the one's Audrey had just bought. They were also covered in the unexplained substance.

"Oh my God, something happened in this car. Something really bad."

"We don't know that, Audrey—we don't know anything for sure." I put the uniform down and headed back to the main passenger compartment of the Bel Air to have a second look.

Audrey looked around the darkening salvage yard. "I feel like someone's watching us."

"Audrey, come here. I think I figured something out."

"What is it?" She slowly approached the front seat.

"This car was purposely impaired."

"What do you mean?"

"I mean that these seats didn't get torn with everyday use. They were cut. The speedometer casing is cracked and the needle's been torn off. The gear shift's been jammed with a piece of wood lodged down in the column." I took a look underneath and then popped the hood. "The fuel lines were cut, the engine is in shambles—it looks like a sledge hammer was taken to it."

"But why?"

"How the hell do I know, Audrey? I'm just guessing like you are. It could've been vandalized after it was put in this place. Who knows?" I was trying to hide signs of anxiety, but I was very disturbed about what we'd discovered.

"How do you know that the engine isn't messed up because it was in an accident?"

"It's really obvious, Audrey. There's no body damage. That also makes me think that it wasn't vandals either. Any delinquent bashing in the lights, windows and body panels would've been much more satisfied than they'd have been smashing up a carburetor or distributor. I tell you Audrey, this whole situation is really weird." I gathered the uniform and dog tags; Audrey closed the trunk and shut the doors and hood. "It's dark now. Let's head home. There's got to be something about this in all those papers Conway left for me."

"Do you really think so, Adam?"

"We'll soon find out."

9

I was incapable of driving the mandatory 25 mph along Sherman Avenue to our home. Audrey and I used the few minutes of our drive to discuss whether or not we should go to base security—we decided against it. After all, what did we really know? We hadn't determined for certain whom the car belonged to and we hadn't positively identified the coating on the dog tags as blood. We imagined how it would sound to the MPs if we had to explain what we found and how we found it, so we opted to do our own research. If this whole thing turned out to be nothing and we had gone to the MPs, we'd be known base wide as Nancy Drew and Joe Hardy. We both agreed if we discovered anything really concrete, we'd contact the police.

At home, I went into my bathroom where the light was best and took a good look at the dog tags. I wanted to preserve as much of the suspected dried blood as I could, so I was careful to scrape only across the name.

"Do you have anything yet?" Audrey asked.

"Yeah, I think so. Get a piece of paper to write this stuff down as I tell you. I want to handle it as little as possible."

"Got it. What does it say?"

"It looks like it says, LORING, D. J."

Audrey thought for a moment. "That name seems so familiar to me."

"Come on, Audrey. You have no idea who this is."

"No, I'm telling you! That name seems familiar. Do you think that it's really blood?"

"I'm not sure, but I'm leaning towards yes."

"Oh my goodness! I just remembered where I know that name from!" Audrey ran out of the bathroom and into the back bedroom like a flash of light. I was quick to follow her.

"What is it? What do you think that you know?"

"I'm right! It's right here in an old clipping from the base newspaper, from 1958. Listen:

TRAGEDY IN GUANTANAMO BAY

On Christmas Eve, tragedy struck our small community when Marine Lance Corporal Daryl Loring of Pittsburgh, Pennsylvania mysteriously disappeared and is now presumed dead. In what appears to be a drowning, Lance Corporal Loring's uniform, identification and some personal items were found on one of the picnic tables at Kittery Beach on Christmas morning by Hank Moore, Exchange manager, and his wife Sandy while on a diving trip. At first the Moores thought little of the discarded belongings, but when they returned from their dive and searched the area, they reported what they had found to Harbor Patrol. "We figured that it was probably some Marine sleeping off some heavy drinking the night before, but when we couldn't find anyone on the beach or surroundings, we naturally became concerned. We decided that safe was better than sorry," said Moore. Lance Corporal Loring had been not been reported as being missing by the Marines. "Sometimes these youngsters stay out late with their friends, and the other Marines cover for them. That was the case with Lance Corporal Loring, which is why he was not missed sooner," said Marine Platoon Sergeant, Gunnery Sergeant Elliot Gaultier. "He was an outstanding Marine and we're deeply saddened by his death."

A memorial service will be held for Lance Corporal Loring at Windmill Beach on Sunday afternoon at 2pm. All base residents are invited to attend.

"I have goose pimples running down my whole body!" Audrey exclaimed.

"Stand in line! The hairs on the back of my neck are at

attention. Do you realize what this means?"

"I don't know what to think, Adam. Did he stage his own death or was he killed?"

"Well, let's go over what we know. We know that he didn't drown."

"Actually Adam, we don't know that for sure."

"Of course we do! That's the one obvious thing!"

"No, it isn't. Just because his dog tags were found in the car, encrusted in blood, that doesn't mean it's Daryl Loring's blood."

"Ok, you have a point. But what were the dog tags doing hidden in that trunk?"

"Who says they were hidden? It's an old car and maybe they just fell underneath the flooring. How do we know that the car didn't belong to Loring himself and maybe there's blood in the car because he got hurt once. Maybe he bled all over his car trying to find a towel to wrap his wound."

"Come on, Audrey. That's too much blood to be from a cut."

"If it is blood," she argued. "We still don't know that for sure."

While Audrey had some good points, I was frustrated. I reached into my pocket to try and get more information from the old car title that I'd found in the thrift shop uniform, and I almost stopped breathing as I began to read.

"Audrey. You won't believe this. Remember how I told you that I couldn't read the owner's name on this title? It was partly because it's old ink and partly because the handwriting is so sloppy."

"And?"

"And now I can read it." I handed it to her and she read the name aloud.

"EL...LI...OT... GAUL...TIER?" Audrey and I locked eyes. The car belonged to Loring's platoon sergeant?"

I took a moment to gather my thoughts. "Where's the bloody uniform?"

"Over here. Why?"

"Pass it over."

"Are you going to try to read the name tape?"

"Nope, Marine uniforms didn't have name tapes on the front back then, but there should be a name stenciled inside the collar." I pulled carefully on the antique fabric. "This blood has dried like concrete. I'm scared that if I pull too hard that I might tear it."

"Just be as careful as you can with it."

"I am." After a few strategic pulls, I managed to separate the two sides of the uniform that seemed to have been fused together for years.

"What does it say, Adam?"

"Take a guess."

⫷⫸ ⫷⫸ ⫷⫸

The next morning, I ended up having to take back all of my hateful comments about the roosters. Had it not been for them, I would've slept too late Saturday morning and missed my very first Northeast Gate tour, which was a base-wide excursion to the only remaining passageway between American and Communist Cuba. Missing it wouldn't have been so bad, except I was the one *giving* the tour. Once a month, the Barracks hosted a tour of the Northeast Gate. Except for these tours, most residents would never see much of the base, because about eighty percent of the land area of Gitmo was off limits to them. Much of the off limits area were bombing ranges or magazine (ammo storage) areas and the rest were restricted to Marines due to its proximity to the fence-line. Because of the allure of normally off-limits areas, most residents and visitors made time to take the tour.

I'd tried to do some research on the subject so I'd be an interesting tour guide, but my mind kept wandering back to Gunnery Sergeant Gaultier's blood-soaked uniform. Audrey and I made the decision to contact the base police, but we thought we'd start with an MP my wife came to know at the migrant camp. Her name was MA2 Lydia Voorhees, and she agreed to meet with Audrey at the house while I was giving the tour.

There were three white buses waiting to be filled with enthusiastic base residents when I got to the top of Marine Hill at 0745. I quickly ran into my office to grab the handouts I'd prepared the day before, and to check out a pistol and ammunition from the armory. The colonel was very strict about all Marines being armed when on the fence-line. I didn't mind; it added a little intrigue to the tour. After waiting until the morning colors was done at 8am, I instructed the tourists to board the buses. I took a count on each bus then boarded bus number one, giving the driver the go-ahead to start the small convoy. We made a left after leaving Marine Hill and traveled North on Sherman Avenue towards Communist Cuba.

After we'd cleared the residential areas, we came upon vast salt flats to either side of the bus. While they were a natural part of Cuba's landscape, they proved to be an effective defensive barrier for the Marines. For most of the year, the salt flats were so marshy, Cuban tanks wouldn't be able to travel through them, thereby forcing the soldiers and their equipment onto Sherman Avenue. Even during the dry season, the salt flats remained a part of the base's barrier plan because long trenches, called tank ditches, were cut across the flats to further delay and deter vehicles. The road which traversed the flats had been constructed with metal cylinders built into it so cratering charges could be inserted to blow the road, making it difficult for the Cuban tanks to advance. The idea was to put the enemy in a dilemma; if they stayed on the road, they would have to stop to traverse the breech, while Marine anti-armor missiles picked them off. If they chose the flats, the same fate awaited them.

Our next point of interest that day was Camp X-Ray, a holding pen for the most dangerous and unruly Haitian detainees, which had been used during the Haitian insurgence back in 1994. At that time nearly fifty thousand Haitians had flooded the shores of Gitmo in make-shift rafts, hoping for passage to America. They were organized into camps, but while a political solution came slowly from Washington, the Haitians periodically rioted against the Joint Task Force (JTF) sent in to guard them. On one such occasion, the Haitians nearly managed to take over McDonald's—no joke. There are even pictures of Mickey D's with concertina wire and heavy machine guns on the roof. During that particular riot, the JTF got overrun and, as America always does, they called in the Marines. As it turned out, the Marines were not equipped with riot shields and billy clubs, but they did have bayonets. Not surprisingly the prisoners backed down almost immediately and retreated up to the top of nearby Chapel Hill, and the next morning they were returned to the camps.

Thank goodness that all military families had been evacuated prior to this, as it would have complicated and perhaps aggravated the situation more. However, it did highlight the need for a place to segregate the rabble rousers—hence Camp X-Ray. If you were in a migrant camp, and just couldn't manage to play well with others, tan Chevy Blazers, with blacked-out windows and a scorpion stenciled on the side, would arrive to take you to Camp

X-Ray. In a place where 50,000 people had lost hope, the discipline of the standard camp was immeasurably improved by the general understanding that there was someplace worse to be sent.

After Camp X-Ray, we came upon a Marine check point in a small valley called Sherman's Gap. I pointed up to a mountain on the Cuban side, straight in front of the bus, called Las Malones which means *the melons*. I explained that, a long time ago, there had been a bar on the side of that mountain called the Silver Dollar. Back in the day when military personnel could take leave into the Cuban territory, many would go to that bar, and, for a silver dollar, the bartender would explain the Cuban point of view on all events regarding our base.

Upon our arrival at the Northeast Gate, I shuttled all the visitors to a shaded observation area, gave out my handouts, and began my spiel.

❧❧ ❧❧ ❧❧

"So what do you think Lydia?" Audrey asked her. "Do you think that we need to take this to your boss?"

"Let me get this straight. You bought an old Marine uniform at the thrift store, found an old car title in the pocket, went to the junkyard and located the car, went through the car and subsequently found the trunk *allegedly* blood stained, discovered an *alleged* bloody uniform which belonged to it's owner—Gunny Sgt Elliot Gaultier—and then read an article about a missing lance corporal. I guess I'm not catching on. Why am I here?"

Audrey sighed, frustrated. "Because something's not right. Everyone on base at that time said that Lance Corporal Loring drowned, even though his body was never found. But, his dog tags—blood encrusted dog tags mind you—were found underneath the flooring in Gunnery Sergeant Gaultier's trunk. That doesn't seem a little odd to you?"

"Odd yes, but hardly a crime. Besides, my boss has other things on his mind right now."

"Like what?"

"Like me! He's totally obsessed with me!" Lydia fell back against the couch, rolling her eyes and making a nasty face. "He sends me romantic e-mails, he's always complimenting me on my looks and he actually had the friggin' nerve to leave a gold bracelet in my car with a note."

"But aren't you married, and to a Marine?"

"He's married too, and with kids! And he way outranks me, which makes me his subordinate and this whole situation way out of control."

"Have you told him you're not interested?"

"Many times, but he won't let up. I think people in the office are beginning to talk. They see that he treats me a lot different than he does the rest. I'm so upset."

"I understand how you feel and I hate to sound unsympathetic, but I have to know what to do here. I have the bloody uniform of a gunnery sergeant who was on this base almost fifty years ago, and a huge suspicion that Lance Corporal Loring didn't drown. What should I do?"

Lydia walked over and took hold of the uniform. "I don't know what you should do, but I sure as hell know what you shouldn't do. Don't take this to Harbor Patrol—they won't care."

"How could they not care?"

"Because, my dear Audrey, most MPs are wash-outs from other military fields. They're slackers looking for an easy ride. Look, you may have something here, but no one wants to get off their butts and do anything about anything. For heaven's sake—this would require paperwork!"

"How do they get away with it, with doing nothing? Isn't it their job to investigate things?"

"Can you keep a secret?" Lydia said, lowering her voice.

"Sure."

"No! I mean a major dome-of-silence secret?"

"Yeah, what's up?"

"Well, Captain Pickard got to the island a couple of months before Mimsey did, and one of the MPs caught Pickard getting down and dirty in a car at Kittery Beach with one of the ladies who works in the exchange."

"No way!"

"Yes, way! So now, all of us at security have a get-out-of-jail-free card. Pickard kisses our butts big time so we'll keep his little indiscretion under our hats!"

"He seems so conservative, so self-righteous. I'd have never suspected. I almost feel sorry for Mimsey. The lady in question must have been something else."

"Actually, she's a load! She must weigh 300 pounds!" Lydia

said, laughing.

"Well, now I understand why no one will care about my hunch."

"I'm sorry I can't help you, but that's the way it is in Gitmo Bay!"

"I understand. Hey, are you going to Lois Ranagan's tea today?"

"Ah, no. I'm here to tell you that none of the enlisted wives will show up, or at least most of them won't."

"Why?"

"Because Lois is so fanatical about proper dress, she intimidates the ladies. A lot of the enlisted women don't have fancy tea clothing because they're working moms. Many of them don't have the money to buy a nice suit, so they just don't go. Besides, they all think that officers' wives are bitches anyway."

"Isn't your husband enlisted?"

"Yeah, but I'm different because I have a career and I stay away from all the Marine wives' functions. Personally, I don't pay much attention to all that pomp and circumstance, but Lois is huge on it. Are you going?"

"Yeah, I'm kind of being made to go."

"Screw that! There's no way that lady could make me go into her house. Hey, but make sure you tell me all about it!"

"Oh, I will."

10

The moment I walked in the door, Audrey shouted to me to sit down on the living room couch. I knew what she was doing—the game is called, "Guess What Audrey's Bought Today?"

"Close your eyes, Adam!" Audrey called from the bathroom, "Are they closed?"

"Yes, they are."

"Ok, open them!"

I don't know what happened to my wife, but Minnie Pearl was standing in front of me.

"What do you think?" Audrey said as she spun around and flung her arms in the air.

"Well,...you look...well..."

"Come on—do you like my hat and white gloves? What about this flowery old lady dress? Doesn't it just become me?"

"Become you? No. Beg to be torn off and burned? Yes."

"So you hate it?" Audrey said excitedly, which alarmed me.

"Audrey, all that's missing is a little tag hanging off your hat. What's this all about? And, are those support hose?"

Audrey plopped down on the sofa beside me. "As it turns out, I have a tea today at the beloved Mrs. Ranagan's, and I just wanted to dress appropriately."

I knew exactly what my wife was trying to do. She knew she couldn't have it out with Lois, so she was going to mock her instead. While I thought the whole outfit thing was funny, and a great laugh between us two, I hoped and prayed she wasn't going to actually go to the party like that.

"So what are you really going to wear?" I asked kindly.

"This," she said with confidence.

"I don't really think that's such a good idea. You don't have to like her, but you sure as hell don't have to piss her off."

"Goodbye, Adam. I have to go now," Audrey said coolly as she headed for the door. "By the way, happy anniversary."

"Wait a minute! Don't be like that."

"Be like what?" she said in an angry voice. "Look, Adam, I don't even want to go to this absurd party. I told her that we had plans for our anniversary and she pulled rank on me! If she wants me at this damn party, I want to make damn sure that she remembers I was there! I'm sorry you have a problem with this, but I didn't ask for any of this and I sure as hell don't remember asking for your permission!"

I stood there, knowing we were both right. I didn't want Audrey to play with fire, but Lois had bullied her into going. I had no idea what to say, so I just spouted off the first thing that came to my mind. "Have fun." She hugged me goodbye and smiled as she walked out the door. I was mildly curious about how the tea would go, but annoyed I'd forgotten to ask Audrey what Lydia had said. I decided to spend the time without Audrey doing some research myself.

Audrey stopped by Regina McCarran's house on the way to Lois'. Audrey had bought a matching outfit for Regina. The two of them giggled all the way down the street as they walked side by side.

"Well, hello!" Lois said excitedly. "I feel like I'm looking in the mirror! You two come in! Did you get those dresses at the exchange? Of course you did! How else could we've all bought the same exact dress?"

Audrey had forgotten we lived on an island with one clothing store. Lois had fallen in love with the dress Audrey was wearing, and, instead of Lois feeling insulted, Lois thought that Audrey had an unimpeachable sense of style. Feeling defeated, Audrey removed her wide-brimmed hat and delicate white gloves, and took her place at one of the tables. To her surprise, the sergeant major's wife took the seat next to her. They had not spoken since the day Audrey had confronted her in the exchange parking lot.

"Pardon me," the sergeant major's wife said to Audrey as she extended her hand, "but I don't believe that we've met."

Audrey wasn't sure what to do. There was no question that the sergeant major's wife knew precisely who Audrey was. "I'm Audrey Claiborne," she said returning the handshake.

"My name is Dorthia Ormond. It's nice to meet you, especially since we're neighbors."

Audrey wasn't sure what to make of it, but decided that Mrs. Ormond was a classy lady who refused to let one incident spoil an entire tour. Gitmo was way too small to be living amongst enemies. The awkwardness Audrey felt sitting next to Dorthia was broken when Lois began to speak.

"Well, it's half past two, but only the officers' wives have arrived," Lois said with a small sigh.

"Lois, I'm not sure anyone else is coming," Maura Geller whispered.

Lois snapped her head in Maura's direction. "And why would you say that?"

Maura looked around the room as if she were trying to muster support before answering. "Because a couple of the enlisted women I know said they weren't coming—they said they don't really feel comfortable in your home."

Lois was taken aback. "How can that be? Everyone is made to feel welcome in my home. I just don't understand."

"I think it's because you tell people what they're supposed to wear and that makes people feel uncomfortable," Maura added diplomatically.

"That's ridiculous! I've *never* told anyone what they have to wear when they come to my house. I want people to wear what *they* want to wear."

"But that's not true, Lois," the XO's wife, Drew Ray, chimed in. "You specifically told the ladies that they needed to dress 'smart and snappy' and I dare say that there are a lot of wives who haven't a clue what that means."

Dorthia Ormond jumped in to defend Lois. "Lois didn't mean it to be a hard fast rule. It was merely a guide, as so many people often inquire about what they should wear."

"But that's also not true," Rhonda Romero injected. "The wife of the Marine my husband replaced once told me that you sent her home from one of your parties because her shirt was too tight across her chest."

"Well, good taste would dictate that—" Dorthia said, but was interrupted by Lois.

"I don't believe any of what you ladies are saying!"

Maura spoke sweetly to Lois, "It's not that you have done anything wrong. I was just pointing out that some women would rather just skip your party rather than feel badly that they don't have the money to buy something dressy."

"I've heard that too," Audrey said to Lois and Maura.

Lois turned to Audrey and spoke callously. "Oh, Mrs. Claiborne? You've only been here a couple of months. Who do you even know yet, and why would anyone tell you something like that?"

"I'd rather not tell you their name," Audrey said, backing down.

"Of course," Lois returned. Then, as if the discussion had never begun, Lois became a charming hostess and began serving her tea and cake. "Well, ladies, let's get started on some of the food that I've prepared. I've made some of my favorite recipes."

❧ ❧ ❧

"Sir, Colonel Ranagan would like to see you," Warrant Officer Razor told me. I immediately stood up and walked down the corridor to his office. I hadn't even been in the White House for more than three minutes that morning.

"Colonel Ranagan, sir, you wanted to see me?" I asked as I stood in his doorway.

"Come in, Captain Claiborne."

I stood near his desk, but he had his chair turned away from me and was looking out the window facing the Bay—I couldn't see his face. He had a pen in his hand he kept clicking, and, after a while, it became irritating.

"Captain Claiborne. Do you know what the word insulted means?"

"Yes, of course, sir."

"You see, I don't think you do. Why don't you tell me what you think it means."

"Well, sir, it's when someone hurts or offends someone on purpose."

"Hmm...I guess you do know what it means." After a dramatic pause, he began to speak in his syrupy voice again. "Do you think your wife knows what it means, Captain Claiborne?"

My jaw tightened. There was no reason that a wife, especially mine, should be talked about in a military setting. "I believe so, sir, but if you want to know for sure, you're free to ask her yourself."

"No, Captain Claiborne, I asked you."

"And once again sir, you'd need to ask her. If you don't mind, sir, what's this all about?"

"Captain Claiborne, do you know what the word liar means?"

"Yes, sir."

"Please tell me what it means."

I took a deep breath to keep my cool and I probably raised the volume of my voice. "It's a person who says something that is untrue with the hope of passing it off as being accurate or real."

"Hmm...you know that one too."

"Yes, sir. Again, I respectfully ask you to clarify what this is all about."

Colonel Ranagan spun his chair around and continued to click his pen. "Your wife, Captain Claiborne, is a God damned liar!"

"With regards to what, sir?" I tried not to look visibly shaken, but I was.

"She told my wife that someone had told her something, but you and I both know that your wife made the whole thing up to make my wife look bad at her own party!"

"Sir, I'm unaware of anything being said, especially out of spite."

"Claiborne—this is the last time I'm going to say this—teach your damn wife some manners!"

"Sir, I feel that you—"

"What do you feel? Try feeling what my wife felt when your wife made up some cockamamie story so that all the other wives would think badly of her! Dismissed."

I was halfway down the hall before I heard him summon me back. "Yes, sir," I said coldly.

"Go home during your lunch hour and mow your damn lawn. That's all."

I couldn't get back to my office fast enough. I slammed the door behind me and threw a book across the room. About a minute into my tantrum, Evan Gellar, Manny Romero, and Tony Razor came in to see me. They all had the same look on their faces. However, instead of consoling me, I was basically told to get used to it. Tony told me he'd been counseled because his wife had gone shopping with a sergeant's wife. It turned out that Lois didn't approve of officers' wives and enlisted wives becoming friends. Evan told me he got counseled because his wife went jogging in a tank top and Lois didn't believe an officer's wife should go around dressed like that. Their stories went on and on. None of us could believe that differences among the wives could cause us so much grief for us at work.

🙐🙐 🙐🙐 🙐🙐

I waited as patiently as I could for Audrey to get home from work. I was anxious to hear what she'd said at the tea to make the Ranagans so angry. I kept looking out the front window to try and spot her car, but no matter how much I looked, it didn't make her come home faster. When she pulled up, I reached for the doorknob and then stopped when I saw Lois Ranagan pull up behind her. Lois walked up to Audrey with a big smile and they talked for about ten minutes. Audrey seemed to enjoy the conversation too, and just when I thought things couldn't get any weirder, Lois handed Audrey a huge bouquet of hand-picked flowers and a card.

Audrey was speechless when I told her about my conversation with Colonel Ranagan. She told me what had occurred and I found absolutely nothing wrong with what she'd said. We tried for an hour or so to understand why a wounded and insulted Lois would pick a bouquet of flowers for Audrey. To change the subject for a while, I switched the conversation to Lydia Voorhees, the MP.

"I can't believe it, Audrey. I can't believe that the base police wouldn't be interested in what we discovered."

"Yeah, I know what you mean. I saw Lydia again today and when I began to talk about the blood and car and stuff, she changed the subject."

"To what? What could be more important than a possible murder investigation?"

"She thinks that her hubby's screwing around with another Marine's wife."

"Who?" I asked, unexpectedly hungry for gossip.

"I'm not sure of her real name, but Lydia likes to call her the Scumbag Ho'."

"Lovely.".

"Yeah, I thought you'd like that. But all kidding aside, what do we do now? I mean, we have a mysterious blood-soaked uniform, a missing corporal and the Keystone Kops of Gitmo Bay not giving a damn about any of it. Do we just hang up the ol' uniform in the closet, or maybe I should just box it up and send it to the FBI lab in DC?" Audrey groaned.

"What if Lydia's wrong? What if we asked someone else?"

"We could, Adam, but what if Lydia is right? The colonel and his wife already have it out for us, and I don't really think the Pickards like us all that much either. We have no allies here—not yet anyway. I think even though it seems a little creepy; let's just put the uniform away until we get more information."

"From where?"

"From there," Audrey said, pointing to the mound of old books, letters and journals we had stacked on our kitchen table we'd yet to read.

"Ok, Audrey. I'll give you a month or so to find out something, then I think that I'll call NCIS."

"NCIS?" Audrey looked at me puzzled, and then it clicked. "The Naval Criminal Investigative Service—I got ya. Sounds fair."

≼≽ ≼≽ ≼≽

At 4am the next morning, I awoke to the phone ringing. Ryan Hill, the minefield maintenance officer, had apparently asked me once if I ever wanted to see a minefield burn. He informed me that I needed to get dressed and meet him in twenty minutes. Like a good Marine, exactly twenty minutes later, I walked outside to the minefield maintenance truck parked in Ryan's driveway.

We turned south down Kittery Beach Road, which took us past Marblehead Lanes, the bowling alley named after the USS Marblehead, to the left, and Cooper Field to the right. As we passed it, I couldn't help but picture that Cuban, hatchet in hand, chasing the sailor across the soccer field.

Ryan turned off the radio to brief me a little on what to expect. His tone was very serious. "Today we're going to begin the process of clearing the Kittery Beach area of all its mines. The first thing that we'll do is saturate the ground with thousands of gallons of diesel fuel and set it on fire."

"Why are you setting it on fire?" I asked.

"Because that area's become overgrown. Before we can take our maps out and locate the mines for extraction, we need to see the land as it looked when they were first placed in the ground forty years ago. Once the weeds, shrubbery and thickets are gone, we'll be working with only soil and explosives. Well, that's the idea anyway."

"So when the land is cleared, what happens next?"

"We take out the maps that our predecessors used to originally plot the mines and try and match them up without getting killed."

"I should say so," I added.

"Once we believe that we've correctly identified them, we send a team into the field to disable and extract the mines, one by one."

"How many men have we lost over the years in these fields?"

"Ten or so. We lost an officer about twelve years ago—a first lieutenant. He was out in the field and tripped. He went ass-over-tea kettle and sat right on a mine. The Marines who saw it happen said it was gory as hell. He actually lived for a while before he died."

"God, how awful. At least he didn't suffer too long."

"You say that, but as he was stumbling, he knew that he'd land on a mine. He knew he was going to die a horrible death. That's almost worse."

Suddenly a sergeant called out to Ryan from the back seat. "Sir, tell Captain Claiborne about the USS Boxer."

"Back in the sixties, the USS Boxer was docked in Guantanamo Bay for sailors to take R and R. A bunch of them had come out to Kittery Beach for a party, and they did quite a bit of drinking. No one knows why, but a group of sailors—I think four or five—started to walk along this very road that we're driving on now. As drunk as they were, they took a shortcut through minefield eighteen. They hadn't been walking long before one of them stepped on an anti-personnel mine, which bound up and exploded at head level. There were no survivors."

There was silence in the car as we came to a fork in the road. In front of us, surrounded by darkness, was an old Haitian migrant camp and a rocky cliff which edged the sea. As we drove toward Kittery Beach, we passed numerous lengths of bob-wire fencing and signs declaring *PELIGRO MINAS!* (Dangerous Mines!) Sadly, over the years, many Cubans have swum to our shores and tried to cross those fields. The signs haven't worked as a deterrent in their quest for freedom. While placed there as a defensive tactic in the event of a Cuban military invasion, the minefields had only ever caused the death of innocent refugees seeking asylum. That's the main reason the minefields had been ordered to be cleared by the President.

During our stay in Gitmo, Audrey and I would occasionally hear explosions that weren't made by our training Marines, but rather by the weight of an unfortunate animal upon a well disguised mine, and occasionally, by the weight of a Cuban body. I came to Gitmo neither hating nor loving the Cubans, but, as I came to know them, I embraced them and their horrible plight. Week after week these poor souls would risk everything they had just to have a taste of the liberty upon which we engorge ourselves. I had enormous contempt for Castro, but immense compassion for his people.

I watched with great interest as the field burned, knowing that we were obliterating our first line of defense against a Cuban incursion. After all, the Cubans would never eradicate the mines from their own fields which surrounded the base, and, as the years passed, the Department of Defense had stripped our resistance capability to bare bones. Our tank platoon, bomber squadron, artillery battery, weapon systems and manning had all been decreased, left in disrepair or been taken away all together. Mesmerized by the flames, I realized all that stood between those of us on base and the Cubans was a chain-link fence and three-hundred fairly well-armed Marines. Not to toot our horn, but one Cuban general told Captain Pickard, "If you ever send your Marines away like you have your other defense capabilities, we'll be shopping in your stores, living in your homes and watching movies in your theatre by sundown."

After several hours, the fields were nothing more than smoldering pockets of soil, ready for the first team armed with metal detectors to enter its confines. It was amazing to watch these men at work. They had nerves of steel and a sincere respect for the danger that accompanied their job. The Men in Black, as they called themselves, were a true brotherhood working in uncommon unison. Methodically and systematically, they found each mine, exposed it, disabled it and removed it. I held my breath more than once. The hairs on the back of my neck stood on end when one of Ryan's men shouted to him from the center of the field. Hill approached the area quickly, but with great caution. I stayed behind, but looked on intently as Ryan talked with the Marine. I couldn't hear anything, but I saw the corporal put something in Ryan's hand before he walked back to me.

"Well, Captain Claiborne, are you ready to hold a piece of history?" Ryan asked me.

I held out my hand and Ryan placed an old, beat-up lighter in my palm. I looked at him, puzzled, and Ryan reached down and turned the lighter over. My eyes grew big as I read the words: USS Boxer. I was transported back to the night those sailors wandered away from the beach and into the arms of death. I looked at the path they might have taken, and I could even hear the party music in the background as the men began their walk.

It was a clear night, I supposed, and they must've been ecstatic to finally be off the ship. Someone on the morale bus had told them about the party at Kittery Beach earlier that morning and they'd made the decision to go. When they got there, a fire was already roaring and someone tossed cold beers at them as they sat down on the warm sand. For hours, they laughed, took turns looking after the barbecue, told dirty jokes, smoked and drank up a storm. Maybe it was getting late, maybe they missed the morale bus back to the ship, or maybe they were looking for a place to take a piss—who knows—but something drew them to the minefield.

Now, instead of a bunch of old men getting together at a navy reunion, all that was left to remember that night, and those young men, was a souvenir lighter recovered from a God-forsaken minefield. Ryan took the lighter back and said he'd be turning it over to the lighthouse museum. What a way to be remembered.

11

Before we knew it, October was upon us and so was the next Marine Wives Association meeting. Audrey debated going, but in the end, she thought not going would send the wrong message to Lois. Audrey was by no means afraid of Mrs. Ranagan and showing up at the meeting would make that clear.

As always, the ladies filtered into the White House conference room and took their place around the large table, and, as usual, Lois took her place away from the table and behind the podium. This time, she pulled up a folding chair and sat in it, making herself hardly noticeable to the gathering group. At six sharp, Drew Ray called the meeting to order. After the reading of the minutes, Drew began with the first order of business.

"Ladies, the first item up for discussion is a request by Jackie Razor to give money to needy Marine families for their scuba gear. Jackie? Would you like to tell the ladies what this is all about?"

"Yes, thank you, Drew. I would like the MWA to donate money to needy Marine families as it has come to my attention that some Marine children aren't allowed to join the youth scuba club because they don't have the equipment. Since we're the *Marine Wives Association*, I felt it made sense for us to donate the equipment to the children so that no child is excluded."

"Absolutely not," Lois Ranagan said sternly.

"I beg your pardon?" Drew Ray responded.

"I said no. That's not what this club was set up to do."

"Actually, Lois, the by-laws clearly state that our club is a charitable organization, as well as a social one, and we're allowed to spend our money in any way that supports the social and benevolent aspirations of the ladies in Gitmo—as long as the activity is approved by vote, of course."

"The colonel won't approve it even if you do vote on it," Lois said, as if the colonel was someone other than her husband.

"It's not the colonel's place to approve what we do. Last time I looked, he wasn't a Marine wife," Drew said, locking eyes with Lois. "Ladies, let's call for a vote." Lois bit the inside of her cheek.

"One moment," Audrey said. "How will we decide the definition of need? I've seen plenty of women claim to have no money and then go out and get a thirty dollar manicure."

After some discussion, the item was defeated.

"The next item up for debate is the budget for our monthly socials."

"Drew, it's a fixed budget of twenty-five dollars," Lois said.

"Maybe it was last year, Lois, but this is a new board with new members." Drew replied. "That figure will hardly buy anything."

"I agree," said Arlene Hill. "Maybe we can double it? A lot of the enlisted women refuse to host a social in their home because of the cost. If we want to get across the notion that the MWA is a club for all wives and not just officers' wives, this might be a good first step."

"I totally agree," said Audrey enthusiastically.

"Well, ladies, let's take this up for a vote then," Drew said.

"No!" Lois commanded. "The MWA funds are not for parties. We need to keep our money for more charitable events."

"So what you're saying, Lois, is that these women can raise money all they want, come to every meeting, and spend their personal time trying to grow this club, but they can't enjoy any of the benefits? This club was meant to foster a solid relationship between all the wives here. It's the one place they can gather on common ground as women, not just as military dependents."

"You heard my answer, Drew."

"And you heard mine. Ladies, let's take a vote." The women unanimously voted to raise the budget. The only thing Lois did was scribble in her notebook.

"We also need to come up with a budget for the Fall Festival. Does anyone have a starting place?"

"Well," said Maura Geller, "we need to buy decorations, face paint, prizes, pumpkins, food and drinks for all the families. We need to anticipate at least 100-150 people coming."

"What do you say to a $350 budget?" Drew offered.

"That's ridiculous! That's way too much!" Lois called out.

Drew looked down at her papers. All the other ladies sat quietly, looking around at each other. The fireworks between the CO and the XO's wife were only beginning. "Mrs. Ranagan, our latest bank statement says that we have almost $5,000 in our account. I think that $350 to feed and entertain 100-150 people is less than ridiculous."

"One hundred dollars. That's all you need. Let's go to the next order of business."

"Of course we will, Lois, as soon as the board takes a vote."

"Drew," Arlene said, "what if we compromise, say $225? McDonald's could supply the punch for free and maybe we can all bake a treat. What do ya'll think about that?"

The ladies jumped on Arlene's solution to keep the meeting running smoothly.

"Lastly, we need to decide on the goodie bags for the single marines," Drew said.

"Actually," Lois interrupted, "the colonel informed me that many of the Marines have gained too much weight and are restricted from snacks outside their meals until November first."

Rhonda had no idea what to say next; her blood felt like it was boiling. Drew spoke for her. "Excuse me, Lois. The entire Ground Defense Force is on a diet? I find that hard to believe."

"Do you doubt the colonel?"

"I just find it curious that when you didn't get your way, your husband put an entire battalion on snack restriction until the day after the party, which I subsequently find absurd since most of the Marines here are eighteen with amazing metabolisms!"

When Drew finished, Lois put her pencil in the spiral binding of her notebook, folded her chair, placed it against the wall, and walked out of the room confidently. The sergeant major's wife and Rosie Bradshaw soon followed.

When the only people left in the room were Arlene Hill, Jackie Razor, Maura Gellar, Rhonda Romero, Regina McCarran and Audrey, Drew shut the door and walked back to her seat. She told the ladies they had to keep secret what she was about to tell them. Drew apologized for her own behavior during the meeting; she realized she wasn't as diplomatic with Lois as she could have been. She went on to explain that a week earlier, Lois had invited her to her house. The meeting began cordially, and Lois couldn't have been nicer. What Lois said next was too much for Drew to handle alone: "I think part of your problem here in Gitmo is that you don't understand what you're dealing with. You're far too naive and you don't see these ladies for who they really are. Take Arlene Hill. She's a country bumpkin if you ever saw one and we need to help her with culture, guide her. Jackie Razor is a very common girl from New York, and she hasn't any real understanding of what it means to be an officer's wife. Now Maura Gellar suffers from depression. Her insecurity will lead her to try and destroy other people's lives through rumor and innuendo. Rhonda Romero is a trouble maker and we need to keep our eye on her. It's obvious that she cares nothing about anything but herself. Audrey Claiborne is a true introvert, and sadly, she has no friends, and I don't think she has much education. I also think that she and her husband are having money problems since she's working with the migrants. I think if we work on her, she might be ok. Regina McCarran is the only truly decent one in the whole bunch."

The ladies sat back in their chairs, almost unable to believe what Drew had just told them. Drew went on to say when she questioned Lois about how quickly she passed judgment on the ladies without really getting to know them, Lois became irritable and unreasonable. When Drew started to leave, Lois stood in front of the door and refused to let Drew out of her home until Drew agreed with her comments.

I was able to stay in my little corner of the White House all the following day without being summoned by the CO. Lt Colonel

Ray wasn't so lucky. We could hear him being hollered at all the way down the hall, and while none of us spoke about it, we all felt badly for him.

It wasn't until it was almost time to go home that I spoke to him. "Sir, I need your signature on these papers." When I walked into his office, he looked pallid and distracted.

"Yes, come in, Adam," Ray said. I was surprised he called me Adam. "Close the door, would you please." This also surprised me since doors are usually kept open unless it was something important or someone was in trouble—and an XO rarely says please.

"Is there something you want to talk to me about, sir?"

Lt Colonel Ray took a deep breath. "No, not something that I want to talk to you about, but something that I've been ordered to talk to you about."

"Sir?"

"I've been in the Marine Corps for a long time and I've never been in a situation like this one. Earlier this morning I was counseled by the CO and, quite frankly, I'm still staggered." He threw the files he was looking at down on his desk and let out a huge sigh. "For forty-five minutes, I was lectured about how badly my wife behaves and how almost every Marine wife is a bitch." Lt Colonel Ray cleared his throat. "I'm supposed to tell you your wife is rude and I'm supposed to *strongly suggest* that you keep your wife in line. I think his exact words were, 'I might not be able to control their wives, but I can damn well make sure that my Marines won't see their wives very often.'"

"Sir, what are we expected to do? Audrey tries not to say very much, but no matter *what* she says, there's hell to pay afterwards. It's like we can't ever win."

"Captain, you're preaching to the choir! My wife is enemy number one in Colonel Ranagan's eyes. Every time I try and discuss Marine business, all the colonel does is talk about the situation with the wives! It's gotten to where this office can no longer function effectively. Because of his hatred of Drew, he refuses to listen to any opinion I have on any administrative or tactical policy for Gitmo. I feel utterly useless."

I stood there listening to Lt Colonel Ray, realizing I was standing before a man who needed a friend. It was hard for field grade officers, majors and above, to have friends on the island since there were only a handful on the whole base. I found out during this conversation that the Ranagans and the Pickards hated each other, and that Colonel Ranagan had told Lt Colonel Ray that Marines were permitted to be cordial to the Navy personnel on base, but we could never befriend them. Ranagan said the Navy was out to get the Marines, so the Marines had to stick together. From my own experience, most Navy people on base were absolutely wonderful.

"Again, sir, what are we supposed to do? Should my wife quit the Marine Wives Association?"

"No, absolutely not! Our wives are doing a great job and the other Marine wives on base need them to sit on that board. Besides that, if our wives quit, Lois can run the association any way she likes. As far as what to do to keep Lois happy, I'm clearly at a loss. By the way, the colonel has informed me that Lois is going to have the officers' wives over to her home tomorrow evening, minus my wife. He says that it's her last-ditch effort to rescue the ladies from Drew's poisonous influence."

"He didn't really say that, sir, did he? You can't tell me that Colonel Ranagan said that about your wife and was left standing!"

"He said it and I took it. He's my commanding officer and that was his word."

Lt Colonel Ray was right. While Ranagan was completely out of line, there was nothing any of us Marines could do about it. He was indeed our commanding officer and we had to treat him with respect at all times, no matter how much we disagreed with the way he did business. Besides that, how would it have looked for any of us to go whining to the general? What would we say? Colonel Ranagan is mean to our wives? It was a really bad situation to be in, but we had no choice but to accept this was our life and would be as long as Ranagan was the CO. "Sir, it kinda makes you wonder what side of the fence we're living on sometimes, doesn't it?"

The XO was quiet for a moment and then nodded his head. "Yeah, sadly it does."

Audrey met up with me in the parking lot outside the White House as I was about to stick my key into the door of the Gremlin. She had a smile on her face from ear to ear.

"Guess where I've been?"

"Why don't you tell me."

"I just bought us an anniversary present!"

"I thought that we'd decided not to buy anything for each other this year. Didn't you want to save up for a luxury cruise?"

"Yeah, but then I began to think about it more. Here we are in the beautiful Caribbean every day and we should take advantage of that. Look!"

Audrey handed me a receipt for diving lessons for the two of us, paid in full. "Fantastic! I had no idea you were interested in diving. As a matter of fact, I specifically remember you telling me that there was no way in hell I'd ever be able to get you to go diving."

"I know, but I talked to the people in the dive shop and they made me feel really good about it. Did you know that the dive shop is right next to the White House? It's called Oceanic Adventurer's Incorporated."

"When do we start?"

"Next Monday night. Our instructor's name is Donny. You know that funny lady in the video rental place, Becca? It's her husband. We have to attend classes from seven to ten each night until the weekend, and then we have a pool dive. After that, we'll have another week of classes and then our first ocean dive. Aren't you soooo excited?"

I was extremely excited, but I had my doubts about how Audrey would do. She'd always been petrified to even snorkel. "Yeah, I'm very excited. Thanks for doing this for us."

I tried to be as animated as I could, but I was still thinking over the conversation I had with the XO just a few moments before. Audrey noticed my distraction and asked me what was wrong. When I told her, she just let out a long sigh and leaned up against the side of the car.

"Adam, I just don't know what to do. Lois Ranagan doesn't just affect me, but also my friends. I found out that she called Regina yesterday and asked for Regina's help in tightening the reigns on us, and asked her to help all of us to understand the chain of command among the wives."

"The chain of command among the wives? There's no such thing! I can't believe the balls on that broad! What arrogance!"

"Tell me about it! But the thing is, just when you think she's a total bitch, she does something really nice for you and then you're left there saying 'Okay, is she a bitch or am *I* the problem?' I just don't get it! Oh, and what's worse is when I was buying our lessons, Donny said that Mrs. Ranagan had told him that she just loved all her wives and how wonderfully everyone was getting along."

"She didn't?"

"She did! She even told Donny's wife, Becca, that the association was throwing a marvelous Fall Festival for all the Marine families and how proud she was of all of us for doing all the planning."

"Wait a second here. I thought she hated the idea of the party and even tried to restrict your budget?"

"Bingo! Now you see how frustrated we all are. When I'm not working, I sit in the park with the other wives and we talk about how stressful this all is."

"This reminds me, I have a message from the XO for you and all the other wives who sit in that park each afternoon."

Audrey tilted her head. "What?"

"Mrs. Ranagan feels that all of you ladies aren't waving to her enough when she drives by. The XO says the husbands have been ordered to tell their wives to wave to her more."

"Wave to her? Screw that! Next time, I'll be sure to give her the one finger-salute!"

To try and get our minds off of the Ranagans, we went to Phillips Park to watch the sunset. While we were there, Audrey began to tell me about her day at the migrant camp. A sixty-three year old Cuban refugee had joined her group the night before. The woman had warm brown eyes and an almost toothless smile. Her face was worn, the wrinkles deep. She looked as if she were a much older woman, with her gray hair in an unkempt bun. There was something about this person, Lupe, that drew Audrey to her. She spent several hours talking with her.

"She had such a sad story to tell."

"Don't they all? I can't imagine anyone with a good story braving shark-infested waters and a minefield."

"That's not what I mean. She told me her husband used to work on the base a long time ago and one day he just never came home."

"Does she know what happened to him?"

"No, but she thinks that it was Castro's men. After Castro took over, he still allowed Cubans to work on the American side, but often, when the workers would leave the base at the end of the day, Castro's thugs would be waiting to rough them up."

"I see, he wouldn't *make* them quit, but he tried to intimidate them into resigning on their own by causing them severe bodily harm."

"Exactly."

"So, what makes her story so much sadder than all the rest?"

"I don't know. I think it's because she never remarried and she never stopped loving him. Of course, not knowing if her husband even died for sure has haunted her all these years. She said she even took a job on base as a housekeeper way back when—in our housing development—to try and learn what happened, but when the Cuban missiles crisis happened, she had to make a choice—leave the base or stay on it forever. She went home."

"You mean she used to live above the old garages?"

"Isn't that kind of neat?"

"It is. Where was she off to when she got caught?"

"She was within sight of the Florida coastline when the Coast Guard caught her a day ago. She and thirteen other Cubans were in a fifteen-foot boat. Can you believe it?"

"Imagine going all that way, risking everything, and then finally being in sight of your dream, only to have to have it ripped out from under you. Wow, I sure feel badly for her."

"Yeah, but you're right, all the stories at the camp are equally as tragic. I can't favor one over the other. But I really do like her. She even told me to call her *Abuelita.*"

"Doesn't that mean little grandmother?"

"Yeah, screw protocol. I think that's what I'll call her from now on—Abuelita Herrera."

12

The next afternoon, Gordie Shaw invited me to join him and the other single officers for a drink at Rick's. I was looking forward to going, since I hadn't had a chance to really sit down and talk to these guys about anything outside of Barracks business since I 'd arrived. I rode there with Gordie and when we walked inside the bar, Guy Armstrong and Chet Dingle were already there, along with another officer who worked on Leeward, Aidan Foster. We had never met. I soon discovered Aidan and Chet were inseparable.

As soon as Chet saw us, he got up and reached out his hand to me, as if to welcome me into their modest-sized gang for the afternoon. His demeanor was friendly and he made a place for me at the table next to him. He, then, took control of the conversation and rarely let anyone else do much talking. If he didn't ask you a question straight out, nothing said was important to him. He came across as a nice person, but he was the kind of individual your little voice warns you about. I wanted to like him—everyone else seemed to—but he had an air of overconfidence about him that was unsettling.

"So, Adam, how's life in Gitmo?" Chet asked me between sips of his Corona.

"I like it here. I mean, it's by no means perfect, but there's something about this place that really fits my personality."

"Glad to hear it. I think all of us here can toast to that. Why else would we've all extended our tours here?" Chet said as he raised his bottle.

"Extended? Why? It's not like there is a lot to do here and last time I looked, there weren't many single women."

All the men looked at each other sheepishly and Guy started talking. "Chet doesn't have to worry about that, now do ya, pal?" He stopped to clink bottles with Chet. "Let's just say his mattress doesn't ever get to cool down."

"So you consider yourself to be quite the ladies' man, do you?" I asked, trying to fit in, hardly believing that Chet was the Casanova they were describing.

"Oh, he's a ladies man all right—he's our hero!" Gordie said as he too clinked bottles with Chet. "Shit, the only reason I hang out with him is because I hope he'll throw me his sloppy seconds."

Sitting there talking with these men, I felt so much older than they. We were all in our late twenties, and yet I felt a decade older. Nothing they discussed was of any substance and they were bigger gossips than any woman could ever hope to be; and they were cruel gossips. They talked about people in such a careless manner that it made me livid. At one point, they all turned to look out the window, cutting down every person who passed. One sailor was labeled a fag, and another was a dirt bag, and it went on and on like that until they started cutting down on a group of moms with their kids. I won't repeat the things they said about those ladies, and their less than perfect figures— especially Chet's comments—but needless to say, I found their annotations to be offensive and totally inappropriate. When I made a comment to that effect, the group became cold toward me. Chet nursed his beer for a moment, maintaining eye contact with me every second.

"Mr. Claiborne," he said, wiping the beer from his lips with the back of his hand, "it seems that you've been married so long, you've forgotten how to be a man." His comment drew chuckles from the others.

I looked off for a moment as I cracked a smile, and then looked right back at Chet. "Actually, Chester, I know everything about being a man. It's just pathetic that you're twenty-eight and have yet to become one."

I put my beer down, threw a couple of dollars on the table for the waitress and told Gordie I was walking home. As I opened up the door to leave, I could hear their hushed tones barraging me with insults for what I'd said to Chet. It was clear nobody dared to stand up to him, and I had no idea why. When I reached the parking lot, I heard Gordie call to me. I stopped as he ran to join me. Gordie was a nice guy who was hanging around with the wrong crowd. He was the kind of man who couldn't lie his way out of a paper bag, which I actually appreciated.

"Sorry about that, man. That's just Chet being Chet."

"Not a problem. It was time for me to meet up with Audrey anyway."

"Ya know, he's actually a really great guy—you just have to get to know him."

"I'm sure he is," I said, trying to keep things cool.

"He's one hell of a Marine too," Gordie went on. "All his men think he's the bomb."

I almost had to smile when I heard Gordie say that since it was very much out of character for him. "Can I ask you a question? Why are all the women on this base so ready to jump into his bed?"

Gordie smiled big. "Who the hell knows man? But he sure as hell gets 'em."

"How many woman has he had since he's been here?"

"He says it's about fifteen, which for this place makes him a god, but he thinks he's lost count."

"Wait a minute—he says? Are you all going by his word? How do you know that he isn't just saying that to string you guys along?"

"No, Chet wouldn't do that. He's telling the truth. The girls are always around him when we go out."

"Gordie, I learned a long time ago to believe what I see, and I'm not overly impressed by what I've seen thus far. And by the way, there aren't fifteen single female officers on the whole base—especially his rank. That makes him a liar right there!"

"Well, Adam, I guess you haven't opened your eyes too much since you've been here, have you?"

"What do you mean?"

"Let's just say that there's a whole lot of screwing going on here, and nobody says a word."

I stopped and looked right at him. "You can't be serious! Are you telling me that officers and enlistees can get it on and nobody cares?"

"Adam, our quarters should be renamed S and M. Think about it—we have senior enlistees and officers living side by side with no chaperones. Everyone is tan and undersexed. It's just understood that people have needs and those needs are being addressed in anyway they can be."

I 'd reached my home and was thankful to be there. Gordie and I finished up with work issues and I stepped inside my air-conditioned home to find Audrey waiting for me at the kitchen table. Did I say air-conditioned? Because what I meant to say was refrigerated. Normally, I don't say anything, but I was so agitated by Chet Dingle and company that I switched off the AC unit when I walked in. Audrey grimaced since she likes the house cold, but I told her I wasn't in the mood to hear anything negative. I went on to point out it was my home too, and that I didn't feel like freezing my ass off that evening. Of course she asked me what was wrong, but instead of answering her, I walked into the bedroom and shut the door. Life in Gitmo was starting to affect me.

❦ ❦ ❦

"Is there something that you want to talk about?" Audrey said softly.

"No...yes...maybe...I don't know." I was so frustrated. She came into the room and sat down next to me. "I like it here, Audrey, but this place...there's something strange about it. It's like it's this perfect utopian society: everyone knows everyone, the weather is pleasant, the scenery is beautiful, everyone's willing to help each other. But it's almost as if it sort of...you know...brings out the worst in people too."

"Yeah, I know what you mean. I think I was more even keeled in my emotions before we arrived. Instead of minding my own business, I find my mind wandering down the street and into the Ranagan's home, trying to figure out her next move so that I can be ready with mine. I have to tell you, it takes a lot of energy to be in two heads at once. Knowing that I can't speak my mind without getting you in trouble; knowing that my neighbors across the way hate us because we're officers and they think we look down on them; knowing that I've been labeled by a woman who's never even sat down and talked to me, well, it's beginning to take its toll. And what's worse is that my friends are getting hit by Lois even harder than I am. Lois called Maura the other day and made her cry. She told her that if she didn't start acting the role of a good officer's wife that Evan won't get very far in the Marine Corps. I don't know about you, but that sounded like a threat to me."

"But I worry that maybe it's just us. Maybe we're seeing things that aren't even there. Maybe we're bringing this on ourselves."

Audrey looked at me and her face hardened. "What's that supposed to mean? You're blaming this all on me, aren't you? Do you think that I'm the trouble maker? Do you?"

"Well, come on, Audrey...you can't exactly say you've been an angel here!" I heard my voice growing louder to match Audrey's. "You picked a fight with Mimsey Pickard in DRMO, you wore that stupid dress to Lois's party, and you open your mouth at every Marine Wives Association meeting when you know damn well that no matter what you say, I'm going to be the one to pay for it in the colonel's office!"

"How can you say those things to me, Adam?" Audrey sounded hurt. "I might have done what you said, but they were retaliatory acts, not offensive posturing! I think the historian in you has become revisionist." She stormed out of the room and I stayed where I was for a while, thinking about what we both had said. I felt horrible Audrey and I were fighting, but we were so filled with stress, and had no idea why. My mind began to recall the conversation I had with Conway before he left. He'd warned me this might happen, and I didn't pay attention to his advice.

After about an hour, I walked into the living room to find Audrey sitting on top of the old desk, staring out the window into the backyard. "Hey," I said, as I began rubbing her shoulders, "I'm sorry that we had a fight and I'm sorry that I tried to blame everything on you."

"I'm sorry too. I've been sitting here, trying to make sense of everything, asking myself if there was any truth in what you said. I'm still standing by the fact that I don't go looking for it, but I'll confess I can probably find more diplomatic ways of handling these situations. Adam, I think that I'm going to go see one of the chaplains on base."

"What for?"

"Just for some guidance. This can't be the first time something like this has ever happened, and maybe if I took a more Christian approach, we might find ourselves happier here."

"Sounds like the best idea I've heard all day."

❦ ❦ ❦

At 2am, my beeper went off and the phone rang simultaneously. I jumped up out of bed, my heart pounding, and picked up the receiver, "Captain Claiborne."

"Sir, this is Lance Corporal Smithwick. Patrolling Marines over on Leeward just came across five strange objects that appear to have washed up on shore near Hidden Beach."

"Have they been opened yet?"

"No, sir. The Marines are waiting for instructions."

"Tell them to stand guard until I, and the OPS O, can get over there. Make sure we have a Fast Boat waiting at the dock on Marine Hill. I'll call Major McCarran myself."

McCarran and I drove together to Marine Hill and hopped on the Fast Boat to Leeward Point. What usually took twenty minutes by ferry took us ten. When we arrived at the dock, a Humvee transported us to the site. Hidden Beach was on the opposite side of the airfield and was rarely visited by base residents. Tucked away among rocks and high cliffs, Leeward Marines were about its only visitors.

The Humvee came to a stop at 2:37 am and Major McCarran and I made our way down the stairwell to the shore in total darkness. The warm sea wind was blowing in my face and the surf against the rocks sounded much more intense with the absence of light. Marine spotlights, seven gathering Marines, and five members of Harbor Patrol aided us in our expedition.

"What's the situation, Corporal?" McCarran asked the Marine who had first spotted the strange objects.

"Well, sir, it was less than an hour ago when my patrol came across these right here. There was nobody around them, and we didn't see any suspicious activity on the water. We did a survey of the beach in case there was anyone hiding behind the rocks, and then ,sir, I called it in over the radio."

"Have you opened them?"

"No, sir. Captain Claiborne gave specific instructions to wait until you arrived before they were opened."

"Private, get a crow bar and let's see what's inside," McCarran ordered. The private took the crow bar and wedged it into the seam of the first crate, all of which were identical in size and shape, and, after a minute, the top was off and its contents were visible.

"Just as I'd suspected," McCarran said, reaching his hands inside.

"What is it, sir?" I asked as I drew closer to the crate.

"Marijuana. I was briefed this occasionally happens here. Drug-runners in their high-performance racing boats get spotted by the US Coast Guard and race into Cuban waters where the Coast Guard can't go. Sometimes, if they're being followed by Coast Guard aircraft, they'll dump their cargo at night to avoid being arrested when they go back into international waters."

"What do we do with it?"

"We put it under lock and key until Customs arrives from Miami to take custody of it." Major McCarran walked up to a sergeant and gave him instructions on what to do next. "And make sure these four bales are well guarded around the clock."

Major McCarran and I began to walk up the stairway toward the Humvee when I stopped. "Sir, what did you just tell those Marines?"

"I told them to take the crated bales to the hangar and stand guard over them until US Customs arrives, why? Did you have a better idea?" His arrogance was well noted.

I stood there thinking. "No, sir, but I'm confused. How many bales were on the beach just now?"

"Four. Why?"

"Just a moment," I replied as I took my radio in hand and called Lance Corporal Smithwick, the Marine who had originally contacted me. After receiving the information I was seeking, I raced back down the beach, more or less commanding Major McCarran to follow me. I was nearly out of breath when I'd reached the Marines left in charge of transporting the drug-filled crates to the hangar. "Hold everything!" I said full of authority. "Where are the Marines who originally discovered the crates?"

"What's this all about, Claiborne?" McCarran asked.

"Just a moment, sir. I'm trying to find that out." Three Marines stepped forward. "But I thought there were five Marines on this patrol. Isn't that right?"

"Yes, sir," one Marine answered, not looking me in the eyes.

"Where are the other two now?" I asked. No one returned an answer.

"I believe Captain Claiborne asked you all a question—one that deserves an answer," the major hollered in support of me, even though he had no idea what I was doing.

"They're back in the Leeward Barracks, sir," a Marine replied nervously.

"Sir," I turned toward Major McCarran, "when I received the call about this incident tonight, I was told there were five crates that washed up on shore tonight, not four. I reconfirmed that just now with Smithwick. If my hunch is right, the absent patrolling Marines went against my orders and opened one of the crates before we got here tonight. While I hate to say it, sir, I think if we swing by the Leeward Barracks right now, we will find our missing crate and two Marines in possession of a tremendous amount of marijuana."

"You're sure about this, Claiborne?"

"Positive, sir."

McCarran and I got into the Humvee and drove hastily to the Leeward Barracks. The major had already sent word to the company first sergeant to secure the area, and when we arrived, the two Marines who'd abandoned their fire team were sitting in the first sergeant's office.

"Where is the commanding officer of this rifle platoon?" McCarran asked, obviously angered by the absence of the Lieutenant.

"Sir, we've tried to page him and we've tried calling his room numerous times, but we've yet to get a hold of him," said the first sergeant.

"Well, then go knock on his door, call the other officers, put the word out—whatever you have to do, but get him the hell over here now! Tell him that two of his men are about to get busted for possession!" Major McCarran was quite an authoritative man, with his deep voice and large physical presence. He started down the corridor to find out where the two Marines had hidden the bale and I was quick to follow. "Sack of shit, Lieutenant. He's probably out getting laid somewhere."

After the major and I surveyed the lockers of the two Marines and discovered their not so ingenious hiding place, McCarran put me to action on the SITREP, or situation report, while he phoned the XO and the CO to give them an update. It wasn't until he and I had the whole thing wrapped up, many hours later, when the door to the office flung open. I saw a very cocky Chet Dingle standing in the doorway.

"What's the situation, First Sergeant?" Chet said without acknowledging Major McCarran or me, trying to sound in control.

"I have a better question," McCarran interrupted, "where the hell have you been for..." the major looked at his watch, "...for the past four hours?"

"Well, sir, I was reading Shakespeare in one of the abandoned MOPs," Chet answered in an overly respectful way.

"*Shakespeare?* Why the hell would you read Shakespeare in an abandoned MOP at night, Lieutenant? That sounds totally fucking stupid!"

Chet moved closer to the major, softened his voice and attempted to endear himself to him. "I recognize, sir, it's a little odd, but one only gets the full effect of Shakespeare when one can read it aloud. I would've done it in the Barracks, but I didn't want to keep anyone awake." He smiled and gave a little laugh. "It's been my hobby for some time."

McCarran looked at me. We didn't believe a word Dingle said. Chet had a certain snake-like quality you really have to see to believe, and McCarran immediately caught on to Dingle's slimy routine. "Lieutenant, two of your Marines are in the brig right now awaiting a court marshal hearing for stealing, possession of drugs, and with intent to disobey a direct order. What do you suppose Bill Shakespeare would say about them apples?" McCarran moved towards the door. "Be in my office at 0700. You were culpable in this too since I've come to understand it's seldom that your men can reach you. Perhaps if you'd stop chasing nurses around this island, you might begin to realize this is not a game, Lieutenant. If you don't watch out, someone on your watch will get hurt."

"Yes, sir." Dingle, for once, kept his mouth shut.

As I started out the doorway behind Major McCarran, I paused. "By the way, Chet, which play were you reading tonight?"

Without missing a beat, he said, "*The Taming of the Shrew.*"

I nodded my head with enthusiasm "That's a great one. Fortuno is one hell of a character, isn't he?"

"Yes, he's the reason I read the play to begin with," Chet answered, as if he and I shared a special devotion to the English playwright.

"Goodnight.   See you tomorrow."   As McCarran and I walked to our vehicle, the major told me I was a geek for knowing Shakespeare. In return, I told him Chet Dingle was a liar because Fortuno wasn't a Shakespearian character, but rather the lead character in *"A Cask of Amontillado"* by Edgar Allen Poe

It made me wonder what Lieutenant Dingle had really been up to that evening.

13

"Pardon me," Audrey said as she walked into the chaplain's office, "is there a chaplain available for counsel this morning?"

"Father Blankenship has an opening. Would you like to see him?" the church secretary asked, as she took off her reading glasses.

"Yes, please."

"Right this way. He'll be here in a minute, so please make yourself comfortable."

Audrey sat anxiously in the office on Chapel Hill. It was medium-sized, with brown paneled walls, an abundance of books, numerous crucifixes and lots of paperwork stacked on the floor. Besides his desk, the only other pieces of furniture were two wooden chairs and a couch against the far wall. Audrey felt a little uneasy; she'd never sought the advice of a clergyperson before, but she was a Christian who believed in God.

After about five minutes, Father Blankenship greeted her as he walked through the door. "Good morning!" He was an average sized man with a protruding stomach. His hair was gray, but he still had several strands of blonde streaking through it. His face had red blotches on it and his nose seemed too small for his size. His eyes were bright though, and Audrey liked him right away.

"Good morning, Father. My name's Audrey Claiborne and my husband is the air officer at the Marine Barracks. I have to tell you I'm not a Catholic, but I'm Christian and I need to ask your advice on something."

"Please feel free to talk to me about anything," he said with great warmth.

"Father, it's like this: Lois Ranagan, the Marine CO's wife, has made my life, my husband's life and the life of many of the other Marine wives almost unbearable. When we first got here a couple of months ago, I really liked her, but now, I can't stand to hardly hear her name. She tells us how to dress, she tells us who we can become friends with, she won't let us run our association the way we want to, and when we do something she doesn't like, our husbands get in trouble for it."

"And why does she do these things, do you think?"

"How the hell should I know?" Audrey exclaimed, without thinking. Her cheeks turned red, but she carried on. "I don't know. It's like some sort of freaky control thing with her. That's all I can think. She has her idea of what the perfect wife should be and none of us fit into her mold. Maybe it's an age gap or something."

"Well, that could be, but let's talk about you for a while. If it takes two people to have a disagreement, then two people are responsible for the discontent. What things have you done that you aren't proud of—here or perhaps at another duty station?"

"I'm not sure what you mean. Of course I'm not perfect, but I can't say that I've ever done anything that I'm not proud of. Well, I guess I do egg Lois on, but she asks for it! She told me if I didn't go to her stupid party, my husband would get in trouble."

"Did she say that or did you assume that's what she meant?"

"Well, she pretty much said it, but, to be fair, she didn't exactly use those words."

"Perhaps the problem here is you," he said gently. "Perhaps you're looking for her to act a certain way, so that's all you see now. Surely, she has done nice things for you too, right?"

"Well, yeah. She did bring me flowers."

"You see! There is good all around! I suggest you leave here with only expectations of goodness and that's what you'll see in her from now on." The two continued to talk for a half hour more, until the father had another appointment. Audrey thanked the priest and drove home. She wasn't sure if the talk had done any good, but at least she'd been able to release some of her tension by talking it out. She wondered why the Father had asked so many questions about her personal life, but she assumed he had to get to know her first before he could provide any guidance. He told her to come back again the next week to see if things had improved.

When Audrey drove up to the house, she noticed some of the other wives sitting at the picnic table in the neighborhood park; she decided to join them. After the usual greetings and small talk, Audrey jumped right in.

"I went to see the Catholic chaplain today," Audrey told Regina, Maura, Arlene and Rhonda.

"Why?" Rhonda inquired.

"Because I'm tired of living like this! I'm sick of wondering what Lois is going to say or do next to upset us, or get our husbands in trouble."

"What did you tell him?" Arlene asked.

"I told him everything. I told him that she tries to control us and that none of us feel like we have any freedom here—we can't say what we want; we can't do what we want. I just told him what we've all been going through."

"And what did he say when you told him all this?" Rhonda asked suspiciously.

"He told me that maybe it's us—well, me. Maybe we're looking for Lois to do bad stuff all the time, so that's all we see. He suggested that we try and see what's good about her and maybe things will change for us."

"Hmm," said Rhonda.

"What's that supposed to mean?" Audrey asked.

"Nothing, it's just that the next time, see the protestant chaplain. He's new to the island and doesn't know Father Blankenship very well."

"Why should that matter?" Maura chimed in.

Rhonda rolled her eyes. "Guys! Haven't you opened your eyes? The Ranagans are Catholic and Father Blankenship is very close to them. I wouldn't be surprised if he marched right to their front door and told them everything you said."

"No way, he wouldn't do that. He's such a nice man." Arlene said.

"He already did it to Jackie. She went to be counseled by the father on another matter and the next thing you know, Lois is at her front door telling Jackie she's heard that she's having personal problems and would like to help out in any way. Needless to say, since the matter was regarding Tony's temporary inability to perform in bed, Jackie and Tony were mortified."

"How could he do that to her? That's not allowed. What Jackie told him was in private. What reason would he have to betray her like that?" Audrey demanded.

"As I understand it, Lois has a standing order with everyone to report matters having to do with her girls. She feels that she's the mother figure here and she needs to know everything. Just wait, Audrey. I bet you get a call from her sometime soon. The only way you're guaranteed privacy is in a confessional, and to be honest, I wouldn't even trust that."

"That sure doesn't make me feel very good," Maura said, putting her head down on top of the picnic table. "I've told Father Blankenship a lot about my personal life. I'll just die if he's been telling Lois all those things."

"Look ladies, let's not jump to conclusions here. Right now, I feel very good about the father. Let's not let our imaginations go wild. This is exactly the point that the father tried to make — we're assuming again," Audrey said.

"Ok, Audrey," Rhonda said, "but don't be surprised if he turns out to be an ally of Lois's. By the looks of it, there are seven of us against one of her. That makes Lois the underdog and he'll likely side with her."

"I'm confident the father will side with who is right and that's us," Audrey replied. "By the way, how did Lois' officers' wives meeting go the other night? I missed it."

"It was rescheduled for tonight, so you didn't miss anything."

⟐⟐ ⟐⟐ ⟐⟐

I sat in my office most of the day waiting for Major McCarran to give me the low-down on Chet Dingle's meeting with Ranagan. I was eager to know if Dingle was going to get his; I thought it was about time someone be held accountable for something even vaguely related to Marine business and not just the MWA. Chet

Dingle was lying and every fiber in my body told me not to trust him. Day after day I was amazed at how many people seemed to admire him, but not me and not Major McCarran.

McCarran entered my office at 2pm, but, instead of speaking, he motioned for me to follow him outside. We jumped into one of the pick-up trucks owned by the Barracks and drove away. I didn't ask any questions; I knew the major would speak when he was ready. Although we were headed out to the fence-line, I knew it wasn't for any inspection; he wanted to talk freely.

After five minutes or so, I decided to engage the major on another matter of business, but instead of giving me an appropriate answer to my question, he started in on what was eating him.

"I swear to God that Dingle must be smokin' Ranagan's pole!"

"Sir?"

"I've only been here half a year, but it's just incredible what that guy gets away with! I mean, it's just not explainable any other way! Dingle must be Ranagan's butt buddy—I'm totally convinced!"

"Sir, what happened today? Are you telling me that Dingle didn't get in trouble, or at least counseled for the drugs that his Marines stole last night?"

"Trouble? He didn't even get a slap on the wrist! No, he's probably getting his slaps on the ass!"

"But, sir, we caught him in a lie. He was supposed to have been on watch and he wasn't. He didn't even respond to his pager for over an hour. How did he not get in trouble for that? It's text book."

"After Dingle told that horse cock story about reading Shakespeare, Ranagan glazed over. After a few minutes, Dingle told the colonel, 'Don't you remember, sir? I was practicing that sonnet to read for your wife on her birthday like you asked me to.' Can you believe that shit?"

"And what did Ranagan say to that?"

"He suddenly recalled asking Chet to do that and told Dingle not to worry about anything, and that was it."

"Son of a bitch! So Chet Dingle is Ranagan's boy—but why?"

"I don't have a damn clue, but Dingle's got to have something over Ranagan. Keep in mind this isn't the first incident like this."

"I'm not aware of anything else. What are you talking about?" When McCarran reached one of the deserted MOPs along the fence-line, he hit the brakes, threw the truck into park, and took his cover off to wipe the sweat from his brow.

"I flew to Gitmo to check things out a few months before we moved here, so while I was being hosted by the Barracks, I wasn't officially a part of the administration. I met Chet Dingle a few times during my ten-day stay. I can't say that I knew him well, but I knew him enough to know that he was responsible for what happened.

"What happened?"

"It was New Year's Eve and some of the junior members of Dingle's rifle company were partying down at Windmill Beach. Although they were all under twenty-one and not allowed to drink, there was plenty of alcohol there and a great deal of pot too. At about 3am New Year's Day, five of Dingle's Marines decided to drive home. They ended up driving off the side of the cliff. They were all decapitated upon impact."

"Jesus!" I called out. "So what did the investigation turn up? Where did the alcohol and drugs come from?"

"Well, that's the funny part. They went back and looked at the surveillance tape from the exchange and none of the people at the party had purchased any alcohol within four weeks of that night. They investigated if there were any missing narcotics from the NCIS evidence vault, but, according to the Marine officer of the watch, nothing was missing."

"Let me guess—Chet Dingle was the officer that night."

"Bingo. Of course he denied buying his men any alcohol, and not surprisingly, none of the Marines could remember who bought it for them. I should also mention that he denied being there that night, but he was lying."

"How do you know that?"

"Because I saw him there. Since I was away from home, and I didn't know anyone on the island, I decided to spend New Years' Eve diving off the Ig House."

"Ig house? What the hell's that?"

"Right before you round the last turn to get to Windmill Beach, there is a small building sitting up on top of the cliff called the Iguana House. It's a research facility for various universities to study iguanas in their natural habitat. Just beyond the parking area is a ladder down to the water. At approximately 11pm, I was heading down the ladder and I saw Dingle's car pulling up at the beach. When I got out of the water, about an hour later, it was still there, and as I was loading my gear into my trunk, he zipped right past me."

"So, sir, you actually saw him, not just his car."

"Yes, I actually saw him."

"Did you say anything to anyone?"

"Yes, but keep in mind, I wasn't attached to anyone here and I had no authority. I told the colonel what I saw, but when I did, he completely ignored what I said about Dingle and focused on the fact I was diving without a buddy, which is a major big deal here. After my one hour lecture on diving safety, he dismissed me and no one ever mentioned Dingle's name again in association with the accident."

"That's such bullshit! Are you telling me that he probably had a hand in the death of five of his men and not only did he not step forward, but Ranagan covered it up for him? That's total, mind-boggling bullshit!"

"Tell me about it. Think about how I felt! I knew all this and I still had to go back home and get ready for my move here. I had months of doubts about this place and the leadership."

"Something's going on here that's really strange. Dingle must have something on Ranagan."

"I don't know. I've been trying to figure that out for months now. Let me know if you come up with anything because I'd sure like to have some answers."

14

I arrived back at the house just after sunset and the only sign of Audrey was a note she left for me on the seat of the toilet bowl. I always have to hit the head at the end of the day. I can't tell you how many notes she's pinned on the refrigerator I never even saw. I guess she gave up on my brain, and began to rely on my intestinal tract. Whatever her reasoning, it was a suitable place to read what she'd written: Audrey had gone down to Lois Ranagan's house for an officers' wives meeting, which she assured me was quite different from a Marine Wives Association meeting. Personally, I couldn't have differentiated between the two if I had a gun to my head. What I did know, however, is that they needed to stop calling them meetings, and start referring to them for what they really were—pissing contests. Even though she was a lady, with her husband's rank behind her, there was no doubt in my mind Lois Ranagan could write her name in the snow, if you get my drift.

Until Audrey came home, I decided to dig into the materials that Conway had left for me to read. I began with the *Book of the Dead* to study the New Year's Eve accident in as much detail as I could; but there were no "MVA's" or Motor Vehicle Accidents listed around that time. I couldn't even find an article about it in any of the archived copies of the Gitmo Gazette. I sat there wondering how five marines could be killed and not have one word written about it, and no mention in a legal hospital record. I went back and looked again, and I came across the names of five marines who had died within a week of each other, in that particular time frame—but the causes of death were listed as drownings. I jumped out of my seat and ran to the kitchen to call Major McCarran.

"Hello, Regina, it's Adam. Can I please speak to your husband?"

"Hi, Adam. I'm sorry but he's not home yet. He's still dealing with that riot at the migrant camp that started this afternoon. Have the Cubans settled down yet?"

I had no idea what to say. I'd been with McCarran until the hour before I called her, and there were no riots at the migrant camp. Even if there were, the Marines didn't handle the migrant camps—base security did. Although I hated to do it, I kept McCarran's lie going for him. "I'm not sure, I've been tasked with something else now. I wasn't sure if the major made it home or not. Can you have him call me when he gets in?"

"Sure, if it isn't too late," Regina said as sunny as usual.

"Hey, how come you aren't at the Wives Association meeting down at Lois's?" I asked, trying to change subjects.

"You mean officer's wives meeting? My youngest is sick, and I didn't want to leave him."

"Ok, tell your husband I called please, and I hope your little one feels better soon."

I hung up the phone and walked back to the pile of news clippings, hoping to find some answers. As I continued perusing the materials, I heard the door in the kitchen open and close. I put what I'd been reading down, anxious to meet Audrey.

"So, how'd it go tonight?"

"Well, you're sooooo not going to believe what happened!"

"What this time?"

"Well, to make a long story short, I had a lot of fun. We all did."

"Define fun."

"Adam, I'm just as surprised as you are, but all of us decided to really try to get along with her before we went over there, and that positive thinking really worked for us. Don't get me wrong, she was still way out there on a lot of things, but we decided to focus on the good and not the bad."

"What do you mean that she was way out there?"

"I just mean that she's born to a different generation. She has totally different ideas on marriage and the role of a wife—especially the role of an officer's wife. When she'd go off on one of her tangents, we'd all start thinking about something else and tune her out."

"So you think she had fun too?" I asked with skepticism.

"She seemed to, but at least she can't report to her husband that we said anything, because we let her do all the talking. I think the problem is, and has always been, she's a woman who considers herself to be a modern woman, but she's not. She's pretty much old school and there's the clash. Look, I don't think she's so terrible; I just think we're all different types of women who got off on the wrong foot. Hopefully all of this is behind us."

"Just for clarification, you said she did all the talking, so what did she talk about?"

"Hmm...she covered a lot. Mainly we talked about the Marine Corps Birthday Ball, which is in four weeks and I've nothing to wear! I should add I had to fight pretty hard to keep quiet when she told me they're holding the ball in the abandoned hangar out on McCalla Field."

"Cool."

"Cool? Adam! There's no air conditioning in there! We live in the tropics! How can I put on a ball gown without sweating all my makeup off, not to mention my hair frizzing in all directions?"

"I didn't think about that."

"I've no idea why they want to hold that ball in that crumby old hangar, with busted windows and shards of glass still visible, when there's a perfectly wonderful facility at the Windjammer."

"I can answer that one. The ball is the one night when the Ranagans are king and queen of the island, and they invite everyone on base who's even remotely important to be honored guests. The Windjammer couldn't possibly hold that many people all at once. You should see the guest list."

"Well, it's clear to me, once again, the Ranagans are more concerned with appearances than they are about the Marines and the Marine families. Oh, before I forget, she did say Captain Pickard is going to tear down our garages."

"Surprise, surprise. When?"

"I'm not sure, but I think pretty soon."

"Figures. Anything else?"

"No, but how was your day?" she asked innocently, not realizing how sorry she'd be for asking. I thought about not saying anything because to tell her the story would re-ignite the frustration I felt earlier, but I thought Audrey could help me make sense of the *Book of the Dead* and the mysterious Major McCarran. We talked for a couple of hours and really got nowhere fast. McCarran either made up the story, Ranagan covered it up to protect Dingle, or there was more to everything and everyone than we could have ever imagined.

In the middle of our conversation, I looked over at the prized desk Audrey had stolen from the clutches of Mimsey Pickard and noticed something; it looked great! I was very impressed and was quick to tell her. After a few minutes of complimenting her on the outstanding job, I followed Audrey into the back bedroom to grab a stack of research materials. We were bound and determined to find something of use.

We began with the *Book of the Dead*, and we copied down the names of the five Marines who had supposedly drowned in the weeks right before and right after New Year's. Next we took a roster from the Leeward rifle company during that time and we had a match: all five had come from Dingle's platoon. Next we searched the *Gitmo Gazette* from Christmas to two weeks after New Year's for any stories on the Marines, and came up with nothing—at first. Audrey looked closer and found an article written by the president of the Student's Against Drunk Driving club at the high school on base, who seemed to have referenced the crash in her story. She'd written, "In light of our recent tragedy, we need to be even more vigilant in getting our message across to the youth of America—drunk driving kills." It was a stretch, but we ran with it. By putting these together, we were able to establish that five Marines from Dingle's platoon all died around New Years Eve, tragically. The *Book of the Dead* stipulated that all the deaths occurred by way of five separate drownings, on different dates, but McCarran stated the deaths had been caused by a DUI-related car accident. The accident the girl's article referenced led us to believe alcohol was somehow involved.

"Adam, who keeps the original Death Log?"

"The Naval Hospital, of course. Why?"

"I think I've found something." She walked across the room and sat next to me on the edge of the guest bed. "Look here. The Death Log we have is the property of the Barracks, and clearly, it's a photo-copy version of the real thing. Because it's a photo-copy, it's nearly impossible to see erasure marks on the original entries."

"You said nearly."

"That's right, but if you're looking for them, they get clearer to see." She took her pencil and circled something above where it said 'Drowning' on one of the five Marine's entries. "Right here, on this entry, you can see there is clearly a quotation mark next to the *D* in Drowning, but on the other end of the word, there is no quotation mark."

"Ok, so maybe the guy forgot the other quotation mark when he wrote it."

"That could be, but if you look throughout the log, the only other place where quotations are written are in the cases where MVA is the cause of death."

"Wow. I don't think I'd have caught that!"

"Adam, my desk has been painted for a week and you never caught that, so I'm not exactly surprised you overlooked this. Women, as it has been proven time and time again, have a better eye for detail."

"Stop your gloating and finish your theory, Wonder Woman."

"Well, it seems clear that drowning wasn't the cause of death. I think someone used white-out, wrote in drowning and recopied it. If we could get our hands on the original, we could prove I'm right."

"Ok, I'll give you that, but I don't understand why they're not listed all together. These five Marines deaths are spread out over two weeks. How did they fudge that?"

"Don't know. My theory isn't perfect, Adam, but at least we're getting a little closer. Hey, on another note, I need your help with something, Mr. Barracks' Historian."

"What do you need?"

"I need you to get me special permission for something. I want to take Abuelita out of the migrant camp and bring her here, to where she used to live. It would only be for one day," Audrey said, pleading. "I want to bring her to Marine Site Housing so she can show me which garage she used to live above, and hear the stories about Marine wives back in the sixties."

"It's a nice idea, but I've no idea what I can do to help you. That sounds like something you'd have to work out with the COMNAV, in other words, with Captain Pickard."

"No, you're wrong. Tell Ranagan you want to interview her as a former Marine Site resident. Tell him you want to document her memoirs for posterity. That way, he'll get the permission for you."

"That may work. I'll see what I can do tomorrow."

We heard the kitchen door slam and before we knew it, Regina McCarran was standing in the living room.

"I want the truth, Adam," a tense Regina demanded. "Was there something important going on tonight? Has my husband been out doing official stuff tonight or what? Tell me the truth!"

I stood there unable to utter a sound. I really liked Major McCarran and I really liked Regina, but I felt badly for her because I knew while she was sitting home with the kids, he was up to no good. I had no idea how I could look her in the eyes and be another man who lied. "No, Regina, nothing out of the ordinary went on today or tonight. As a matter of fact, I was with your husband most of the day and we had no pressing events of any kind."

Regina had a blank look about her. "Thank you Adam. It's nice to hear the truth for a change. Do you know where he has been tonight?"

"No, I can honestly say I've no idea where he's been. Do you want me to try and find out?" I hoped she'd say no.

Regina shook her head. "No. I just needed confirmation of what I guess I'd already suspected. Sorry to barge in like this you guys. I'll see you tomorrow."

There was no way I was going to let her leave like that. I glanced over to Audrey and she called Regina back. I made a believable excuse about being tired and went on to bed. I think Audrey and Regina must have talked the rest of the night, because Audrey was a walking zombie when the alarm clock rang the next morning. Since we both were racing to get out the door in time, I decided to wait and ask questions later at dinner.

⋑⋐ ⋑⋐ ⋑⋐

As I made my way to my office, I heard a familiar voice summon me to his: Major McCarran was sitting behind his desk looking quite puzzled, and asked me to come around to his side to have a look at his computer. In front of him was an assortment of photographs and a digital camera filled with pictures, all of which were shots of him in suggestive poses. I bit my tongue to keep myself from laughing.

"What can I do for you Major?" I asked respectfully.

"How can I scan these photographs into the computer, and then how can I attach them to an e-mail?"

"Sir, if I could sit down for a moment, I can take care of this for you in about two minutes." The major stood up. I'd not been sitting there long before Guy Armstrong, the Communications officer, entered the office.

"Hey Adam, are you and Audrey coming down to Windmill Beach for the cook-out tonight?"

"I hadn't heard about it. Who's going?"

"Everyone. There's supposed to be a meteor shower or something. Anyway, just bring a dish to share with everyone and be there around 1900."

My eyes were darting back and forth between Guy standing there in front of me, and McCarran's computer screen, but I managed to utter a "I'll check with Audrey." As I scanned his photos, the major went outside to talk to Guy, Gordie and Chet Dingle, except their conversation was anything but work related. I strained to listen, but the gist was "a new piece of meat" had arrived on the island by the name of Lieutenant Junior Grade Holly Humphries. The men seemed downright jovial about the new arrival, and apparently, they had invited her to the festivities later that night at Windmill Beach. All along I was wondering to whom McCarran intended to send those photos, and why he seemed to be chummy with Dingle all of a sudden. I definitely had my radar up, and I wanted to be at the beach for the cook-out, if to do nothing else but to get a peek at Miss Humphries and to watch how Dingle and McCarran related to each other outside of work. After a quick call to Audrey, I shouted to the men we'd be there, and I also let Audrey know Ranagan had obtained the go-ahead to let Abuelita out of the migrant camp for a day.

15

As we pulled up to the parking lot at Windmill Beach, everyone else was already there and were beginning to gather around the food. Our group had taken over an entire picnic shelter with dinner on one side, appetizers and desserts on another. This was our first such beach gathering, but it certainly wouldn't be our last. Due to the size of the base, most social events involved the beach.

The sun was still shining brightly in the early evening sky, but had begun its decent into the sea as I waited anxiously to see the meteors. I walked with Audrey to the shelter, which was only a few yards away from the car, and said hello to the gang. Rhonda and Manny Romero were the first to greet us, and then Maura Gellar and Arlene Hill quickly found their way to us. The bachelor officers—Guy Armstrong, Chet Dingle, and Gordie Shaw—were gathered around the barbecue, with the naughty Holly Humphries in the center of them all. The married Evan Geller had even strolled over.

Holly was petite and slender, with artificially red hair and eyes so blue, I knew she had to be wearing blue shaded contacts. Her curves were slight and her smile bright, but she was nothing to write home about. Miss Humphries was attractive—Audrey said cute was the best she could do—but she was no raving beauty by anyone's standards. However, one would have a difficult time telling that to Holly, as the men were drooling and she knew it.

"Well, it's time I get my husband to roll in his dribbling, pink tongue and get him to heel," Maura said with humor, making her way over to him. That's the thing Audrey and I loved most about the Gellar's—their sense of humor.

"Where's Ryan?" I asked Arlene as I stretched my neck to find him.

"Oh, he's telling dirty jokes with Aidan Foster and Tony Razor down the beach somewhere," she said, rolling her eyes.

The last time I'd seen Aidan was at Rick's Lounge the day I had drinks with him and Chet Dingle. Normally, he worked on Leeward with Chet, so I rarely saw him. Standing beside him was a pretty lady, about twenty years old, with strawberry-blond hair pushed back with a pink head band. Her name was Kelly and she was one of the college students from the States who had recently arrived in Gitmo to study the iguanas. Even though they hadn't been together long, rumor had it that Aidan and Kelly were serious and thinking into the future.

"So? Did you get your invitation yet?" Arlene asked Audrey, as I excused myself to go join the men.

"What invitation?"

"The invitation to the Ranagan's cocktail party before the Marine Corps Birthday Ball."

"No, I haven't gotten one."

"Well, that's funny because the McCarrans, Romeros, and Gellars all got one."

"I guess she must not like us too much."

"You probably just haven't gotten it yet, that's all," Arlene said. "Come on! Let's dig into this food before the flies attack it."

Do you remember the Hitchcock movie *The Birds*? A village was besieged by birds and no matter what the citizens of that town did to keep the birds away and out of their homes, the birds kept coming. I lived this movie almost every day for months on end, but we called it—no shocker—The Flies. When any of us would leave our home and walk to our car, hundreds of flies would swarm and it was a mad dash to get to your car before you swallowed a fly or they got tangled in your hair. We all had Captain Pickard, and his unreasonable quest to save money, to thank for this. He'd reduced funding for the fumigation of the Gitmo dump. None of us lived farther than two miles from that breeding ground and others lived a lot closer.

Just as I reached Ryan and Aidan, my pager went off and I had to walk across the parking lot to use the phone mounted on the side of one of the pavilions. As it turned out, LT. Bradshaw had taken ill and they needed someone to stand over-night duty that evening, so I volunteered. I wasn't sure how Audrey was going to take the news, but just before I arrived back at the picnic shelter, the skies opened up and it began to pour. Everyone raced around collecting their belongings and headed towards their cars. Within minutes, the whole get-together had ended without meteor one showing its face. Audrey was just as happy to ride home with me, and I was happy I'd get to spend a little more time with her before I reported to the White House.

"Adam, did you get an invitation to the Ranagan's cocktail party? I think everyone else has."

"Do you mean the one they're throwing before the ball?"

"Yeah."

"No, and we're not getting one. Only department heads get invited or company commanders, and since I'm neither, we get the night off!"

"Do you think that's right? I mean, that's kind of rude to invite most of the people who live on our street, but not everyone."

"I wouldn't want to go anyway. I see enough of that man at work."

"Yeah, I know, but still." I heard the gears turning in her head. "Hey! What if we throw our own party and invite everyone else who wasn't invited to the Ranagan's?"

"That would be an awesome idea. Let's do it. I'll spread the word next week."

"By the way, what did you think of Miss Hump-a-lot?"

For a moment, I had no idea what she was talking about, and then I got it. "Oh, you mean Lieutenant, JG Humphries? She was ok. Where did you come up with Hump-a-lot?"

"I didn't, Maura did. All the girls say she's a total mattress— she'll sleep with anyone."

"I'd buy that. The Gitmo Naval Hospital better get ready for Nurse Hump-a-lot."

"Oh? She's a navy nurse? Nope, no stereotype there! Adam, aren't there any nice women in the military who want a serious career?"

"Yeah, we call them lesbians."

"No, seriously!"

"Of course there is Audrey. I just don't think they're stationed here. From what Gordie told me, the BOQ is a sex palace—everyone doing everybody."

"Lovely. You're not allowed to go over there ever again."

"Wouldn't dream of it darlin', wouldn't dream of it. Okay, I might dream about it, but then again, I'm a man."

Let me paint a picture for you: standing duty sucks. It's boring, uneventful and absolutely ridiculous on a base the size of Gitmo. Once in a while an important matter arose that needed immediate attention, but since every Marine who stood duty could throw a rock at the White House from their back door, it was absurd to spend a night away from family. Nonetheless, since nobody had sworn me in as Commandant of the Marine Corps, my fate was clear; twelve hours of complete tedium lay ahead, and I'd volunteered for it.

I spent the first few hours doing the regular paperwork and making the usual rounds around the White House before doing something a bit more stimulating. Upon securing the safe in Major McCarran's office for the night, I decided to linger a few minutes to see if I could figure out where he'd been lately and what he'd been up to. He never showed up at the cookout, nor did Regina, so I figured they were home together. Proceeding on that assumption, I rifled through his papers and desk drawers, hoping I was right; the last thing I needed was to have my boss find me ratting around in his desk. I'm not usually the kind of person who spies on others, but something didn't seem right, and I felt compelled to check things out.

Since I didn't want to stay in the office too long, I wasn't able to find very much in the way of personal items, but I did come across something I didn't understand. The Marines of the Ground Defense Security Force in Gitmo have a Defense Action Plan, or DAF, to be used in case of a Cuban attack, and we'd been revising it for the last several weeks. It was a diagram for war, with all our tactical plans laid out in black and white, and we needed to send a copy to SOUTHCOM, or Southern Command, in Miami. As you might imagine, it needs to be under lock and key at all times, unless it's either in use or being revised, as it had been that morning. It was McCarran's responsibility to make sure the DAF was locked in his safe at the close of operations for the day, but there it was, just lying on his desk for all the world to see. If that wasn't enough, on a sticky note he placed on top of the DAF, he'd written: TOTAL BULLSHIT!!!

As I held the DAF in my hands, I thought I heard footsteps in the main operations office, so, with a sickened feeling, I quickly closed the folder and shut the door behind me. As I peeked around the corner, I didn't see anyone, so I proceeded to lock McCarran's office and headed back to my watch station. On my way, I turned my walk into more of a stroll as I came to the part of the corridor where all the historical photographs were hung. At first glance, it looked like every photo was of a former CO, but there were actually many photographs of Marines and Marine events throughout the years that I'd overlooked. There were pictures of the first defense force and of the old barracks; Marines shooting at the old abandoned range; the primitive base facilities in the 1920s; and, then finally, the most intriguing of all; down on the bottom left was a photograph of a group of Marines entitled "Liberation, July 18, 1958." I stood there, staring into the framed snapshot, trying to figure out what had been liberated and why. I bypassed the watch office and went to my own desk in OPS to see if Conway had left anything in that file cabinet that might shed some light on this moment in Marine history.

After an hour or so of serious digging, I came across several old newspaper articles, written in Spanish, which had been stapled together and stuck in the back of the cabinet, behind the drawer. Given that the only language I knew was English, I called Audrey and asked her to translate them for me. I felt badly that it was almost midnight, but when I realized one of the editorials in my hand was accompanied by the same photo I'd just seen on the wall in the corridor, I knew I wouldn't be able to sleep without an explanation.

Despite my butcher job on Cuba's native tongue, Audrey understood what I was reading to her. All the articles pertained to an event which began on June 27, 1958, when twenty-nine

Marines and sailors were kidnapped by Cuban rebel forces, under the command of Raul Castro, as they were returning to base from liberty. After twenty-one days as hostages, the group was released—apparently unharmed—as a result of diplomatic efforts. Under the photograph, there was a caption listing all the men who had been held. I read them to Audrey as well, although the American names obviously needed no translation. When I came to the eleventh name, my mouth stopped working; I literally could not speak.

"Adam? What is it? Why did you stop?"

I attempted to match him up to one of the men in the photograph. For a moment, I'd forgotten I even had Audrey on the line.

"Adam! What's going on? Why won't you answer me?" Audrey demanded.

Then I saw him. I couldn't believe I finally had a face to go with the name.

"If you don't answer me this instant, then I'm going to come up there."

"It's him Audrey," I said, interrupting her. "I'm looking at him right now."

"Who? Who are you looking at?"

"A murderer," I said calmly. "Gunnery Sergeant Elliot Gaultier."

"He was one of the men who were kidnapped in '58?"

"Yup, he was," I said with disbelief in my voice. "I can't believe I know what he looks like."

"Well! What does he look like?"

"He's very tall, athletic-looking, light hair, strong jaw line.... you'd approve."

"So, what does this mean Adam?"

"It means there must be more written on the good gunnery sergeant somewhere—a debriefing, a testimony, something."

"Can you get your hands on it?" Audrey asked, unconvinced.

"I'm sure as hell gonna try."

16

The big day finally arrived for Abuelita, and my wife picked her up promptly at 8am, taking her straight to our housing area. Abuelita was dressed in an orange and yellow gauze skirt, covering almost all of her legs, with a yellow cotton blouse and tan leather sandals. Her gray hair was tucked neatly in a bun and she was sporting the new glasses that she'd received from the base optician. Abuelita was a beautiful woman at one time, with warm eyes and high check bones; her skin, while wrinkled, was olive and without blemishes. I met the two ladies right on time and began the mock interview.

Audrey told me later Abuelita had not said very much on the way there; she appeared to be surveying her surroundings, searching her memory for stories to tell. However, when Audrey drove the car onto our street, the Cuban woman conveyed her excitement upon seeing her old home. As it turned out, she used to live in the small apartment above the McCarran's garage. Abuelita was amazed at how tall the trees had gotten in the neighborhood and described in detail how the houses looked when she lived there in 1959. As she spoke, Audrey translated for me, although, from time to time, Abuelita would stick in an English word when she knew it; it was quite charming when she did.

"She says on her first day here in March of 1959, she was surprised to see how big the homes were that the Marine families lived in. Back then, the houses were sided with wood, instead of vinyl, and they were painted white to match the garages. She's unclear if the houses had the same orange tiled roofs like the garages do. There were no glass windows, only wooden louvered coverings, so it was really hot in the homes during the day and bug infested in the afternoon and at dusk. The area of the house she is pointing to...there...where the living room protrudes into the back yard...that extra space wasn't a part of the actual house at all—it was a screened-in porch. The porches were a necessity because the insects could be very bad, especially after a big rain storm." Abuelita waved her hands around her head as if pretending to fend off flies and mosquitoes.

She walked toward our house, across the street, and began to speak again. "She says there used to be some sort of apartment complex or dormitory behind our house, which is why we can still make out the edges of a parking lot. She thinks it was for married officers who didn't have any children, but she is not sure."

Abuelita turned towards our garage. "Her friend Daniela lived in the space above our garage. She says Daniela gave her strength to carry on each day when she couldn't find her husband, when no one would even talk to her about her husband."

"Ask her what happened to him exactly? When did he go missing? What was his job on base? See what you can find out," I told Audrey.

"She says her husband's name was Miguel Herrera, and he was thirty years old. He worked for base maintenance, but sometimes he'd be loaned out to help the construction battalion, but that was rare. He'd worked six days a week, from 7am to 7pm, almost without exception. But one day, right before Christmas in 1958, he left earlier than usual and he acted strange. He hugged her and kissed her incessantly, until she finally sent him away. She says she stood in the doorway to say goodbye, and, before he got into the truck, he blew her a kiss." Abuelita made the motion of blowing a kiss. "And that's the last she saw or heard from him."

The Cuban took off her glasses to wipe the tears in her eyes, and took a deep breath before continuing to speak.

"She waited for three days thinking he'd been asked to stay on base for extra work—that wasn't entirely unheard of—but when he didn't come home on day four, and since he'd missed Christmas, she called the husband of her deceased sister, Chico, who also worked on base, but he never answered his phone. On the tenth day, she walked for four hours to the Northeast Gate to try and find someone who could help her, but she didn't speak English and the Marine guards weren't interested in helping her. When she realized she couldn't find any answers there, she walked the four hours home, to Guantanamo City. There, she filed a missing person report, but she felt the Cuban police would be of little help to her since a new leader had just assumed power in Havana, Fidel Castro."

Abuelita spat on the ground after uttering his name.

"The whole country was in chaos and then...then the killings began. She says by that summer, Castro expressed his allegiance to Marxist ideology and mass imprisonments and mass executions were widespread. US military members couldn't go into Cuban territory anymore, but Castro allowed Cubans to continue to work on base. In March, she decided to take a job there to see if she could find Miguel herself, and was made a housekeeper for a Marine officer and his family. At first she went home each evening on the commuter bus, but in 1961, everything changed."

"Wait a minute. She just jumped from 1959 to 1961. What did she find out about her husband?" I asked, totally enthralled.

"She says she didn't try to find out anything right away because she didn't want to lose her job. After six months, she told the Marine officer she lived with the whole story, and he promised to help her."

"*And?*" I said, wishing Audrey could translate faster.

"She says he called one day to say he'd found something out about Miguel, but he'd wanted to check something out first, and he'd tell her what he knew later that evening. But he didn't ever tell her, because he never came home."

"What? Why?" I asked. Abuelita continued, Audrey covered her mouth with her hand, gasping.

"WHAT? What did she say?" I demanded.

"She says he couldn't tell her what he found because...because he'd been killed in the minefields that same afternoon."

Retelling such an unpleasant story wasn't easy for Abuelita, so I took her arm and escorted her to the sheltered picnic area in the center of our neighborhood. Audrey ran to the house to get her some water and a few slices of apple. She drank the water, but refused the fruit. Since we didn't want to make her uncomfortable, we stopped asking questions and waited for her to begin speaking. After a few minutes, she carried on.

"She felt compassion for her employer's wife; she knew what it felt like to lose a husband. She also felt sorry for herself because he'd been her last and only hope. She wondered, night after night, what information he'd discovered, and prayed God would allow him to return to earth to tell her what he knew."

"Ask her if she remembers the name of the man who died," I prompted Audrey.

"Yes. She will always remember that name. Captain Haggar— the dapper Captain, as she remembers him." Abuelita smiled when she recalled that expression. "His wife, Mrs. Haggar, was devastated, and was only allowed to stay on base for thirty days after his death. They became very close during that time, and Mrs. Haggar swore she'd find out what she could about Miguel before she left."

"And did she?"

"No, she was too distraught to be of any help that way, but Daniela told her something that frightened her. Her friend, Daniela, had been secretly dating an enlisted Marine, and she asked him to help Abuelita find Miguel. One night, a terrified Daniela ran over to her house and begged Abuelita to stop looking for Miguel. Daniela told her that her Marine had been warned to stop asking questions."

"Does she remember the enlistee's name?" I asked, getting my pen and paper ready to write.

"She only remembers his name started with an O, and she is not sure whether it's his first or last."

"What happened to her after that?"

"Hoping that something might turn up about Miguel, she continued to work on base, but only until 1961. Castro began to send his thugs to the Northeast Gate to beat any Cuban who continued to work on base, and life became unbearable. The Americans offered to let Cubans live on base permanently, but she knew her home was in the only place where she'd lived with her husband, and she returned there."

"Then why did she try to escape? I mean, how did she end up in the migrant camp?"

"She had a son named Miguel in 1975, out of wedlock. About a year ago, he left for America and was captured by the US Coast Guard and sent here. She was hoping to find him on base so they could be together again, but none of the other detainees seem to know who she's talking about. She says it's the same nightmare all over again."

Audrey began to rattle off something to Abuelita that made her smile as big as the Grand Canyon.

"Translation please," I said with a grin.

"I told her when Cubans are brought to Cuba, they stay here until the US can determine if they require political asylum, and if so, the State Department brokers a deal with a third country, like Costa Rica or Peru, and sends them there. I told her there's an excellent chance he's alive and well in Central or South America."

"That should be easy to verify, right?" I asked Audrey.

"Piece of cake!" Audrey said as she snapped her fingers. "I can find that out on Monday."

But Washington paperwork turned out to be a long and winding road.

Donny and Becca Mancuso, the dive instructor and his wife, met our class at the Phillips Park dive platform on Saturday morning for our very first saltwater dive. Despite the early hour, Audrey, our fellow classmates, and I were eager to utilize our newly learned skills. After Donny briefed our dive, which included entering the water, a fifty-yard snorkel, and a trip to the bottom thirty feet down, each of us hooked up with a buddy and we helped each other put on our gear. Audrey had some difficulty correctly positioning her tank on her BCD, or Buoyancy Control Device, due to an impromptu anxiety attack, but I helped to calm her with an unequivocal guarantee that she wouldn't see any sharks that day. Donny, sensing her unease, walked over to her and promised the title to his car if she, or anyone else in the class, spotted a shark of any kind that morning. Audrey's eyes hastily shifted to the parking lot where she caught a glimpse of Donny's 1976 brown, VW van with gold pin-striping, and a plywood rear window. I think the Gremlin even looked good to her at that moment.

Donny and Becca were super fun people, with off-color jokes never-ending. He'd been a Marine diver, but had retired out a few years before. She'd been in the Navy, but left after only five years in service. They met at a wedding the year before and the rest is history. Becca spent her days running the video store and Donny worked as a civilian electrician. In the evenings, Donny kept Becca company until closing time at the store, and Becca would accompany Donny on weekend dive classes whenever she could. There was a rumor, of some magnitude, going around the island that Becca and Donny were swingers, but Audrey and I refused to believe it; they were just too in love.

Donny was the first to enter the water, followed by me. I floundered in the ocean, waiting for Audrey, but she kept letting the other five students go in front of her. I was beginning to worry if she'd really have the guts to do it. When it was finally her turn, she took a deep breath and rejected the idea of diving entirely by sitting down on the edge of the platform. Donny and I swam over to her to find out what had gone wrong.

"I can't do this!" Audrey said, fumbling with her BCU, trying to take it off.

"What can't you do?" Donny said in a very soothing voice.

"Dive! I can't!"

"What the hell, Audrey! Come on already!" I said, embarrassingly losing my patience with her. Donny shot me a look and motioned for me to swim away, so I did. He climbed out of the water and sat beside her for a while, talking to her quietly, reassuring her. After about five minutes, he slipped back into the water and the whole class watched as Audrey did the same. The Cubans in Caimanera must have heard our fervent shouts of encouragement as we all took part in Audrey's victory over fear. As I swam towards her, Donny informed me he'd be Audrey's partner for the day. I was to buddy up with the odd-man-out in the group, Harvey Gross, the Jamaican elementary-school janitor. I gave Donny the thumbs up on his call, but inside, as I swam away from my sexy wife and towards a man who cleaned kiddy vomit for a living, I knew Donny had gotten the better end of that deal.

When we completed our snorkel activity, the moment of truth had arrived for our little group; at Donny's signal, we began to let air out of our BCUs which initiated our descent into the shadowy

THE GHOSTS OF GUANTANAMO BAY

Caribbean abyss. Every ten feet we submerged, we had to take a moment to equalize—pop our ears like when flying—before continuing our downward slope. None of us, including Audrey, seemed to have a problem, and, after a few moments, we had all reached the sandy bottom. My first inclination was to look up at the surface, at that crystal blue ceiling. At my feet were literally hundreds of sand dollars littered about, and the occasional sea biscuit—a puffy sand dollar—which everyone excitedly scooped up into their mesh bags.

Donny ran through his checklist of must-do items, such as taking our masks off underwater, and buddy-breathing. I glanced over at Audrey and there she was, sucking on Donny's air like there was no tomorrow. I was a little jealous, but she needed an experienced diver at her side—which I was not. My mind stayed busy thinking about all the dives she and I would go on once she had her confidence, and of course, the dive at hand.

After our final exercise in the sandy area, Donny motioned for us to follow him. Experienced divers said Phillips Park had the least attractive reefs, but for me, it was heaven. There were purple and pink coral, blue and yellow fish, orange lobsters and visibility you wouldn't believe! We could see for fifty-yards in any direction, with the rays of the sun illuminating an unspoiled world of absolute perfection. I'd never known true peace and relaxation in my life until that moment.

🦐 🦐 🦐

The next day was the day of the Marine Wives Association Fall Festival. Everything went without a hitch and 104 people showed up; there were smiles from wall to wall and everyone had a wonderful time. When the party was at its liveliest, Lois Ranagan meandered into the room with a sense of confidence about her, and surveyed the crowd for about ten minutes; none of us could believe she had even shown up. On her way out the door, she stopped in front of Audrey and said in the same voice as a high-school cheerleader, "Now see, Audrey! See what a little effort can do for morale! I know you all worked very hard, and even though you had a good turn-out, had only one family shown up, this all would have been worth it just the same." She actually had the audacity to pat Audrey on the shoulder before leaving with an accompanying, "Ya done good."

17

The first day of November set the tone for the rest of the month as the next meeting of the Marine Wives Association was called to order. Audrey wasn't in good spirits to begin with; she'd been unable to unearth information about Abuelita's son that day. She couldn't even find a paper trail, and, nobody remembered a Miguel Herrera ever being in the migrant camp. I begged Audrey not to go to the meeting since she was already feeling so dejected, but she didn't want to let the others down.

After making myself a snack, I headed into the back bedroom to rummage around for a register of enlisted Marines stationed in Gitmo in 1959. Abuelita said the Marine who'd been warned to stop looking for Miguel had an 'O' as an initial in his name, and, while I knew it was a long shot, I felt obligated to try. I wasn't sure what I'd do with the name if I came across it, but her story intrigued me so much, I was a slave to my own curiosity.

"Well, ladies," Drew Ray began, "I want to congratulate you all for the outstanding job you did on the Fall Festival. I've heard from many of the families and they said they all had a wonderful time.

Do you have anything to add, Lois?" It was apparent Drew only asked Lois that question to force her to admit she'd been wrong for not wanting to have the party in the first place.

Lois, who had taken a seat in the back of the room, made a feeble attempt to look at the group before uttering an unconvincing, "Yes, the people I saw seemed to be having a nice time."

Drew locked eyes with Lois for a moment and then continued with the agenda. "It has come to our attention, sadly, that First Sergeant Howard's wife has been medically evacuated off the island for cancer treatment in the States. I'd like to take a vote to see if you ladies would like to send a gift basket. The card would read 'From all the Marine Wives in Gitmo'."

"Drew, that won't be necessary. A gift has already been sent," Lois interjected.

"What do you mean one's already been sent?" Drew asked. "By whom?"

"The Marine Wives Association," Lois said bluntly.

"How could the Wives Association have sent a gift when we haven't voted on it yet?" Drew said, her voice rising.

"Because I sent one," Lois said plainly.

"And how may I ask did you pay for it?"

Lois was growing tired of all of Drew's questions, but managed to keep her composure. "I simply went down to the bank and drew off the association's account."

"While I recognize your name is on the account, the only person this club recognizes to write checks is the Treasurer. You can't just go and use club money the way you want, no matter how noble the purpose," Drew snapped.

Feeling the immense discomfort in the room, Regina jumped in to change the subject. "I've heard that on Friday's flight, four new enlisted wives will be arriving. Do we have hospitality bags ready for them?"

"Yes, I do as a matter of fact," Arlene said, smiling, but Drew was quick to take back the floor.

"The next item up for discussion is regarding Christmas. Gunnery Sergeant Braun contacted me the other day about setting something up for the single Marines. He told me the Marines would really appreciate some sort of holiday party. He even went so far as to say they wanted to do holiday crafts and would sure love some home-baked goods. As I understand it, only one Marine is tasked with putting up the Christmas tree, so what do you say we make it an event and invite all the Marines and Marine families to decorate the tree? Gunny Braun has secured the activity room for November thirtieth, just in case. So, what do you all think?"

"I love it!" Rhonda exclaimed. "What a super idea!"

"Now, wait just a minute," Lois interrupted. "The single Marines have a fund for their own parties. I really think it would be inappropriate for us to host one for them."

"Not if we combined it into a Christmas party for Marine families too," Rhonda said, looking directly at Lois. "Personally, I can't think of a better way to spend the holidays. I'd love nothing more than for my children to sing carols, make ornaments and decorate cupcakes alongside the Marines. Sharing what we have, including strangers in our traditions...well, that's what puts the magic into Christmas as far as I'm concerned."

"That's my sentiment exactly," said Drew. "Anyone else have an opinion?"

With great hesitation, Maura began to speak, cautiously directing her question at Lois. "I like the concept, so, I don't really understand why you're against this."

"It's not that I'm against this," Lois said, feeling picked on, "I just think it's not a good idea for young men to be around married couples and their kids. I just don't see the need."

"The need is there are 400 men, who are barely men because most of them are only eighteen or nineteen, who have recently left home for the first time in their lives, who have no family support here, no home-cooked meals, no little brothers and sisters to talk with about Santa, and no tree of their own to decorate. In other words, there's nothing but a hot, sweaty MOP for them to look forward to this Christmas!" Drew stopped, never having lost control but obviously full of many emotions.

"Do what you want, but don't expect me to be there," Lois said without feeling, "and don't expect the colonel to be supportive." Everyone hated when she called her own husband the colonel.

"Drew, I'd like to say something if I can," Rhonda said, her hands trembling. "I'm resigning from the association tonight."

Everyone looked puzzled and even more uncomfortable.

"Why?" Drew was obviously disappointed.

When Rhonda spoke, she either looked down at the table or

off to a corner of the room where no one was sitting. It was apparent she was attempting to remain calm and chose her words deliberately. "I joined this association because I wanted to do some good for the Marine wives on this base. In my past experiences, the MWA has been an organization of inclusion. Yet here in Gitmo, it's done nothing but cause discord, friction, and dissention among us, and in my family. I feel as though there's a force in this room that does not wish for us to succeed in any way which is...which is not according to their own particular scheme. I feel our ideas and opinions aren't respected, and, therefore, I have little to no respect for this force which divides us, or attempts to divide us. Lois, I think you're unreasonable, unfair, and as long you use your husband's rank against our husbands, what we have here is not a club, but a vehicle for your tyrannical agenda."

Rosie Bradshaw, who had great affection for Lois, stood up and began to speak faster than her mouth could move. "I'm resigning too, but for a different reason! I'm resigning because all of you treat Mrs. Ranagan terribly! She doesn't deserve the negative way you act towards her. All she wants is to do wonderful things for the people we share this base with, and all you can do is to criticize her. You!" she said, pointing to Rhonda, "should be ashamed of yourself for saying the things you did. I bet your mother never thought she raised a little bitch like you!"

With that said, Rosie stood up and left the room. Lois remained, as if totally unaffected by what had happened. Rhonda had no idea what to do or say; none of the women did.

"Ladies, in light of what occurred here tonight," Drew said, her voice quivering, "I motion to table the remaining items on our agenda until next month." When she finished speaking, Drew left the room as quickly as she could, heading down to her husband's office where he'd been working late. Lois left too, but walked in the opposite direction.

The debrief that followed a MWA meeting was always both stressful and entertaining; however, what those ladies should have been able to discuss in thirty minutes, usually took hours. I wasn't sure if I'd be able to stay up for Audrey's return; I was dead tired. But, Audrey came home only forty-five minutes after she'd left, and by the look on her face, I knew there was definitely a story to tell. Needless to say, I was flabbergasted when she told me what had transpired, but I understood it. The guys at work told me what they had gone through—being counseled for their wives befriending enlisted wives, or for their wives' attire while gardening in their yards or while jogging—so, I knew the breaking point was fast approaching. Audrey had been doing well, but her moment with Lois was inevitable.

"Adam, I just don't get it. Lois obviously thinks nothing she does bothers us. I mean, I can see how she saw nothing wrong in sending the gift to that lady in the hospital, but the right thing to do was to wait for a meeting...or at least call for a phone vote. This is what she doesn't understand: it's not her private club, it's our association. God! It's so frustrating."

"Yeah, I bet it is. I think the big problem here is that each of her individual acts is not so bad all by itself, but when you combine them all, there's a whole lot of something."

"You know what I heard? Mimsey Pickard calls herself the advisor of the Navy Wives Association too. She also refers to her husband as the Captain and votes down a lot of what they want to do. But none of those ladies or their husbands get in trouble when she doesn't get her way."

"Ya know, on any normal military installation, there is a general/admiral at the top of the pyramid and colonels/Navy captains are a dime a dozen in most places, but not here. There are only three full bird's on the entire base: Pickard, Ranagan and the hospital CO. Also, when Gitmo had more people, the house Pickard lives in used to belong to an admiral and the quarters Ranagan lives in used to house a Marine general. Basically, they're living in a dream world for their rank. Had they been here even ten or fifteen years ago, they would have never been living in such grandeur, and they certainly wouldn't have the clout they seem to have created. I think they do what they want because they feel as though they're protected on this base—accountable to absolutely no one but themselves."

"But that's not true, right, Adam? They've got to be accountable to someone!"

"Of course they are, but Ranagan's chaperone is General Crane, who's stationed in Quantico and Pickard's is some admiral in Jacksonville, Florida. As long as there are no deaths or military skirmishes, and as long as each honcho receives their flowery monthly report describing Gitmo as heaven on earth, Ranagan and Pickard can do what they want, when they want. And so can their wives."

Audrey let out a huge sigh. "Well, at least that explains it."

"Explains what?"

"Why everyone says that when a CO first gets here, he's totally cool, but as time goes on, he becomes a dick. Remember what Conway said? He told us Ranagan was the best when he first got here, and so was Colonel Vandermeed—the guy who tried to have Conway court-martialed—but then they both turned into total butt-wipes the longer they were here."

I stood up and mimicked the voice of a high-powered southern attorney. "Ladies and gentleman of the jury, I'm here today to accuse Colonel Ranagan of the scandalous crime of being a dick and his wife of being a total butt-wipe. Thank you very much." I sat back down and put my arm around Audrey. "Your father and mother would be proud of that college degree now...the way you articulate your opinions."

"Hey, I'm just tired. Let's change the subject. What did you do to entertain yourself tonight, and there better have been two hands involved in whatever it was."

"Very funny. I think I've found that Marine—Daniela's boyfriend."

"How?"

"Well, I didn't actually find him, but I was able to narrow it down some. In 1959, there were three Marines with O first names— Otto, Orlando, Oliver—and five with last names beginning with O—Osterman, Outlaw, Olsen, Orcher, and O'Malley. Now I just have to figure out which one it was."

"Oh, is that all?"

"Guess who I'm going to start with first?" I asked her with confidence.

"Haven't a clue."

"A Mr. Oliver Orcher. He was the only one in the bunch that had an O first and last name. I figured maybe that's why Abuelita remembered the O to begin with. After all, it was like fifty years ago."

"I suppose that's as good a place to start as any," she conceded.

"Hey, you never did tell me what you and Regina talked about the other night when she was so upset."

"Oh, nothing. It felt like she wanted to talk about something really big, but in the end, I guess she wasn't ready, so we just talked about Lois. Can you believe Lois has been calling her, asking for her help with the rest of us? Lois said Regina was the only one who was mature and the only one who had any sense of reason in the whole bunch."

"And what did Regina tell her?"

"All she said was that the rest of us feel as though we're being controlled by her, and then Lois shot back that the only real problem here was Drew Ray, since she filled our heads with nonsense."

"What did she mean by that?" I must have missed something along the way.

"I guess she found out that Drew tells the wives what the colonel says. It seems that Ranagan goes off on his tirades about us—how much he dislikes us—and he does all of this in front of Lt Colonel Ray. When Ray gets home, he tells his wife, Drew, everything the colonel said that day, who tells us what he's said behind our backs."

"Whew, that was a mouthful. Anything new to report?"

"Not since I told you that Lt Colonel Ray was told to counsel us on waving more to Lois. I still can't believe that woman gets upset because we don't wave to her enough! She told her husband that she thinks that we're going out of our way to ignore her if we don't wave to her. But the thing is, sometimes I see her like twenty times in a day. I'm not going to wave to her every time."

"You know who I've been thinking a lot about?" I asked, changing the subject.

"Who?"

"Elliot Gaultier. I want to try and find out where he is."

"And why would you do that? I mean, really, what are you going to say? 'Pardon me, but did you murder Corporal Loring and subsequently hide the body?' That would sound stupid."

"I don't know. I just want to know where he is. I want to know something about anything right now!" I said irritably. The late hour had started to affect me. "Just as a general recap for you, in case you forgot anything, we have a car and uniform that are bloodstained; a missing lance corporal; two missing Cubans; a missing migrant; a little old lady who is heart broken and displaced; five dead Marines who have no reasonable explanation for their death; an asshole Lieutenant named Chet Dingle who gets away with every illegal and unethical thing he does; two CO's wives who are totally out of control; a boss who goes mysteriously absent from time to time; and a CO who is completely out of his mind on most days. Now, can you see why I want to have something tangible? Keep in mind that we've only been here four months."

18

Every Marine couple who lived on our street received an invitation to our Birthday Ball cocktail party, even the ones who had already been invited to the Ranagan's. Audrey and I made sure all of our friends and acquaintances—including the weirdo Mosers across the street—had a place to go. For the ones who were already committed to the other party, we were told to expect them at the earliest possible moment, meaning that they intended to blow the Ranagan's party as soon as they could. In all honesty, we only invited everyone so no one felt left out; we never expected nor needed any of the Ranagan's guests to actually show up at our home, even if they were all good friends. Twenty people were more than enough for Audrey to cook for and for us to entertain.

Three days before the ball, after we had already done all the shopping for the food, and after we had bought cases of beer and wine, Audrey received a call from Lois before I arrived home for the evening.

"Good afternoon, Audrey, this is Lois," she said nicely, but as if she were in a hurry. "I'm calling because I'm not sure if you know this, but the colonel and I are hosting a cocktail party at our home just before the Ball in General Crane's honor and we'd like you and Adam to come."

Audrey bit her lip and paused for a moment, realizing Lois had obviously gotten word of our party and was trying to get us to cancel by offering an invitation to her own gathering. Once Audrey collected her thoughts, she spoke politely, yet firmly. "Wow! Thank you so much, Lois! That's so sweet of you to invite us to your cocktail party, but I'm afraid we're having our own party that evening at the same time. We wouldn't have planned one, of course, if we had had more notice about yours."

"Well, I don't know anything about that. All I know is that your husband is the second in command of operations and he's required to be at our party to greet the guest of honor, General Crane." Lois had apparently forgotten that she originally had only invited department heads, not second-in-commands.

"He will be," Audrey said knowing Ranagan could absolutely order me to go, but Audrey also knew the colonel had no power over her. "I, on the other hand, have guests to consider at my own home. Adam will be there right on time, but I need to stay here with my guests. I'm sure you understand. But thank you again for the invitation. It was very thoughtful."

"Audrey, I think it would be best for you accompany your husband. After all, what would people think?" she said as if she were aghast.

"People would think that I have my own party to consider and too much food here to go to waste. Again, Lois, thank you, but I really won't be able to make it."

"Fine. Whatever you want to do," Lois said impersonally, right before the phone went dead.

Even though it was early evening, Audrey jumped in her car and drove to Chapel Hill with the hopes of talking to Father Blankenship, but he'd already left for the day when she arrived. In his place was Pastor Penelope Dooley, who was more than happy to talk with Audrey.

"You're the Protestant Chaplain?" Audrey asked. "I was told that the new chaplain was a man."

"I'm sorry someone confused you, but I'm a woman, or at least I was the last time I looked!" she smiled. "I may not have the man parts, but I assure you that I have the same heart and mind, so feel free to discuss anything you like."

"I'm sorry. You misunderstood me. I have no problem with you being a woman; I just had expected to see a man, that's all."

"Well then, please speak your mind." Pastor Dooley kicked her legs up on her desk and began to eat an apple. "Pardon me for eating, but I was about to go to dinner when you walked in. I'll assure you that I can eat and listen at the same time."

"That's fine, Pastor," Audrey began.

"Please, call me Penny," the pastor insisted.

"Okay, Penny, I will," Audrey said with a bright smile.

While some people might have been put off by Dooley's laid-back style, Audrey embraced it. The new thirty-three year old pastor was a plain-looking woman with short black hair and small tortoise-shell glasses. Her eyes were bright and she had two rosy checks that looked like round balls when she smiled.

"So what do you think Penny? I've done everything that Father Blankenship has asked of me, but this phone call today...Lois only invited us so that we'd give up on having our own party."

"Personally, she sounds like a control freak and a real pain in the butt," Penny said bluntly.

"Tell me about it!" Audrey snapped back. "Also, the other wives told me that Father Blankenship tells Lois everything we tell him. Can that be true?"

"Could be, but to be honest, I've only been here a short time and I don't really know the man too well, but I'll see what I can find out for you. I know he's not supposed to say anything. I can tell you that Mrs. Ranagan came up here today to remind Blankenship of her party right in front of me, and she never even offered me an invitation. Come to think of it, she never even acknowledged me."

"Penny, how long have you been a chaplain?"

Penny looked at her watch. "Officially? About seventy-two hours now. Why? Do I look a little ripe around the ears?" she said, folding her ears back for Audrey to see.

"Not ripe, but you sure don't act like any chaplain that I've ever met before!"

"No? I don't know what to say about that. I guess I should thank you. During my time in seminary, I thought that everyone seemed so uptight and stuffy. My goal was to be approachable and relaxed. How am I doin'?"

Audrey smiled. "You're doing great! I think your attitude is refreshing, but I need to know: do you really think Lois is the wrong one?"

"Sounds like it to me. Just ignore her for now."

"That's easy for you to say. I've been kind of dreaming about doing mean things to her to get even," Audrey admitted. "She's such a bitch."

"Yeah, I'd probably do the same. Some people just like to fuck with other people."

Audrey burst with laughter. "Did you just say what I think you said?"

Dooley smiled."Yeah, why? Pastors are people too. Did I offend you?"

"Oh no! I just never heard a God person say that before."

"God person?" Penny started to chuckle. "Well, I've never heard that expression before! For your information Audrey, we're all God people, or, People of God. Not a one of us is, or can ever be, as perfect as He. So I curse from time to time. Sue me."

"I don't have a problem with it. I can curse as good as the next sailor myself," Audrey answered.

Penny put on a bright red clown nose.

"Are you trying to impress me or are you just dressing for dinner?"

"Actually, I'm getting dressed up, but not for you. I have a children's clown ministry tonight."

"What's that?"

"It's a way of teaching children who are normally introverted to be extroverted. You should come sometime." Penny looked at her watch and began rushing. "I'm sorry, Audrey, but I'm out of time. Let me think about what you told me...give me a call on Friday. I'll see what I can come up with. In the meantime, don't sweat it. She's a power-hungry old bag and that's all you need to know."

"Okay, but since you were left off of the Ranagan's cocktail party list, how about coming to mine?"

"Time and place is all I'll need."

BY THE TIME AUDREY GOT HOME, her whole demeanor had made an about face. She was the most relaxed and the happiest she'd been since we arrived in Gitmo. When she told me about her conversation with Lois, she didn't let herself get upset. I wasn't sure if she'd gotten used to the Lois-isms, or if Penny in her corner was the reason for her change. In every regard, Audrey seemed like the woman I once knew, and, for three days, I knew true Gitmo happiness.

The day of the Marine Corps Birthday Ball arrived and Audrey was racing around the house cleaning and cooking for most of the afternoon. At 4pm, she took her shower and by 5pm, she looked like Cinderella heading for her pumpkin stagecoach. The table was laid out, the candles lit, and the music was playing by 5:30. Miserably, I kissed Audrey on the cheek, told her how wonderful she looked and walked down to the Ranagan's house.

I had not been disconcerted about having to go to the colonel's until that moment. It was then I realized I had to leave my own home and my own friends, so that the Ranagans could prove a point, or, at the very least, parade me around in front of the general. My fellow Marines were drinking top-shelf liquor and high priced beer at my house, while gorging themselves on Audrey's gourmet appetizers. At the Ranagan's, we were treated to wine in a box, hot poppers and a cheese platter from Post 46. They were all class. The real kicker was that the general never showed up at the Ranagan's; as a matter of fact, he never even made it to Gitmo. He had called earlier that day and told the colonel that something had come up. Needless to say, the Ranagans were fit to be tied. However, you'd never have known that. Lois pretended everything was just as she had wanted it to be.

Since Lois and the colonel knew I had a house full of company, and since the general was a no-show, I fantasized that they might find it in their hearts to let me leave early. Who was I kidding? Lois actually followed me around, making polite conversation for almost an hour. When I could take the tedium no more, I respectfully thanked the Ranagans for their invitation and made my way back to my house at the opposite end of the street.

When I opened the door to the kitchen, the volume of the music was unleashed, and would have swept away a bald man's toupee. I could hear laughter and thunderous conversation throughout the house. By the time I reached the food table, most everything had been devoured and a few of the Marine officers were feeling quite loose, if you know what I mean. To my astonishment, Master Sergeant Moser and his wife were ear-to-ear smiles and having a wonderful time. These were the folks who hated officers and hated us for receiving their paper invitation to the Labor Day picnic.

I saw Tony Razor talking to the new chaplain and walked over. I introduced myself and felt the warmth from Penny Dooley that Audrey had described; she had an enlivening personality and a cheerful disposition.

"So how was *the party?*" Penny asked, making quotation marks with her fingers.

"It was...it was...how can I describe it?" I searched for just the right words.

"It sucked," Penny said unreservedly. "Is that what you were trying to say? Hey, look, like I told your wife, please feel at ease with me. The last thing I want is for people to feel all uncomfortable."

I excused myself from Penny when a new crowd of people arrived. They surrounded the coolers looking for a libation. By my count, almost all the Marines I'd seen down at the Ranagan's were now at my party. I walked up to Ryan Hill, almost embarrassed.

"So who's left at the CO's house?" I asked, afraid of the answer.

Ryan took a swig of beer and grinned widely. "Hmm...that would be...ah...nobody." He took another swig of beer.

"Nobody? Really? Why did you all leave at the same time?"

"Come on Claiborne, you were there! The party was boring and tense. Besides, there's just so much wine in a box you can drink before you start to get a headache."

"But did you really leave the house empty?"

"No. We stayed our hour and then left when the Ranagans started to talk to Dingle and Father Blankenship. We thought that was our ticket out."

"Were they mad you all left?"

"They didn't seem to be. Hey, what time is it? We need to be at the hangar by 7:30 sharp."

"It's 7:10," I answered, after looking at the kitchen clock.

"Well, then," Ryan said as he finished his beer, "I do believe I have time for one more!"

We pulled up to McCalla Field later than expected as we had to ensure that all of our guests had a safe ride to the Birthday Ball. Audrey and I wanted to talk about the success of our party, but were inhibited by the presence of Guy Armstrong and Gordie Shaw in the back seat. We weren't sure how well they would do that evening; they had already started to snicker like little girls at the most inane things. At one point, they were laughing so hard, I had to stop the car to see if they were still breathing. While too intoxicated to drive, they could still walk without assistance, so I dropped them both off at the entrance while Audrey and I parked the car. By the time my wife and I entered the hangar, the ceremony had begun.

The decorating crew had done the best they could under the circumstances, hanging camouflage netting from the ceiling as some sort of an adornment and parachutes to cordon off the area we were using. The flags of all fifty states were draped in front of the broken window panes to class the place up some. While there had been talk of installing AC in the building just for the night, the air in the hangar was exceedingly humid and the tropical climate was amplified by the heat of our assembled bodies. When Audrey started to whine about the temperature, I reminded her there were 500 Marines there who were dressed in long-sleeved, woolen uniforms. The sweat was pouring down my face too.

It took us a few minutes to find the seating chart, but, in the end, it turned out to be of little use to us. There were not enough tables to accommodate the people invited. Fifteen of us stood in the back throughout the forty-minute formal procedure, and that—combined with the heat—ensured that most of us couldn't concentrate on anything the colonel was saying. At first there was the presentation of the Colors and the National Anthem, followed by the Commandants' Annual Birthday Address, read by Lt. Colonel Ray. The last part of the formalities was Ranagan's speech, which I actually enjoyed.

"I want to thank everyone who came here tonight to share this special day. I apologize that General Crane couldn't be with us, but he was otherwise occupied, as Generals usually are. However, even though we're without a guest of honor, there is still a tremendous amount of honor in this building tonight and it should be recognized." He walked towards the enlisted men who stood watch in the MOPS. "These fine young men here have a very difficult job to do, far more difficult than you could ever imagine. Thirty, twenty, even ten years ago, the men who stood in their place knew their mission and had the support and respect of every bureaucrat in Washington. Today, sadly, our government is in conflict. Some say that Guantanamo Bay Naval Base should be closed down, since the threat posed by the Cubans has greatly diminished. Others say that Guantanamo Bay is essential to our national security and the stability of this region. You can have your opinion since neither one can be proven right or wrong at this time. But keep in mind that while Washington is making a decision, these men have to continue to do their job."

He moved closer to the Marines and personalized the speech. "How difficult it must be to stand watch for twenty-four hours a day in the desert-like heat, ready to take action at a moment's notice, knowing that lives depend on your quick thinking. And, all the while, people are telling you that there is no threat. How can you take your own job seriously if no one else will? I tell you all here tonight that the people of Guantanamo Bay take what you do very seriously and we have total respect, and total admiration, for the risks you take in the name of our safety. So let us all make a toast to our heroes: to the men who are told by Washington that they have no mission, as they stare across the fence-line at the last vestige of the Cold War, at the guard towers and the minefields of Communist Cuba, waiting for someone up North to realize that we are not a game."

When the colonel finished speaking, he shamefully motioned for the Navy guests at the forward tables to head for the buffet first. Mimsey Pickard and her husband were first in line, followed by the next power tier on the island, and so on. It was almost thirty minutes before the enlisted Marines—the men Ranagan had just praised—were allowed to eat. Audrey and I felt badly. Not only were they not allowed to leave their tables to eat or drink until Ranagan gave them the go ahead, but Ranagan had ordered the floor fans be aimed at the head tables instead of on the Marines. The poor guys were in agony. I'd been so proud of the colonel for his speech, where he'd given deserved recognition to the people who gave the Marine Corps Birthday Ball it's very purpose—the enlisted Marines. But in the same breath, he made the evening all about grand impressions and forgot why we were all there. To Ranagan, Gitmo was a one-man performance and the Ball was showtime.

19

When dinner was complete and the cake-cutting ceremony had concluded, nearly every one of the enlisted Marines left the Ball. By 10:00, the dance floor was empty; most people had left for air conditioned spaces. Audrey and I followed the rest of the usual gang to the Hangar Deck, located in the bowels of the Bayview. It was the watering hole of the fighter pilots stationed on Leeward, but when they left in the early nineties, the Marine officers took it over. Without Guy and Gordie in our back seat, we were able to speak our minds about the evening.

"Adam, this ball was the worst one I've ever been to. It was disorganized, impersonal, and, above all, hot. It was like Africa hot."

"I know what you mean. I was quite disappointed myself," I admitted.

"Notice I didn't even mention that we had no place to sit? What were the Ranagans thinking? I mean, come on, Adam, no one wanted to stay at their cocktail hour and everyone left the Ball before 10pm! Don't they ever sit down in their living room and ask themselves what they're doing wrong?"

I shrugged my shoulders. "Obviously not."

"What's wrong with you? Why aren't you talking? You're giving me one word answers. Don't you have anything to say?"

"Yeah," I said, sighing. "I just don't know what good it will do to say it all out loud. Ranagan is the sorriest excuse for a Commanding Officer I've ever met. He doesn't think logically, he lets his wife dictate policy most of the time and he abuses his authority when it comes to the wives."

"Well, let's do something then!"

"Audrey, there's nothing to do. There's nobody here to help us. Look, let's just go to the Hangar Deck and hang out with everyone. We'll make our own fun tonight."

On the right side of the Bayview, a set off steps led to a doorway in the basement of the club. The room was dark and small; about the size of an extra large living room, with a bar for eight and two worn couches. Straight forward was a pool table, and various tall cocktail tables were appointed throughout the room. Several neon Budweiser signs hung from the rafters, and eighties music was blasting from the three speakers placed behind the bar. There was a second entrance to the far back left, which led to Rick's Lounge located right above. The floor, which was often sticky with spilled beer and other assorted beverages, was made of concrete. The air was musty.

Major McCarran and Holly Hump-a-lot were conversing in the back corner. Their conversation was obviously quite stimulating based on the way they were looking at each other, and their body language. Regina was telling jokes with Arlene and Maura on the opposite side of the room, but every so often, Regina's eyes would wander over to her husband and panic would flit across her face. Audrey and I saw this, and decided to spoil McCarran's fun. "Well, Howdy Dan! Hope I'm not interrupting anything over here."

"No, no. Holly—I mean Lt Humphries—and I looked familiar to each other and we were just trying to figure out where we'd met before."

"Did you figure it out?" Audrey said, playing along.

"Yeah, did you figure it out?" I interjected.

"Yes. We went to the same gym out in Camp Pendleton," Holly concluded.

"How nice," Audrey said, sarcasm dripping, but neither one notice. Knowing Audrey could take it from there, I went to the bar and was talking up a storm with Guy until Aidan walked over and leaned down to talk privately with Guy. Because they had been drinking heavily, they spoke far louder than they would have otherwise, and I could hear every word.

"Hey, man," Aidan said, "you got plans to do Holly tonight or what?"

"Plans, no. Fantasies, yes," Guy shot back. "Why?"

"Cause someone's gonna have her tonight and I was just looking out for my friends first."

"Chet doesn't want her?" Guy asked, sounding suspicious.

"Oh he does, but he's making her come to him. Chet told me to spread the word that she was available tonight."

"Why don't you have your way with her?" Guy suggested.

"Man, I would, but I have Kelly now. It wouldn't be right, even though she went back to Leeward tonight because she felt sick. I mean, I could totally get away with it if I wanted to, but Kelly's special. I really care about her and I wouldn't want to hurt her. I'm kinda thinking that she might be the one." Aidan was interrupted by Gordie handing him several cases of beer. "So why don't you go after her, Guy?" He asked as he began to stack the cans. "Look at her over there talking to Major McCarran. She totally wants to be ravaged."

Guy put his glass down and stood up straight. "Okay, man. It would be my pleasure. Well, actually her pleasure. I'll just walk over there and tell her that she makes me as hard as Chinese algebra."

Audrey had gotten bored with Dan and Holly, so she found her way over to Regina; after a few moments of conversation, Audrey and Regina joined me at the bar. All three of us spun our stools around so that we had a front row view of Guy Armstrong making a play for Holly. It took a second or two for Holly to peel her eyes off of McCarran, but eventually she did, and within ten minutes, Holly and Guy left together.

"What a slut," Regina said, her eyes on Holly as she walked out the door. "I can't believe that anyone can be that easy."

"Did it bother you that she was talking to your husband?" Audrey asked. "I know I wouldn't be happy about that."

"Well, it sure as hell didn't make me feel good," Regina said, tossing back a glass of wine. "What did he say to you when you went over there?"

"Not too much. He only said that they had met before."

"They know each other? From where?" Regina was ashen and there was a shudder in her voice.

"They worked out at the same gym in Pendleton. Why? Is everything okay, Regina?" Audrey asked.

Regina didn't have time to answer before McCarran himself sat down beside her. She turned her frown into a smile and pretended to be having a wonderful time. He put his arm around her and told her how beautiful she looked. If we didn't know better, we would have thought they were the perfect couple.

"So, Claiborne, what did you think of our little Ball this evening?" McCarran asked, his tone filled with disdain.

"Well, sir, if I can be frank,"

"Shit, Claiborne, you can be Frances as long as you give me your friggin' take on the evening." While the major was usually quite blunt, drinking made him mean.

"It was the worst ball I've ever been to, sir. Ranagan's idea was nice, but totally not do-able. It was way too hot, they didn't have enough seating or servers, and honestly, I think Ranagan should have let the Marines eat chow first."

"I totally agree. I was sweating like a pig myself. I must've hit the water coolers a hundred times, and those Marines weren't even allowed to piss on themselves," McCarran answered back.

"Hey, who was Chet Dingle's date tonight?" Audrey asked.

"Well, who he went with, is not as important as who he's doing now," McCarran smirked.

"What do you mean?" Regina asked.

"Well, keep this under your hats, but Dingle went with Lt Humphries to the Ball, but decided somewhere along the way she was too easy a mark for him, so he chose someone else to finish the night with. You could say he wanted a challenge."

"Who?" the three of us said in unison.

"Aidan's girlfriend, Kelly." We gasped. "I guess that near the end of the dinner, Kelly started to feel ill because of the heat and too much to drink, so Aidan took her home. With Aidan here with us at the Hangar Deck all night, Chet knew he could make his move."

"But aren't Aidan and Chet best friends?" Audrey asked with great interest. "Why would he do that and how do you know?"

"Yes, they're the best of buds, and Holly was the one who told me. Chet thinks she's as dumb as rocks, but she's not. She's actually pretty damn smart," McCarran retorted.

"Does Aidan know any of this?" Regina asked.

"No. He thinks Chet got paged and had to return to Leeward, which, of course, is where Kelly's room is." McCarran let out a large burp. "You have to admire him. He's quite the player, always thinking of the next move."

"Admire him?" Regina exclaimed. "He repulses me."

"Oh, lighten up, Regina. It's not like Aidan and Kelly are married," McCarran said, not making eye contact with his wife.

"I'm with her Dan," Audrey shot back. "Chet Dingle has no moral compass, no sense of what is ethical or decent and Aidan is his friend. Shoot, with a friend like Chet, not one of us on this base needs an enemy."

Just as Audrey finished speaking, Aidan Foster stood up from behind the bar where he'd been stacking beer. He flew over the counter like a bat out of hell. Aidan heard every word we'd said, and was racing to the White House to catch a Fast Boat over to Leeward. We knew from his face and the enormous amount of alcohol he'd consumed that night, Aidan was capable of killing Chet.

Because we'd all been drinking past a safe limit to drive, I called the duty driver at the White House who drove me and Major McCarran to our own Fast Boat. We briefly thought about calling base security, but we knew Ranagan would never forgive us if we contacted Harbor Patrol and had a Marine Corps officer arrested on the night of the Birthday Ball. An internal handling of this incident was our only option to save face for the colonel and the Corps, however, there was a standing order—given by me—to all Marines to stop and restrain Aidan if spotted.

The Marine who piloted our boat to the other side of the base told us Aidan had left a few minutes earlier and was all alone in his watercraft. We pressured the Marine to go faster and faster across the moonless bay, desperate to intervene before it was too late, but the wind picked up and the surf had begun to swell significantly. With each wave that crashed against our eighteen-foot vessel, and with the wind and nightfall blinding our vision, hopes of an intercession appreciably decreased. The only saving grace was that Aidan's boat was experiencing the same elements, and with any luck, slowing him down as well.

When we docked at the pier, another duty driver met us and delivered bad news: Aidan had inexplicably beaten us there by fifteen minutes, and had already been to the armory to check out his weapon. The Marine armorer had not received my order and had handed Aidan his sidearm without question or concern. Our vehicle transcended all speed records as we raced to the barracks. We took some comfort in knowing every Marine had become aware of the situation, but were sickened when none of the three could be found. Our minds were rushing and our stomachs were churning as each room turned up empty.

Twenty minutes after we'd arrived, we received a call from one of the patrolling Marines; he'd caught a glimpse of Aidan running into the Leeward work spaces. McCarran and I were close. We headed in that direction, but when we took sight of Lt. Foster coming out of Chet's office, we backed off. He had his firearm at his side, and, when he saw us, he moved back inside the doorway.

"Get out of my way!" Aidan cried out with immense desperation. "This has nothing to do with any of you! This is between him and me!" Aidan hit his chest expressively with the side of his gun as he shouted.

"Don't do anything stupid, Lieutenant," McCarran said calmly. "All we want to do is help you resolve this peacefully."

"No, sir! I have to teach that son of a bitch, piece of crap a lesson! He thinks he can fuck with everyone! He only cares about himself! He doesn't care who he hurts!" Sweat was pouring down Aidan's face and his breathing was labored.

"Aidan, it's Captain Claiborne. I think he's an ass too, but this *way*...it's not the answer. What do you say we get everyone together, put the boxing gloves on and do this the old-fashioned way, huh?"

"No, sir!" Aidan roared. "I want to do it my way!"

"Son, your way is going to get you a lifetime of hard labor in Leavenworth. Chet Dingle isn't worth that. Hand me the weapon and let's talk about this over a beer."

As McCarran talked, the doors at the far end of the corridor flew open and Chet Dingle proceeded arrogantly down the hall. He stopped and looked at me with an expression of disgust. "Could someone tell me what the hell is going on in my office?"

Before Chet could get an answer, Aidan lunged out of the

doorway, threw his gun to the floor, and landed on top of Chet. With all the force and fury Aidan could muster; he took his fists, and, with a relentless hammering, gave Chet as much pain as he'd caused Aidan. The major and I pulled the Lieutenant off of Chet, but Aidan's powerful barking continued. His voice trembled, and he went almost hoarse at times from the strain of hollering.

"You son of a bitch! I told you, man! I told you she was off limits! You get every piece of ass on this island you want, but that wasn't good enough for you!"

Chet stayed down on the hallway floor, his head propped up just enough to wipe away the blood that had seeped from his nose.

"Don't you remember? I told you I loved her! I told you I wanted to marry her! I told you to leave her alone! It's all I asked of you! You're a fucking whore, Dingle! All you had to do was leave her alone!"

Aidan tried to break free as Dingle stood up, but we held on. When he'd gotten to his feet, Chet took a few steps backward before speaking with a deadpan tenor, looking Aidan straight in the eyes. "For the record, I'm not the fucking whore. She is."

McCarran ordered Chet to back down and angrily accompanied him down the corridor, and eventually outside. With the gun at a safe distance, I escorted Aidan into the office, and, when the door was closed, he collapsed into the closest chair and sobbed. He knew he'd made a horrible misjudgment and knew there would be painful consequences to pay for his conduct. I sat there trying to mentally write my report to Ranagan. The truth would mean Aidan's career was almost certainly over.

20

Pulling up in the driveway, I could see the light was still on in our bedroom. I stood outside for a short while, watching the duty driver back out onto the street, and then shifting my gaze up to the stars. I leaned my body against the chain-link fencing surrounding our yard, but eventually, I just sat down where I stood. Exhaustion had begun to consume me and I wanted time to think before I went inside to my wife.

When I saw Aidan leap on top of Chet, I felt like the first right thing was happening to the right person since I'd arrived in Gitmo. With every punch the lieutenant threw, someone inside of me applauded. Even though I'd only known Chester Dingle a short while, I felt I'd only seen the tip of the iceberg: he was nothing but trouble. If the major had not initiated the move to pull Aidan off of Chet, I can't be sure I would have bothered. I know that's the wrong answer, but it's the truth. I won't apologize for feeling that way and I don't exactly feel badly either. My inability to think objectively disturbed me, which is why I chose to stay outside and contemplate my outlook. Aidan was wrong for doing what he did, but if presented with the same circumstances, I don't think there's a man in the world that could've pulled me off of

Chet. In a morbid way, I felt badly that I didn't allow Aidan to achieve the satisfaction he needed.

When I finally tired of the isolation I'd created for myself, I stepped inside the house, tripping over the mess left by the party we'd hosted earlier that evening. There were empty beer cans, balloons that had lost their ability to float, and chairs scattered all about. The only light I had to guide me was the one from the bedroom. Once in the doorway, I could see my wife lying asleep atop the covers of the bed, still dressed in her evening gown. She was stretched out on her back, her hands near to her head, and the portable phone still clenched in her hand from when I'd called her earlier in the night Both of her shoes had been tossed haphazardly to the floor.   I soon got in bed beside her; within seconds, I was asleep.

On Saturday morning, I awoke to much awaited news; our name had finally reached the top of the internet list. In the first few weeks we were in Gitmo, I had access to commercial/private e-mail at the White House, but within a month, Ranagan installed a firewall so none of the Marines could use the computers for anything but government business. Normally, I could understand this and even defend the policy, but not in Gitmo. Every phone call we made to the States cost twenty-five cents a minute, and even 1-800 calls cost us fifty cents a pop. To make things a little easier, the base authorized free-of-charge morale calls once a week, but two things were wrong with their plan: the time allowed per call wasn't to exceed fifteen minutes, and, for someone with a family, that's not enough time to re-connect. Secondly—and I was told this by an employee—the phone operators would listen in on the calls whenever they desired. I recognize that listening to someone else's conversation, in and of itself, wouldn't be so horrible—except for the fact that this was Gitmo. Our personal e-mail became our only way of communicating freely with the outside world; the colonel would often have the tech sergeant pull random e-mails from the Marine Corps server. Of course, we even began to distrust the internet when Rhonda told the gang a story—later corroborated by Jackie Razor—that before she'd gotten to Gitmo, copies of e-mails between Rhonda and Jackie, from Jackie's private account, were sitting on Colonel Ranagan's desk. Nobody, not even Jackie, knows how he got them.

I spent the first part of the morning explaining the situation between Aidan and Chet to Audrey. I hadn't wanted to say too much on the phone the night before—for obvious reasons—but I'd needed to let her know everyone was okay. She was just as disturbed as I was by what had occurred, but there was no use dwelling over it. The situation was totally out of our hands; McCarran had set up a meeting with the XO and the CO for early that morning; I figured he'd call to let me know what happened.

I sat in the chair behind the computer desk, where I'd a wonderful view of the banana trees in our yard and of the White House. Audrey dragged her chair beside mine as I pulled up a search engine and typed in the name: Orcher. Within seconds, my search drew nine results, but none of them were OLIVER. Of the nine names, seven were women and two were men. Audrey wondered if one of the two men might be his son, so I got offline and made my calls. The first name got me absolutely nowhere, but I struck gold on the second.

"Hello?" I heard the female voice answer in a very flat Midwestern accent.

"Hi, my name is Adam Claiborne and I'm a Marine stationed in Guantanamo Bay Cuba. I'm looking for a former Marine by the name of Oliver Orcher. Is he related to anyone who lives at this number?"

"Who did you say you were again?"

"Adam Claiborne. I'm a historian for the Barracks here in Guantanamo and I'm writing a book about the history of Gitmo," I lied. "Do you know the person I'm looking for?"

"Why do you want him?"

"I'd like to interview him for my book. I'm actually looking up many of the Marines who used to be stationed here in the fifties. Is he related to you?" I asked politely.

"Yeah, he's my father-in-law, but he doesn't live here. How did you get this number?"

"On the internet. Fortunately for me, there aren't many Orchers in America," I said with a chuckle. The lady was giving me the third degree and didn't seem to like me very much.

"Well, he's retired now and he lives on a house boat in Florida. He doesn't have a phone, so I guess you'll have to write him a letter. You got a pen?"

I wrote the address down and was excited to learn his PO

Box was out of Jacksonville, Florida. If I could get Commander Cleary to put me on the C-12 flight schedule, I had a good chance of talking to him in person. I thanked the lady and hung up the phone. I raced back to the computer to get online again. This time the name I plugged in was Elliot Gaultier and I came up with nothing. After a diligent attempt, I ended my hunt with thirty-three Gaultiers nationwide. While I realized I wasn't dealing with something as enormous as Miller or Smith, thirty-three names were a lot to sort through.

"Adam, remember the night you were on duty and you read me those Spanish articles about the kidnapping?" Audrey said in deep thought.

"Yeah."

"That wasn't the first time I'd heard that story. I think because I was translating, and not actually reading myself, it didn't register; but Conway included something about that incident in those papers he left for you to read. I actually read it out loud to you, along with the story about the crazy Hatchet Man."

"Okay, so what's your point?" I asked, disappointed I hadn't found what I'd wanted to find.

"Maybe there are other articles on the internet where a family member is quoted. Newspapers call relatives when something tragic happens to help build their stories. If one of Gaultier's relatives had been quoted, we might have another name to look up."

"That's an awesome idea, Audrey!" I turned back to the computer and hurriedly typed in: Marines Kidnapped Cuba. Nothing happened. "Son of—," I exclaimed, as I pushed my rolling chair away from the desk and threw a pen on the floor.

"What? What's the matter?"

"I got knocked offline! I can' believe it! I can't friggin' believe it! I pay for this!"

"Now, Adam, just reconnect and calm down."

"Calm down? It's the principle Audrey! Nothing works right in this place! Nothing is easy here! I should be able to point and click and be online—it's not too much to ask! I should be able to have opinions; you should be able to voice concerns; we should be able to go more than a week without mowing our lawn without Ranagan ordering me home on my lunch break to clip it per his particular specifications!"

I got back online, but within moments, was disconnected again by the ringing of our phone—yet another Gitmo charm. It was Ryan Hill telling me the colonel wanted the word passed down that he was completely dissatisfied with the condition of our yards. This particularly bothered me because I knew Colonel Ranagan had absolutely no authority to judge the condition of our properties, and more importantly, to make us maintain them. The housing director periodically drove around to each of the housing areas and said she'd never had a problem with anything she saw in our neighborhood. Clearly, the yard thing was just one more way in which the Ranagans tried to control us.

You may be wondering why we didn't just mow our yards once a week to make the colonel happy. It's like this: Guantanamo is built upon one gigantic piece of coral, and the dirt that holds the grass is intermixed with a highly concentrated coral dust. That dust got sucked into the engines of our mowers each time we mowed. Any mower, high priced or otherwise, didn't stand a chance against such a beating. Two months was the most any of us seemed to be able to go without our mowers breaking down, and it's not like there was a small engine repair shop around the corner. What we ended up having to do was to share mowers, or mow each other's lawns to avoid face time with the colonel.

WHILE AUDREY AND I were waiting to borrow Ryan's mower, Major McCarran and Lt Colonel Ray pulled up in front of our house. They were both dressed in their camouflage utilities.

"It's about damn time you did something about this farmland!" Lt Colonel Ray shouted with a smile on his face, as he remained in the vehicle. "I don't think you need to mow it, I think you need to harvest!"

I walked over while Audrey raked fallen branches. "Good morning, sir. Good morning, Major. Just felt like starting my morning with a little yard work. There's nothing like slaving in the ninety-degree heat to make your lawn look a little less dead." I wiped the sweat off my face with the bottom of my T-shirt. "What brings you by on this fine day?" I wanted them to tell me what happened to Aidan without me asking.

"Funny you should ask," the Lt Colonel said. "We showed up at 0700 like he asked, and waited an hour before he arrived. When he got there, we briefed him on the whole Dingle/Foster matter and then he didn't say a word for, what Dan? Wasn't it like five or six minutes?"

"Yes, sir." McCarran answered. "Something like that."

"Then, when he did speak," Lt Colonel Ray went on with a funny look on his face, "all he said—and stop me if I'm wrong Major—all he said was 'So someone else thought they needed to have their own cocktail party. I sure as hell don't remember authorizing any party!' Can you believe the balls on that guy?"

"Sir, you've got to be kidding!" I said. "He didn't really say he hadn't authorized a private party, did he? He's pissed I had a party?""

"No shit. He really said it," Ray said, laughing.

"And then what?"

"And then he told me how much he likes you, but he absolutely detests Audrey. I think his exact words were 'She's a fucking bitch'. Isn't that right, Major?"

"Yes, sir. But don't worry, Adam. He said the same about a couple of the other wives too."

"Well," I said, trying not to fly off the handle, "what did he do about Aidan and Chet?"

"That's a funny story too. All he said was, 'Women have a way of making men forget who they are' and 'snatch is snatch wherever you go'. He told me to refer Aidan to counseling with Father Blankenship and then he went diving."

"And Chet?" I asked. "What happened to him?"

"Chet? Hmm, well, I'm sure he and the colonel are enjoying their dive together."

"Are you telling me Chet is diving with the colonel right now, after what happened last night?"

"By Jove, I think he's got it!" McCarran quipped.

"Well, Captain, I must return to my lovely Drew. Have fun with your lawn care!"

Audrey was standing there, leaning her weight on her rake, very curious to hear what I had to tell her. When she heard the words come from my mouth, she took the rake and heaved it across the lawn like an Olympic javelin thrower, and marched around the lawn espousing the repeal of public hangings.

"Go to hell Maura! You're totally wrong!" Audrey and I heard Rhonda shout from several houses away.

"Oh yeah? Well, I don't think so! You broke it and you know you did!" Maura retorted as she slammed the door to her house.

"Just so you know, I'm not buying you another one!" Rhonda screamed back as she, too, went into her house.

Audrey looked at me and we both shook our heads. "Be right back," Audrey said, jogging to that end of the street.

My curiosity made me follow her, but I was careful to stay out of sight. I watched her knock on both ladies' doors and motion them to a middle ground.

"What's going on here you, guys? You're friends and friends don't talk to each other this way," Audrey began.

"I loaned Rhonda my ceramic pasta bowl from Mexico and when I got it back, there was a crack in it that wasn't there before!"

"That's bull, Maura Gellar! I did borrow it, that's true, but I took excellent care of it while I had it. I've no idea where that stupid crack came from, but there's no way on the world I did that!"

"Let me see the bowl," Audrey said. After a close inspection, she was able to find a hairline crack that was almost unnoticeable. She handed the bowl back to Maura and told them both to go sit on the picnic table, under the shelter. Audrey proceeded to go to the homes of Arlene, Jackie, Regina and Drew and instructed them to do the same thing.

"Ladies, I want you to listen very closely to what I have to say," Audrey said firmly. "Our time here in Gitmo's been short, but the stress and strain we've endured day after day has sometimes been more than we think we can handle; that's the good news. There's no doubt in my mind things will only get worse for us before they get better when it comes to the Ranagans. She wants to control us and we refuse to give her that power. Until one side gives up, this tense situation will remain a constant struggle for us all. There will certainly be more casualties, namely our husbands. The bottom line is we're all we have here, and when we've lost the ability to draw off of each other's strength, we're finished. From this day on, there will be no fighting, no arguing, no talking about each other behind each others' backs, no fussing, no name-calling, no finger pointing—nada! We'll support each other, stand by one another and be a family in every sense of the word."

Her words were magic. From that moment on, those women became a close, cohesive group. They cared for one another's kids, helped with chores, made a fuss over birthdays, listened to each other's personal problems, kept secrets, and made a point of gathering together in the playground area of the neighborhood each afternoon for support and conversation. There was no further gossip, no backstabbing and they even used their own individual talents to educate each other. Every lady became better, stronger and more able to handle the pressures of life under the tyrannical Ranagans.

While Audrey remained in the park to talk with her friends, I finished mowing the lawn and decided to cool myself off with a warm Gitmo shower. As I stepped back out of the shower stall— totally unrefreshed—something struck me. Abuelita told us that the Marine officer whom she'd worked for died in a minefield explosion. With the towel still wrapped around me, I began to search for the small notebook I'd used when I interviewed her. I checked my uniform pockets and my dresser before I remembered I'd put it in Audrey's desk, top drawer, left.

I grabbed hold of the handle to open it, but found the drawer was stuck. I wasn't sure if it was Audrey's paint job or the humidity in the house, but it was immovable. I decided to put my foot up on the edge of the desk for leverage and tug again. Within seconds, I was sitting on the floor with the drawer in my lap. I thought I heard my tailbone crack upon contact with the tile floor, but it ended up being a loose CD case that broke my fall.

When I fell, I managed to scatter most everything that had been in the drawer, so I busily crawled around the floor finding what I'd dropped. The notebook had made it all the way to the couch and the paperclips found their way to the back door. As I assembled all the items and put them back inside the drawer, I noticed the back wood panel was busted up pretty good. With the force of my pull, I cracked the section that held the two sides together. I took the drawer to the kitchen where I kept my tools and wood glue. After surveying the situation for a few moments, I knew I'd have to take the whole drawer a part and reconstruct it completely. Although I didn't have enough time to fix it that day, I disassembled it so I could take accurate measurements of each piece. When the back panel was completely off, I saw that a very small piece of white paper had gotten wedged in the crevice of the drawer and panel. Once I picked it up, I realized it wasn't a piece of paper at all, but a thumbnail-sized photograph of a child. I was unable to determine if the black and white photo, with very tattered edges, was of a little girl or boy; it was a whole face shot of a Caucasian child, and the hair was dark and short. I assumed the kid was around three or four, but nothing was written on the back to indicate gender or age. When the novelty of finding the picture faded, I placed it under the cookie jar for safe-keeping and finished taking the drawer apart. I almost immediately forgot all about it.

21

Thanksgiving Day turned out to be a much better day than I'd thought it could be. The Ranagans invited the single officers to their home and Lieutenant Colonel Ray and his wife invited all the married officers and their families to their home. The Rays were very gracious and warm hosts, making everyone feel at home even though we were thousands of miles away from our relatives back in the States. There was a large formal table set for the adults, and a smaller, yet equally festive-looking table for the children. Drew managed to seat the Romeros, the McCarrans, the Razors, the Hills, the Gellars, us and themselves together. Drew also did all the cooking herself and made a point to accommodate everyone's likes and family traditions. Although he was my executive officer, on this day, Lt. Colonel Ray was like a father and a friend to me, and to the rest of the Marines who joined him for the holiday. Both he and Drew had enormous smiles on their faces and seemed pleased to have us all in their home.

For most of the afternoon, the conversation focused on football, diving, diets, and child-rearing, however, before the day was complete, the Ranagans became a popular topic of conversation. With the children playing safely outdoors, the XO and Drew spoke openly about their feelings. It was odd a man of his rank would speak so freely about his extreme dislike of the commanding officer, but it also seemed strangely appropriate. We were all experiencing the same myriad of emotions, and, clearly, we needed to express them.

"You want to hear something amusing?" Lt Colonel Ray began. "The other day I was in a meeting with Colonel Ranagan and Captain Pickard, and Ranagan's private line kept ringing. I don't mean once or twice, I mean every thirty seconds it would ring. Finally, an hour later, the meeting was over and Captain Pickard left Ranagan's office. Just as the door closed behind Pickard, the phone rang again and the colonel picked up the receiver. Well, before Ranagan could even speak, I heard, from the other side of the room, Lois screaming at the colonel. She was telling him he had no right to ignore her call and who does he think he is not to take her call. I actually felt sorry for the guy. He finally was able to ask her if something was wrong, but as it turned out, there wasn't anything the matter at all. She told him point blank that when she calls, he answers!"

"Not surprising," Major McCarran quipped.

"Well, get a load of this," Drew jumped in. "You know when she told us about how all the navy people on base hate us and how they're out to get us? Remember how she told us not to be friendly with them? I found out she's been going over to Deer Point and kissing up to all the wives of the naval officers. She's been telling them about how badly we treat her and how we're all a bunch of vindictive and mean-spirited ladies."

"But that's so not true," Regina said. "If anything, she's the mean one. All we've tried to do in the Wives Association is have fun with the other Marine wives on base, and maybe create some fun for all those young guys who stand guard. Perhaps she doesn't agree with us, but that doesn't make us vindictive."

"But wait, there's more," Drew added. "You know how the base is going to knock down our condemned garages? Well, I found out Lois told the housing director that she wants all the orange tiles off the roofs."

"But why?" Audrey asked.

"I can answer that," Henry Ray said. "She says it's because they were hand-made by Cuban workers back in the forties. It seems they would put the clay on their laps and mold the shape of the tile by using their thighs. Lois thinks they should be preserved as historical pieces."

"And she's just the lady to do it, I bet," Audrey interjected.

"Yeah, but wait until you hear the real reason," Drew interrupted. "Go one, dear. Finish the story."

"I went fishing with the husband of one of her gardening pals, and you won't believe this. Lois and the colonel have bought a house in Florida and it needs a new roof. Instead of paying for a new roof, they're going to take all of our garage tiles and use those."

"Cheap bastards," Ryan Hill exclaimed.

"Hey, do you think those tiles are worth any money? I can't believe hand-made Cuban tiles aren't worth something. Do we know if any of them were signed?" Rhonda asked.

"Signed?" Arlene questioned.

"Yeah, signed. Out west, when an Indian sculptor's finished a piece, they always sign it, even if the pottery's for his or her own use. If any of them are signed, especially if any of the workers did anything famous, they might be worth something."

"We could find out," Jackie said. "The workers took down a couple from my garage roof when they went up there the other day—I guess so they could see what they were dealing with."

"Be right back," Tony said, heading to his house. Ryan joined him.

"What makes you suspicious?" Audrey asked Rhonda.

"Come on, guys, if Lois really wanted those tiles because she needs a new roof, I hardly think she'd actually tell anyone that. There must be another reason."

"I don't know, Rhonda," Drew said. "She's pretty cheap. She told me—back when we were still speaking—that she grew up dirt poor. She even had an out house until she was a teenager. Look at how tightly she's held onto the association's money. No, I believe she's beyond frugal and just plan stingy!"

The door to the Ray's house flung open and in walked Ryan and Tony. Each had an orange roof tile in their hand. "Rhonda's right. Some of these are signed," Ryan said, a bit out of breath.

"I knew it! She knew these were worth something and she wanted to keep it all to herself!" Rhonda exclaimed.

"Well, guess what? I have news for her!" Drew began. "I'm

going down to base housing to ask if we can each keep our own tiles off our own roofs."

"You know what the funny part is?" Henry Ray asked. "Since her house was refurbished a year or two ago, her house doesn't have any tiles, just regular roofing shingles. If Drew finds out we can all keep them, Lois won't get any."

As the table kept discussing the Ranagans, I pulled Ryan Hill off to the side. "Hey, Ryan, do you know how I can get a list of the people who died in all the minefield accidents over the years?"

Ryan looked puzzled. "Yeah, I have a list in my office. I can get you a copy. Why?"

"Just curious," I said untruthfully. I wanted to verify Abuelita's story about her boss dying in a minefield explosion. After I retrieved my notebook from the drawer, I looked up his name in the *Book of the Dead*, but his name wasn't there and I wanted to know why.

❧ ❧ ❧

We thanked the Rays after we had our dessert and strolled back to our end of the street with overly stuffed stomachs.

"Hello Claiborne's!" Gordie came up next to us.

"Howdy, Gordie! Happy Thanksgiving," Audrey said back.

"So how was your dinner at the Ranagan's?" I asked.

Gordie rolled his eyes and motioned that he'd meet us at our house in a minute. We were a little curious about his secretiveness, but didn't think too much about it. Audrey and I waited for him in our driveway, but he walked right past us, rounded the corner and met us in our backyard.

"So what's with the Mission Impossible act?" I asked Gordie.

"Mrs. Ranagan told all of us single guys we're not allowed to hang out with any of the married Marines anymore. Technically, I'm not supposed to be here."

"What? She can't tell you that!" I said, angrily. "We work together. We're friends. Why would she say that?"

"Look man, I didn't ask why, I'm just telling you what she said. Speaking of which, Audrey, did you tell Father Blankenship he was forbidden to come to Marine housing?" Gordie asked, almost embarrassed.

"Absolutely not! Why would you ask me that?"

"Man, I hate chasing down rumors. Ok, it's like this: Chet and the Ranagans told all of the single officers today that you told Blankenship he's not welcome in Marine housing anymore. I just wanted to know if it was true."

"Of course not! I'd never say that! Why would they think I said that?" Audrey was clearly upset.

"I don't know. I'm just telling you what was said. It's obvious Mrs. Ranagan and the colonel don't like you. Your name was brought up all during dinner. Come to think of it, so was Rhonda's. Chet was telling them a bunch of stuff about you guys. None of it was very favorable."

"Well, it's all bull since I've never even had a conversation with Chet. What could he know about me?" Audrey demanded.

"A lot, as far as he's concerned," Gordie replied. "I hate to say this, but sometimes the truth doesn't matter so much in Gitmo. People believe what they want to believe."

It was creepy to hear Gordie say that. I'd heard those very same words from Conway before he left. I thought back to what he'd told me that day, and all of it was coming true. I blew his advice off thinking I knew more than he did, but the fact of the matter was, I had no idea what I'd gotten myself into.

"So, where are you off to now?" Audrey said, calming down.

"Me, Chet, Guy and Aidan are going fishing. We heard a bull shark was hanging around Phillips Park dive ladder."

"Did you say Chet and Aidan? Don't they hate each other after the whole Kelly thing?" Audrey asked.

"No man, they're still friends. Closer than ever if you ask me. Well, I've got to get out of here and get my gear together. You guys have a great rest of the day."

Audrey and I were speechless, but not entirely shocked. It seemed par for the course, after all, it was Gitmo. The only way I know to explain it is this: Each day you wake up on a beautiful and isolated island that relatively few Americans have ever seen. You feel fortunate to be able to explore its wonders and become a part of its history; however, you also feel alone and disconnected from the real world at times. The remoteness makes you experience mixed emotions, so even when you're sad, you're also elated. Mole hills become mountains, and mountains become mole-hills. Your perception becomes skewed and you aren't really sure how you feel about anything on most days. There are moments when you want to extend your tour another year, and then there are days when you're actively seeking the next plane out. As we learned at the Ferry Landing when Conway left, the people are what make Gitmo special. For whatever reason, Aidan and Chet felt they still needed each other's friendship despite, the conflict, and managed to work things out. Many times, citizens of Guantanamo Bay befriend individuals they would never normally befriend in the real world. It makes for an extremely interesting tour, but it also causes a lot of trouble.

❧ ❧ ❧

Ryan Hill dropped by the house at around 9pm that night and gave me the documentation I'd asked him for while at the Ray's. The name of Abuelita's former employer, Captain Haggar, was on the list of Americans who had been killed in a minefield-related incident. With the minefield maintenance company's official chronicle in hand, I went back to the *Book of the Dead* to try and locate Haggar's name by comparing dates, but again, I couldn't find it. I also couldn't find any name of any service member who had died in the Guantanamo minefields at all. Considering the fact that twelve people had been killed in years past, I expected to have seen at least one or two entries and I couldn't imagine why the names had been omitted.

I did locate several minefield related deaths listed as "Unknown Cuban". Two of them occurred on Christmas Eve in 1958 and it made me wonder: Did Abuelita's husband and his friend try to defect from communist Cuba, and die in the attempt? I passed on my theory to Audrey.

"But it doesn't make any sense, Adam. Miguel and Chico could already come and go as they pleased on base. Why would they run across a minefield?"

"I get what you're trying to say Audrey, but look at this. This entry clearly states that two unknown Cubans were killed on the exact date Miguel and Chico went missing. What's the chance that's just a fluke?"

"Castro was about to take over. I bet a lot of Cubans tried to flee."

"But there aren't a lot of entries for Cubans who were blown up in the minefields! There are only two. Come on, Audrey! You have to admit it's at least an interesting theory, right?"

"Fine. Let's assume you're correct in your thinking. That still doesn't explain why Haggar's name isn't listed. What's your theory on that?" Audrey asked, folding her arms.

"Well, this would only be a guess, but Ryan told me the minefields have always been a serious point of controversy since day one. For years, human rights organizations have been on a campaign to rid the globe of every last mine, no matter how significant the mines were to those who used them. Even Princess Diana jumped on the band wagon. The press followed her all over the place as she launched her crusade against the utilization of mines. So, knowing the minefields played an essential role in Guantanamo Bay's first line of defense against a Cuban onslaught, I could see how former base commanders wouldn't want to advertise any minefield-related deaths. If they did, they might have drawn attention to the base and been forced—through political means— to extract every last one."

"Isn't that what happened, though? I mean, isn't that what Ryan and his company are doing now? Getting rid of all the mines?" Audrey asked.

"Exactly my point! The President signed an order to remove all minefields in Cuba, North Korea, anywhere we have them, in response to this growing global movement. I guess some intelligent person, way back when, knew this was inevitable, and the former base COs concealed the casualties to circumvent their removal."

"All right, I'll accept that. But what I want to know is this: Let's assume Miguel and Chico died in the minefield. Don't you think it's odd that Abuelita's boss, Captain Haggar did too?"

"Not if he was a minefield maintenance officer. Stuff like that just happened sometimes. It was unfortunate, but it did happen."

"But do you know for sure he was a minefield officer?"

"Well, actually, no I don't. I just assumed."

"So then, find out for sure, and then we can put my over-active imagination away for the night," Audrey pronounced.

"Ok, I will." I walked over to a stack of company year books and thumbed through the 1959 edition. I located Haggar's stats in a matter of minutes and discovered his MOS, or method of service, had been logistics, not minefield maintenance. "Hey, Audrey, you may be on to something," I said, focused on Captain

Haggar's photo. "We need to find more information on Haggar's death. Something's not right. I can't think of one scenario where a logistics officer would be out in the minefields."

"Maybe he wandered out there or got lost on maneuvers."

"No. I don't buy that at all. Something drew him out there."

"Do you think it had something to do with the information he found for Abuelita? Remember? She said he called her and told her he'd established a lead on Miguel's death, but he needed to check something out first. Do you think he was murdered and his death wasn't an accident?"

"Come on, Audrey, you sound paranoid now," I said, dismissing her idea.

"I'm not paranoid! I'm being pragmatic! Think about what we found out in some of those readings Conway left for us. Remember the one Marine who found out a former CO was stashing weapons? When he reported it to the Naval Criminal Investigate Service, they told him he and his family had fifteen minutes to leave their home and get off the island! Remember? The CO had arranged for him to have an accident. Maybe something like that happened with Haggar."

I took a deep breath and let it out slowly. Audrey and I were getting in way over our heads and beginning to believe in our own suppositions. "I respect your opinion, honey, but don't you think we're going a little overboard here? Doesn't it seem a little strange to you that we're the ones who keep coming across unexplained deaths and disappearances wherever we look? Remember, when everyone else around you is the problem, sometimes you have to look in the mirror," I said rather condescendingly.

She walked to me, leaning down to whisper in my ear and placing her hands on my shoulders. "Well, actually, Adam, for that statement to be relevant to what we're talking about, you'd have to say 'If everyone else is dying and disappearing around us, how long before we're next?'"

"Very funny," I shot back. "It's obvious we're going to have to come up with some kind of strategy for making sense of all of this. We also need to get organized. I'm sure if we look long enough, we can come up with a logical explanation for everything we've come across. Don't you agree?"

"Yes, but what if we don't? What if we can't find anything to help us understand all these events? Then what will we do?" Audrey sat down at the table alongside of me.

"Don't worry about that. I think if we spend some time and really put our heads together, we can come up with something. What do you say we devote our Christmas vacation to finding some answers? I have two weeks off and you have a week. How does that sound?"

"Count me in," Audrey said, giving me the thumbs up. "Now, what do you say to going to bed early and waking up for a sunrise dive?"

"You don't have to ask me twice."

As I lay in bed, about to drift off, I kept wondering what Captain Haggar had been doing in the minefields. I racked my brain trying to figure it out, and then I turned over in bed and shook Audrey. "Wake up. I think I have an idea of why Haggar and Miguel were in the minefields!"

"Why?"

"What if Miguel and Chico were involved in something illegal, maybe having to do with the minefields, and Haggar went out there to check it out? That would explain everything."

"Well, it wouldn't really explain everything, but it's sure a start. Good work," Audrey said as she rolled back over.

At that point, I couldn't sleep. I played out every scenario I could until my body gave in to fatigue. At the very least, I knew Miguel's disappearance and Haggar's death were related. I was sure of it. Proving it, however, would be another thing, but I was bent and determined to try.

22

Audrey reached over to shut the alarm clock off at 5am, and we hurried to get our equipment ready for our first dive without an instructor. After a few minutes of discussion, we decided to make our dive at Kittery Beach, which had been named for the supply ship that had brought provisions to the base residents back in the early part of the 1900s. When we'd finished gathering all our gear, we hopped in the Gremlin and drove towards the southeast boundary of the naval station.

Kittery Beach was the most distinctive of all the beaches for one important reason; it was a true microcosm of the last vestige of the cold war. Three-quarters of the beach belonged to the Americans, but the eastern fourth was Cuban territory. A simple eight-foot, chain-link fence was all that separated the two opposing nations. A Marine observation post stood directly across from a Cuban guard tower. For twenty-four hours a day, Marine guards were eyeball to eyeball with Cuban soldiers. Minefield warning signs littered the area, as did remnants of rusting barbwire fencing from years long past. Oddly, Kittery was dubbed a family beach, due to its kid-friendly tidal pool, but, at first sight, I'd never have believed it to be the best setting for children and their parents.

Occasionally, a child would run into the water and attempt to swim to the other side of the fencing, since the fence stopped at the water line, but a parent would always intervene before any infringements occurred. Once when I was scuba diving there, my head bumped into something on the sandy bottom, about twenty feet under. When I looked up, I saw a black sign with a white skull and cross bones painted on it. The sign read: DANGER! YOU ARE ABOUT TO CROSS INTO COMMUNIST CUBA. Needless to say, I swam back quickly, visions of Cuban gun boats swarming above my head.

One of the most unique and magnificent things about Guantanamo Bay was its diving. While there were some who chose to dive off a boat farther out to sea, it was completely unnecessary. Breathtaking underwater views were only yards away from the shoreline. At Kittery, we would wade through the tidal pool for about fifty feet before we submerged into a world unlike anything I'd ever known. There was a sturdy rope that ran along the sea floor to help divers navigate the narrow gaps in the rocks at the mouth of the lagoon, through which the waves would rhythmically break. Exiting that zone, you were free to explore to your heart's content.

The water was crystal clear and the most wonderful ocean creatures would come alongside us without apprehension. Large sea turtles paddled effortlessly, and exquisitely-colored parrot fish glided through the deep as if they were there to observe us. Fields of foot-long conch shells lie untouched and the barracuda shadowed us, always keeping a watchful eye. There were times when we would follow a school of tropical fish, or just float weightless in their center while they carried on as if we weren't even there. For a few hours a week, it was like becoming the scuba man inside God's personal fish tank. My only responsibility was to appreciate and admire the marvels of that undersea world.

As Audrey and I were nearing the end of our hour-long dive, Audrey took hold of my arm and stopped me as I began to swim towards the shoreline. She reached down and grabbed her writing board, scribbling: "GLOWING...MY LEFT....10 YARDS." I scanned quickly then wrote on my own board: "CAN'T SEE. YOU LEAD?" She nodded, and after we both checked the air level in our tanks, she tapped the regulator in her mouth and gave me the "OK" sign to let me know she had enough air. I replied with the same and she led off in the direction she'd pointed.

The sun was beginning to rise and the sea floor was visible, yet we had no idea what was producing the light. Initially, I didn't even see what Audrey had described, but then I managed to pick out a glowing object ahead. She picked up her writing board again: "WHAT IS IT?" Shaking my head I indicated I wasn't sure. We both skimmed the floor of the ocean as we approached the glowing object.

I snatched my wife's hand and immediately drew her closer. With my free hand, I made a symbol on top of my head that resembled a shark fin. She began to breathe deeply and too quickly, which she couldn't afford to do with such little air remaining. While we were fairly close to shore, we didn't want to attract the five-foot, black tip shark swimming by. We huddled together to look bigger than we were, and continued to sit close to the bottom, since sharks like to attack from underneath. As I continued to watch Audrey panic, I became nervous myself; her air level fell deeper into the red zone of the tank's gauge. We'd have to do something soon. Then, as quickly as it had come upon us, the shark's attention was diverted elsewhere and we were able to make it back to the rope. Hand over hand, Audrey feverishly made her way through the rocks and surf to the lagoon, and, from there, to the security of the beach. As she came out of the water, her fins flew in one direction and her snorkel in another. I watched her struggle with her BCU; her hands were still trembling.

"Audrey!" I called loudly from the entrance to the lagoon. "Wait a minute and I'll help you!" I hurried up the beach, looking like a wobbling sea lion with the weight of my gear upon me, and aided her with her tank. She walked to the showerhead to rinse the salt water off her body. "Are you okay?" I asked calmly. "I know you were pretty scared out there, huh?"

She nodded her head. "Yeah, I'm okay. But our diving instructor owes me the title to his piece of crap VW van!" She said, growing stronger. "That jerk told me I'd never see a shark and I see one on our very first instructorless dive!"

"Well, I was pretty proud of you," I said excitedly. "Actually impressed is more like it."

"Really?" Audrey was doubtful.

"Really. I don't think I've ever met anybody who can suck down air as quickly as you did! Now, I've heard of women who can suck the chrome off the side of a—"

"Chrome! Adam, was that *chrome* we saw in the water?" Audrey asked, her attention obviously refocused. It was clear she hadn't been listening to a word I'd said.

"Chrome? No, I don't think it was chrome. Hell, Audrey, I've no idea what we were looking at. All I know is it was shiny, or glowing. That's all I can say about it. Do you want to get new tanks and go down for another look?"

Audrey ignored my question and continued to shower; the shark had quelled her enthusiasm for another dive, so I dropped the subject.

We had only been home long enough for Audrey to eat her breakfast when she received a call from Drew Ray. Something important had come up and the regular gang was headed down to Drew's to talk about it. Audrey had no idea what the problem was, but she slipped into some shorts and headed down the street. Drew asked the ladies to not to be obvious about the gathering since Lois lived near the Rays.

"Well, we're all here," Arlene said as the last woman took her seat. "What's this all about?"

Drew and Regina were standing, while the rest of the women were sitting. "Regina has brought something to my attention recently and I think you all need to know." Regina and Drew had grave looks on their faces. The ladies knew whatever Regina had to say wouldn't be very pleasant.

"As you all know, the Marine Wives Association makes the vast majority of its money by selling Northeast Gate flags. The Marine guards will hoist a flag up over the border between the American sector and Communist Cuba, and the Wives' Association gives that flag to the buyer for fifty dollars, accompanied by a certificate of authenticity signed by Colonel Ranagan. Each certificate has the date the flag was flown and the name of the person the flag is dedicated to."

"Yeah, we know all that. What's your point?" Maura asked, trying to hurry Regina along.

"We sell so many of these flags that our bank account is overflowing. Most everyone on this base thinks of the Northeast Gate flag as a real Gitmo treasure, an irreplaceable souvenir."

"Go on," Maura again urged Regina.

"Ladies, it has come to my attention that the flags, well, that the flags—"

"Go ahead," Drew encouraged Regina.

"There's only one way to say this: The flags are never actually flown. The boxes are sent out to a MOP, refolded by some privates and then Colonel Ranagan picks some random date and signs them as having been flown."

"Are you *sure* about this? How do you know?" Rhonda said angrily.

"My husband was out checking on his men when he found a stack of them. The thing is, he found them at a MOP with no flagpole, not the one at the Northeast Gate. He inquired and the men told him Ranagan ordered the Marines to just refold them and keep their mouths shut."

"But why? This makes no sense!" Audrey exclaimed.

"For one, the flags we sell to the base residents don't fit on the pole at the Northeast Gate. The hooks on the rope are set up for a much larger flag."

"Are you sure Colonel Ranagan knows this?" Rhonda asked.

"Yes, I'm afraid he does," Drew said, sounding defeated. "My husband put the question to him and he was told to keep his blankety-blank mouth shut."

"So what you're saying," Audrey asked, "is that we have a bank account filled with money we acquired through fraud? Are you telling me we've been lying to everyone?"

"I'm afraid so," Drew said sadly.

"That loathsome old goat!" Maura said under her breath. "How long has this been going on?"

"We're not really sure. At least since the beginning of the summer," Regina said.

"We have over $5000.00 in our account! Isn't fraud basically stealing? And if so, isn't this grand larceny or something like that?" Arlene said.

"It's obvious that we have a serious problem here. What do you want to do about it?" Drew asked.

"Well, for one, none of us will sell the flags anymore!" Audrey said. "I'm not having my name associated with such dishonesty."

"I agree," Drew said. "But I think there's more to it than that, but I don't want to go into it. Ladies, I'm in such a precarious position. There's so much I know about the Ranagans and about the horrible things they do and say about all of us, but I don't think it's really my place to tell you all. Besides, by husband would kill me. The bottom line is, things aren't right and we have to make them right. I suggest we all put our thinking caps on and try to come up with a solution."

WHEN AUDREY TOLD ME, I was pretty shocked. I couldn't understand how the colonel could shame us all. But it wasn't until Lt Colonel Ray and Drew came down later that night to talk to us, when I fully understood the convoluted political situation in the Barracks.

"Hello, Adam," Lt Colonel Ray said, "I'm sorry we're bothering you, but I want to talk to you about something if you've got a few moments."

"Sure, come on in, sir" I replied. Seeing Lt Colonel Ray in my home after work hours seemed odd and felt strange. I really liked the man, but his visit seemed out of place.

"As you know," Ray started, "the situation between the ladies and Colonel Ranagan has gotten out of control. Something has got to be done about him and his wife."

"I agree, sir, but what?" I said, shrugging.

"Someone needs to write to the general," Ray stated plainly.

"What do you mean, sir?" I asked.

"Someone needs to write a letter to General Crane. Here," he handed me sheets from a notebook, "I've written my own letter, but then I thought this shouldn't come from me. It should come from the wives. I think Audrey should write a letter to the general as soon as possible. Use my words if you want, but whatever you do, we need to move quickly."

"Why, sir, what's the rush? If we do nothing, he's still due to move by the summertime." I said, trying to avoid the whole matter. "He's leaving in only five months."

"Adam, I can't tell you everything I know, but Colonel Ranagan is a hateful man. He's already dismissed me completely. I do nothing all day. He won't assign me tasks, he won't ask or heed my advice, and he won't let me handle the Marines. I feel useless."

"Why does he treat you like that?" Audrey asked.

"Because Lois hates my wife and because I get along with everyone else's wife. Lois is extremely jealous that Drew has managed to get the respect of the ladies. As we speak, the colonel's trying to have Drew removed from the island. I don't want to go into it, but it's true, and Pickard isn't trying to stop him."

"Sir, I'd like to help," I said.

"Me too." Audrey jumped in. "I'd be happy to write that letter for you."

"Wait a minute," I said to Audrey, and then turned my attention back to the Rays. "We will gladly support the two of you, sir, but we need to know the whole story before we do."

"I'll tell you," Drew said, looking at her husband affectionately. "We went to see Chaplain Dooley about our conflict with the Ranagans last week. She was just as lovely as you said she'd be, but then she asked a lot of personal questions and I admitted to her I'd once suffered from bulimia. Within the week, Ranagan called my husband into his office and held my medical record in his hand. He said it had come to his attention that I'd not been entirely truthful on my medical screening form—the one which allowed me to come to Gitmo. He asked about my eating disorder and said, with my medical history, I shouldn't have been allowed on the island and he's started the paperwork to have me removed."

"Can he do that?" I asked.

"He's doing it as we speak. We've gone to the hospital CO, but he won't listen to us. Pickard won't take our calls, and the family service center says they can't intervene. Nobody wants to help us," Drew said.

"Are you saying Pastor Dooley leaked that information to Ranagan?" Audrey asked.

"She's the only one who knew," Drew said despondently.

"But why would the fact that you're a recovering bulimic have anything to do with being able to live in Gitmo?" Audrey asked.

"It all comes down to medical staffing," Lt Colonel Ray began. "Any individual who may require extra medical attention, or the services of a specialist, are prohibited from coming here. Gitmo isn't really capable of handling situations outside of normal everyday care. Over the years, just like the base, the hospital has downsized by closing whole departments. They feel bulimics need constant psychiatric attention, and right now, the base psychiatrist is completely overwhelmed with his patient load."

"But the thing is, I was bulimic over ten years ago. I haven't had any problems or relapses since then. That's the reason I didn't mark it down on my Gitmo form. It's not a part of my life now."

"Why do you think Dooley would tell Ranagan though?" Audrey asked.

"I don't think she told Ranagan," Lt Colonel Ray said. "I think she told Father Blankenship, and he told Lois. But I hope this will allow you to see things from our perspective. They've told me I can stay in Gitmo unaccompanied, but Drew only has thirty days to leave."

"Well, if she's forced to leave, will you go with her?" Audrey asked.

"We talked about it," Drew said, "but if he leaves with me, then the Ranagans will have won. They'd love nothing more than to see us go."

"We think the best thing is to have Audrey write the letter, telling the general what's going on here, and then maybe Drew will be able to come back again. We don't see any other way."

My wife and I told the Rays we'd do whatever we could. After they left, Audrey and I sat on the couch totally depressed about what we'd just heard. We couldn't understand why the Ranagans were so callous and uncaring toward the Marine families. And we wondered why the Rays had chosen us to write the letter.

"How do you think Ranagan got her medical record?" Audrey asked.

"Beats me, but then again, nothing those people do surprise me anymore."

"Hey Adam, do you think," Audrey paused. "Do you think that—"

"Do I think what?" I said, frustrated.

"Well, I swung by the hospital the other day to get a prescription for one of the refugees at the camp, and I had to pass medical records. Guess who I saw behind the counter?"

"Who?" I said, giving Audrey my full attention.

"Lt. Humphries, you know, Miss Hump-a-lot."

"So?" I said. "She does work in the hospital. What's the big deal?"

"Isn't she dating Chet Dingle now? She probably got a copy of Drew's record and gave it to Chet, who then gave it to Ranagan. That would explain why Chet gets away with so much. Think of it! I bet Chet gets information for Ranagan whenever the colonel needs it.   He sleeps with women at the internet company, which is how Ranagan probably got Jackie's e-mails from the server. He always seems to know what's going on, even with the married Marines—you know—who we talk to and what we're doing. Chet must tell him everything that's going on in our private lives and in return, the colonel looks a blind eye to Chet's misdoings. Shoot, he must get an earful about our telephone conversations from the signal intelligence company. Aren't they the guys who listen to our calls when they're bored?"

"Okay, you're definitely making sense, and I agree that your theory explains a lot, but why?"

"Ranagan is obviously paranoid or something.   Look who he lives with! Lois probably emasculated him years ago. She's obviously the pants wearer in that house and she probably verbally abuses him just like she did that day on the phone in front of Lt Colonel Ray. He exercises unreasonable control over the Marines to punish their wives, which makes Ranagan look good in front of his wife. Obviously, through surreptitious means, he finds out what he can about people and screws with their lives. Lois doesn't care how he does it, she's just glad when it's done. He ends up looking like a real hero."

"Wow, that's a lot to mull over," I said. I began to mentally replay all the occurrences regarding Chet and Ranagan. Audrey's words seemed to put it all together. "Hey, honey, I don't suppose you'd like to befriend Miss Hump-a-lot, would you? I'd sure like to see what the unexpurgated *Book of the Dead* looks like."

Audrey gave me a devilish grin and winked. "I'll think about it." She walked to the phone in the kitchen. "However, first I have a phone call to make."

"To whom?"

She picked up the phone and dialed. While she waited for someone to answer, she held up her finger and mouthed, "You'll see." I was only able to hear Audrey's side of the conversation and wondered what Lois was saying to fill in the blanks.

"Lois? This is Audrey. I was wondering if...well, no...that's not...actually....but if you'd just let me...I'd like to be reasonable... Can we meet and talk this...that's completely untrue! Well, you're misinformed...fine...goodbye!"

My eyes grew large and when she hung up the phone, I had to ask. "What the hell was that all about?"

"That was me giving that queen bee one last chance to talk this out and be reasonable! I thought I could express the feelings of the wives in a way she could understand. I wanted to make her aware of how bad things have gotten for the Marine families here because of her controlling attitude!"

"So, now what are you going to do?"

She stormed over to her desk and sat down with authority. "That's easy, Adam. I have a letter to write."

Dear General Crane:

My name is Audrey Claiborne and I am stationed with my husband at Guantanamo Bay. He is the Air Officer for the Ground Defense Security Force and I am writing to you because I am in need of guidance. Ever since we have arrived on the island four months ago, the Commanding Officer, Colonel Ranagan, and his wife Lois, have made the climate in which to live and work almost unbearable for myself, and for many of the other officer's wives and our husbands.

Much of the trouble involves Mrs. Ranagan and the activities surrounding the Marine Wives Association. When her ideas and requests are not met with complete enthusiasm by us, our husbands are reprimanded by the colonel. Through the executive officer, Lt Colonel Ray, the wives have been absurdly counseled by the CO for such things as not waving to Mrs. Ranagan enough as she passes us in the street. Mrs. Ranagan has told the ladies that we "do not understand the chain of command among the wives" and she uses veiled threats to make us comply with her wishes. We are told whom to befriend, how to dress and when our association attempts to offer social activities that she does not approve of, she reminds us that "the colonel can and will remove his support at any time".

General Crane, we have tried to work this situation out with Mrs. Ranagan, but to no avail. We have even sought the advice of the two base chaplains, but we have been offered little comfort. Mrs. Ranagan appears to have an archaic definition of the appropriate role of an officer's wife, and when we do not live up to those expectations, our husbands are reprimanded by the colonel, both in their work life and in their home life. I ask that you provide us with guidance so we may all work through this tense situation favorably. Thank you for your time, and I will look forward to hearing from you at your earliest convenience.

Sincerely,

Audrey M. Claiborne

23

Audrey finished writing her letter just before midnight and then she asked me to proofread it. Although I was proud of her for sticking to her guns, I was uncomfortable with her actually sending the letter. Of course, I never told her about my apprehension because I didn't want her to think for a moment I wasn't supporting her; but there were days that followed when I'd wished I'd forbidden her from going through with her plan. It's one thing to have a verbal accusation of impropriety among friends, but putting it in writing and forwarding it to a general was a whole other game.

The following morning, she gathered the ladies, with the exception of Drew, in the picnic shelter to tell everyone what she'd done. Intentionally, she made no mention of Lt Colonel Ray's visit to our home. If she was going to write a letter, it would be to explain the circumstances of her own life; she didn't feel like she had enough information to speak on behalf of the XO and Drew. As she read her letter aloud, it was met with enthusiastic nods from all. When she stopped reading, she offered the ladies the opportunity to sign their names to her letter as well. Audrey believed it was possible for one woman's complaint to fall upon deaf ears, but the general would have a hard time ignoring it if numerous names were attached. After some deliberation, each woman decided to write their own letter.

Every day, for over a week, they would get together in the park to review what the others had written. Some of the ladies were strong writers, and some were weak. Together, they assembled a collection of eight letters. Most letters were one or two pages, some were six and seven. For the first time in months, the women felt empowered to do something to make their lives better for themselves and for their families. Every Marine supported his wife completely and encouraged her to send her letter. Morale was intolerably low and an appeal to the general seemed like the only way for all of them to regain a sense of normalcy.

The morning after the letters were sent, Audrey told me she'd finally been able to sleep soundly for the first time since we'd arrived. In her heart, she knew she'd done the right thing. Her confidence was contagious and I began to believe it too.

➤ ➤ ➤

Audrey waited a week before she phoned Pastor Dooley. When Drew and Lt Colonel Ray told her Dooley had leaked the details of their personal lives to Blankenship or the Ranagans, it incensed Audrey. She wanted to wait a little while before speaking to Dooley so she'd have time to cool off. Unfortunately, a week had not been long enough. She made the call on a Friday afternoon, just before the close of business.

"Penny, ever since I met you, I've been so much happier here in Gitmo. Your sense of humor, your compassion, and your way with people has been refreshing and encouraging. But I want you to know I'm calling today because I'm terribly upset."

"Oh-kay," Dooley said, condescendingly. "With whom?"

"I'm not sure. Maybe you."

"Me? What have I done?" Dooley said dismissively.

"I think you were disloyal to the Rays. They came to see you for direction, and within days of that meeting, the intricacies of their private lives were on Colonel Ranagan's desk. Could you please tell me how that happened?" Audrey's tone was biting.

"I've no idea what you're talking about. What's more, clearly you have no idea what you're talking about," Dooley snapped.

"Oh really? I happen to know you were the only one on this

whole island who knew about Drew's bulimia! A day later, Colonel Ranagan knows too. Now, how do you suppose that happened? Did you tell Blankenship, or did you run right over to the Ranagan's and tell them yourself...hmm?"

"Who I speak to and what we discuss is absolutely none of your damn business," Dooley said, frustrated by Audrey's accusation.

"Nice mouth, pastor. Did they teach you that in seminary?"

"Judge ye not," Dooley said, fighting back.

"So, are you denying you told another party about Drew's bulimia?"

"I've nothing left to say to you, Audrey."

"Well, that's just perfect because I have a whole lot to say to you! You were wrong to betray her like that!" Audrey scolded, losing control of her temper. "She's going to have to leave the island now, and it's all because of you and your inability to uphold the trust that the Rays placed in you. How could you do that to her? You know what the Ranagans are like! How many times have you and I talked about them? How many times have I told you what they're capable of? How many times have I told you how miserable they make us all here and then you go and give them ammunition like that! How could you?"

"You're obviously upset," Dooley said calmly, yet coldly, "but I'm beginning to resent the tone you're taking with me. Being a Chaplain is a job you'll never understand. I do what needs to be done and that's all you need to know."

"Well, Pastor Dooley, then all you need to know is that you have helped to ruin someone's life. I'm sorry I ever trusted you."

"I'm truly sorry you feel that way. Maybe if you knew more of what's going on, you could speak more intelligently. If you don't mind, Audrey, I'm done being yelled at. Goodbye."

Audrey stormed out of the house and down to the playground to talk to the ladies. She recounted the conversation she had with the pastor, and inadvertently spilled the beans about Drew leaving the island. When Drew made it down to the park a half hour later, Audrey apologized, but was made to feel better. Drew intended on telling the rest of the ladies anyway.

As they sat there talking in the park, I drove my car up to the picnic shelter and headed over to the table. Audrey looked puzzled since I was home a few hours earlier than normal.

"Nice to know the air officer doesn't do any work!" Maura joked.

"Yeah, must be nice working half days. I wish my husband did!" Regina added, but I wasn't in a joking mood.

"Hello, ladies," I said as cheerfully as I could. "I actually have to go back to work, but there's a buzz going around the White House and I thought you should know about it."

"What's going on, honey?" Audrey asked.

"Well, it seems a group of wives wrote some letters to a general, and Colonel Ranagan has been informed that a JAG investigation is being launched against him."

"What charge?" Rhonda asked wide eyed, her mouth hanging open.

"Abuse of power," I reported. "I have to go now, just wanted you ladies to know."

"Wait, Adam," Audrey called out to me as I walked to my car. "What does that mean?"

"It means you got what you wanted. My advice? You all better get ready for one hell of a fight."

As I drove away, I slammed my fist on the dashboard of my car. There was a part of me that was happy to know Ranagan was about to have a succession of sleepless nights. There was a larger part of me that was so unbelievably angry with Audrey for instigating the investigation. When I drove to see her at the park, I was genuinely happy for her and the other ladies, but as I stood there, I became uncomfortable in my own skin. When I said the words, "JAG investigation" and "Abuse of power", it became real to me and I wanted to get as far away from Audrey as I could. It's not that I was unhappy with her, and of course I loved her, but I needed space. Knowing that, I probably shouldn't have gone home that night; I should've gone fishing with the other husbands who needed the same space.

"How was your day?" Audrey asked me, as she gave me a hug when I walked through the door. I hugged her back, but not as tightly as usual.

"Long. How was yours?" I asked, distracted.

"Shoot, I'm not sure how to answer that," she said, following me into the bedroom as I changed out of uniform. "I mean, we got what we wanted, but, wow! A JAG investigation."

"Yeah, I know what you're saying." I walked into the bathroom, but this time I shut the door, which I usually never do.

"Is everyone talking about us at the White House?" Audrey said, sitting on the bed waiting for me.

"Oh, yeah."

"What are they saying?"

"You name it," I said coolly.

"Are you okay, Adam? You seem distant."

"Nope. Just tired."

"Hey," Audrey began spiritedly, "I haven't gotten a chance to tell you about my phone call with Pastor Dooley."

"Why did you talk to her? Did you call her?" I asked, my tone agitated.

"Yes, I called her! I wanted to give her a piece of my mind, that's why!"

"About what?"

"About betraying the Rays! Oh, you should have heard her! She was so condescending and callous. I sure gave her a piece of my mind!"

"God damn it, Audrey!" I exploded as I came back out of the bathroom. "Can't you keep your damn mouth shut for once? Can you?"

Audrey was stunned. I'd gone from zero to sixty in about three seconds. "What are you talking about, Adam?"

"You!" I shouted. "That's what I'm talking about! You! Why are you always causing trouble?"

"Me, causing trouble? I don't really think I'm the problem!" Audrey shot back.

"Well, I happen to differ with you, and so do a lot of other people too!" I said as I threw my boot across the room, hitting the wall just above the dresser mirror.

"If you've got something to say, then just go ahead—have the balls to say it!"

"You want to know, fine!" I said, getting in her face. "Audrey, I'm sick and tired of finding your nose in everything that's wrong about this place. So Lois is a bitch—let her be a bitch! So Ranagan is an asshole—let him be an asshole! We only have to live with these people a short time. Why make so much trouble? First it was Mimsey, then it was Lois, then it was Father Blankenship, then it was Chet Dingle, now it's Pastor Dooley. Do you see a common thread, Audrey? It's you!"

"You son of a bitch!" she shouted with tears in her eyes. "How dare you say those things to me! We've already had this conversation, by the way. I never asked to be brought here! I never asked to be observed and questioned by Mimsey in the Norfolk terminal! I never asked to be treated unfairly by Lois! I never asked to be bullied by the Ranagans! I never asked to be betrayed by a friend, who happened to be a chaplain! I never asked for any of those things! I actually got less involved by taking the job at the migrant camp! And by the way, Mr. Innocent, I had your approval to send that letter to General Crane. I told you that night I'd never send that letter if you didn't approve of it. And, another by the way: Don't you remember the look on your XO's face when he came down to your door? Do you? Don't you remember a lieutenant colonel came down to your home—a lowly, insignificant Marine captain's home—and begged you to help him? I don't know about where you come from, but where I come from, when friend asks for help, we help! Do you have any idea what Lt Colonel Ray's life must be like for him to ask us for help? Do you? I bet not! You haven't once stopped to think about how any of the Gitmo crap has affected anyone but yourself!"

"That's the first right thing you have said to me tonight!" I hollered at the top of my lungs, and I pointed in her face. "Maybe your pride feathers got ruffled a little, and maybe you didn't enjoy being told what to do, but this is my career Audrey! This is my career!"

"Well then Adam, why don't you take your career and cuddle up to it tonight because I want nothing to do with you! This place has made you like stone! You used to be feeling and understanding, and now you're selfish and I don't recognize you anymore! After the desk incident, which I apologized for, I promised you I wouldn't do anything you didn't approve of and I kept that promise. If you're upset right now for me writing that letter, then be mad at yourself! And by the way, you're right! It is your career, but it's also my life. Try and remember that sometime."

"That's just beautiful, Audrey! Put it all back on me!"

"When I married you, I married *you*! But somehow along the way I managed to become married to a military career. I'm not a Marine, and yet I'm treated like one and I have to live by those rules. I don't think that's fair. I do my best to fit in and be a good officer's wife, but I won't be treated like a second class citizen to make you look good. And for your information, if you want a Lois, then you married the wrong lady!"

"Obviously!" I said, throwing my hands up in the air.

Audrey paused and gave me a hard stare. "I've had enough of this, and of you. I'm leaving."

"Go ahead, but the plane doesn't come back again until Tuesday."

"I'd rather live under a rock for four days than live with you!"

"Be my guest."

Audrey left sobbing. I watched her drive away through the living room window and then I took my frustration out on whatever crossed my path.

24

"Hey, Audrey? Is that you?" the kind, warm voice called out.

Audrey wiped her tears feverishly as she sat on a rock overlooking the ocean at Cable Beach. "Yeah," she said, making her voice stable, attempting to hide her emotions. "What's going on? How are you?"

"How am I? I think the question is how are you? You look like you need a friend?"

"No, I'm okay," Audrey said, continuing to compose herself. She watched as her dive instructor, Donny Mancuso, climbed up the rocks and sat beside her.

"So what's a nice girl like you doing on a rock like this?" he said to make Audrey smile.

"Oh, just thinking," Audrey said quietly. "It's so beautiful here. I love watching the sunset."

"Well, you don't have long to wait," Donny said, looking up at the sky. "The sun's on its way down. Mind some company?"

"No. Company sounds nice."

Donny Mancuso was born in South Dakota but grew up in Nebraska before joining the Marine Corps. Although he was in his late forties, he was very popular with the women on base. While he was sitting next to Audrey, he took off his T-shirt to get more sun, exposing his fit and overly tanned chest. Donny Mancuso was the last man a Gitmo husband wanted comforting his wife.

"Feel like talking about it?" Donny asked.

"Talking about what?" Audrey said, pretending there was nothing wrong.

"The reason you're sad," Donny said, pushing the hair out of Audrey's face.

"I'm not sad. I'm just frustrated."

"Yeah, I know how that feels. Sexual frustration is the worst." Audrey laughed out loud. "Hey! I got you smiling!"

"You did. Thanks."

"So then, why don't you tell me what's on your mind. Maybe you just need a friendly ear."

Audrey, engaged by Donny's comforting tone and sunny disposition, poured out her heart. He put his arm around her for support as she spoke and when she was finished, rested her head on his shoulder. Me? I was home, wishing I hadn't said all those horrible things to Audrey. Had I known about the hedonistic subculture in Guantanamo Bay, I would have never let her leave the house in her condition. Gordie had once told me a whole lot of screwing went on in Gitmo, but when he told me that, I'd assumed he meant single people—not so. Everyone's tan, everyone's no more than six hours from an alcoholic beverage, everyone's bored, there aren't many single people to choose from, and everyone feels like they're a million miles from reality. While we were there, the veterinarian ran off with a Marine wife; Pickard did the exchange chick; a married doctor did a married corpsman in the medical supply closet; a group of enlisted navy personnel did the wife-swapping thing; the contractors hosted numerous naked hot tub parties; the Jamaican workers got it on with the Philippine workers; enlisted Marines tried to bed officer's wives; and officers would bed whomever they could get away with doing. That's not to say there weren't faithful, monogamous couples on base, because there were. I just happen to think the amoral kind outnumbered the faithful kind, two to one.

When the sun had completely descended, and after Audrey had given Donny the entire unadulterated version of the day's

events, Donny convinced Audrey to spend the night at his and
Becca's house. Later on, she told me she'd really wanted to come
home instead, but after the "four days under a rock" comment,
her pride wouldn't allow her to be with me just yet. So, with
some reluctance, she got into his car and they drove together to
an area of the base she'd never been.

"Where are we going?" Audrey asked as Donny drove along
several unpaved roads.

"To the Magazine area, you know, by the old cemetery."

"No, I don't know. What's the Magazine area?"

"That's where most of the base's ammunition is stored. We had
a couple of power outages on this side of base today and I need to
check something out. Actually, that's what I was doing at Cable
Beach when I saw you. Sometimes when there are power outages,
followed by power surges, a lot of damage can be done." His car
stopped by the old cemetery. "Be right back—won't be a minute."

Audrey stepped out of the car, too, and began reading headstones.
Even though the sun was down, there was still a decent amount
of light; otherwise my wife wouldn't have gone near the place.
As she looked around, she came upon an excessive quantity of
graves marked with the words: HAITIAN BABY or CUBAN BABY.
Donny explained that during the times when there was a surge
of refugees, many children arrived ill, or were born to unhealthy
mothers and passed away soon after birth. Audrey also found
numerous grave markers for the infamous fifties' babies, when
122 babies who were born to American mothers and mysteriously
died soon after birth. As Audrey continued to survey the area,
she came upon an interesting tree.

"Donny! Do you know anything about this tree? I see ones
like it all over base."

"Yeah, it's an East Indian fig tree called a banyan. Its branches
send roots to the ground to become new trunks. It's actually
pretty neat." Donny motioned for Audrey to get back into the
car, and, when she did, she noticed a pathway. "Where does that
lead?"

"That's the path to Cuzco Wells. That's where the battle for
Guantanamo Bay began, or was won, I forget. You need to ask
your husband. He has to give a tour to all the base residents
soon."

"Can we go see it?"

"I'm afraid not. Cuzco is off-limits because of its proximity to the Magazine area. Sorry."

WHEN AUDREY WALKED through the front door of Donny's house, she immediately became uncomfortable when she saw Becca sitting on the couch wearing only a purple thong.

"Hi, sweetie!" she called out to Donny, completely unconcerned with Audrey's presence.

"Hi, baby," he answered, stepping over the coffee table to make out with her. "You look so hot. I'm gonna have to get me some of that tonight." He pinched her left nipple and went on to massage her crotch.

"Okay, guys!" Audrey said, utterly embarrassed. "What do you say we call it a night and I'll walk home?"

"Absolutely not!" Becca announced firmly. "You need a place to stay tonight and we've got one."

"Yeah, I called Becca from the Magazine area. She already has dinner made," Donny insisted. "She figures this will be a regular slumber party."

"Well then, thank you. I really appreciate it." Audrey's mouth turned dry.

While Audrey helped to set the table, Becca threw on a cover-up, which really didn't cover much, and Donny returned from the bedroom wearing nothing but black silk boxers and baby oil on his chest. Audrey pretended not to notice either one.

"So what's for dinner, sexy?" Donny asked his wife.

"*Long...hot...thick....juicy...sausage,*" Becca said seductively. Audrey began to thumb through a coffee table book as a distraction—until she realized she'd been reading the *Kamasutra.*

"I'll give you some of my sausage if you think you'll need more than what's on your plate," Donny returned.

"Ooooo, baby, you got me squirming," Becca said after she licked his stomach.

"Well, I don't know about you two," Audrey said, overly upbeat, "but I sure am starved!"

"For what? Anything I can help you with?" Donny said playfully.

"Hot sausage! I mean long sausage! I mean Becca's sausage!" Audrey blurted out, as the two of them giggled at her.

"I know what you mean," Becca answered, laughing. "Hand me your plate."

As the three ate dinner, Audrey was careful to steer the conversation away from sexual innuendo. "Adam and I sure love diving. Thanks for being such a great instructor."

"No problem. To be honest, I wasn't sure if you were ever going to get into the water. You were sure scared that day."

"You're right, I was.   But thanks to you, my fears were alleviated. Becca, if it wasn't for your husband making me feel so safe underwater, I'm not sure I could've gone though with it."

"Yeah, he's the best." Becca said, winking at her husband as she played footsy with him under the table.

"Do you get jealous? I mean, with your husband teaching so many young girls to dive. I'm sure there are some that must get a crush. I think it would bother me," Audrey said.

"No way! Besides, I like to share."

"Excuse me?" Audrey almost choked on her food.

"Share! I love to watch my husband being pleasured by another woman as much as he loves to watch me be pleasured by another man. Isn't that right, honey?"

"You know it, baby."

Audrey decided to just ask the question on everyone's mind: "So it's true? The rumors are true? You guys are swingers?"

"It's not like I go home with one guy and then he goes home with some girl. We invite others into our bed. There's a difference." When Becca finished speaking, Donny got up to answer the phone. Becca leaned in to talk quietly to Audrey. "You know, my husband absolutely adores you!"

"Well, that's nice to hear. I'm fond of him too."

Becca drew in even closer and began to speak like an excited teenager. "He totally wants you! I haven't stopped hearing your name since class."

Audrey was caught off guard. "Doesn't that bother you?

"Hell no! I want him to be happy and if he wants you, then I want you for him—besides, it's fun to watch."

"I'll take your word for it."

"Hey, girl, take more than my word!" Becca said excitedly. "Question: Have you ever had lesbian sex?"

"No, can't say that I have!" Audrey said, with a blank stare.

"You have no idea what you're missing! It's totally awesome. You've got to try it!"

"Maybe another time. I think I need to get back to Adam. He's probably worried sick."

Donny came back to the table. "That was Tiffany and Bill. They said they'll be over in about ten minutes."

"Wahoo! Bill and Tiff are awesome! Are they in a mood to party?"

"They said they were," Donny said and resumed eating.

"Honey, I think Audrey isn't comfortable with us. Look at her. I think we scared her," Becca said, pointing her fork at her.

"No, no! I'm just missing Adam. I want to thank you both for being really great friends to me tonight, but I think Adam and I need to sort this out for ourselves. Hiding won't solve anything."

"Well, if you're sure. Let me throw some jeans on and I'll drive you home," Donny offered.

"No, you don't have to do that," Audrey insisted.

"I want to. Just a second."

Donny got dressed and walked Audrey out to the car. He talked to her about how much he loved his wife, and why they were meant to be together, the whole way back home. When they pulled up in the driveway, she gave Donny a quick appreciative hug, but, before Audrey could exit the car, Donny reiterated his invitation to stay at his house that night, and she politely declined.

LOIS APPARENTLY KNEW what she was doing when she forbade the single Marines from hanging around the married ones, even though no one listened to her. As time went on, the single Marines became entirely too close to the wives. It wasn't because they were after them, but the isolation of the island, and the sense of loneliness, made people feel much stronger bonds than they normally would have. Our wives cooked for them, listened to their problems, danced with them at social functions, paid them wonderful compliments, gave them much needed hugs and emotional support, and somewhere along the way, the lines got fuzzy. No one was the 'bad guy'; sentiments of all kinds were amplified on our base. The episode with Donny was a perfect example of a Gitmo friendship about to cross the line.

I DIDN'T SEE AUDREY PULL UP for a very good reason—I wasn't home. After she'd been gone for a couple of hours, I went looking for her. She and I had experienced our share of arguments over the years, but none had been so terrible. After thinking it over, I knew Audrey was right. She'd apologized for the trouble she'd caused, and asked my permission to send the letter to General Crane—I even helped her write it. I came to realize, as I drove around, I wasn't mad at her, but rather, irritated by the circumstances. Everyone was drowning in stress, but I'd lost the ability to keep my feelings in check. I'm not saying Audrey couldn't have handled some situations better, because she could have, but hindsight is always twenty-twenty. I couldn't hold her responsible for what we should have done. Besides, I reread the letter that Audrey wrote to the general and I believed in every word. Something had to be done, and maybe she, more than we, needed to be the color in an otherwise back and white Guantanamo Bay.

After what seemed like forever, I decided to go back home to see if Audrey had returned, and if so, explain what she'd found. When I walked into the living room, I saw Audrey sitting near a pile of wood that had once been her desk. I'd become so infuriated, I tossed the desk over on its side a couple of times, eventually busting it up pretty good. Had it not been so old, or in such bad shape, it might have survived my tirade.

"Hey, I'm really sorry," I said speaking softly, walking slowly toward her. "I'll buy you another one—whatever one you want." I was so humiliated I'd lost my temper.

"I don't care about the stupid desk, Adam. I want to know what happened tonight. This isn't us. We don't act like that with each other."

"I know. I've felt badly all evening. I even went out to find you."

"I guess you looked in all the wrong places."

"Yeah, I guess so. Where were you by the way?"

"Oh, that's its own story. I'll tell you later," she said, rolling her eyes. I really wanted to know, but I knew she'd tell me when she was ready. "Adam, I'm sorry too. There're a lot of things I could've done better. I'm entirely too outspoken, for one."

I quickly interrupted. "And I should've continued to support you on the letter. It wasn't fair of me to tell you it was okay and then chastise you later. I'm so sorry for making you feel the way I did. You're the best thing that ever happened to me," I said, hugging her.

"You are too," she replied, lovingly.

"Do you want to put this all behind us?"

"Yeah, I do." I leaned over to kiss her, but before my lips touched hers, she said, "After you clean up this mess."

"I guess I need to do that, huh?" I said sheepishly. I knelt down to sort through the broken pieces.

"How about some help?" Audrey offered, but I didn't reply because something had caught my eye.

"There's something written on the underside of the desk," I said, sounding like a character from a TV crime drama.

"What is it?

"I've no idea."

"It looks like symbols. Do you think it has any meaning?" she asked.

I looked at the writing more closely before I answered. "I have a strange feeling it does, and whoever wrote this, never wanted anyone else to see it."

25

The lamplight in the living room was too dim to see the details of the faded wording, so we carried the desktop into the kitchen and turned on the much brighter fluorescent ceiling lights. In the top left corner was a name: R. Mercado. Right underneath it was a number, 56-6902, and a small notation: 0530, NEG, LB3T.

"Who in the world is R. Mercado?" Audrey wondered. "Do you think it's the guy who used to own this desk?"

"Not sure, but I tend to doubt it. If the name was written all by itself, I might go with that answer, but clearly, the number and notation refers to him," I said, trying to sound like I knew what the hell I was saying.

"What's that in the middle there? It looks like a really bad drawing of some kind?" My wife said, pointing.

"Your guess is as good as mine."

About a half a second later, Audrey's face lit up with excitement. "It's a map!"

Instead of immediately dismissing her idea, I opened my mind, thinking outside the box. If it was a map, it was quite rudimentary, lacking a compass, key and legend. I then recalled every map Audrey had drafted since I'd known her: Random lines on the paper; no direction indicated; landmarks in place of mileage markers or cross roads. I was obviously unequipped to decipher these hieroglyphics, so I moved aside to watch my wife at work. "Okay, if you're so sure, tell me what it's a map of."

Audrey moved in closer, scrunching her face. I sat back, arms folded, leaning my body against one of the kitchen cabinets as detective Audrey surveyed the aged sketch. I began whistling, which echoed wildly in the kitchen with its high ceilings. My eyes darted back to the map as I saw the light bulb go on over Audrey's head.

"What? What have you found out?" I asked eagerly.

"Just a sec."

"What? The look on your face is telling me you know what this is about."

"Shh, give me a minute."

I sat there, trying to be calm. "Throw me a bone!"

"It's not a map," she said with great confidence.

"Not a map?" I said, throwing my arms up. "Then what else could it be?"

"A plan."

"A what?"

"A thought process."

"Spell it out for me, Audrey. It's late."

"Whoever wrote this was unquestionably stationed here in Gitmo, and going on that fact, we know he or she knew this base like we do. Think about it, why would anyone who lives here need a map? Maps are for people who are new to the island— one would hardly draw a map for someone else on the underside of his or her desk."

"Ok, you have my attention."

"This person was mapping out a route of some kind for planning purposes, but for what and for where I don't know. Here on the bottom left is a big X, and here up at the top is another large X. I'll assume the first X is the starting point since about an inch down the line is a very small number one. The numbers increase to four until the second X. This hump here by the four looks like a mountain or hill. That's all I've figured out so far."

My skin began to crawl with goose bumps. I thought back to my helicopter flight and the stupid drawing began to make sense. "Audrey, I think the first X is the Northeast Gate and the hill is John Paul Jones Hill!"

"What makes you think that?"

"Because I've seen this base by air, and with so few roads, this sketch makes sense. I need to copy it down and beg Commander Cleary to put me on the flight schedule this week. Tomorrow if I can make it happen. I've no idea what we're looking for, but wouldn't it be amazing to actually find it?"

Commander Cleary came through for me, putting me on the schedule the very next afternoon. Captain Pickard had received new orders the day before and would be replaced within the month, so Cleary didn't care what Pickard thought of me anymore. Before I lifted off, I took a long look at my copy of the drawing since I couldn't take it out in flight. This was my first opportunity in the air since my cowboy day, and I didn't want to betray Cleary's confidence in me by raising any eyebrows.

Since I'd suspected the first X had been the Northeast Gate, I flew there first. With only an air crewman in the helicopter with me, I was free to do whatever I pleased. From there, I flew along Sherman Avenue, hoping the small drawing etched under the desk would come alive on land. I wasn't disappointed. It took everything I had to continue with the flight. I wanted to set the bird down, scoop Audrey up, and tell her what I'd uncovered. However, that wasn't to be. Not long before we were supposed to land, we experienced engine trouble and had to make an emergency landing on Leeward. It took the mechanics less than an hour to figure out what the trouble was, and it wasn't good news. A major component in the engine had sheared and needed to be replaced immediately. At that particular time on the base, one of our two Hueys was in Corpus Christi for its annual maintenance check. The one I'd been flying was the only search and rescue bird left on the island. Since we were required to have a functional helicopter at all times, I had to pilot the C-12 with Commander Cleary to Jacksonville, Florida for the new part. With so much flight planning to do, I only had time to leave a short message for Audrey on the machine, telling her I'd call her that evening.

Cleary and I went through the pre-flight check list and taxied down the runway at 5pm. He was the PIC, or pilot in command,

and I was the second-seater. Usually we invited base residents to hop a ride to the States in the eight-passenger, commuter-type airplane, but today we had to hustle. Cleary and I needed to be landing at Jacksonville Naval Air Station before 9pm to get the part we needed for the Huey. Otherwise, we had to wait until 9am the next morning. The weather was fair upon take off, and we anticipated no problems with the flight plan we filed with Miami Center.

Once we were airborne, we engaged the auto-pilot and took in the view of the Cuban coastline. Our route would take us around the eastern end of the island, through the Windward Passage, across the Bahamas, and into Jacksonville. Except for my infamous helicopter flight when I first arrived on the base, I'd not left Guantanamo Bay in the whole five months I'd lived there. Within a few minutes of take-off, I felt completely stress-free and totally relaxed. Audrey and I had been told by many people to leave the island at least once every two months to avoid Rock fever, but we never took their advice. I was sorry we hadn't taken a weekend to the States sooner—it might have made our adjustment easier. As Cuba faded into the horizon behind me, I knew Audrey and I were going to take a trip out of Gitmo when I got home.

"Does it always feel this good, sir?" I asked the tall, forty year-old Commander.

"Does what feel good?" he answered as he thumbed through a copy of *Men's Health Magazine*. Of course it was two months old, but all the magazines shipped to the island were way out of date. No one seemed too upset by that; we were just happy to have news from the States.

"Getting away from Gitmo? I mean, Audrey and I love it there, but I can feel my blood pressure decreasing exponentially with each mile we travel."

Cleary didn't look at me, staying focused on his magazine, but he let out a muffled chuckle. "Yup. I love it there too, but like dead fish, it begins to smell after a while."

We received word from Miami Center that we were getting too near a Delta flight, so we had to change our altitude. When I finished making the adjustment, I noticed Commander Cleary had put his magazine away and was reading some sort of list. "So what are you bringing back, Claiborne?" he asked me.

"What do you mean, sir?"

"I mean, what are you bringing back for all the people who found out you were leaving the island?"

"Nothing actually. Nobody but Audrey and Colonel Ranagan knows I'm even gone."

"Well, you're luckier than I am because I've quite a list here. Becca Mancuso wants a dozen Dunkin Donuts; my wife's bridge partner wants face cream; my daughter wants moisturizing shampoo; one of the crew chiefs asked for loose tobacco and wrapping papers. Oh here's a beaut! Becca also wants strawberry-scented douche. That one's for you," he said, ripping the bottom off of the paper and handing it to me. "Captain Pickard wanted us to pick up a set of tires for his car, but I told him we wouldn't have the time. However, his wife needs red glitter for a craft project and he seemed adamant we locate some for her."

"You're kidding, right sir?"

"Don't worry, Claiborne. It's kind of like playing Santa Claus. You'll get used to it. Besides, it's the least we can do. We have the best job on the whole base. Who else can leave whenever they want? Shit, sometimes I jet off to Nassau just to get conch fritter soup and Cuban cigars."

"Is that legal?"

"It is when you tell everyone you're flying to maintain proficiency." Cleary reached for his can of skoal and placed some in his mouth. "I'll tell you what does suck: when you get back from a long trip and then the MF-er CO orders you back to JAX to pick up some moron who missed the regular flight. Once, I flew so much in one day that my balls turned black!"

"No shit?"

"Literally! And if that wasn't bad enough, they began to swell until they reached the size of cantaloupes!" I shifted uncomfortably in my seat, making sure my boys had plenty of breathing room. "Have you any idea how it feels to walk into the Gitmo Emergency Room with an ice pack on your nuts and see everyone you know? How about when I told the nurse, who I saw at McDonald's like an hour later, that my balls were on fire!"

"I'm surprised she didn't slap you across the face. You didn't phrase that very well." I said, chuckling.

"Well, that was a couple of months ago. Hopefully that nurse is gone now, anyhow." Cleary's laughter died down and he became more serious. "But you know what? You'll miss it when you leave. You'll miss Gimto in a way no one else will ever understand. You gotta live there."

"What makes you say that, sir?"

"I was stationed in Gitmo in 1983 and I've spent the rest of my career trying to get back. I don't know if it's the sense of community, the beautiful scenery, the simple way of life or the friends you meet, but Gitmo is a special place and you're damn lucky to get to be a part of it. Never forget that."

"What was it like back then? I'm sure there've been quite a number of changes."

"Well, there was no cable, so forget about any good television. We did get America Forces Network, but it totally sucked. Honestly, most everyone on base was on a sports team and there wasn't a moment of the day when there wasn't an event to participate in. There was an outdoor skating rink, a dirt bike track, soap box derbies, parties galore, fantastic USO shows and concerts. It was better back then—much better. There were also a lot more people. The recreation office even used to plan inexpensive trips to the other Caribbean islands. Now, we've gone from 10,000 military members and families to 500. Guantanamo Bay was the Navy's best kept secret. It still is."

"Audrey and I like it, but the Ranagans have made things really difficult for us."

"Yeah, heard all about that from my wife. Lois, who used to shun her, has now buddied up to her like there's no tomorrow. I guess she's doing damage control for her reputation. Look, don't worry about her. They'll be gone in six months anyway."

"Well, maybe sooner. A JAG team is coming to investigate the colonel on abuse of power charges."

"No shhhhit! I guess I'll wish you good luck then." Cleary continued to thumb through his magazine.

We began to notice a change in wind direction, accompanied by aircraft instability. Commander Cleary took control of the plane and we made a call to Miami Center. They advised us that a violent storm system had developed along the eastern coast of the United States, from Savannah, Georgia all the way to Key Largo, and was expected to last several hours. Miami Center recommended we land at the Key West Naval Air Station for the duration of the storm. We complied with their recommendation.

As we got closer to the coastline, the turbulence became more intense and Commander Cleary and I were struggling to maintain control of the aircraft. I had never experience such volatility while flying, later learning Cleary hadn't either. As we came upon our approach, we knew wind shear was a definite possibility and braced ourselves. The sky grew black and visibility fell to almost nothing. We had no choice but to land, so we lowered the flaps and added power to the landing. Just as we were about to touch-down, a gust of wind blew the aircraft to the side and one of our wings struck the runway. By working together, Cleary and I avoided a disastrous incident and managed to gain control of the plane. While we came out of the ordeal unscathed, the same could not be said for the C-12. The damage wasn't as bad as we had thought it would be, but we both knew she wasn't going anywhere any time soon. When we'd finished surveying the wing for our preliminary report to Captain Pickard, we ran across the runway towards the terminal, attempting to evade the severe lightning and rain that had come upon us so suddenly. In the commotion and darkness of the squall, I lost sight of Commander Cleary. When I arrived at the building, I turned around towards the runway in time to witness the commander being thrown into the air by the violent impact of a rushing fuel truck against his body. I was sick inside as I called out to him, racing back to his still body. I'd never felt so helpless in my life.

I knelt beside him, but was only able to see his face when the lightning lit the sky. There was blood coming out of his nose, mouth, and ears. He didn't respond to my voice and I feared if he wasn't already dead, he'd soon be. The fuel truck driver had already radioed for help and I could see the glaring red lights from the emergency vehicles headed our way. "Hold on, Commander, hold on," I repeated to him over and over again until the paramedics pushed me aside. One of the MPs asked me to follow him inside the terminal to give a statement. By then, the wind and thunder had gained tremendous strength and talking turned to shouting due its earsplitting volume. I walked backwards a few steps, keeping the Commander in sight, before I entered the building.

"Where's he being taken?" I asked the MP with great interest.

"Fisherman's Hospital out in town," he replied coolly as he took out his clipboard.

"Do you think he's going to be alright?" I said as I moved to a window in time to see the ambulance pull away.

"Hard to tell." The MP had the personality of a cotton ball. "Now, could you please give me your name and rank?"

"Ah, Adam Claiborne. Captain. Can I go to him?"

"When we're through. I understand you're stationed in Guantanamo Bay. Navy or Marine Corps?"

"Marines."

"Hey, what's it like there? I've always wanted to know. Are the Cuban women easy?"

"I don't understand your question. How's that relevant to what happened to Commander Cleary? My Flight Ops O was just hit by a truck and you want me to describe life in Gitmo? I'm out of here." The MP followed me to the front of the building where there was a taxi waiting. Before I got into the cab, I stopped to say one more thing to him. "If you want to know about the accident, you can meet me there, but you'll have to find your own damn ride."

I'D NEVER BEEN TO KEY WEST before, although I'd heard a lot about it from my squadron mates over the years. Originally, the Navy built the base as a submarine port, but changed its mind when they realized the clarity of the southern waters made the submerged subs visible for great distances by air. Within months, the Navy turned the facility into a thriving air station. All my friends had spoken of Key West's allure—exciting street parties, a laid-back lifestyle, spectacular sunsets, and enviable weather—but that wasn't the Key West I saw that night. For most of the trip to the hospital, I saw few other cars and absolutely no other people.

"Some weather we're having, huh?" the cabbie noted between fierce bursts of thunder.

"Yeah," I answered unenthusiastically. I didn't give a crap about the weather. All I could think about was Cleary.

"It's gonna make that hurricane out there look like a puppy taking a whiz!"

"What hurricane?" I asked concerned. "It's not hurricane season."

"Ah, don't worry. It's still way out there—whatever it is—but of course when there's a hurricane brewing, it's always a topic of conversation."

We finally arrived at the hospital and I jogged to the front doors at an accelerated pace. I was directed—and redirected—until I finally ended up in a waiting area outside of surgery. The nurse told me Cleary had suffered massive internal trauma, and they had to open him up immediately. I asked if he'd ever regained consciousness, she told me he hadn't. When she walked away, I took a seat in an uncomfortable vinyl chair and waited. I did a hell of a lot of praying too.

26

The doors to surgery flew open five hours later and a short, balding man approached me. He introduced himself as Dr. Byron and asked me to sit back down.

"Commander Cleary is a very lucky man," the doctor began. "He had a large amount of internal bleeding. He also suffered a ruptured spleen, a broken tibia, four broken ribs, a shattered collar bone and a concussion. The good news is that man's as strong as an ox, and, with time, he should heal completely."

"How long will he have to be hospitalized?" I said, concerned yet completely relieved.

"That's hard to say right now. At least several weeks to be sure."

"Well, he's going to be alright. That's all that matters."

"True," he said, patting me on the shoulder. "You should get some sleep now. It's late. There won't be any chance for you to see the commander until tomorrow anyway. Go on back to the BOQ and get some shut-eye."

"I will. First I need to phone my CO and brief him on Cleary's condition."

"I understand. You can use the phone in that office right over there." He held out his hand to shake mine. "Take care and I'll see you in the morning. We will phone you if we have any problems during the night."

I thanked Dr. Byron and called Captain Pickard. When I was sure he was comfortable with the situation, I asked if he could call Audrey for me to let her know I was okay. Pickard informed me Audrey was spending the night with Commander Cleary's wife to help comfort her. I was happy she was where she felt needed, but I'd really wanted to talk to her myself. I could call her at the Cleary's, but I just didn't feel right doing that. Instead, I took the doctor's advice and headed back towards the air station.

Outside the hospital, the storm had dissipated, with the thunder only faintly audible in the distance. While the wind had died down considerably, the streets were still littered with fallen palm branches and an assortment of debris. As I rode in the cab, I saw the city beginning to come alive again and decided not to go back to the BOQ. I asked the driver to take me to center of Key West's action, flight suit and all.

Cleary and I hadn't expected to be in Florida for more than few hours, so we hadn't packed anything. Despite my positive attitude, as I walked down the street, I began to feel uncomfortable wearing my flight suit out in town. I stopped at a souvenir store and did a little shopping. I purchased a pair of lime green shorts, which had been adorned with blue martini glasses, and a white T shirt. I also bought some green flip flops since my black boots wouldn't go well with my new outfit. In case you have any question to the contrary, I went cheap.

With my flight suit in a shopping bag, I continued down the street and came upon a bar called Jack's Martini Shack, owned by the town gigolo. It was a typical bar, gaining notoriety more from its owner than its décor. I took a seat at the bar and ordered an ice cold beer from the bartender. Normally I would've never had a drink before a flight, but it was clear to me I wouldn't be going anywhere fast. Between the wing strike and the commander's accident, I'd be marking time in the southernmost city in America until the C-12 was fixed.

I wasn't in the bar long before an older gentleman in his late sixties walked in and sat down beside me. He was dressed as loudly as I, and appeared to know a few of the others in our general area. He was about five-ten, with receding gray hair and a handle bar mustache. His girth proved he'd seen a few too many beers and hot wings in his time.

"Well, if it isn't Double O!" shouted the bartender at the older man. "Haven't seen you in a while. Where have you been?"

Quite gregariously, the gentleman shouted back over the music, "Oh, I've been a little bit all over the place, if you know what I mean."

"How long you gonna be in the Keys?" the bartender asked.

"Not long at all. I'm just waiting for this weather to pass. I only came into port because of this crazy storm. I'm heading to Mississippi to play me some slot machines."

"Still dreaming of hittin' it big there, Double O?" an older woman near his end of the bar asked.

"Tryin'. I'm gonna die tryin'!"

"What can I get you?" the bartender leaned in to ask Double O.

The man looked down at my beer. "I think I'll have what he's having. Lord knows I deserve it after battling that ocean this afternoon."

"Did you hit some bad weather?" I asked, hoping for a little conversation.

"Yeah, but it wasn't too bad until around Key Largo, and then the wind picked up out of nowhere."

"I know what you mean. I was headed for Jacksonville, and we were told to divert here. I guess we have something in common—stranded in Key West"

Double O held up his beer bottle to propose a toast. "To two salty seamen! Cheers!" The man took a swig of his beer. "What the hell kind of boat were you piloting?"

"I wasn't in a boat. I was flying."

"Where were you flying from?"

"The Caribbean," I said as I put a quarter in the jukebox.

"Where about?"

"Cuba."

"What's a nice American boy doing in a place like Cuba?" The man asked, joining me at the juke box.

"I'm stationed in Guantanamo Bay." I was chatting with the stranger, but my mind was on Cleary.

The man leaned his side against the machine, as he looked out across the crowd and pulled on his mustache. "Well, that's a name I haven't heard in a while. What a place."

"Have you been there?"

"Afraid so," Double O said, on the way back to his bar stool.

"Sounds like you didn't like it there," I said, following right behind him.

"No, it's not that. It's just when you said that name, well, I started to think about things I'd tucked away—things I hadn't thought about in a long time." The man took another swig of his beer. "People I've tried to forget."

"When were you stationed there?" I asked, signaling the bartender for another round.

"A long time ago, son, a long time ago." Double O finished his beer, placed some money on the counter and thanked the bartender. "Well, I need to get some sleep. I have a lot of sailing to do tomorrow." He held out his hand. "It was a pleasure to have met you. Good luck back in Gitmo."

"Need a lift to the marina?" the bartender asked. "I'm getting off in about a half hour."

"Naw, I'll walk. It's not too far. Besides, I might meet me a cute little thing on the way!"

I wasn't sure why I said this, but I said, "I'll join you on that walk." The man seemed surprised, but shrugged his shoulders and walked out of the bar.

"My name's Adam, by the way," I told him as I caught up to him.

"Nice to meet you," the man said as he walked at a steady pace down the street, never making eye contact. For a larger man, he could sure move quickly.

"I'm a Marine stationed at the Ground Defense Security Force. Where were you stationed when you were in Gitmo?"

"Same place."

"Really? A Marine too? What was your MOS?"

"I was an administrative clerk back then, but that was a long time ago."

"When was back then?" I was unrelenting.

The man stopped in the middle of the sidewalk. "What's with the third-degree, son? Do you want to walk with me or interrogate me?"

"I'm sorry if I appear to be prying, it's just...," I knew I had to come up with something reasonably true so my mind went to work. "I'm also the Barracks historian and I'm trying to put together a history of the Marines in Guantanamo. I'd like to interview you if you don't mind."

"Well, actually *I do* mind," Double O said.

"Ok. I'm sorry to have bothered you." I fell back a little and began to walk the other way. After about thirty seconds, I heard the man's voice call after me.

"Hey kid, are you hungry? I'm smelling something wonderful and I'd sure like the company. I've always hated to eat alone."

I looked around and saw The Hoochie Mamma Hot Dog Hut a few yards away. "I think that's what you smell," I said, pointing.

"Care to join me for a bite to eat? Looks like an interesting place to go."

"I'd love to," I said as I walked back to him. I wasn't sure why he called back, but I fully intended to take advantage of it.

After he'd finished one of his three hot dogs and pinched one of the scantily dressed waitresses, he was more sociable. He took a napkin and wiped mustard from his face before speaking. "Okay, what's the jig?"

"Excuse me?"

"Why are you following me around? I just met you at a bar for less than ten minutes and now we're eating hot dogs together. I know you want something so let's have it." His tone was much more serious, but still friendly.

"I want to know about when you were in Gitmo—everything you can remember."

"Why?"

"I can't tell you why exactly, partly because I don't even know everything myself."

"Start from the beginning, son and then maybe I can help. Maybe."

I moved my seat closer to his and began to speak in a hushed tone. I wasn't sure why I was acting so secretive. "My wife and I have come upon some information we don't quite understand. There was a lance corporal name Daryl Loring who disappeared in 1958 and his body was never found. My wife and I have reason to believe he was murdered."

Double O's grimaced and put down his hot dog. "You don't say?"

"That's why I was curious as to when you were there. I was hoping you might know something."

"Well, I was actually there twice—once in the late seventies and once in the fifties. I know the kid you're talking about." Double O pushed his remaining food items away. He had lost his appetite.

"So you were there when it happened?" I pressed.

"Yes. He was a good friend of mine, actually. I never believed that manufactured yarn then and I still don't believe it now. Daryl Loring didn't drown. Case closed!"

"How can you be so certain?"

"Because he was scared to death of the water, that's why. If he was at the beach, he was there to get laid, that's all. There's no way in hell he'd go swimming, especially by himself."

"Did you tell anyone about his fear of water?" I pushed.

"I was a buck private nobody. No one asked my opinion, so I never gave it," he said, walking towards the garbage can.

"What's your theory? What did you think happened to him," I asked, following him around like a lost puppy.

"I don't want to talk about this right now. Let's walk to my boat. We can talk there."

🐟 🐟 🐟

"Guantanamo Bay is a funny place," Double O began as he pulled up two folding chairs on the deck of his ancient white house boat. "It changes people."

"How do you mean?"

"If you live there, Adam, then you already know that answer, don't you? I bet you aren't the same man you were before you got there. Am I right?"

"I guess so, yeah," I nodded my head.

"The seclusion, the remoteness, the loneliness—they all take a toll on a man." He reached over and poured a cup of coffee from a thermos, but didn't offer me any. "Now don't get me wrong, it's a great place and I had my share of fun times, but there's something about Gitmo that never leaves you. Sometimes it even haunts you." Double O fixed his eyes upon the water and his mind seemed to drift off to another place.

I waited a few moments before I pressed him further. "Tell me about Daryl."

"He was a wiry fellow, with an amazing sense of humor. He was a real practical joker. I remember on one occasion when a major general came for a visit, Daryl got a hold of the CO's speech and, well, let's just say he changed a few lines."

"I'm not sure I'm ready to hear this," I said with a smile.

"The CO, of course, welcomes the major general and then says in a booming voice, 'What can you say about General Daniels? A major general is an officer who has his men behind him before the battle, and in front of him during it!'"

"Did he get away with it?"

"Absolutely." Double O grinned. "He did a lot of other pranks like that, but he was a good guy."

"Did he have any enemies?"

"No, everyone seemed to get along with him. He was a real likable Marine."

"Did you know a Gunnery Sergeant Gaultier?" I said, fishing.

The man's face fell instantly and his voice lowered in tone. "What did you say, son?"

"Gunnery Sergeant—"

"I know what you said and that's the last time you'll say it!"

Double O was uncomfortable, but I had to keep asking. "So you knew him?"

"Yeah, I knew him and I'd just as soon like to forget him," he answered, shifting uncomfortably in his deck chair.

"Why?"

"Because he was an arrogant, good for nothing, selfish bastard, that's why! He treated his men like garbage and bullied anyone else he could get away with messing with. He even threatened my life one day. No, that man is no good—to the core."

The wheels of my mind were spinning. "You never told me your name—what's your name?"

"Huh?" the man seemed caught off guard.

"Everyone in the bar called you Double O. Why?"

"They're my initials."

I ran my hands back and forth across my hair with anticipation. "When I first heard them call you that in the bar, I just assumed you were a huge James Bond fan, but now I get it. Are you Oliver Orcher?"

The man put his cup down on the deck. "Now how on God's green earth did you know that? Who are you, boy? You'd better not lie to me." Double O pulled out a gun hidden under his chair.

I had no idea what to do, so I just began to speak as quickly as I could. "I'm exactly who I said I was. I know your name because a Cuban woman by the name of Lupe Herrera said her friend, Daniela, had dated a man by the name of Oliver Orcher in 1958. You're him, right?"

Oliver, lost in though, put his gun down. He looked up at the sky and back at me. "Yeah, I'm him. I'll tell you what I know, and maybe together, we can help poor Daryl find some peace after all. By the way, that was only a flare gun."

27

"Daryl and I bunked together. As a matter of fact, we arrived in Gitmo on the same day: September 14, 1958. I hadn't met him before that first morning. He was infantry and I was a squadron clerk. His mother was at the dock seeing him off, and I remember he wasn't embarrassed by it either. She must have kissed him a hundred times, and he let her. He kept reassuring her he'd be fine, but for some reason, she just couldn't bring herself to say goodbye. It's like she knew her son wouldn't be coming home again." Oliver choked up a little when he said that, but cleared his throat and continued. "He and I sat next to each other at first mess, and if I remember correctly, he found a fly or a roach in the spaghetti sauce. We began talking and hit it off. We both loved baseball, banana splits and a girl named Betty. We called them our three B's. Yeah, he was an easy fellow to like."

"Sounds like it."

"We pulled up at the dock about five days later, and what a beautiful sight to see. There were mountains, palm trees, and some of the clearest blue water I'd ever seen in my life. The line to get off the ship was long and in that heat, we had to hold ourselves back from jumping overboard into the bay."

"Some things never change. That was the first thing we noticed about Gitmo—the heat."

Oliver continued as if I hadn't said a word. "Daryl and I walked together to a bus and I got on first, but before Daryl could follow, another Marine stood in front of him and ordered him to another bus. We both thought that was odd, but of course he complied."

"Let me guess. That Marine was Gunnery Sergeant Gaultier?"

"Yes." Oliver moved back to his deck chair. "That was the first time either of us had laid eyes on him. He was a brawny man, tall and lean. His jaw line was pronounced and his arms were like cannons. He was an enviable man by anyone's standards, physically. Morally, he was rotten."

"Why did he tell Daryl to get on the other bus?"

"Because that's the kind of ass he was. He did things just to be a ballbuster. He wanted everyone to know he was in charge and he spent a lot of time proving it."

"How did you end up as roommates with Daryl?"

"That wasn't hard. Gaultier found someone else to mess with and Daryl and I worked it out with one of the NCOs when we arrived at the barracks."

"What can you tell me about Daryl, his life at Gitmo? Who did he hang out with? Did he date anyone?"

"Honestly, there isn't much to tell. He was an infantryman, which meant he spent twenty-four hours on duty at a time guarding the fence-line. I worked 7am to 6pm, and had most weekends off. When Daryl was off-duty, he usually slept, or wrote letters home to his girl. Once in a while, he and I would go to the pool, but he'd only stay in the shallow end, waist high."

"Did he ever tell you why he couldn't swim?"

"Actually, he could swim, but he only did it when he had to and when there were other people around. He mentioned something about being at a beach when he was nine, and he'd gotten caught in the undertow. He said that he got pulled under and the lifeguard never even saw him. It was his mom who saved his life. After that, he just hated the water. That's how I know he'd have never gone into the ocean alone."

"What was his relationship with Gaultier?"

"Sickening. Daryl actually looked up to that bane on humanity, but why I'll never know. He always went out of his way to please the gunny and the gunny seemed to take a special interest in him." Oliver stopped to think. "Wait, actually that's not true. In the beginning, Gaultier thought very little of Daryl and really had no use for him, but around Thanksgiving, he took Daryl under his wing and really showed him quite a lot of attention."

"Did you ever find out why?"

"Daryl told me the sergeant thought he had a lot of potential. Daryl tried so hard to live up to Gaultier's expectations. I found Gaultier's interest in Daryl suspect though, because Gaultier wasn't even in Daryl's company. Back then, maybe even now, platoons were tight and there was almost a rivalry between each of the companies. A platoon sergeant taking an interest in a private from another company seemed out of place to me. "

"Gaultier had a car. Do you remember what kind?"

"Wow, you're making me think. Let me see...if I'm not mistaken, it was a blue and white car. Yes! It was! I remember because a couple of the Marines used shaving cream to write something on his car and he made them clean it with a toothbrush, right outside my office window. Damn prick, couldn't even take a joke."

"Did he ever give Daryl a ride in his car?"

"Not that I can recall, but honestly I have no idea. Why?"

"Audrey and I found his car and Daryl's dog tags were in the trunk covered in what we think is blood."

"Are you sure?"

"I'm sure about the dog tags, but the blood is a guess. That's why I need you to help me piece all of this together. What occurred the last time you saw him?"

"He got up at 0500 and went to chow. After that, he made his way to the fence-line and never came home."

"Did anything unusual happen the night before?"

"No." Oliver stopped and played with his mustache again. "Gaultier was missing at company formation the morning Daryl disappeared."

"How do you know?"

"Because I was in admin and there was a hullabaloo in my office trying to track Gaultier down."

"Did they ever find him?"

"Yes. According his story, he'd gone out on a morning jog and had fallen while trying to scale the side of a hill. He had to walk back to Marine Hill on the injured leg. He banged himself up pretty good. He'd lost a good bit of blood."

"Audrey and I read about a number of Marines and sailors who'd been taken hostage in July of that year while out in town. Gaultier was one of them. Had you heard anything about that?"

"Did I! Every chance he could, Gaultier would tell the story of his capture and his heroic efforts to escape. He really thought well of himself for surviving the conflict."

"Was he ever in any real danger?"

"Who knows? What I can tell you is this: Gaultier lied about being on that run that day he got injured."

"How do you know?"

"Because there was this Marine—I've long since forgotten his name—who said Gaultier was at the Northeast Gate that morning. He said the Gunny took charge of a pair of Cubans Daryl had detained. He also saw them drive off together—Gaultier in a Jeep and the Cubans in a blue truck. About fifteen or so minutes later, he thought he saw Daryl get into the Jeep with Gaultier, but he wasn't positive."

"And no one mentioned this when Daryl disappeared?"

"Nope. I told you, we were private nobodies and Gaultier was a hero. That's all that mattered. The truth had no place."

"Why do you hate Gaultier so much? I mean, I know he was a dick and all, but you seem to have a lot of anger towards him."

"Adam, you have no idea. Gaultier was full of himself, and he got that way by deflating the esteem of others. I've tried long and hard to forget the humiliating things he did to people, and if you don't mind, I'd like to keep it that way. I always felt sorry for his wife, being married to such an awful man."

"She was there too?"

"No, she was back in the States. Poor thing, she was UHG-LEE." Oliver cracked a smile.

"How do you know?"

"He kept a photo of his family on his desk. None of us could understand what he saw in her. He was the kind of man you'd expect to have a trophy wife." Oliver got up and urinated off the side of the boat. When he was done, he shook off the last drop and turned back to Adam. "Sorry about that, but at my age, ya gotta go when ya gotta go."

"Oliver, I want you to know I respect your wish not to talk

about your own personal doings with Gaultier, but I do have a specific question."

"You can ask, but I sure as hell don't have to answer."

"I'll accept that. I want to know about the incident that Daniela told Lupe about. Lupe's husband had been a Cuban worker on base who disappeared one night, very close to the night Daryl went missing. Lupe's employer was a Marine by the name of Captain Haggar."

"Well, if that's not another name I hadn't heard in forever. Fine man, he was. What about the captain?"

"Captain Haggar told Lupe he'd uncovered something about her missing husband, but he had to check something out first before he could tell her what he knew. Before he could, he was killed."

"Yeah, in the minefield."

"Lupe asked Daniela to ask her boyfriend—-who was you—if you could find anything out. Daniela told Lupe someone had scared you off the scent. I need to know what you found out and who it was that threatened you."

The rosy color in Double O's cheeks turned pale, his breathing slower and deeper. "Adam, there's something you should know. Once, when I was complaining to Daryl about how I didn't make friends very easily, he said to me—and I can remember this as clear as day—-he told me that when I didn't have a friend, I should be a friend to someone who had nobody. Tonight, when you walked away from me on the street because I wouldn't answer your questions, Daryl's face came into my mind and I heard his voice: He said, 'be a friend.' There's no doubt in my mind Daryl's the one who brought us together tonight. He wants us to know what happened to him."

"Well, I'm not sure I believe in ghosts, especially a ghost in Guantanamo Bay."

"Oh, my friend, there's more than one ghost," Oliver chuckled softly, and then grew serious. When he spoke, his words were as elegant as a Harvard man, not what I'd expected of a salty sailor. "There are many ghosts there, I'm afraid. Each of us leaves a piece of ourselves when we're stationed there, and that makes up the unique character of the island. The spirit we feel when we're there and the feeling we take with us when we leave is derived from an incomparable history we share with those that came before us, and those who will come after. The ghosts of Guantanamo Bay aren't unearthly apparitions, but rather the things that consume you while you're there, and the things you'd like to hold on to long after you're gone. They're the memories we cherish and the nightmares we stare down. You'll see what I mean when it's your time to move on. You'll be a better man in many respects for the time you spent in Guantanamo Bay, and no matter where you go on your life, a small piece of you will remain there. There is a lot to learn about life, and, for some reason, many of us learn our lessons there."

"I'll take your word for it. But for now, I really want to know what Daniela was talking about."

"I went into Haggar's office to see if I could find any notes on what he'd discovered, but before I could find anything of any value, Gaultier entered the room. After he dressed me down for being in the deceased captain's office, he said that, off the record, from that moment on, my life was in his hands. He told me he was God and if I wanted to live, I'd better sing his praises."

"So what did you find?"

"An appointment. He was to meet with Gaultier the afternoon he was killed."

I talked to Oliver for many more hours, and he and I eventually ended up in his sparsely decorated galley, jotting down notes about certain time lines. We realized an unremitting pattern: Gaultier was present just moments before Miguel, Daryl and Haggar went missing or died. The why of it all was difficult to discern. It was late into the night, or early into the next morning, when I realized I'd not thought about Commander Cleary in hours. I headed back onto the dock, telling Oliver where I was off to. He took my phone number and told me he'd call me if he thought of anything else.

Although I had refused to give it any merit in his presence, I thought a lot about what Oliver had said about Daryl while I rode back to the BOQ. Could a Marine lance corporal, who went missing almost fifty years ago, really be guiding us? It seemed odd, but then again, most everything in my life at that time was.

I WANTED TO GO BACK to the hospital to see Cleary, but I needed to lie down for a little while. I'd not slept in about twenty-two hours. Audrey was also on my mind. With the C-12 in the Keys and damaged, not to mention the regular flight wouldn't come around for a few more days, I was sure Mrs. Cleary was in need of much support back in Gitmo. I was glad Audrey could be there for her.

When I checked into my room, which was a standard BOQ room with concrete block walls painted in a blue pastel, my first inclination was to phone the hospital. As I reached for the phone, I paused. I wanted to know the commander was going to be fine, but I was in no state to hear the news if he'd taken a turn for the worse.

28

"Adam? I've been trying to get a hold of you all night, but the BOQ attendant said you never checked in," Audrey whispered.

"Huh? Yeah, I only got here a short time ago," I said, rubbing my eyes and clearing my throat. "How are you doing? How's Cleary's wife?"

"She fell apart when we got the news."

I sat straight up in bed. "What news?"

"Commander Cleary... he's dead."

"Oh God, oh God...I knew it. I saw when the truck hit him. It was awful, Audrey, just horrible."

"What truck, Adam? What are you talking about?"

"What do you mean what am I talking about? The truck...the fuel truck...the one that hit Cleary on the tarmac," I said, growing frustrated.

"I'm confused, Adam. I don't know what you're talking about. We didn't hear anything about a truck."

"The truck on the runway. The storm—he couldn't see. It was raining and dark, and then he just stepped in front of it."

"I don't know what you're talking about. You must be

exhausted. I have to go but I wanted you to know they found him. He's under arrest for what he did to the commander and to the others."

"Audrey, who's under arrest?"

"Gunnery Sergeant Gaultier, of course! He admitted everything. He's the one that killed Commander Cleary and he admits he killed Miguel and Daryl Loring. He said it's a good thing he got caught because he was going to kill you next."

"How is that possible? I saw the truck hit Cleary! Gaultier had nothing to do with it! Don't you get it? He had nothing to do with it! Audrey! Are you still there? Audrey!"

And then I woke up, sweating profusely and out of breath. I'd torn my blankets off the bed and pushed the items from the night table to the floor. I went straight into the shower, leaning my head against the cool tile wall. I felt like I was falling apart. I turned the water off after a few minutes and put my flight suit back on. My tee-shirt and tropical shorts were sopped with perspiration. Before I left the room, I tried calling Audrey at home, but she didn't answer. I was disappointed, but I knew I'd be able to call her in a couple of hours at the Cleary's. By then, I'd know his condition.

At the hospital, I was ushered to his room where I found the commander sitting up and resting comfortably. He still looked weak and badly beat-up, but I knew he'd be okay. There were tubes sticking out of him no matter where you looked, and monitors beeping up a storm, but he smiled when I walked through the door. It was all I could've asked for under the circumstances.

"So you decided to hang around for a while longer, sir?" I asked. "I thought you'd bought a one way ticket outta here."

"You and me both. Hey, Adam, you know what really sucks? I mean, really sucks?"

"What?"

"Getting run over by a truck."

"I'll take your word for it. So what's the good news? When can you fly us home?"

"I'm afraid you're on your own for a while. It appears I'm going to take the long way home, via Bethesda Naval Hospital. They haven't been so blunt, but I think my body's pretty messed up. I need to see a few specialists up there. They're keeping me here just so I can remain stable for a few days. They don't want the internal bleeding to start up again."

"Well, you and the C-12 might be ready about the same time. She took quite a hit last night."

"Have you assessed the damage?"

"No, but the mechanics are giving her a going-over now. I can't imagine her back in the air before a few weeks."

"Well, Gitmo can't go without a pilot or plane there that long. I assume Pickard is making arrangements for a replacement from JAX or Norfolk."

"Yeah, I have to call him in a little while. Speaking of which, have you talked to your wife?"

"Yes. She seems much calmer now that she's heard my voice."

"Glad to hear it. I guess I should probably call Pickard now and get my orders."

I walked down the corridor and asked to use the phone in the small office I'd been in the night before. While I wanted to stay with Cleary until his wife arrived, Pickard wouldn't have it. He ordered me to get on a commercial airplane to Norfolk to pick up the new bird. A temporary pilot was going to accompany me back to Gitmo, which was expected. What was completely unexpected was who I'd be ferrying back to Guantanamo. If someone had asked me this as a what-if question, I would've thought it too far fetched.

So there I was, introducing myself to Marine Colonel Bill Minter and Lt Colonel Sandra Brogan, the appointed investigators of the Guantanamo Bay Marine Wives Association Scandal. Also on board accompanying the two investigators, was a Navy chaplain, Commander Edwin Anders. All I could glean was that the chaplain had been requested by Colonel Ranagan himself. But why? I had absolutely no idea, especially since Anders was protestant and the Ranagans were obstinate Catholics. I couldn't even begin to imagine what Ranagan had up his sleeve.

I greeted the passengers cordially, but didn't introduce myself. I'm sure one or more of them might have glanced at my name-patch, but I wasn't going to go out of my way to let them know who I was. Part of my discomfort was in knowing those senior officers were on their way to Gitmo because of my wife, and the other part of me didn't want them to ask me any questions about Ranagan while in flight. I knew I'd eventually have to sit down and answer their prying inquiries, but I refused to do it while I was flying. Occasionally, I'd turn my head to view the passengers since we hadn't closed the door to the cockpit, and I was struck by two things. Colonel Minter, a dark green Marine—or black—had an exceedingly pensive look on his face the entire flight. He was totally uptight. I wasn't sure if he was thinking about the case at hand, or of he was merely scared of flying. The other thing that struck me is how much the chaplain looked like the actor Jack Lemmon—I mean, a real dead-ringer. Lt Colonel Brogan slept the whole way. With her glasses lying crooked on her face and her mouth hanging open, she was nothing to really write home about. She was a medium-build, plain-Jane—totally average. Colonel Minter, on the other hand, was tall and lean, and much more cerebral-looking.

We arrived in Guantanamo just after 5pm, and Colonel Ranagan was standing just outside the hangar waiting to greet the investigators. It was uncharacteristic for him to be there, but then again, he wanted the team to have a positive first impression of him and the base; I couldn't blame him. Curiously, the two interrogators greeted Ranagan with genuine affection, and not just professional courtesy. It made me recall a conversation Audrey had with Lt Colonel Brogan just after the letters were received by General Crane. Audrey had asked her point blank, "How do I know the investigators you'll be sending won't be friends of Colonel Ranagan? How do I know they'll be completely impartial?" Brogan answered, "You'll just have to take my word for it." I pondered those words while I sat in the cockpit—the situation on the airfield was a little too awkward. As a matter of fact, I decided to call the White House for a Fast Boat so I didn't have to see them aboard the ferry. As I walked into the hangar to make my call, I saw an incredibly familiar sight out of the corner of my eye: my Audrey.

After a long embrace, we got in the car and drove to Leeward Point, which looked out across the bay towards Windward and Glass Beach. We walked hand and hand, approaching the shoreline.

"Guess why Glass Beach got its name," I instructed Audrey.

"I don't know. Is it because of all the pretty glass that washes up there?" Audrey said, shrugging.

"Yes, but do you know how the glass got there?"

"Nope. But I bet you know."

"Many, many years ago, there used to be a bar up on that cliff—above the sand and ocean. After the sailors and Marines had a few too many, they would walk outside and throw their bottles off the cliff, watching as the glass broke into a thousand pieces when it hit the rocks."

"How do you know that?" Audrey asked skeptically.

"A friend told me."

"What friend?"

"A guy by the name of Oliver Orcher."

"But how? Where? Did you ask him everything?" Audrey was visibly energized. "What did you learn?"

"I learned that Elliott Gaultier was as big of a son of a bitch as we thought." I sat down on the sand, prepared to tell Audrey everything I'd learned from Oliver, when I noticed a shift in the wind's direction. Within seconds, the breeze went from gentle and pleasant to stinging and bothersome. The skies darkened and the surf turned gray as it began to swell. I could see the ferry at its midpoint in the bay, fighting with the current as the clouds unleashed an eruption of chilly rainwater. Audrey's hair began to fly all over and impede her line of sight. The skirt she was wearing made great attempts to reveal her with every gust, so we made a dash for the car. Blowing sand had gotten into my eyes just as I reached out to close the door, and Audrey's sunglasses flew right off her face. Running after them, she tripped on something buried just under the surface of the sand. Not knowing how hurt she was, I cleared the sand from my eyes and went to help her. I tried talking to her, but the wind was howling so intensely, it made all other sounds inaudible. Instead of wasting any time on indistinct conversation, I picked her up and carried her to the car.

"That wind is unreal. Are you okay?" I asked her.

"Yeah. I think I just twisted my ankle or something. No big deal."

"Where on earth did that come from?" I asked as I looked up at the sky.

"Maybe it's the first bands of the hurricane. I think that storm is only a day or two away."

"Hurricane? It couldn't be. It's January!"

"Well, then it's just a regular old storm."

"I'd better check in. I might be needed."

Audrey and I drove to the Leeward rifle company's office, where I found Aidan Foster. He briefed me on the weather, calling the current storm a spontaneous squall. However, he did confirm there was an anomalous storm headed toward our island and was expected sometime that week. He also briefed me that I was to be the acting operations officer, as of the following morning, since Major McCarran was going to be leaving on TAD, or temporary assigned duty.

"Where's he off to?" I asked, baffled. I'd not been aware of the major needing to be anywhere but Gitmo.

"Ranagan told him to mail the Defense Action Plan off to SOUTHCOM, but McCarran thought it was too important to send. He asked to hand deliver it."

I stood there trying to maintain my calm. The Defense Action Plan was the document I'd found lying on his desk—for the entire world to see—the night I stood duty. It was the same plan he'd deemed ridiculous and worthless, even though it was the literal diagram of our defense of Guantanamo Bay. I couldn't even begin to understand why he'd want to hand deliver it. Then I remembered. On the day I'd helped him scan photos, McCarran was e-mailing cheesecake shots of himself to the account: MIAbeachbunE. It wasn't a stretch of the imagination to see what was going on. McCarran was an adulterous letch and the hard part was I'd really liked him. I wondered how many other women he had, and if any were on the island. Lt. Humphries came to mind. It was true that he and Hump-a-lot had worked-out together at a previous duty station, and they both seemed to have very lax morals. I had no proof, but I did consider that maybe, in between trysts with Chet, Humphries was getting it on with McCarran. It wasn't an unlikely scenario, especially considering where we were.

The weather deteriorated even more, so Audrey and I decided to get a BOQ room on Leeward instead of fighting the waves across the bay. Just as we were walking out of Aidan's office, Kelly passed us in the hallway and jumped into Aidan's arms! We had thought Chet and Aidan being friends after the blowout over Kelly was bad enough, but seeing Aidan and her together again was just too bizarre. I kept repeating that phrase over and over again: Gitmo...a strange little place. Whoever thought that up knew what they were talking about.

Our Q room was just as any other we had ever been in: cinder-block walls, all purpose carpeting, and lots and lots of functional furniture. The bed was surprisingly comfortable, and the awful weather allowed Audrey to relax her weirdo hotel room standards; she had nowhere to go. As long as I promptly placed the bedspread on the floor, and washed my hands, we were good to go.

Audrey's ankle was still bothering her, so I offered to rub it until it felt better. I went into the bathroom and took one of the little complimentary lotions. I opened the cap and attempted to pour some in my hand, but I was having some difficulty in getting the lotion to leave the container. After a moment or two, Audrey lost patience with me and grabbed the bottle. She pounded furiously on the bottom of the bottle until an explosion of lotion flew all over the place! There was creamy, white moisturizer on the floor, the ceiling, the headboard, the covers, and even the television set. She looked at me with an innocent Oopps! stare.

"My dear Audrey, do you realize you've just made me the king of Gitmo?" I said smugly.

"How's that?"

"Because the housekeeper's going to think this is all my work." I lay on the pillow, with my arms folded behind my head, sighing. "They'll be talking about me for generations to come. Even the Cuban army will hear of this."

"Adam, dear, you may get off on the fact that other men will think you detonated like a popcorn kernel in hot oil, but have no fear, by the time I get through cleaning this place, they'll think you were in here with a nun."

"A man can dream," I said wistfully.

I spent most of the evening with Audrey going over the conversation I had with Oliver. She was surprised Oliver always had his suspicions about Daryl's fate, and happy to know we finally had someone taking us seriously. However, my wife was most interested in my theory that the drawing on the underside of the desk was a route Gaultier had planned to follow, although the reason for the route was still unknown. Gaultier apparently needed to go from the Northeast Gate to what appeared to be the Magazine area. The marks along the way were not immediately apparent at first, but, by air, I could see that each place on the drawing was a location where a checkpoint of some sort existed. The only mark that wasn't a checkpoint was Marine Hill. Obviously, he was trying to avoid being stopped or seen by other Marines. We still had no idea who R. Mercado was, what the series of numbers meant, or the significance of the seemingly random letters that had been written beside the drawing. Audrey and I eventually took a piece of paper and began to scribble down a timetable of sorts.

"Okay," my wife began, "if I understand this right, Gaultier arrived in Gitmo in 1956. Except for winning a diving competition, he did nothing that really draws attention to himself. That all changed in July of 1958, when he went out in town—back in the day when anyone could leave the base—and became one of the twenty-three random Marines and sailors captured by Castro's thugs. He was held prisoner for nearly a month and was released to return to duty. About a month and a half later, Oliver Orcher and Daryl Loring arrived in Gitmo. Almost immediately, Gaultier started in on Daryl, making life difficult for him."

"Yeah, but about a month before his disappearance, Gaultier more or less befriended Loring and paid him an over abundance of attention. Also, Oliver told me all of the hostages were sent home to the States after their ordeal, but Gaultier requested to stay. I find that strange, especially since he had a family back home. Why would any man want to stay in that isolated place after such a harrowing ordeal? I know I'd want to be back Stateside."

"Excellent question and one I can't answer," Audrey said, frowning. "But moving on, at some point he took the top of his desk off and drew a map or plan of some kind, along with a name, numbers and letters that seem to have no meaning. He was careful to be mindful of checkpoints, clearly his plan required secrecy."

"Evidently. But I want to know why he needed to use the bottom of his desk and why he didn't just use paper like a normal person?"

"He was probably paranoid. Whatever he had up his sleeve was going to be damaging and he didn't want to leave a paper trail."

"But writing on a permanent piece of furniture? That seems a little ridiculous." Audrey stopped speaking, deep in thought.

"But maybe not as much as we think. Adam, what happens to furniture the military no longer needs?"

"They send it to DRMO. That's where you bought it in the first place."

"Yeah, but what if it's damaged, then what happens?"

"I imagine they destroy it somehow or haul it to a dump. Why?"

"Maybe it was slated to go to DRMO, and he had plans to buy it, that way, when he moved, it would go with him."

"That's a possibility, but probably not likely."

"Well, then, maybe he planned to paint over it when he accomplished his goal—I don't know."

"The only thing I can imagine is that he was paranoid, mentally messed up from the capture, arrogant, and, therefore, probably not thinking right. I doubt we could ever get inside his head."

"You're right about that. But my next question is: What do Abuelita's husband, Captain Haggar—her ex boss—and Daryl have in common?"

"We know Miguel had to come through the Northeast Gate each morning, and we know Daryl stood guard there, so there's a connection there."

"And Captain Haggar?" Audrey asked.

"Oliver said Haggar was supposed to meet Gaultier the afternoon he was killed. Whether or not that meeting ever took place, we don't know."

"Yeah, and we know Haggar had stumbled upon something relating to Miguel's death, so he's tied in by way of that information alone."

"So it seems," I replied, rubbing my tired eyes.

"But what could he have found out?"

"Isn't that the million-dollar question? If you ask me, Haggar must have found out Gaultier was the last person to see Miguel alive. That's all that would make sense. Think about it: if Haggar knew Gaultier had killed Miguel, he wouldn't have met with him, he'd have called the MPs. No, Haggar had a suspicion with nothing to back it up—that's why he wanted to meet with him first."

"But in the minefield? Isn't that totally bizarre?"

"Yeah, I agree. We may be way off here."

"Unless, there was something in the minefield that had to do with Miguel's death."

"Do you mean a body?"

"A body or papers or something—maybe the thing that was worth killing Miguel for!"

"You may be on to something. We should talk to Ryan Hill and see which field Haggar was killed in. Maybe they uncovered something when they cleared it that would be the missing link for us."

"Ok, but what about Daryl? How does he fit into all this?"

"He must have come across the plan or been a witness or something."

"I feel like we're really close now."

"Me too. Our next step should be to find out where Miguel was supposed to go that day, talk to Ryan about the minefields, and try and decipher the letters and numbers on the bottom of the desk. I'll start by doing an internet search engine for R. Mercado."

It hit me. In all my enthusiasm to tell Audrey about Oliver, I'd forgotten about the Wives' Association investigators. When I told her they were on the island, all she said was, "Bring it on."

29

I f looks could kill, I'd be dead. Walking into the White House the next morning was painful. Enlisted Marines who looked up to Ranagan were incensed by the inquisition. Every one of them knew my wife had led the movement that ended up as the investigation, and while they didn't say it, I knew they couldn't believe I'd allowed my wife to write that letter to Crane. I refused to let that all get to me. The Marines who passed judgment on me and on Audrey without knowing the facts were the ones with the problem, not me. Of course I did feel badly that each shop had to spend hours rummaging through their file cabinets so each service member's jacket could be scrutinized. Those enlisted men had enough work to do on a normal day. But, as it was explained to me, the investigators wanted to see for themselves if any notations had been made in anyone's folder with reference to the wives. Also, they were looking to see if anyone lost a promotion based on Ranagan's opinion of his wife. After a while, even the single officers like Chet, Aidan and Guy looked irritated.

In the meantime, abandoned housing on another part of the base was turned into office spaces for the team. Flintstone furniture was moved in and antiquated air conditioning units were repaired. Ranagan made sure his best foot was forward and left nothing to be desired by the investigators. During the day, Lt Colonel Brogan handed out appointment slips to each of the officers, married and single. Each Marine was required to visit the new offices and give a written deposition. When I got home, I found out my wife would be the very first to be interviewed by Brogan the following morning. She wasn't nervous, or anxious; she was completely confident in her original decision, and, while mildly overwhelmed, she knew the facts would eventually speak for themselves. The Ranagans had misused their authority and they needed to allow the Marine families to live their lives in peace.

Audrey arrived at the investigator's workplace five minutes early and found no one in sight. Promptly at eight, Lt Colonel Brogan and Colonel Minter drove up to the old house. They were courteous to Audrey and Minter engaged her in polite conversation while Brogan set up her desk for the interview. However, just moments before Audrey was invited into Brogan's office, Minter said something that set off an alarm in Audrey's mind.

"So how do you like it here in Gitmo?" Audrey asked Colonel Minter, the lead investigator.

"Oh, I love it here. I was so happy to hear I could come back again," Minter replied cheerfully.

"You were stationed here before?" Audrey asked inquisitively.

"No, I was never stationed here. I came down last summer for temporary duty, which is when I first met Colonel Ranagan. What a view he has from his back veranda, huh?"

Audrey's stomach dropped to the floor. The lead investigator had been an acquaintance of the Ranagans, just what we we'd hoped to avoid. Audrey had specifically asked Brogan if any of Ranagan's friends would be doing the investigating and Brogan had assured her that wouldn't be the case.

Audrey had no idea what to think. She walked into Brogan's office and answered each of her questions as truthfully and completely as she could. After Audrey finished speaking, Brogan sent another blow her way.

"Look, we see this kind of thing anywhere there's an isolated base—Iceland, Okinawa, Guam, Diego Garcia—it happens. You get a few colonels who have no one to answer to and this ensues. They go a little crazy. I can assure you this is very common in the military."

"Does that make it right?" Audrey shot back. "Does that make the way they treat us acceptable? Because of the isolation?"

"No, of course not. I'm just saying we need to be reasonable here. These people put in a lot of years, they take a lot of shit along the way and look forward to the day when they're on top to dish some shit back out, that's all. It's harmless, all in all."

Audrey couldn't believe what she was hearing. "Then why are you here? Why did you come if that's what you'll write in your report?"

"We're here to investigate and disprove or substantiate your claims."

"And then what?" Audrey asked evenly.

"Then we will give our report to General Crane and he'll decide what to do from there."

"But it sounds like you've already made up your mind," my wife acknowledged.

"No," Brogan said coolly, "I'm just telling you your complaint is not new to the military, that's all. We're not surprised. Of course when I worked for Ranagan about ten years ago, he wasn't the man you seem to describe, but I guess people can change."

Audrey couldn't move when she heard Lt Colonel Brogan say she'd worked for Ranagan, and obviously had a very different opinion of him. This was the same woman who had given her word to Audrey about sending an impartial team to investigate the colonel. Her confidence had been betrayed.

"Now, if you can give me the names of the other wives who wrote letters—"

"Pardon me, what did you say?" Audrey was distracted by Brogan's earlier words.

"The other wives. You were the only one to sign your letter. We would like to interview the other wives, but we don't know which ones wrote them."

"There are others," Audrey said, trying to come to grips with the reality of the situation. "There are other wives who didn't write letters who would also like you to know their stories." She took a piece of paper and wrote the names of all the women she could think of who could add value to the inquiry. She handed it to her and thanked the Lt Colonel.

When Audrey opened the office door, Chet Dingle was sitting in the makeshift waiting area. He looked rather anxious, rubbing his hands intently. As she exited the old house, Audrey nodded in Chet's direction, and he returned the nod.

The drive back home was difficult for Audrey. Her mind would race and then her thoughts would just stop all together. The uneasiness she'd once felt on a daily basis, which had subsided once she'd written the letter to Crane, had returned. Audrey didn't feel at ease with the investigators. That sense was heightened when she met with the ladies later that afternoon in the park.

"How long did she talk to you?" Arlene Hill asked Maura.

"About twenty-five minutes, what about you?"

"The same, I guess. How did she treat you?"

"Cordially, but not overly friendly," Maura responded. "How about you, Regina?"

"The same, but she did tell me she was surprised I wrote a letter. It seems Lois had told her exactly who had written the letters, but my name wasn't one of them. Brogan said Lois considered me a friend."

"I had the opposite happen to me," Drew cut in. "Brogan told me Lois was sure I'd written one, and of course I didn't."

"But what do you guys think? Is this doing any good?" Arlene asked the crowd.

"To be honest," Regina answered. "I'm not sure. My gut feeling is no. I think they're just going through the motions. I never got the sense that they were on our side."

"Ladies," Drew said exasperatedly, "I hate to agree, but I do. I think this is a horse and pony show and nothing will change."

"Great!" Maura exclaimed. "We make fools of ourselves on base, jeopardize the careers of our husbands and we still have to live behind The Ranagan Wall!"

As the women sat there feeling deflated and discouraged, a Navy exchange rental car pulled up alongside the park, and an older man got out of his car, walking directly to the ladies. He looked just like Jack Lemmon. When he was close enough, Audrey could see a cross on his collar and realized the man was the mysterious chaplain Ranagan had requested.

"Well good afternoon! Lovely day, isn't it?"

The women were suspicious, but managed to mutter, "Hello."

"My name is Commander Anders. As I understand it, you ladies have had quite a time here lately, huh?"

"You could say that," Arlene said lightheartedly.

The chaplain looked off across the bay and spoke in a gentle tone. "You know, people are just people and sometimes they make mistakes. We all can understand that, because God understands that. But sometimes, people are just mean, or abusive. Sometimes people use other people to make themselves feel better and that's not right." All the ladies began to tune into the chaplain's words. "What I think we have here is a situation that is shameful, especially since it could have been avoided. I blame myself because I'm the one who assigned the chaplains here. They were completely inexperienced in handling concerns like yours, and, for that, I'm sorry. Places like this have a way of bringing out the other side of us—the side we're not proud of. I think maybe the people at the end of this street," he said, motioning to the Ranagan's home, "just forgot who they were. Had there been better suited chaplains, then I think we could've handled this a long time ago. It's not right what you ladies have had to go through."

"Amen to that!" Drew said.

"All you want to do is raise your families and support your husbands, not have to live under a dictatorship," The chaplain continued. "This should never have happened."

For the first time in a long time, the ladies felt like they had someone who understood their plight. The chaplain offered them comfort and support, right when they needed it the most. "I have to go now and visit with Mrs. Ranagan, but I wanted to stop by and tell you I'm thinking about making some changes—maybe sending another chaplain here who will answer directly to me. I want you ladies to feel good again, to feel like you can live your lives freely and peacefully. Would you support a new chaplain?"

"That would be great," Maura replied. "Change would be welcome."

"Well, alright then. I'd better go. I want to hurry because after I meet with Mrs. Ranagan, I have a fishing boat to catch!" The chaplain chuckled like a happy grandfather. "I'm with you and God is with you and we will make this all better, I promise." They all said goodbye to him as he walked away from the picnic shelter. Before getting inside his car, he turned back and shouted,

"What a great little place for all you ladies to fellowship, right here in the middle of your neighborhood! It's wonderful you have each other and this place to spend time together!"

Audrey watched him drive away. "God sent him, I just know it. He's here to restore our faith and to remind us of all that is good and right."

"I feel it too," Arlene said. "He made me feel warm inside."

"I sure needed that today," Drew chimed in. It was unanimous. While the ladies had no idea why Ranagan had requested him, Chaplin Anders was their ally and would help to make life better for them in the coming days. For the rest of that day and night, Audrey and all of the other wives felt as though someone had heard them and actually cared. Knowing that, Drew Ray's call the next day overwhelmed my wife to the point of tears.

"Audrey, we need to talk," Drew said, obviously troubled. "The chaplain—the one we talked to yesterday—I know why he's here. Father Blankenship and Pastor Dooley told Ranagan they wanted to support him through the inquiry and....and...they wanted to help by disclosing information about all of us that they'd acquired while in confession and in pastoral counseling. They wanted to discredit our characters. Since they can't disclose that information to Ranagan himself, they had Ranagan request another chaplain so that they could disclose it to him. The new chaplain can then write his own report and submit it to the investigators."

Audrey remained silent. One hand covered her mouth, the other held the receiver. She shook her head in disbelief.

"And that's not all," Drew continued. "Last night, the chaplain went fishing with Gordie Shaw and the chaplain told Gordie, 'They need to burn down that gazebo where those women congregate!'"

"How do you know? He specifically told us that he liked how we meet there and supported each other."

"I know. I was there too. My husband told me everything. I shouldn't be telling you any of this, but I know how much you trusted the new chaplain and now we know we can't. All we have is each other."

Audrey hung up the phone and went outside for some fresh air, sitting in the shade of a large tree in our front yard. She wasn't there long before Nelson Moser, the enlisted odd-ball neighbor from across the street, marched up authoritatively.

"Have you been saying things about me? Have you been trying to get me in trouble?" Nelson barked.

"I've no idea what you're talking about."

"Yeah? Well, I fuckin' happen to know you asked someone why I get home so early! That's none of your fuckin' business!"

Nelson was making no sense to her. Then it clicked. "All I said to Arlene, and it was completely innocent, was a general 'I wish my husband had Nelson's job because I like his hours better.'"

"You're just a fuckin' nosey bitch, that's what you are! And you want to know something else? Everyone on this base thinks you're a shit stirrer—did you know that? You're going to ruin your husband's career!" His finger was pointed in Audrey's face.

All Audrey could think to say was, "Well, I don't think we will be staying in the Marine Corps much longer anyway!"

"That! That makes me happy! The Corps will be better for it!" Nelson shouted at the top of his lungs.

"Can I quote you on that?"

It was at that moment Nelson Moser realized the severity of his words. What he said was disrespectful and a border-line offence.

WHEN I GOT HOME, my wife relayed the conversation to me and I practically flew to his front door. I knocked with force and the door was answered by his extremely overweight and homely wife, Phyllis.

She didn't allow me to say one word before she began to bellow at me. "So I see you're here to pull the officer card, huh? You think you're the shit, don't you? Just because you have those officer bars, don't you?"

"I want to speak to your husband," I said calmly.

"Why? So you can be some tough shit? Well, the answer is no! I won't let you say one damn word to my husband, so screw you!" Phyllis screeched.

"Phyllis, I can talk to your husband calmly outside, as neighbors, or we can talk tomorrow morning in my office."

When I finished speaking, I saw Nelson standing behind his wife, although her enormous size and his scrawny physique almost obstructed my view of him. "I'll handle this, honey," Nelson said tranquilly.

"Don't you let him give you any crap, Nelson!" she hollered as she walked back into her kitchen.

Nelson Moser and I had a straightforward talk, and let's just say I never again heard a word from him—or his hideous wife—until the day they moved from Guantanamo Bay. It had been Colonel Ranagan's idea to have enlisted Marines live with the officers. All it did was foster bad feelings and make the enlisted Marines bitter toward the officers and their families. It also made it hard for all of us to relax once we got home. They had to call us "sir" and we had to mind our Ps and Qs in their presence. No one was ever able to fully unwind and be themselves.

After that altercation, I began to understand what Oliver told me in Key West about learning life's lessons. That experience made Audrey and I look at each instance of controversy with new eyes. Instead of looking for what was bad in everything, we looked for what we could learn from it. We knew to be careful about what we said in the presence of others; even an innocent comment can be misconstrued. And we went to great lengths to get along with those we live around.

I walked back across the street to our house after confronting Nelson, but didn't even make it to my front door before my beeper went off. Punching the numbers into the key pad, I realized I never wanted to be that connected to my job again. However, it ended up being an important call: Our modest base was under weather condition I, which meant an exceedingly violent storm was imminent. The change in the weather pattern meant considerable planning for the Marines, and as acting OPS O, an especially sizeable amount of work for me.

30

The investigators had arrived on a Monday, and took the normal Friday flight back to Norfolk. Both Colonel Minter and Lt Colonel Brogan kept their poker faces the entire time, so none of us had any idea what their findings were. We all figured it would be a month or so before the report was submitted to General Crane. In the meantime, the storm continued to head in our direction and it was up to me to make sure the Marine families were evacuated to safer accommodations. The sheer age of Marine housing, coupled with non-hurricane-strength construction to begin with, meant Audrey and all the other wives and children had to ride out the storm in the gymnasium of the high school.

By 7pm Friday night, all the officers and senior enlisted Marines had assembled at the White House, per Ranagan's request. We were formally debriefed on the weather situation by the chief meteorologist on base. He explained that everyone at the local weather center, and at the National Weather center back in the States, was absolutely perplexed by the projected conditions. Hurricane season runs from June to November. Storms that replicate hurricanes, but occur in months outside of the normal season, are called Nor'easters. Since we weren't in hurricane season and we weren't living in the Northeast, what we'd be experiencing in the next twenty-four hours was somewhat baffling to every weather guesser in the business. A storm such as we were anticipating was, essentially, downright strange.

At the conclusion of the update, I was instructed to ensure that each Marine family member was re-accommodated and accounted for by midnight that night. Once I'd finished with that task, I was to report to Leeward and stand duty as a search and rescue pilot in the event of any calamitous incident. With the winds being forecasted between eighty and ninety mph, I knew I'd never be able to fly that old bird very far or very precisely. I wasn't sure how much use I'd be over there on the other side of base.

Needless to say, none of the wives seemed very happy about being separated from their husbands, but herding them into the gym for two days was the easy part. Informing them they would be shut inside the gymnasium with Lois for that period of time was excruciating. Honestly, Lois is the one I felt sorry for. Even though she brought much of the commotion upon herself, being essentially locked up with one's enemies couldn't have been easy for her. Besides that, all the ladies had each other and she was alone.

Audrey was beside herself when I went to kiss her goodbye. It was about 9:30pm and I needed to check in with the White House before I left for the airfield, but she wouldn't let go of me. She was nervous about me flying in the storm, and, she had no idea how she'd survive "civil internment" with Lois. I took a few minutes to talk her through some of her concerns. I reminded Audrey that once Ranagan had gotten notice from HQ about the letters, Ranagan and his wife backed way off of us. We never knew why it happened, but we assumed Ranagan had gotten a call telling him, until the charge was investigated, he and his wife needed to maintain a low profile around the wives, which is just what they did. For a period of several weeks, Lois and the colonel out and out ignored the wives. There were no phony airs, no intimidating calls, no plastic greetings out in town, and, most importantly, no mention of the wives in the White House. I convinced Audrey that with the investigation still in an active state, Lois wouldn't do anything to make her husband look bad.

My wife agreed and began to relax. Before I left she made a quick comment. "We never needed for her to like us, we just wanted her to leave us alone and for her husband to let you guys do your jobs. I know the letters caused a lot of grief for you and the other husbands, but look, we got what we wanted. We got our lives back. I don't care what the investigators come up with; the Ranagans are already giving us that."

With that, I hugged her goodbye and wished her luck. Inside, I was totally convinced Lois would forget about the investigation and sink her teeth into the ladies when I left.

It was 10pm when I left the high school and hopped into my Gremlin. I pushed in the eight-track that came with it and began jamming to Earth, Wind and Fire. It's not usually the kind of music I listen to, but the one and only English radio station was relaying weather information exclusively, and Spanish music never quite did it for me. As I drove, the dark evening and blowing palms trees reminded me of that horrible night with Cleary. I rubbed my eyes, as if to wipe away the memory, but it was still there when my eyes focused on the winding road. The rain had not yet begun, but the potent breeze was picking up strength by the minute, turning into an unremitting succession of impressive gusts. Conversely, the bay looked calm. There were some breakers, but it was eerily still compared to what was headed our way. I boarded the last ferry of the night and climbed up to the bridge since I was one of its only passengers.

"Good evening," I called out as I opened the bridge door. "I heard you like company up here."

"Yup, come on in. Make yourself comfortable," the ferry boat captain replied.

I stepped inside what was essentially a small cockpit. It had windows on all sides and its dimensions were roughly twelve by six. To my left and to my right were consoles enabling the captain to drive the ship. When he pulled the craft up to the dock, he didn't turn the ship around, but just moved to the controls on the opposite side of the deck to begin the trek across the bay. In front of each console were large, grayish-blue vinyl chairs, positioned high enough to allow the driver visual access across the bow of the ferry.

The captain was a scruffy older man in his late fifties. He was of medium height and build, but very thin, with a face older than its years. His gray hair, while short in the back, was growing longer around his ears. He was dressed in jeans and a T-shirt, with a package of cigarettes in his left pocket.

I closed the door behind me and maneuvered up next to the captain. "Wow, what a view you have from up here!"

"Yeah, and I never grow tired of it neither."

"I bet. So how long have you been doing this?"

"Well, I started in the Navy back in 1962, but I've been running this particular boat for nine years now." Once the ferry had left its berth, the man reached over with one hand and pulled out his cigarettes. "Care to join me?"

"No, thanks, but please feel free."

"Damn right I'm gonna feel free, after all, this is my boat!" he said, with a slight smile. "So who are you?"

"I'm Adam Claiborne, the Marine air officer."

"I'm Vern Lambert, but everyone calls me Lam. How long ya been here?"

"Oh let me see, going on seven months now."

"You like it here?"

"Yeah. Of course it's got its ups and downs, but for the most part, my wife and I are happy. We have a lot of time with each other and that's always nice. What about you, do you like to here?"

"Are you kidding me? This is a salty dog's paradise. God invented places like this for people like me. I never want to leave."

"But after nine years, doesn't this place begin to lose its charm?"

He laughed. "More than you could know. But it's kinda like being married. Some days you love your wife, some days you want to shove an old sock in her mouth, but you never leave her, do you? Same goes for Gitmo. It's an odd love affair, I'll agree, but I'm sticking with her."

"Have you ever been married?"

"Yes, sir—still am."

"Does she like it here too?"

He was quiet for a moment. "As long as I'm here, I think she must be too." He nodded his head vigorously.

"Do you dive?"

"I live in Gitmo, don't I?"

"Ever find anything exciting?"

"There's a couple of sunken jets that crashed off the runway a number of years ago. They're kinda neat to look at. Other than that, I just enjoy the peacefulness of the underwater world."

"I'd love to dive off of Cuzco Wells, wouldn't you?"

"Who wouldn't?" Lam took a long drag of his cigarette before continuing. "After such an amazing battle, that place must be crawling with artifacts, but good luck. Nobody's ever been able to dive there and nobody ever will."

"So I heard. Not only is it historically significant, but it's proximity to the munitions stored at the Magazine area makes it dangerous too."

"You got that right. So, Adam, what brings you out on such a creepy night?"

"Colonel Ranagan wants me to stay at Leeward in case we need SAR."

"I see. Well, good luck to you. After I drop you off, me and this baby are heading for the Windward dock and I plan to ride the storm out in my office. I want to be there if she begins to come loose. Lord knows how bad this storm's going to be."

"Pretty odd, isn't it Lam? What do you think of this weather?"

"Mother nature's a woman. That's all you need to know."

I felt a slight jolt as the ferry pulled into its Leeward docking space. I turned to Lam and said goodbye; he pulled out another cigarette.

"Take care Adam," Lam said in a cheerless, unhurried voice. "It was nice meeting you. Hope you'll visit me again. I get mighty lonesome sometimes."

When I disembarked the ferry, I walked toward an awaiting HumVee, but took a second to look back at the ship, up to where Lam was. I wondered what was underneath his smooth surface. He came off as a simple old sailor, but my gut told me there was far more to learn about him. I've always believed that each of us walks around with an incredible story to tell; reaching deep to find that story is what's so difficult. Lam's face was like a map to that place; each wrinkle a road, each sunspot an X. His eyes spoke volumes and I knew there was something I could learn from him, but what, I had no idea.

A few minutes after Audrey entered the gymnasium, the queen bee stood up on a chair, clapped her hands zealously, and mandated 10pm lights out for everyone. The Wives Association gang reacted predictably; they shrugged their shoulders, shook their heads, gave her a few cold stares, and insulted her under their breath. Lois went on to assign bunks, and Audrey was placed next to Phyllis Moser, of all people. Lois thought everyone needed to sleep in "house" order.

At 2am, the winds began to wail and strengthen substantially, and the rain began to pummel the roof of the high school. The doors to the outside rattled with each explosive gust, and without a warning, a set of doors flew open and the entire gymnasium was illuminated by lightning. The thunder of the storm ricocheted against the concrete walls and shot straight into everyone's eardrums. Audrey raced towards the doors and attempted to pull them closed. Loose papers and other debris flew wildly in her face. With the door handle in her grasp and all her weight pressing down to close it, she called out for assistance, but she couldn't be heard. Audrey turned to her right and saw Lois making her way to help her. Communicating through shouts and body language, they worked together to secure the doors.

"Thank you," Audrey told Lois.

"No need to thank me. It needed to be done," Lois returned politely. She ran her fingers through her hair to repair her style, and walked back to the chair. "Ladies, may I have your attention? Everything is back to normal now. Even though we've not yet lost our electricity, we need to resume our lights out. Let's all try and settle down—there are children here who need to sleep."

Audrey couldn't even begin to think about sleeping, and, as it turned out, she was glad. Later that night, after Gitmo had lost electricity and everyone was sleeping in the oppressive heat, Audrey heard Lois whispering to Maura. If Audrey hadn't seen it, she never would've believed it. Lois told Maura, who was very pregnant at the time, to sleep in her bed—the one closest to the fan which, was running off Lois' portable generator. Maura, who was miserable sleeping in the stifling gym, jumped at the chance. In return, Lois took Maura's cot—the furthest from the fan.

Audrey became a believer that night. There *is* good in all people—even Lois Ranagan.

For me, the night was endless too. I spent the time securing the hangar and airfield, keeping my ear to the radio in case my services were needed. At around 5am, just as the brunt of the storm seemed to have passed through, Ranagan ordered me to take a quick tour of the beaches and of Leeward Point. Visibility was next to nothing and the weather was extremely violent, but, of course, I complied. When I got to Leeward Point, I saw in the beam of my flashlight that one of the beach signs was coming unhinged from its post, becoming a potential projectile. I unscrewed the corner that was still attached, putting it under my arm to carry it to the humvee. As I approached the vehicle, I tripped on something just below the sand. Since it was the same general area where Audrey had tripped the day before, my curiosity was piqued. I placed the sign under my knees to hold it steady and began to push away the wet sand. After a few seconds, the stone object was completely cleared. I shone my light upon it, realizing it was a plaque which read:

IN MEMORY OF JESSICA LAMBERT
On June 15, 1986, Jessica Lambert arrived on this beach to find two Marines struggling in the intense surf. She fought the current and rescued one Marine, but drowned in her attempt to rescue the other. She will always be remembered as a true hero and we will never forget her. May her light always shine.

I WONDERED. He said he was married, but he also said, "I think she is happy as long as I'm still here." I found it odd. A man knows whether or not his wife is happy. He was also sad and sounded so empty. His last words to me were about being lonely. I wasn't sure, but I had a feeling Jessica Lambert was related to the ferry captain, Lam, and probably the very thing that kept him from leaving Guantanamo Bay. He needed to be where he'd remember her best.

That plaque was a good example of why I appreciated Gitmo so much. People die on military bases all the time, and are hardly missed—but not in Gitmo. When someone died, heroically or otherwise, the entire community took it to heart and commemorated his or her life with extraordinary sentiment. Even when we didn't know the individual personally, it felt as though we'd lost family when someone passed away. They may have ended their lives in Gitmo, but all those people continued to live in us.

31

When the ominous clouds finally parted and the threatening sky turned a beaming shade of blue, I stepped out of the hangar to find a miraculous sight. The landscape all around the base glimmered in an emerald hue. The brown, desert-like backdrop had been infused with color and Guantanamo Bay finally looked the part of an exotic, tropical island. For so long, we'd been satisfied with the sunny weather and clear waters, but now Gitmo was lush, painted with the vibrant blooming flowers I'd not yet seen. Pollution from the surrounding Cuban cities and smoke from the sugar-plantation fires had been whisked out to sea, and in their place was a breeze crisper and far more salubrious than the days before. Even though there were trees downed and rubbish strewn about, Gitmo was strikingly beautiful.

I was pleased there were no casualties during the storm, and the only major damage was sustained by McDonald's. The golden arches in front of the building had collapsed and flying debris had pierced the drive-thru speaker. Marine housing survived unscathed, and, as I pulled up to the high school, was hoping the same for the ladies. By the time I arrived, the women had already gotten the "all clear" from Colonel Ranagan and were collecting their belongings. When I finally found Audrey in the crowd, she looked haggard and unkempt.

"You made it!" I shouted with a bright smile.

Audrey pushed her tousled hair out of her face and continued to fold her cot. She sounded tired and annoyed. "Great. I see you did too. Congratulations to us both."

"Can I help you?" I asked, beginning to lift the cot.

"No!" she shot back at me as she wrestled with the sheets and pillow. "I'm doing just fine."

I knew I was in trouble when she used the world fine, so I probably shouldn't have said, "Why aren't you happy?"

"Happy, Adam?" she said with a you-must-be-retarded look on her face. "I've just spent twelve of the most agonizing hours of my life in this gym. First of all, I had to sleep—if you can even call it sleep—on a mildew-infested, surplus cot that only about a thousand other sweaty people have slept on. I bunked next to a neighbor who hates my guts, which happened to be conveniently located in a room with a woman who has controlled my life for seven months—who I'm currently having investigated! This echo chamber, which you call a gym, has been filled with dozens of bored, unruly children whose maddening little voices can crack glass. Looking on the positive side, I don't think we quite made it to a hundred degrees in here, which is why I haven't, yet, been arrested."

"Hey, Audrey."

She placed her hands on her hips, squinted spitefully and growled, "What?"

"This Bud's for you."

Ranagan had given each of the officers a section of the base to assess in case there were any downed power lines or unsafe conditions. Audrey asked to go with me on the inspection and I was pleased to have her company. My area was Cuzco Wells Beach and the Magazine area. Audrey was eager to see the cemetery again, as she'd not been able to stay there long on the night that she'd gone with Donny Mancuso—swinger extraordinaire. Along our way, we saw more damage to the surrounding neighborhoods than had previously been reported.

The golf club, Lateral Hazard, had several blown-in windows and there was an electrical pole that dangled near the entrance to the Windjammer pool. The dormitories for the Jamaican workers, Gold Hill Towers, had numerous roof tiles torn off in the wind, and there had been significant flooding on Cooper Field. All in all, though, the damage had been far less than what we had expected based on the forecast.

The Magazine area was located in the shadow of John Paul Jones Hill, down a long and winding dirt road named, appropriately, Magazine Road. The Magazine area sat perpendicular to Cuzco Wells, and was tucked in the middle between Windmill Beach and Cable Beach, right on the Caribbean Sea. About halfway down the dusty side road, a sturdy, metal-framed gate blocked our passage any further. A large red RESTRICTED sign hung from the locked obstruction. Despite the fact it had been firmly fastened, had we been in an off-road vehicle, we could've driven right around the barrier. Had we been on foot, we could have easily jumped over it.

There were no visible storage buildings because much of the ammunition was massed underground, and there were no paved parking facilities. Magazine Road itself coiled through the vicinity, but had no outlet. Within the confines of the area, the cemetery and dilapidated blacksmith shop were the greatest of attractions. Nevertheless, that particular part of Gitmo was the most sought-after locale because of its enigmatic neighbor, Cuzco Wells. I reached behind my seat and pulled a folder from my backpack; in it was the speech Conway had used during the Cuzco yearly tour, and one that I was suppose to memorize for when I led the excursion. I read it out loud for Audrey:

"On June 6, 1898, Guantanamo Bay awoke to the sound of gunfire from the cruiser USS Marblehead, as Commander B.H. McCalla ordered his guns to engage the Spanish positions on the hill that would eventually bear his name. As the five-inch and six-pound shells forced the Spanish to retreat inland, Cdr. McCalla landed a party of Marines to raid Fisherman's Point in order to cut the communication cable connecting Guantanamo Bay with the rest of the world. This was the first move in the struggle for Guantanamo Bay during the Spanish-American War.

Four days later, the battle continued when the 1ˢᵗ Battalion of Marines, under the command of LtCol R.W. Huntington, landed upon Fisherman's Point and moved up to occupy the Spanish positions on McCalla Hill. The first night passed uneventfully as the Marines fortified their positions against the possibility of a Spanish counterattack. Such a counterattack materialized the following night as skirmishers approached the Marines' positions on three sides. The Marines replied with cannons, rifles and machine guns and the morning found them still in place but with two of their number killed.

The next day, L.t. Col Huntington, reinforced by fifty Cuban soldiers, moved their camp down to Fisherman's Point and prepared their defensive position on the hill in anticipation of another Spanish attack. The Marines had not long to wait because, after dark, the second assault began and continued throughout the night. The Marines' lines held, but another Marine and the battalion surgeon did not live to see morning.

On the third night of Spanish attacks, two more Marines were killed, including the sergeant major, and the following morning they decided to move into the attack. Lt. Col Huntington ordered 160 of his men, reinforced by the Cubans, to march southeast to the Spanish stronghold of Cuzco Wells. The march commenced at 0900 and by 1100, the Marines had taken the ridgeline overlooking the Spanish camp and were engaging the 800 Spaniards in the valley below with rifles and naval gunfire. By 1500, this final engagement of the four-day battle was over. The Marines with their supporting Cubans had killed fifty-eight, and captured eighteen Spanish soldiers while wounding 150 more. As the remaining Spanish retreated to the north, it became clear that in Guantanamo Bay, the United States had won the first land battle of the Spanish-American War."

The base-wide rumor mill was constantly churning out inane reasons why the civilian population of Gitmo wasn't allowed to utilize Cuzco Wells Beach. We heard it all: priceless historical artifacts littered the shoreline; unexploded sea mines lingered in the lapping current; ghosts of dead Marines walked the coast; and we'd even heard that sadistic pirates had buried their treasure there a century and a half before. No matter what the tales were, everyone on base wanted to visit the mysterious place simply because they couldn't. Gitmo was a small place and having an off-limits area like Cuzco only served to stir the imagination.

In reality, there was nothing fantastic or extraordinary about the place outside of its amazing past. The real reason civilians were not authorized access to the beach was because of its proximity to the munitions, and Navy regulations—not the CO of Gitmo— stipulated that non-military persons were not allowed admittance to such a potentially dangerous area. Having said that, the CO of the base applied for—and received—a waiver each year on the anniversary of the battle, so the residents could take a guided tour of the beach. This allowed civilians the opportunity to relive the engagement and hear the answer to the frequently asked question, "Why are we here?" Despite the yearly pilgrimage, the rumors have persisted, perhaps out of nothing more than tradition.

As we drove around the bend, the ramshackle blacksmith shop came into sight and Audrey asked if she could look around the foundation while I did my survey. Knowing full well my wife shouldn't have been in the Magazine area at all, I thought about her request. I couldn't think of any reason why I shouldn't let her explore the long-forgotten structure. Whether she merely sat in the car, or stood by the shack, I'd broken the regulation and would pay equally either way.

The blacksmith shop was reasonably small, looking more like a large room and less like a place of business. The ceiling was partially caved in and the windows were broken. Loose tools, antiquated and rusted, were strewn about the dirt floor, while a covering of sawdust served as a calling card for termites. As Audrey walked around the outside of the late 1800s shop, which had been used by a Cuban farmer before the battle, her attention was captured by something closer to the cemetery.

"Oh no," I heard her call out disappointedly. "The tree!"

"What's wrong?" I asked, walking towards her.

"My tree—it was uprooted in the storm," she said, pointing. I'd forgotten Audrey had been in the Magazine area with Donny Mancuso after our fight. She'd mentioned something about a tree then, but I didn't recall any details.

"Yeah, that's sad." I tried to sound compassionate, but it was a stretch.

Audrey and I met about fifty yards from the banyan and walked together. "I loved that tree, Adam. It wasn't as big as some of the others on base, but it was sure beautiful."

Most of the banyan trees grew to be 100 feet tall, but Audrey's tree stood at about twenty feet. Obviously, it was a much younger tree, and, as we grew closer, I started to share Audrey's melancholy. While we walked, I tried to figure out a way to save it, but there was no way I could. I figured we would approach it, pay our last respects and then I'd get Audrey back to unrestricted terrain.

"Look at it, Adam, just lying on its side like that. I wish we were strong enough to prop it back up," she said as we approached the banyan's leafy top. Audrey paused for reflection as she rubbed one of its leaves in her hand. She continued to walk around to the other end; I was looking up at the amazing blue sky.

"Oh my God, Adam!" Audrey ran in my direction. I grabbed her arms tightly on each side of her body.

"What is it?"

"Oh, God, Adam! It's horrible...absolutely horrible!"

"Audrey, get a grip on yourself!" I was afraid she was going to hyperventilate. "Tell me what's wrong!" But all she could do was shake her head and point to where she'd just come from. I sat her down on the dirt road and placed my hands on her face. "You stay here. I'm going to have a look, okay?" She nodded.

I walked cautiously toward the other side of the tree. With a galloping heart and furrowed brow, I rounded the leafy part of the tree and saw nothing. I continued to walk towards the bottom of the banyan, but could only make out the gigantic suspended root-ball. I inched closer and saw what horrified Audrey. Embedded and entangled in the root-ball was a human skeleton dressed in Marine utilities. There were remnants of blonde hair still attached to the partially-missing skull and there were a few patches of leathery skin located throughout the remains. In a knee-jerk reaction, I backed up hurriedly and tripped on one of the fallen branches. I propped myself up, but remained on the ground, gripped by the vision before me.

"Who is it?" Audrey called, her voice still unsteady. I could not speak. "Answer me!"

My mouth finally caught up with my racing mind. "It's gotta be him."

In the commotion of finding Corporal Daryl Loring's corpse, Ranagan managed to overlook the fact that Audrey had been with me in the Magazine area. It was bad enough to have stumbled upon such a grisly discovery; I sure as hell didn't need a new ass carved out by the colonel. Strikingly though, Ranagan appeared to have genuine sorrow about our lost comrade and ordered a funeral for Daryl, with full military honors. The colonel, himself, called Loring's elderly mother and passed on to her the sympathy and compassion of the entire Marine Corps. I was completely impressed with him for the way he handled everything having to do with the corporal. He gave Daryl and his family everything he possibly could.

The unearthing of the body offered Audrey and me the opportunity to share with the Naval Criminal Investigative Service, NCIS, our theories and findings regarding Gunnery Sergeant Gaultier. We passed on the information we'd gleaned from Abuelita, as well as the newspaper clippings, barracks journals and everything we'd learned from Oliver. I never, however, told them Oliver's name; it was his only request—to remain anonymous—and I intended to honor it. NCIS seemed suspicious when I "couldn't recall" Oliver's name, but they didn't push me. I think they didn't harp on that one point because Audrey and I turned over the desk top and that seemed to hold their interest greatly.

At the end of the first day of questioning, one of the NCIS guys told me to put it all together for him in writing: the whos, whats and whys, which I gladly did. The following is the exact document I submitted to him:

In July of 1958, Gunnery Sergeant Elliott Gaultier was out in town when a band of Cuban rebels kidnapped him and held him hostage for nearly thirty days. Once rescued, he refused a Stateside duty station, and asked to remain in Gitmo for the duration of his tour. In September of that same year, Private Daryl Loring (who was later promoted to lance corporal) arrived on base and was greeted by Gaultier with hostility. Fellow Marines often remarked about the harsh way in which he approached Loring. By Thanksgiving Day, Gaultier had begun to show Loring an inordinate amount of positive attention. Loring and Gaultier became inseparable and it became obvious to all those around that Loring looked up to the Gunny with utter respect and admiration.

On Christmas Eve morning, at approximately 0530, Corporal Loring was standing guard at the Northeast Gate and had detained two Cuban workers, reason unknown. He was relieved by Gunnery

Sergeant Gaultier, who was seen leaving the border checkpoint with the two Cubans following behind in a blue cargo truck. Neither the two Cubans, nor the truck were ever seen again. At around 0600 the same day, a fellow Marine spots Loring talking to Gaultier at the Northeast Gate and is seen leaving with him moments later.

Coincidently, on that same morning, Gaultier failed to show up for morning formation, and, when located, is found injured and covered in blood. He states that he had gotten hurt while running along a rocky ridgeline during personal PT. The next day, some of Daryl Loring's uniform pieces and ID are found at one of the beaches and he is deemed missing.

Forty years later, Gaultier's car is found in the Gitmo junkyard and in his trunk is found his uniform (covered in what looks like dried blood) and Loring's dog tags.

Several months after the disappearance of the two Cubans, Captain Haggar, a logistics officer, is asked by his housekeeper (Lupe "Abuelita" Herrera) to find out what he can about her husband's disappearance. Her husband was one of the missing Cuban workers seen talking to Gaultier. Haggar called and told her that he had come across some valuable information, but needed to investigate further. Later that afternoon, he was killed in a minefield explosion.

A Marine private is asked by Abuelita to try and figure out what Haggar had run across, but is confronted by Gaultier and told to stop looking. Before Gaultier had intervened, however, the private discovered that Haggar had a meeting set up with Gaultier the very afternoon that he died.

The fate of Gunnery Sergeant Gaultier after that period is unknown to me.

32

"She's back!" Audrey exclaimed over the phone to me.

"What do you mean?"

"Lois! She's back to her bossy CO's wife self! Right at this very moment, she's out in our driveway instructing the Sea Bees to hand over our garage tiles to her."

"She has some nerve. I thought Drew talked to the housing office and found out that we can each keep our own tiles if we want to."

"Try telling her that!" Audrey shot back.

"Well, if you don't, then she's going to take them all. But, why do *you* care? Do you even want any of those old tiles?"

"Not all of them," Audrey confessed, "but since they were handmade, and some of them are even signed, I think I'd like first pick."

"Audrey, my only advice to you is this: make your decision based on logic and not feeling. Another confrontation is so not worth it right now. I think we've had our lion's share." She agreed with me and hung up the phone.

"LOIS, WHAT IN THE WORLD do you think you're doing?" she demanded.

"I beg your pardon?" Lois asked innocently.

"These are my tiles, not yours. You have no right to take any of them."

"The colonel told me to come and fetch these out of the dumpster."

"The *colonel* has no authority over housing, and it just so happens that the housing director told us we are entitled to the tiles, not you!"

"Well, I never!" Lois returned.

"Never what? Encountered someone who would stand up to you?"

"What do you want from me, Mrs. Claiborne? I've tried long and hard to get along with you and the other ladies, to no avail. I've no idea what I've done to make you hate me so much. But get one thing straight: I'm taking whatever tiles I want, from whatever house I want to take them from. You, or the housing director, can't stop me." With that, Lois scooped up several tiles and began walking towards the back of her car.

"Oh no, you don't!" Audrey called out, but Lois kept walking. Audrey moved quickly towards her, and when Lois looked over her shoulder to see what Audrey was up to, she stumbled over a tool chest lying in the driveway. With the fall, the tiles flew out of her hand and crashed down on the concrete. Out of genuine concern for Lois, Audrey tried to help her up, but Lois refused and stood up on her own.

"I hope you're satisfied with making a fool out of me," Lois said, brushing her clothes. "Let me say just one thing. I've gotten down on my knees every night and asked the good Lord to bring peace to this neighborhood, but for some reason, he has not answered that prayer. As I'm not one to question God's plan for us, I won't ask why—*however*—be sure, Mrs. Claiborne, what goes around comes around and you'll indeed pay for what you've done here."

"I can say the same for you. All we wanted was to be left alone, but you never stopped. You waved your husband's power like it was a fly swatter. If you'd only been you instead of some Stepford officer's wife, then maybe we could have all gotten along. Each one of us in the Wives' Association has come from a different area of the country, each with a different background and education. Instead of trying to mold us into the perfect officer's wife, you needed to let us each be ourselves. You should've listened to all of our ideas—some of them were very good."

"Good day, Mrs. Claiborne. I believe I've heard enough from you. I only hope your husband's career survives this embarrassing rant of yours."

Audrey stood in the driveway for a few seconds before she reached down to pick up the broken tiles Lois had dropped. The men of the construction battalion were trying to look busy, but they'd witnessed it all. As she walked into the house, Audrey realized that no satisfaction had been gained from the exchange; they were two completely different women who could never see things from the other's perspective. Audrey had always prided herself in being able to put herself in someone else's shoes, but she realized that maybe she wasn't as all-knowing as she'd once believed herself to be. It was the first time Audrey doubted her own motives. The letter to General Crane was warranted, but, like the desk, Audrey hadn't wanted the tiles. They'd merely been an excuse for her to flaunt her own power as an independent woman who wouldn't be controlled.

She entered her home through the side door nearest to the washroom, tossing the broken tiles into a laundry basket; she hardly noticed the loud sound of them breaking as they hit the bottom. My despondent wife had enough and wanted to leave Gitmo and never return. When I came home for lunch, we talked about her taking the Friday flight to Jacksonville, and after an hour, we'd begun to put the plan in motion. Her parents had a winter home on Hilton Head Island, so I insisted she make a visit. She called over to the migrant camp to ask for the days off and began to pack.

The following morning, I accompanied her over to Leeward and watched as her plane taxied down the runway. I knew from my own experience that the minute the plane touched off, she'd be far more at peace. When I could no longer see the aircraft, and after I'd finished some pressing paperwork in the hangar, I drove back to the Ferry Landing to make the trip back to Windward. When the ship pulled into the dock, I looked up at the bridge to see a familiar face. Lam was waving down to me and motioned for me to visit. On my way up, I thought about the memorial I'd found at Leeward Point and wondered if I should mention it to him.

"Good day, Adam," he said cheerfully as I entered the bridge. "What brings you to Leeward today?"

"Seeing my wife off. She's gone to visit her parents."

"Oh? You guys have a fight or somethin'?"

"Nah, nothing like that. She just needs a break from our little island. Hey, Lam, you said you've been here for about nine years, but you said you were also in the Navy. Had you ever been to Gitmo before you took this job as ferry captain?"

"And then some. I was a part of the fleet training group and Gitmo was a staple on those floats."

"Do you remember any memorable events taking place?"

"What do you mean? The base bank was robbed once in the seventies. I'd say that counts as being memorable."

"No, but now I'm curious," I said, folding my arms and smiling. "What happened?"

"Oh it was a hoot! The bank was located right next to a public restroom and the robbers crawled through the ladies' room and into the vault."

"Into the vault? What kind of vault was it?"

"Well, that's what made it so funny. They didn't have a vault like you and I know; they used a reinforced supply closet. The crooks got away with over $350,000!"

"Did they ever catch the guys who did it?"

"Nope, not even to this day. Of course, I have my own theory. I think it wasn't about the money. I think it was someone with something to prove."

"Wow, that must've been pretty exciting for a place like this," I said.

"Sure was. But sorry it's not what you were looking for. What are you looking for? Does this have something to do with the skeleton you found?"

"I guess everyone knows about that now, huh?" I said, shaking my head. "Nothing is sacred in Gitmo." Our attention was diverted for a moment when Lam spotted a shark swimming around the bay.

"So what's gotten under your wife's skin? What's she running away from?"

"She had a run in the other day with Mrs. Ranagan about the

old Cuban tiles on our garage. Lois wants them herself. As the grapevine reports, she's building a Caribbean-style house in Florida and wants to use them." When I finished speaking, Lam had the most intense look of concern I've ever seen. "Something wrong, Lam?"

His face snapped back into a smile. "No, no. Just thinking about something, that's all."

≈≈ ≈≈ ≈≈

It was about noon when I finally arrived back at the White House and I found it virtually empty. A passing sergeant reminded me that all personnel were supposed to report to Windmill Beach for mandatory fun; that's what we like to call all-hands parties hosted by the big guy—mandatory fun. Instead of giving us half a day off, we were expected to participate in volleyball matches, three-legged races and water balloon tosses.

My car engine hadn't finished its last rumble before I was thrown on a team. Despite my poor attitude, I ended up having a great time. People were laughing and enjoying themselves, willing to be amused. After a while, diving groups were formed and I found myself happier than I'd been in a long time.

By the time I'd exited the water and washed my gear, Guy Armstrong had an amazing bonfire blazing in the night. With the CO, XO and junior enlisted Marines long gone, the military function part of the day was over. The beer became free flowing and the mood lighter. Around the fire with me sat Rhonda and Manny, Maura and Evan, Arlene and Ryan, and Guy. Surrounding the food in the picnic shelter was Chet Dingle, Aidan, Kelly, Gordie, Holly Hump-a-lot and a number of senior enlisted Marines. Several more enlisted Marines were still diving trying to get a glimpse of night-time feeders.

At around midnight—with most of my fellow officers passed out on the sand—I said goodbye to their wives and started to walk to my car, knowing it had been four hours since my last beer. When I put my hand on the door handle, I heard a roar of shouting and laughter coming from one of the distant picnic shelters. My curiosity got the best of me, so I moseyed in that direction. In the center of a crowd of enlisted Marines, I caught sight of Chet Dingle with his bathing trunks around his ankles. As a compliment to that, Holly was bent over the picnic table with her sundress hiked to her shoulders. Needless to say, Chet was going to town and Holly gave him and all access pass. Every once in a while, Chet would call out to the enlisted Marines, "How about this gentlemen?" and his words would be met with thunderous applause. Holly's facial expressions ranged from erotically contorted to wide-mouthed grins, while Chet's eyes surveyed the crowd for the fervent approval of his men. The sound of the zealous onlookers caught the attention of Maura, Arlene and Rhonda, and, before I could stop them, they had a front row view of Chet Dingle's porn party. They were obviously disgusted and embarrassed by the scene. As I broke through the crowd to hose down the two performers, Chet pulled away from Holly and allowed the group to examine the fruits of his repulsive labor. When he was done, he slapped Holly hard on her ass and bowed to his company of enlisted Marines.

"Conduct Unbecoming" was written for just such an occasion, but despite the recommendation of the XO, Chet Dingle got off with nothing but a slap on the wrist—again. Ranagan decided to use the incident as a retaliatory instrument against Audrey's letter. Since I was the highest ranking officer at the party— even though it ceased being a military function long before the incident occurred—I was the one held fully responsible and was officially reprimanded for what Chet had done. As I stood in Ranagan's office bearing his rage, I finally understood Audrey's point of view. It didn't matter to the Ranagans what reality was; they simply made up their own truths to fit their agenda. As I stood there incapable of reacting to his words for fear of a more caustic penalty, I thought about the investigators and hoped to hell Ranagan would get what he deserved.

The morning after the beach party fiasco, I had to give another Northeast Gate tour—my fifth. By this point, my spiel was well rehearsed and I'd acquired many interesting historical tid-bits to share with the group. On that overcast day, there were thirty base residents raring to learn about that fascinating piece of real estate. With the jumbling of the bus as we rode, my thoughts turned toward Gaultier, and I tried to consider his experience as a hostage. I wondered if he'd, at one time, been a decent man, but as a result of his capture, had a complete change in disposition.

I wanted to know more about his captors, and I wanted to know more about him before July 1958.

We pulled up to the tour area right on time and the group followed me to the makeshift shelter where I usually gave my speech. Once everyone had found a place to listen comfortably, I began my history lesson:

"For a number of years, the Americans and the Cubans maintained a very cordial relationship. Cuban workers could come and go as they pleased on base, and the base residents were greeted genially in Cuban cities. As a matter of fact, our mail was delivered four times a week from Havana, not by plane or ship as it is today. It wasn't until the late fifties—when America adopted the policy of containment—that our relationship began to take a downturn. A man by the name of Fidel Castro assumed power of Cuba and forced upon his nation Communist ideology. The beginning of the end of our peaceful co-existence came in June of 1958 when twenty nine Marines and sailors were kidnapped by Raul Castro and held for almost a month. While returned largely unharmed, President Eisenhower used that incident—among other smaller political skirmishes—to officially terminate our diplomatic relationship with Cuba in 1961. Almost overnight, the Cuban government poured thousands of unproven soldiers around the border to act as guards and forbade Cubans from obtaining work on base. Cuban workers, who had been working on the base before this time, were allowed by both the U.S. and Cuba to keep their jobs, however, Castro had many of them roughed-up on their return home each night to get them to quit. Since the base depended greatly on the Cuban workers, the American government offered to let many of them make a life here on base. As a matter of fact, there are three families in Gitmo today that have lived here since 1962 and have never left the base, not even once."

At that point, I allowed the visitors to roam around the Northeast Gate and take photographs before moving onto the next part of the tour. On that particular day, I walked off by myself and looked through the chain-link fencing towards communist Cuba. I tried to imagine Christmas Eve night in 1958. Occasionally someone would ask for a quick fact and I'd recite the answer in a professional manner, but my mind was otherwise occupied. One answer I'd given about Cuban commuters, however, started me thinking. "In the fifties, the roads to the base were unreliable due to Cuban troop movements and because they were difficult to traverse. As a matter of fact, the only vehicles that really utilized the roads near the border were cargo trucks carrying supplies to the base."

Cargo trucks! Miguel and Chico must have been driving some type of cargo truck to have come through the Northeast Gate. Next, I looked over to the sign above the border crossing and the N in north, the E in east and the G in gate jumped out at me like I was wearing 3-D glasses. N-E-G! On the underside of the desk, the letters N-E-G were inscribed. Convinced the drawing was a map from the Northeast Gate to the Magazine area, N-E-G meant Northeast Gate. Mentally moving on to the other letters and numbers, I assumed, for the moment, 3T stood for three ton truck. I decided LB stood for the color or make of the vehicle, or the cargo itself.

Excited by my findings, I accelerated the rest of the tour and instructed the bus to head back to Marine Hill—I had work to do.

33

Walking to my car, I thought again about Gaultier's capture. I hadn't known—until a few weeks before that specific tour—Castro's brother, Raul, had been behind the hostage crisis. The newspaper article Audrey translated for me had used the term insurgents, not Raul Castro, but Raul definitely would've been considered a rebel by much of the Cuban population. My thinking led me in the direction of a story I'd once heard about Patricia Hearst, heiress to the Hearst publishing empire. She'd been kidnapped in the 1970s, and, becoming sympathetic toward her captors, helped them fight for their cause.

With that in mind, I made a supposition: Elliott Gaultier was captured by Raul Castro, and, for whatever reason, became his pawn. Raul must have instructed him to do away with Miguel and Chico, maybe for what they were bringing onto the base. I dismissed that idea quickly when it occurred to me Raul could have overtaken Miguel's truck anywhere along the road; waiting until they were on base didn't make sense—unless—they were supposed to bring something off the installation. I was more confused than ever. Then I recalled something Oliver told me;

Gaultier had been an extremely intelligent man with a survivor mentality to boot. What if Gaultier was trying to pull something over on Castro? That theory made as much sense to me as any of them did.

WHEN I GOT BACK TO THE HOUSE, I noticed the usual gang was gathered in the park: the Romeros, the Gellars, the Hills, the Razors, the Rays and even Major McCarran and his wife were there. They were deep in discussion when I got there.

"What's going on?" I asked the group.

"We were just talking about the latest news from Quantico," Regina answered.

"Did General Crane make a decision about the Ranagans yet?" I asked eagerly.

"Not that we know of," replied Drew, "but my husband got a phone call from a friend in Crane's office, and it seems Crane's really upset with Colonel Ranagan."

"Really? That's great news! So why aren't we celebrating?" I wondered.

"Well, first of all, I need to see it before I believe it," Henry Ray said. "Of course my friend was quite adamant that things are going to change here, but I still want it in writing. We've all been through so much."

"But that's not everything," Drew added. "Ranagan won. I'm being sent off island next week because of my medical history."

"Can he do that?" I asked.

"He already did," Drew said sadly.

"What an asshole," Major McCarran growled. "I can't believe that piece of shit has gotten this far in the Marine Corps. What pile of crap promoted him anyway? I'm telling you what, the Corps we have today is not the one I signed up for. I don't know what the hell's happened over the years, but the leaders they have in there now are worthless."

"Amen to that!" Lt Colonel Ray replied. "I'll tell you what's wrong. There hasn't been a war in so long that the colonels and generals we have today aren't battle-proven. They have no way of distinguishing themselves from their peers. In a critical situation, real leaders rise to the occasion. Today, all we have is a bunch of cut-throat officers clawing their way to the top, and kissing quite a lot of ass in the meantime."

"You know," Maura said, sighing, "no one will ever believe this has all happened to us. No one could ever begin to understand what we've all been through; and on top of it, we look like a bunch of cry-babies."

"Yeah, I heard we're the laughing stock on base," Regina said. "Lois has been spreading all sorts of tales about us. Since I got my new job, people come into the bank and look at me funny. I know they want to ask what in the world is going on up in Marine housing—I can feel it."

"This is like a movie. Someone needs to make a movie about what's has happened here," McCarran said. "It's got all the elements of a blockbuster."

"Oh, yeah?" I looked at the major. "Who would play you in the film, sir?"

He thought about it for three seconds and replied, "Arnold Schwartzenegger, of course." His comment, while expected, drew laughter from the group. "Ok then, who would play you, Mr. Pilot?" McCarran asked me.

"I don't know. Maybe somebody simple and down to earth, like Tom Cruise."

"I think that was done already in a little movie called *Top Gun*," Maura announced.

"Well then, what about you Maura?" I asked playfully.

"I've already thought about this. I'd pick Julia Roberts."

"Since I'd pick Robert Redford," Henry Ray added, "it appears we'd be looking at an all-star cast!"

"Guys!" Maura cried. "My water just broke."

Her crude husband retorted, "Well, ladies and gentlemen, if you'll excuse us, I must get Vagina Falls to the hospital." Maura, who was rather used to his odd sense of humor, had little humor on that day; several hours of impending labor expunged it all. However, she and Evan welcomed Phoebe Renee Gellar into the world seven hours later, and Maura was ear-to-ear smiles once more.

Walking back to my house, I passed the dumpster used by the Sea Bee's for the garage reconstruction. Curiosity got the best of me, so I climbed to the top to have a look. Drew Ray had been right. As I left the park, she told me Lois had hired some Philippino workers to scour the dumpsters for the tiles, and it was clear they had paid us a visit; however, at least ours was still half full. I took a deep breath, thought mean things about Lois, and made my way to the bedroom. It wasn't until I'd been lying there alone for a while that I wished I'd made Audrey stay.

After lying there way too long, I went to the kitchen. Dinner consisted of three micro-waved bean burritos and an ice cold beer. I usually saved beans for when I wasn't around Audrey, for all the obvious reasons. After about an hour of finding nothing to watch on TV, I started thinking about Gaultier again, but getting inside someone's head had never been my bag. It was an impressive trait of Audrey's. I'm continually awed by how she can never have met someone, but know their motivation and accurately predict their next move. I've often told her she needs to become a profiler for the FBI, but she only laughs the compliment off.

Perhaps I willed it, but as I sat there, she called.

"So how are things in Georgia?" I said, trying to sound upbeat.

"I'm sure things are fine in Georgia," she said sarcastically, "but I'm in South Carolina."

"That's what I meant." I felt stupid.

"To answer your question: lonely, but surprisingly relaxing. How about you?" she said with equally fake enthusiasm.

"Lonely too. I had no idea I'd miss you so much. I have to say that Gitmo will Git-mo' better when you Git-home. Ha! Tell me that wasn't totally funny! I crack myself up."

"You're a regular Robin Williams. So how was the tour today?"

"I almost forgot to tell you! I figured out what the letters stand for!"

"From under the desk?"

"Yeah! I think 3T means, three ton truck'."

"What does LB mean then?"

"I figure it must mean blue or black—something like that."

"Could be. You just might be on to something," my wife replied encouragingly.

I filled her in on my whole Stockholm Syndrome, Patty Hearst theory. "So do your magic, Audrey. Tell me why he did it. Piece it together."

"It's not that easy."

"Of course it is. You always do it. Just stop and think about it and I'm sure that you'll come up with something."

"Why don't you try it, then? Everything in life comes down to the reasonable man's approach. Your first question is: What would make me do something like that? Next, sort through each scenario and pick the one that most suits the personality of the person you're summing up. Lastly, apply that scenario to the person in question, and then, if you're lucky, you should have your answer."

"Okay, I'd have to be blackmailed, needing money, or have a hatred of all mankind. I haven't heard of any skeletons in Gaultier's closet, well, at least before the one I found dangling in some roots. He seemed to be a great guy before the kidnapping, so it must be money. If it was for money, the Cuban workers must've been involved with something of value, and Loring was either a part of it or got in the way. Which one was it for Loring? My brain's working too hard."

"Because of the way we found him, I'd say he got in the way," my wife said, perfectly confident.

"Alright, then—what thing of value could they've been hauling on base?"

"Maybe they were taking it off base. No one said they were bringing anything on base. They might have stolen something."

I froze in place. "Oh my God, Audrey! Lam, the ferry boat captain, said that the Gitmo bank was robbed about thirty years ago and they never found the guys who did it! The money's never turned up either. Do you think that the Cuban workers came across the money and Castro found out about it? Maybe that's why those sailors and Marines were kidnapped in the first place! Maybe Raul found out about the money, captured a bunch of guys, and worked them over to see who would work for him!"

"Ok," Audrey agreed. "So Gaultier agrees to help. The Cuban workers try to get on base, and are stopped by Loring because Gaultier arrives late—for whatever reason. He drives off with the Cubans, kills them, takes the cargo and heads back to get rid of Loring. But then why Haggar? Why was he killed and why in the minefield?"

We both were quiet. "Are you thinking what I'm thinking?" I asked her.

"Something's buried in the minefields!" she exclaimed. "Remember how we read in the Book of the Dead that two unknown Cuban males had been found in the minefield around that time? That has to be it! I'm not sure what Haggar knew, but he knew

Gaultier was involved and Gaultier killed him."

"Yeah, and that's why the bank robbers were never caught. They hid the money in the minefields. No one would've ever thought to look there, or even dared to. We need to call NCIS and tell them all of this," I said breathlessly.

"All of what? It's only a guess and a wild one at that. They'd only laugh at us."

"Well then, what do we do next?" I threw it back on her.

"We need to assume that Gaultier got the money, but then how did he get it off base?"

Another thought came to me. "Do you think that's why he refused to move back to the States after the kidnapping? Remember, he asked to stay?"

"You're a genius! That's got to be right! Gaultier knew that he'd only be there a few months more and then the military would move his personal property off the island in a big crate, free from any checkpoints or customs officers. Once he got back in the States, he'd turn the money over to Raul through some Swiss bank account or something, and he'd probably get to keep a little of the action in return."

"Bingo!" I shouted.

"So now what? If we've solved this thing, what do we do next?"

"Find the truck."

Since detective work seemed to be agreeing with me, I returned back to the only crime scene I knew—the Magazine area. When I pulled up, I saw yellow crime-scene tape in the area of the tree and I saw Major McCarran near the blacksmith shop banging Lieutenant Humphries. They were both completely naked and sweat was pouring from every sweat gland they had. I thought about getting in my car and backing down the road quietly, but decided to leave my car parked where it was and take the long trail to Cuzco Wells. My decision to do that was two-fold: I wanted to continue with my investigating, so leaving was out of the question; and I wanted McCarran to see my car and wonder what I knew or had seen.

Cuzco Wells looks like every other beach in Gitmo, but it's unlike any other because of its history. I sat on the shoreline, reliving the great battle in my head, wondering what it must have been like. I pictured deceased Spanish soldiers tossed lifelessly on the sand while cannons exploded on the rocky cliffs above my head. I heard officers shouting orders at their Marines, and listened for the inspiring sound of the trumpet as the curtain lowered upon the blood-spattered theatre. Most people had never heard of Cuzco Wells, and I'd been one of them. Fate brought me to Gitmo to learn and understand things that I couldn't know on my own; I began to see that more clearly. Living in Gitmo allowed me to take a step back from the world so I could find my place in it. On that small base, there was so much time to think, so little to do. Like a child measures his growth by a pencil mark on the wall, I too could measure my growth, but mine was all on the inside.

The last day's light caught the tips of the waves; the clear blue water turned dark and shadowy. Further down the coast, closer to Windmill Beach, I noticed a glimmer in the nearly black water I couldn't explain. On our first dive at Kittery Beach, Audrey had spotted something reflective or shinny in the water, but we didn't have any time to examine it up close. I knew my only chance to see what it was meant diving at that moment. Since my dive gear was always in my car—like most divers in Gitmo—I raced back to the Gremlin and gathered it in my arms. As I headed back towards the beach, I saw McCarran still going at it with Holly and thought "Dive buddy!" I put my stuff down and jogged over to where they were. I was so swept away with my possible discovery, I didn't care what I was interrupting.

"Major McCarran!" I called out, partially shielding my eyes. Panic came over them, and they instantly parted company, so to speak, reaching for their clothes.

"Claiborne? What the hell? My kids better be in the hospital or I'm frying your nuts up for dinner!"

"I need a diving buddy, sir. I saw something out in the water and I need to get to it before it stops glowing. I don't know if it's treasure, a piece of spacecraft or what! Anyway, I'll meet you at the beach."

"Spacecraft? What are you on drugs? You do know diving at Cuzco is off-limits," McCarran called out.

"*I won't tell, if you won't.*" McCarran knew exactly what I meant by that. Bidding Miss Hump-a-lot a fond farewell, he grabbed his gear and headed down the beach.

We entered the water around eight in the evening, and I could still see the flicker of light in the far distance. McCarran and I swam on the surface for a while to conserve our air, occasionally using the snorkel and swimming on our backs.

"So what are we looking for?" McCarran asked me as we swam.

"I'm not really sure, sir. Audrey spotted it on our first dive together and I forgot about it until now. I was sitting on the shoreline—"

"Spying on me?" the major interrupted. "What are you a pervert?"

"No, sir, I came to the Magazine area to view the crime scene again. I was curious about the investigating NCIS had done. When I saw you, I decided to sit on the beach until you'd gone."

"Good enough. So what's the story?"

"Well, there is no story. We saw this glowing object near Kittery Beach, but now it's further down the shoreline. I don't know if it's the same object or one like it. I just don't know."

"I guess we'll soon find out," McCarran said as he got ready to head to the bottom. I followed right behind him.

McCarran and I sunk to a depth of about thirty feet, shallow enough to allow us plenty of time under water. When we first went below the surf, I momentarily lost sight of my object, but after a few minutes of swimming around, caught sight of it once more. It seemed far less bright, and I wasn't sure if murky water was to blame or the lack of sunlight. As I grew nearer, the object disappeared. Major McCarran, who had seen it for himself, looked completely puzzled; I felt the same way too. With the surf kicking up, and the sun having set, it was hard to see much of anything. The intense current kept fighting us, and the tossed waters stirred up the sand, algae and everything else that could possibly impede our line of sight.

Just as we were about to call it quits, McCarran signaled me over to his locale. I kicked speedily, my heart racing inside my chest. When the current settled and the bubbles had cleared, I came face to face with Abuelita's nightmare.

34

The object glowing in the water had been the side-view mirror of an old, encrusted cargo truck resting at the bottom of the sea. It had Cuban tags and Spanish writing on the side, but other than that, there wasn't much left to see. Much of the vehicle had rusted and collapsed in on itself. I took my diving knife and scraped away some of the growth to see it was a light-blue color. The front looked like it had been smashed in, so I surmised the truck must have made quite a fall into the ocean, probably from the cliff above. From what I could see, there were no bodies in the front and no cargo in the back compartment.

When McCarran and I returned to the surface, I felt a strange sensation. While I had no real proof, I knew instinctively that LB3T stood for light blue three-ton. I knew Abuelita would never find her husband alive and I knew Gunny Gaultier was to blame. I figured the storm must have moved the vehicle closer to Cuzco, which is why it wasn't where we'd first seen it. I wondered if anything of value had fallen out of the truck when it had been moved by the intense current and wave action of the storm. I asked McCarran if he'd accompany me on another dive the following morning and he agreed.

"Are you going to tell NCIS about this?" McCarran asked.

"Yes, why?"

"Because we need to tell them we came in from the Windmill Beach side, and not Cuzco."

"Good thinking. The last thing I need is another reaming by the colonel."

I promptly called Audrey upon my return home that night. She was as stunned as I'd been about finding Miguel's truck—or at least what we thought was his truck.

"At least you proved one thing," Audrey said convincingly.

"And what would that be?"

"That Miguel wasn't taking anything off the base. He was bringing it on."

"How so?"

"Gaultier wouldn't have gotten rid of the truck if he needed it to bring something off."

"Oh, so you think that Gaultier pushed the truck over the cliff, or maybe forced Miguel to drive it off?"

"Something like that. What did NCIS say?"

"Nothing yet. The two investigators left the island yesterday to head up to Washington. We should hear about the lab results soon. They have a DNA sample from Loring's mother and they're going to try and prove if the substance we found is blood, and, if so, if it's Loring's."

"So we just wait and see?"

"I'm afraid so."

"How do you plan to spend the rest of your weekend without me?"

"I'm going diving with McCarran tomorrow morning, and, other than that, just miss you."

The sun hadn't completely risen above John Paul Jones Hill when Major McCarran and I reached the shopping area of base the next morning. As we drove down Sherman Avenue, an enormous rainbow hung gracefully in the sky, each side of the multicolored arc firmly planted on either side of the bay. It hadn't been the first time I'd seen one like that— many rainbows appeared in the sky while I was there. Audrey once thought we should've renamed the base Rainbow Bay. On that morning, I took it as a sign; something was drawing me into the water and leading my way.

Early mornings in Gitmo—especially on the weekend when everyone is still in bed recovering from their hangovers—were a privilege to behold. The base was quiet and the waters were still. I felt like the only man alive sometimes. I learned to appreciate simplicity and find the fortune in just being alive.

By the time we arranged our gear, briefed the dive and put everything on, the Caribbean Sea had become fully illuminated. As we entered the water, we made note of its mirror-like quality, and when we went below the surface, the view was equally striking; the visibility seemed immeasurable and the sea life more abundant than ever. A sizeable, emerald-colored parrot fish, with purple and black accents, swam alongside of me until I disappeared into an impressive school of tiny tropical fish. Major McCarran, on the other hand, had already shot two fish dead with his spear gun and paddled along with a trail of fish guts behind him. Clearly, we were two very different men.

Since I had no real place to begin, I just lowered myself to the bottom and hunted through every rock, reef and plant I came across. Finding something would be nothing less than a miracle, but I still wanted to try. Although McCarran and I didn't split up, I can't say we swam close to each other either. I could see him in the distance; it was clear he wasn't interested in doing anything but hunt fish. I was fine with that; besides, he was only with me because of the dive buddy rule anyway.

Near the end of the dive, I joined back up with the major and had one last pass of the area near the truck. It turned out to be a Jurassic-sized waste of time until we were on our way back. I noticed something wedged between two rocks. I reached for it, pulled off the growth, and asked myself where I'd seen something like it before. I knew in an instant what it was, but didn't think much about it at the time. I put the object in my dive-satchel and headed back to shore.

"Okay, Columbo, you've unearthed a skeleton, a sunken pansy-blue truck, and that little piece of garbage you just picked up from the bottom of the ocean. Who done it?" The major sneered.

"That's a great question, sir. I only wish I had the answers."

Ryan Hill was standing in my driveway when I pulled up in my purple car with the violet flames down the side. "Damn, man! It doesn't matter how often I see you in that thing, it always makes me want to puke. You need to get yourself a can of spray paint. Cover that shit over and sketch a shark or something. You know everyone calls you Barney behind your back."

"So what brings you to this side of the neighborhood?"

"Can you fly the Huey on Tuesday?"

"I'm sure I can arrange that. What's going on?"

"We're burning the last minefield and it's in an area that's difficult to get fire trucks to. I was hoping that you could fill up the water ball and fly around by us."

"I'll talk to Pickard tomorrow morning," I said, leaning against my car.

"No you ain't."

"Why?"

"Because Pickard is going to be otherwise occupied."

"Doing what?"

"Change of command, old boy. Tomorrow is the base's big day. Captain *Dickard* is outta here!" Ryan made a gesture like an umpire makes when he throws a player out of the game.

"Holy cow! I almost forgot. Who's the new guy?"

"Navy Captain Eugene E. Elgory."

"Never heard of him. What's the buzz on ole' Triple E?" I said, folding my arms.

"Man, I heard he's great."

"I hope so. Gitmo could sure use a breath of fresh air."

"So what are you going to do about flying for me?" Ryan said, walking backwards toward his home.

"Well, if Pickard's really leaving, I guess I'm in charge as long as the other pilots are off-island. I'll still put through a request to protect my ass though."

"Okay, see you Tuesday at 6am."

"Got it." I waved to Ryan, got out of his line of vision, and ran to the phone as fast as I could. All the while he was asking me to fly, the only thing in my mind were his words, "burning the last minefield". If money was hidden there, it was about to be soaked in thousands of gallons of diesel fuel and set ablaze.

I don't know who she was talking to, but Audrey's phone was busy for over an hour. I made my way to the computer desk and decided to do an internet search on R. Mercado, the name on the underside of the desk. As I was waiting to get on-line, I read through some of the notes on the Northeast Gate I'd prepared a few months before that past Saturday's tour. I reaffirmed I'd recounted everything accurately and in an organized fashion, but I realized I'd left something out—something significant.

According to Abuelita and Oliver, Captain Haggar had died in a minefield explosion in 1959. How could that be when the first minefield wasn't constructed until the Missile Crisis in 1962? Both Abuelita and Oliver told me he'd been killed in a 1959 explosion, but there were no mines on base at that time. I picked up the phone and called Ryan, but his wife told me he'd just left to go fishing; she'd have him return my call later that day. As I sat there feeling tense, I thought about the *Book of the Dead* and the entries for two unknown Cubans; it clearly stated that they had succumbed to wounds inflicted in a minefield explosion in 1958 or 1959. Then I remembered how Audrey had discovered that many of the entries had been tampered with and/or changed. I knew I needed to get a copy of the real thing, but Holly Hump-a-lot was my only contact at the hospital and we weren't exactly friends. I hated using blackmail—her messing around with a married superior—but I needed to get down to the bottom of some things.

When I was finally able to get online, I made my way to my favorite search engine and typed in: R. Mercado. Within seconds, hundreds of articles came up as a match. I re-typed: R. Mercado Cuba. Once again, numerous articles came up, but one in particular grabbed my attention. I clicked onto the link and read.

March 9, 1990—Miami, FL—Yesterday, notorious drug trafficker, Roberto Mercado was gunned down outside his home and killed. He had been walking to his car when a red vehicle sped by and assaulted him with a barrage of bullets, witnesses say. His family was not at home at the time. The police admit that they have no suspects, but are actively looking and encourage anyone with information to come forward.

Mr. Mercado, a native of Havana, Cuba, came to this country in 1979. He had been the thriving owner of the Hotel and Casino Esmerelda, which was assumed by Castro during the takeover. Mercado arrived in Florida with enough money to start a small consulting firm, but as a result of declining business, it eventually became a front for his drug empire.

Drugs? Was Miguel bringing drugs on base? It made sense.

My next thought was about the bank robbery money. "So was it drugs or money, or both that Gaultier was after?" I said out loud.

With a knocking at my back door, all thoughts of Gaultier evaporated.

"They've been called to Quantico!" Evan said, sounding out of breath. "I ran all the way down here."

"Who?" I inquired with a nod of my head.

"Colonel Ranagan and Lt Colonel Ray!"

"By whom? General Crane?" I asked with some trepidation.

"Try General Whaley!" he shot back.

"Wait a minute! Start all over again!"

"I guess the report was too much for a two-star. They needed to call in a three-star."

"Ho-LEE-shit. Tell me everything you know."

Evan and I sat in the kitchen. "Actually it isn't much. I was out doing yard work when I saw Lt Colonel Ray getting out of his car. I asked him if he'd been at work—since he was in uniform— and he told me sort of. He said that Ranagan called him in this morning and told him that General Whaley called him personally last night. When Ray asked what the general said, all Ranagan said was that both men needed to be in Quantico on the next plane out."

"But why Lt Colonel Ray?"

"I don't know. Maybe to congratulate him on his new promotion to CO?"

"How does Ray feel about it?"

"Honestly, he seems apprehensive. I'm sure he didn't see Whaley in the picture at all."

"A three-star? None of us did."

Ryan ended up calling me a few hours later and, of course, the first thing we discussed was the call from the general. Both of us tried to figure out why Whaley got involved, but they were only guesses and none of them were very good. We were forced to adopt a wait and see attitude. We were all surprised by the timeline. It had been a little over a week since the investigators left and military paperwork was notoriously slow. We had no idea what Minter's recommendation had been or what made the general move at such an uncharacteristically swift speed.

It didn't take long for Ryan to explain the discrepancy in what I'd read. It was true that there wasn't an operational use of mines in Gitmo before 1962; there was no reason for them prior to that date. However, when the political situation began to get unstable in Havana in 1958, and the takeover by Castro seemed imminent, the US government sent combat engineers to Gitmo to test certain mines for their effectiveness, and to map out the areas that would have mines if the need arose. The test area was only 100 feet by 100 feet, but was indeed a minefield by definition. Haggar, being a logistics officer, had been part of the planning team that scouted out the site and facilitated its construction. Ryan confirmed that no one would have questioned Haggar's presence in the area at any time.

The phone rang again before I'd even set a foot out of my kitchen; this time it was Gil Randall from NCIS. Gil and I had met when I first arrived in Gitmo. It was his son who taught me all I needed to know about hydroids. "Captain Claiborne, just wanted you to know that we found out about Gaultier. Not long before his move from Gitmo, he was caught breaking in to the Sea Bees' supply warehouse."

"What was he doing that for?"

"We don't know. According to his record, once he was arrested he never spoke another word. He did some time in Charleston and then received an OTH from the Corps." That meant the Marines handed him an other than honorable discharge instead of a dishonorable one since his crime wasn't a felony. "After that, he dropped out of sight until 1986."

"What happened in '86?" I was wondering who else he'd killed.

"He died—cancer if I remember correctly," Gil stated as I heard papers rustling in the background.

"What have you learned about the blood in the car?"

"On the dog tags, we have a match for blood—Loring's blood, mind you. We also found Loring's blood on Gaultier's uniform." Gil's tone was upbeat.

"And the trunk? Whose blood is that?"

Gil paused. "Well, that's where it gets a little weird."

He went on to tell me what they'd found, and if I hadn't had so much on my mind at that particular time in my life, I might've been able to put a few things together and end the whole mystery right then and there. Unfortunately, I was a face-value kind of guy and didn't connect the dots. I thanked Gil for his call and made my way over to Ryan's house for a map of the test area. The test area had never been included in the actually minefield, but had its own separate location, so I was free to roam where I pleased. Ryan wanted to go with me, but I discouraged him. I'd already begun to feel foolish as a result of my investigative-diving with McCarran. I hardly wanted to bring another person into my crazy world of amateur sleuthing. On my way out to explore, I stopped by the house to grab a tool and to phone Audrey once more. This time she wasn't there so I left her a rather lengthy message.

With a shovel in-hand, I left my house through the backyard, walked down the hill to Sherman Avenue and began jogging up Tarawa Road. At the top of Tarawa Hill, I left the main road to follow a path once made by tanks in the heyday of the base. The track was curvy, potholed, bumpy and wildly overgrown. Fighting positions that had been constructed during the Cuban missile crisis littered the landscape and were all in desperate need of repair. Seeing the bunkers and jogging the tank track made me nostalgic for a time in Gitmo's past I'd never experienced. Once a formidable combative power, the defense force had become a glorified police squad and we all knew it—even the Cubans.

As I made my way further into the restricted area, I came across neglected warning signs, dilapidated fencing, and tons of iguanas. Occasionally, I'd take out the map Ryan had lent me to make sure I was staying on course, and, for the most part, I had been. At one point, however, I must have taken a wrong turn because I ended up in a shallow valley between two enormous knolls. Dug into the side of one of the mounds was an especially diminutive bunker that made no sense; fighting holes, while seemingly haphazard in their placement, are actually very well thought out. Each bunker strategically supports another; that particular one had been constructed completely autonomous from all the others. Pulling the overgrowth away from its entrance, I pricked myself on numerous cacti and was startled

by the sight of a Gitmo boa. To avoid a confrontation with the
snake, I jumped into the fighting position and realized it wasn't a
bunker after all, merely a hole in the ground. I reached beside
me and yanked up a badly weathered and frayed canvas bag,
the kind seamen and Marines use when aboard ship. Inside was
a nearly-depleted roll of duct tape and a rusty pair of scissors.
While I wasn't sure why or how long they'd been there, I cast
them aside and found my way back to the main trail.

The test area became visible to me in a matter of minutes and
was recognizable by the large chain-link fencing it had around
it and the large sign that read: YOU ARE IN A MINEFIELD DO
NOT WALK WHERE YOU HAVE NOT ALREADY BEEN. The
original test area had long since been converted into a training
area for the Men in Black to certify new members. Looking at
the ground, I could pick out the three-prong fuses of AP mines
protruding from the dirt. Ryan assured me there were no
mines left in that location, but even so, I thought through my
options carefully before I entered the gated section. Eventually, I
decided to trust him and made my way inside the cordoned area.
I winced with each step wondering if it would be my last. After
about five minutes, I let my guard down considerably. If I hadn't
been blown up yet, I probably wouldn't be.

Walking around the fenced-off quarter, I was struck by the
image of the "Dapper Captain" being lured there by Gunny
Gaultier. I couldn't comprehend what must have gone through
Haggar's mind in the moments before he died. I looked around,
absorbing all the details I could because I wanted to see the world
the way Haggar saw it before he left it. Then, I took my shovel
and began to dig; I had no idea where to look, so I just dug in
between the rows of mines. I assumed minefield maintenance
would have found the money long ago if it had been hidden
where the practice mines were actually buried.

After about an hour, I'd drenched my shirt with sweat and was
in dire need of water. The afternoon had been especially hot and
I hadn't thought to bring anything to drink. Looking up to the hot
sun and around me at the desert land, I wondered if I'd fallen off
the deep end in my quest to find answers. Greed also went through
my head. The money seemed attractive, even though I knew I'd
have to return it once found. Despite my many questions and my
dehydrated condition, I persisted with my search.

When the evening sun started to fall gradually from the sky, I realized I would need light to find my way home. Although it bothered me to give up, clearly, it was what I had to do. NCIS needed to be the hero, not me. I was simply one individual sucked into extraordinary circumstances, nothing more, nothing less. Understanding that, I picked up my shovel and started back out the gate. I was disappointed, but there was nothing else for me to do.

35

Holly Humphries was running along Sherman Avenue when I reached the bottom of Tarawa Road. She waved to me and I waved back.

"Hey, Holly, wait up a sec," I called out.

She stopped, but continued to jog in place. "Sure. What's up?"

"What's your schedule for tonight?"

She looked at me strangely. "Why?"

"Because..."

She stopped jogging and bent down to touch her toes. When she did, I could see straight down her shirt. The sweat on her chest trickled down across her breasts. There was no doubt in my mind she did what she did on purpose. "Spit it out already. I don't want my muscles to tighten."

"Well, you see, I was wondering if you had the time to help me out with something tonight."

Holly stopped jogging. Putting her hands on her hips, she smiled flirtatiously. "That's right. Audrey's off-island."

She thought I was coming on to her. "No. Well, yes. Audrey is gone, but that's not what I mean."

"Then just what do you mean because I really need to get back to my run."

I offered to jog alongside of her and explain the favor as we ran. I was lucky she wasn't only a mattress, but a military rebel as well. She agreed to locate the original *Book of the Dead* and let me look through it. Thankfully, she never asked why; unfortunately, everyone else in Gitmo did. Had I been thinking, I would never have run with her so publicly with my wife being gone. Within minutes, the island was buzzing with gossip about Hump-a-lot and the lonely Captain Claiborne. I hated that place sometimes.

In Gitmo, the truth just didn't matter. People thought what they wanted without ever getting both sides of the account. Conway was right; when someone didn't know the beginning or ending to a story, they just made it up to fit their mood. I often wondered how many people witnessed my wife going home with Donny Mancuso that night and how many of them thought she partook in their sexual escapades. For some reason, people often want to assume the worst in life, but in Gitmo, it seemed to be a hard, fast rule. When a couple argued, they were naturally headed for divorce court. When a married woman talked to someone other than her spouse at an occasion, she was obviously having an affair. When a family had a yard sale, they were broke. It didn't matter what the subject was; the outcome was always the most hurtful, destructive scenario imaginable and everyone bought into it—including Audrey and me.

They say idle hands do the devil's work. Well, in Gitmo, so did eager voices. The only way to survive there was to trust your own motives. You couldn't care what other people thought; you just had to believe in yourself and know that whatever you did had been done for the right reasons. This was an extremely important lesson to learn because—no matter where you are— believing in your self is a difficult task to master, yet the most decisive thing one can do in one's life. Frankly, self-confidence became the key to not falling apart in Gitmo.

The message light was blinking when I returned, and as I pressed the playback button, I hoped it would be Audrey.

"Hello Handsome, sorry I missed you, but I was on the other line when you called. It turns out that my dad plays golf with some real muckety-mucks at the State Department and they helped me find Lupe's son! He's been relocated to Costa Rica and I can't wait to tell her. Hope you're doing well without me. I sure miss you, and love you more. See you Tuesday. I can't wait."

I wanted to call her back, but I just didn't have the time. Holly and I were supposed to meet at 9pm at the side entrance of the hospital. Since I had to shower and get something to eat, I didn't have any time to waste.

After my shower, I put on cologne. Is that a crime? I had no interest in Holly's apparent hobby—semen collecting—but for some reason I felt the urge to look good for her. Even though I didn't think too much of her appearance when she first arrived, over time, she began to look really good—borderline hot. It's what we all referred to as the Gitmo Scale. Due to slim pickin's at the ole Gitmo buffet, people who looked unattractive back in the States looked a whole lot better once they arrived on-island. Having said that, the longer someone stayed in Gitmo, the hotter they got. You may argue that the limited amount of people forced all of us to discover inner beauty, blah, blah blah—but really—it was just the horny factor at work. Whenever someone wanted to get laid, he/she surveyed the room and chose the least-worst choice; that person invariably would have been called a Gitmo eight to ten. The bottom line is as long as a woman could hobble on her one good leg—and her dialysis machine had wheels—she could get a date in Gitmo.

"Didn't think you were coming," Holly said as she saw me drive up.

"Sorry, I had to shower," I explained as I shut my door and walked towards her.

"What, did you spend some extra time soaping up?" She asked seductively.

"Nothing like that, Holly." I kept my business face on.

"I bet," she said with a wink and a smile. "It's been at least three days, right? Poor guy."

I'd always read about people like Holly, usually in *Hustler* or *Playboy*. I'd never met a girl so forward in all my life. "I'll be fine. Do you know where to go?"

"Yeah," she said, walking towards the side door. "I did some recon a little earlier."

The Gitmo hospital was located on Caravella Point, sitting on a prime piece of real estate overlooking the bay. The white, two-level building was dedicated in September 1956, and had been adorned with a large red cross on the front, exterior wall. Its drive was circular and a soaring flagpole sat proudly in its center.

Holly and I entered the medical facility by walking up a white metal staircase on the outside of the building. It was the furthest door from the main road, barely lit. We arrived on the second floor in a wing being revamped. Due to the remodeling, it was totally deserted at that hour and we had complete privacy to do as we wished. Holly reminded me of that often, and I did my best to ignore her. Feeling confident we wouldn't be caught, we entered the temporary records room, turned on a small desk lamp and sorted through a lot of disorganized documentation. Stack after stack produced nothing worthwhile until I heard Holly whisper. When I looked up, I saw a large journal in her hands and a tremendous smile on her face.

"Oh Aaa-daaam, I think I've got what you wuh-unt."

"Great!" I called out quietly. "Let me see!" Just as I was about to grasp it, she pulled it back to her chest.

"What's it worth to you?"

"Give me the book Holly."

"I...asked...you...a question," she said, running her fingertips across my lips.

"Stop playing games and give it to me," I responded, pulling away.

"No."

"No? Why are you doing this?"

"Now you're the one playing games! You know exactly why I'm doing this. It's called foreplay." Holly jumped on top of a desk and crossed her legs. She seductively slid the book under her bottom and rubbed herself.

"You know what? You're a real piece of work," I said as I tried to keep my cool.

"I think that accurate terminology is a real-good piece of ass."

"I'll take your word for it. Now, can you please give me the book?"

Holly pursed her lips and then practically threw the book at me. "What are you gay or something?"

"Yup, that's right," I opened the book and began to study it without paying much more attention to Holly. "Gay, gay, gay."

"I can have any man I want on this island!" Insulted by my disinterest, Holly was growing angry. While she kept her voice low, she was getting louder. "Did you hear me? I can have any man I want on this island!"

"I believe that you can get most men here, but you can't get every man."

"You're an asshole, did you know that, Adam?" I ignored her. "Do you know how desirable I am? Did you know that I can make any man's fantasy come true?"

I looked right at her. "Now THAT I believe!" She mistook my comment as interest and moved closer to me.

Her voice became much more sweet and inviting. "Then... Adam...let me make yours come true." She took off her shirt, and stood in front of me wearing nothing but her exceedingly tight shorts and lacy pink bra. Her nipples were hard, her lips were wet and while I'm not proud to say it, my resistance weakened. I put my arms around her waist, pulled her against my body and kissed her. My heart was pounding and I felt short of breath; I knew my actions were inexcusable, but I couldn't stop. My kisses began at her lips, moved down her neck and about the time I'd reached her stomach, my conscience got the best of me. Just as I regained my sense of right and wrong, Holly pulled away from me. Confused, I stood up to meet her eyes and found her smiling smugly. "You see, Adam? Holly can have any man she wants—whenever she wants him. Good luck with the book—and the cold shower." She slipped her shirt back over her head and sauntered out of the room.

Words cannot describe how ashamed I was—how scared I was Audrey would find out. My palms began to sweat and I found it hard to concentrate on anything. All I could picture in my mind was the hurt on Audrey's face if she found out. Feeling completely uncomfortable in my own skin, I slammed the book on the desk where Holly had been posing and left. I walked briskly out of the hospital knowing two things for sure: Audrey had been right about the false entries in the journal, and about Holly. When I got home, I looked in the mirror and had no idea who the stranger was staring back at me.

Early Monday morning, General Whaley's own plane landed in Gitmo to take Lt. Colonel Ray and Colonel Ranagan to Quantico. In the meantime, Lois kept to herself and Major McCarran ran things at the White House. With both the CO and XO gone, the mice played and played and played. I think McCarran's first order of business was lobster hunting at 10am, with a fishing trip planned at two. Five o'clock was happy hour at Rick's, and then everyone was allowed to sleep late on Tuesday. McCarran made us take a time-out to pay our last respects to the Pickard dictatorship and welcome Captain Elgory as the new base CO.

It must have been very difficult for Lt Colonel Ray to leave the island knowing his wife wouldn't be there when he came back; if any two people were soul mates, it was the Rays. Having been officially ordered out of Gitmo for neglecting to write out her entire medical history during the screening process, Drew was forced to move in with her sister in Florida. Her flight was due to leave the day after Henry's, and she was emotional when she found out her husband couldn't see her off. You may be wondering why the XO didn't accept the transfer and move with his wife to another base, as he'd had the option to do. They talked about it and decided if he accepted new orders, they would be admitting defeat. Instead, they hoped Ranagan would be relieved of duty, with Ray being named CO by Whaley. As such, Ray believed he could bring Drew back to Gitmo to live out their original orders. Drew hugged everyone goodbye, cried a lot, and promised everyone that she'd be back as soon as she could.

Audrey and I didn't agree with their decision. While we loved the Rays and wanted them to stay, I'd never have let Audrey leave without me. Pride is one thing, but love is another and Audrey and I belonged together; I felt that more than ever after my encounter with Holly. And, after so many years of marriage, Drew and Henry Ray belonged together too. I'd never known such an awesome couple as the two of them; I only hoped that Audrey and I could be that close after so many years.

Before he left, Henry Ray asked me to check in with Drew before I went to work on Monday, and I did so happily. Although she had the other ladies for support, he wanted to make sure I'd do all the high-reaching and lifting as she packed up her things. As I walked towards her house, which was perpendicular to the Ranagan's, I saw several crates inside the colonel's garage and Lois rummaging through one of them. She must have seen me out of the corner of her eye—she never looked at me directly—

because she hastily threw a lid on top of the wooden box and called out to me.

"Well, good morning, Adam! It's wonderful to see you this morning!" She couldn't have been nicer as she stepped out of her garage to greet me.

"Good morning to you too, Mrs. Ranagan. Doing some spring cleaning?" I was, at best, cordial.

"You can say that. Even though we don't leave until the end of the summer, it's always a good idea to get organized early. I have so many patio cushions to pack. What brings you out to this end of the street?"

"The XO asked me to see if his wife needed me to lift any boxes or suitcases." I hated answering her questions.

"I see. How nice of you to help out!"

"It's actually no big deal. I'm just happy to do what I can."

"Adam, since you're here and in a worker-bee mood, could I get you to help me move something?" She was as cheerful as Mary Poppins on Prozac.

I stood there, wondering what would be the right answer. "Sure, just show me the way." I followed her into her garage, where I saw four more large crates. All of them had lids except the one she led me to.

"Could you please slide this over to the other side of the garage?" she said, pointing.

"Not a problem." As I pushed the empty crate, I stumbled and landed full force into the side of another one, but it didn't budge. "You must have some heavy-duty cushions in those wooden boxes."

"Indeed I do. Actually it's a lot of mixed junk that I've collected over the years, like these old family photos," she said, holding up a decorative frame. I glanced politely, but I was completely disinterested in anything she had to show me.

"Well, anything else I can do for you, Mrs. Ranagan?" Again, I was cordial.

"No, that will do. You have a splendid day Adam. Thanks again!"

I made my way to the Ray's wondering what Lois really had in those crates; only one thing came to mind—the tiles. They would've been that heavy and she'd have wanted to keep them hidden from me. I started to feel like Audrey. I couldn't care less about those stupid things, but knowing Lois wanted them made me want them too. So, I bypassed Drew's home, walked back to my house and peeked in the dumpster. Many of the tiles from our garage were still there. I jumped in and began tossing them out onto our back lawn like a crazy person; there were probably a hundred or so. She'd already snatched up Jackie's tiles, but our garage was the only other one being renovated. If Whaley was going to send Ranagan packing, Lois had already gotten her last one. When there was finally a large stack of them in our yard, I threw a tarp over it and went to work with a stupid grin across my face.

36

onday night was the toughest night of my life; I couldn't sleep a wink. Audrey was arriving the next morning and I had no idea if I'd be able to look her in the eyes after what I'd done with Holly. I tossed and turned, imaging every scenario and hating that I'd done something to complicate my already problematical Gitmo life. I thought about confessing and begging her forgiveness, but I worried she'd freak out and run over to Donny Mancuso's house for paybacks. In the end, I decided to just play things by ear and occupy my mind by planning how I'd get even with Holly.

My intention was to ride in the ferry cockpit with Lam during my trip to Leeward, but that didn't happen. Just as I was about to climb the ladder up top, I saw Holly sitting all alone at the other end of the ferry, crying. With one foot on the ladder rung, I stopped myself and made my way over to her. Curiosity and anger consumed me, and before I knew it, I'd given into it. When she saw me, she tried to hide, but there was really no way she could. Pretending to read, she buried her face in a magazine and quickly wiped her face.

"So what's a slut like you doing on a nice ferry like this?" I had no idea I was going to be so callous. I just opened my mouth and that fell right out.

"Go fuck yourself, Adam. I don't need this today."

"Yeah, I know the feeling." She and I were keeping our voices down, considering where we were. For some peculiar reason, her sad eyes softened me and I began to feel sorry for her. "So, what's wrong?"

"Like you give a shit."

"To be totally honest, no I really don't. But I'm the only show in town right now."

"Just leave me alone."

"I will when you tell me what's wrong," I said with a hint of feeling. I hated her. I really, honest to goodness, hated her, but she looked at me with the most heartbreaking expression and I couldn't turn her away.

"It's a long story," she said softly.

Just as soon as she said that, the ferry stopped in the middle of the bay. From what I could discern, the deck hands were having difficulty securing the car ramp and an announcement was made notifying us of a delay. "Well, Holly, I guess today is your lucky day. I'm all ears."

"I'm on my way to a funeral," was how she began. About a year ago, after the tragic loss of her husband and son in an auto accident, Holly was at the end of her rope and decided to end her life. Being an emotional wreck, she made her way to the pharmacy at the naval hospital in Rota, Spain and snatched whatever drugs she could find. As she went to leave, an enlisted corpsman stopped her. He walked over to her, opened her closed fist, and took the drugs from her hand. Holly was paralyzed with fear because she knew he could report her. Instead, he put her hand in his, and took her out the back door to his car. "I think what you really need is a friend," Brian told her kindly.

From that day on, the corpsman—who was married—cared for Holly and treated her with complete respect. He included her in his family life and never once laid a hand on her. Brian's gentleness and compassion augmented her self-esteem and made her feel worthy of love and excited about life again. She was an officer and he was enlisted, but that didn't matter. He was her family, and the only one she knew.

When Holly developed stronger feelings toward her married friend, she asked for orders elsewhere. Arriving in Gitmo, she felt alone and afraid without him, but was determined to show him that his friendship had made a difference. Brian urged her to respect herself and to find a man who would treat her well. However, within the first twenty-four hours, Chet Dingle came into her life. At first, Chet was charming, disarming, and caring. He paid her numerous compliments and seemed to respect her, but, by the end of the first week, he began to spread rumors about her and date other women. Every time she tried to break it off with Chet, he'd come back after her and shower her with attention—he'd show her a love like Brian's. Nevertheless, inside a week or two, Chet would become Chet again and inevitably damage her delicate self-esteem. The pattern of emotional abuse led Holly to be insecure, which is why she fought back any way she could. Holly hated her reputation, but being desired by men was the only way she felt loved.

She must have apologized a dozen times for what she did to me at the hospital. Holly told me that the way I loved Audrey reminded her of the way Brian loved his wife, and she'd become destructively jealous. I told her I understood.

Soon after Holly left Spain, Brian was diagnosed with cancer and had passed away earlier that week. She was on her way to his funeral. It was clear that she'd lost the only real friend she'd ever known, and had to say goodbye to him way too soon
. "He saved my life, ya know. If he hadn't shown me such a beautiful friendship, I wouldn't be here today—I just know it."

I put my arm around her and this time, I didn't care who saw. That was one of those times when I had to believe in my own motives and not give a damn what everyone else was thinking. I felt badly for Holly and I was worried about her too, but she told me not to be. It was true she was sad, but she was determined to stay strong because she knew that's what Brian would expect of her.

When the ferry finally docked at Leeward, I hugged Holly goodbye and decided to walk the mile to the terminal building. Believe it or not, my talk with Holly became a turning point in my life. Starting in kindergarten, "don't judge a book by its cover" had always been drilled into my head, but I don't think I understood that phrase until my talk with Holly. There was so much depth to her; there was a real person behind the mask. By the time I'd reached the airport, I'd made a decided to not be so judgmental, but to take the time to get to know someone before I drew any conclusions.

Before I knew it, Audrey's plane had landed and I could see her walking across the tarmac towards the ID checkpoint. I hiked briskly over to the fence and I called to her; she waved enthusiastically. Ten minutes later, she stepped inside the terminal and back into my arms.

We rode the bus back down to the Ferry Landing and I could see Lam standing on the bridge. I asked Audrey if she'd like to have a tour and she climbed the ladder without hesitation.

"Howdy, Lam!" I called out as I approached the bridge. "This is my lovely wife Audrey."

"Nice to meet you. I'm Lam the ferry man," he joked as he shook her hand. "Did you have a nice trip to the States?"

"I sure did. Of course I missed Adam, but I really needed the break."

"Understood," he said, distracted. Lam was trying to talk on the radio and speak to my wife simultaneously.

The view of Guantanamo Bay seemed even more beautiful that day, and we were thrilled by the sight of dolphins bounding in our wake. Lam let Audrey drive for a few minutes while he grabbed a few shots of the marvelous creatures as they leaped into the air. "Nope. You never grow tired of seeing that," Lam stated cheerily as he put his camera down on his chair. "They do that so much, I wonder if they ain't following me sometimes."

For the majority of the trip, Audrey stood in front of me with my arms wrapped tightly around her. Somewhere in the bay, I'd made the decision to take the day off and spend the entire afternoon with her. She liked that idea and suggested a dive. But as the ferry pulled up to the landing on Windward, Lam made a passing comment that changed our lives.

"Hey Adam, I've been thinking about something you said to me the other day."

"What's that?"

"Well, when I got here—going on ten years ago—the Ranagans were stationed here too. He was the OPS O, I think. You said something the other night that struck me funny and it made me think back a little." Lam stopped to gather his thoughts. "Didn't you tell me that there's some sort of hullabaloo with the Marine wives up there where you live?"

"Uh-huh."

"You also said that she's trying to steal some tiles or something—isn't that right?"

"Yeah, right out of the dumpsters."

"That's strange, because when I was checking into housing all those years ago, I heard this woman's voice speaking really mean-like with the housing director. It had been Lois."

"What was she so upset about?" Audrey inquired. "Do you remember?"

"Actually, I'd forgotten the whole event until Adam mentioned the tiles. If I remember correctly, she was demanding the garages be condemned. She told the housing lady that they were unsafe for her kids and demanded they be torn down."

"I don't think that's too strange. We've been told they've been in an awful state of repair for well over a decade," Audrey replied.

"Yup, that's true. But after she finished her hollering, she asked the lady if she could have all the tiles when they were torn down. That struck me funny because I didn't know what that woman would want with used garage tiles. It just seemed odd, I mean, she was ranting and raving like a spoiled-rotten child over old roof tiles."

Everything fit into place. I finally realized what it was we'd been looking for all these months. I took Audrey's hand, thanked Lam, and practically flew down the ladder. Audrey asked me to slow down, as I literally ran to our car—but I couldn't. Everything made sense and I wanted to share it with Audrey.

"Adam! What in the world has gotten into you?" my wife asked irritably.

"You won't believe this, but I think that I've figured everything out!"

"How? Because of what Lam said? Lois was a bitch then just like she is now."

"Exactly! She's a bitch and a bully and an over all mean person—just like her father."

"Her father? What are you talking about? You know her father?

"Yes, and so do you." I pulled into our driveway at an alarming speed and jammed it into park. I jumped out of the car and raced into the kitchen, where I took hold of the cookie jar.

"Have you lost your mind, Adam? Audrey stopped speaking

THE GHOSTS OF GUANTANAMO BAY

when I showed her the small, black and white photo I'd found in her DRMO desk. "Who's the child in the picture?"

"Lois Gaultier Ranagan."

"Oh my God—how do you know?"

"Yesterday I helped her move some boxes and she showed me this one family picture. I didn't realize it at the time, but her photograph matched the one I found in your desk."

"My desk? There wasn't any picture in my desk."

"Yes there was! It had been wedged way in the back. If I hadn't broken your drawer, I never would have seen it. Think about it, Audrey. We know your desk belonged to Gaultier and the pictures match. Lois is Gunny Gaultier's daughter. Shoot! Even their personalities are the same!"

"But what was it that Lam said that made you put it all together?"

"When he mentioned the tiles."

"I'm so lost."

"You won't be after I tell you what I know."

She and I sat down in the living room and I told her everything I thought, felt, discovered and believed. In turn, she added a few of her own ideas, interviewed Abuelita again, and together we answered every conceivable question.

In 1958, Roberto Mercado realized he'd eventually have to turn over his lucrative gambling empire to the impending Communist regime. At that time, it was nearly impossible to get money off-shore, and most people considered Castro's presidency transitory. Mercado fabricated a plan to hide his money on the American base at Guantanamo Bay. Not knowing who to trust, Mercado paid off some of Raul Castro's men during the hostage crisis and instructed them to find American military members who could be bought. Mercado had hoped for three or four contacts, but only one—Elliott Gaultier—agreed to play ball. As such, Mercado demanded that Miguel Herrera and his friend Chico, both of whom were indebted to him, participate in the scheme as well. After much deliberation, Miguel and Chico determined they could not possibly sneak money, or any obvious sign of wealth past the Marine Guards, so Mercado had no choice but to enlist the help of his sworn enemies: Enrique Garza and Jose Castagna.

Enrique Garza owned several factories and warehouses in the vicinity of Guantanamo Bay, one of which produced building materials. Jose Castagna was the underground boss of all the docking facilities along the bay and controlled the ferry system that brought workers and supplies to the base. Mercado realized if Garza could conceal the money, his men—Miguel, Chico, and Gaultier—could hide it on base and out of the clutches of Castro. When Castro was overthrown, Mercado's men could then use Castagna's shipping connections to sneak it back out of Gitmo. None of them anticipated that Gaultier had a mind and an arrangement of his own.

Gaultier agreed to work for Mercado, but, in reality, Gaultier had planned to make himself the beneficiary of the three men's wealth. Gaultier had been told the money would be arriving on Christmas Eve, two or three months before he was to leave Gitmo. Gaultier's idea was to kill Miguel and Chico, stay protected from Mercado on base, and ship the money out with his personal property, courtesy of the US Military. His household shipment would most likely never be checked, questioned or inspected. Gaultier never anticipated the shipment would be as gold coins embedded in thousands of clay roof tiles.

Mercado needed to conceal his money from Castro's soldiers as the cargo made its way to the base; he knew every shipment was searched upon arrival at the naval base. Garza came up with the idea of turning their money into gold coins, and hiding it in the roof tiles. The tiles were easy and inexpensive to produce, they could be made quickly, and their presence on the base wouldn't be questioned.

Knowing he'd never be able to take the coins as they were, Gaultier filled his car up with as many tiles as his trunk could hold and extracted the coins. The powdery clay residue from the broken tiles stained the carpeting in the trunk of his car, which is why it looked so much like blood, baffling the NCIS guys.

Daryl Loring died because the gunny got scared. At first Gaultier thought he might need help, which is why he befriended Loring just before Thanksgiving. We'll never know what role Loring actually played in the scheme, but it was clear Gaultier ultimately didn't need the young Marine and killed him.

After Gaultier had taken all the tiles his car could hold, he loaded the remaining tiles in the Sea Bees' supply warehouse, knowing the Sea Bees had no use for them at that time. Conveniently, the warehouse was located next to the practice minefield; it made disposing of the two Cubans rather easy. After he used the truck to relocate the tiles and move the bodies, he drove Miguel's truck back to the Magazine area, and off the cliff at Cuzco Wells. He knew it was a prohibited area and the least likely place to be discovered. At the same time, he buried Loring and faked his disappearance.

Gaultier, covered in the blood of the three men, feigned an injury and reported to formation late that morning. When he realized each car was inspected before it was shipped off island, he rendered his blood-soaked car disabled and stationed it in the junkyard. As the days went on, Gaultier must have tried to sneak into the warehouse to take more tiles, but got caught by the base police. He was arrested on breaking and entering and sent back to the States for his trial and subsequent incarceration.

In 1963 Hurricane Flora hit the island and Marine housing sustained considerable damage, forcing the Sea Bees to use the Mercado tiles in their repairs. The ones that contained the gold were identified by a small signature engraved in the dried clay. Lois knew all this because of her father.

Lupe "Abuelita" Herrera became Robert Mercado's mistress and gave birth to his son, who she named Miguel, in 1975. Mercado tried desperately for years to retrieve his fortune, but eventually stopped trying. He defected to America and left his son behind. While in Miami, he turned to drug smuggling. He hadn't anticipated Castro's staying power and ended up near penniless. Drugs were his only way back into the world of privilege.

In a birthday letter to his son, he told Miguel all about the money hidden on the American base, explaining it was rightfully his. Armed with that information, Miguel faked a defection later in life so he'd be sent to the migrant camp in Guantanamo Bay, and, once there, he'd try to obtain the concealed fortune. Unfortunately, he was relocated to Costa Rica soon after and never had the chance to find his father's gold.

"What about Captain Haggar? Why did Gaultier kill him?"

"He got in the way or he scared Gaultier by asking too many questions. I'm afraid we'll never have all the answers. Personally, I bet Gaultier didn't need a good reason to kill another man; he was probably used to doing it."

"When did you start piecing this together?"

"When I went diving with McCarran, I came across a broken tile. It was so encrusted with sea growth that it really didn't register. Then, when I came into the kitchen just now, I looked into the basket by the door." I stood up and went into the laundry room to grab the laundry bin. "You'd thrown some tiles in there when you got mad at Lois the other day, and all of them broke when you threw them. Some of the broken pieces resembled what I'd found off Cable Beach. That's when I felt sure."

Audrey reached into the basket and took hold of the largest tile. Along one of its edges, she could make out the curvature of one of the coins. "This is all so unbelievable. What do we do now? There must be a fortune in all those tiles."

I held out my hand and took the broken tile from Audrey. "Honestly, Audrey, I think there's only one thing we really can do."

37

Audrey and I contacted NCIS and told them what we'd discovered. After a short investigation, Lois' crated tiles were confiscated, along with all the others in the neighborhood. No charges were filed against Lois because the crimes had been committed by her father, who had long since died. She was only guilty of wanting the same tiles we all wanted; her reasons were different.

When they came to our house to take the remaining tiles from our dumpster, we told them Lois' workers had already toted our tiles away the week before; they bought into our story hook, line and sinker. I neglected to tell them I'd hidden a large quantity of them in my storage shed, and spent many hours busily extracting the coins. I figured what they didn't know wouldn't hurt them. In the meantime, Audrey's father's golfing buddies arranged to have Abuelita relocated with her son in Costa Rica. About a month after Abuelita arrived there, a check in the amount of $50,000 came to her anonymously in the mail. Audrey and I wouldn't have felt comfortable keeping the money; there had been too much blood attached to it. The only way we saw to make everything right again was to see Abuelita with her son, using the money to finally live.

Colonel Ranagan and Lt Colonel Ray came back to the island just two short days after being summoned to Quantico by General Whaley. According to Ray, Ranagan was found guilty of creating a poor command climate for his Marines and their families, and was severely reprimanded with both a permanent letter in his service jacket and a verbal lashing from the general. Ray told us that Ranagan's meeting with Whaley lasted two hours and he could hear Whaley's voice berating the colonel the whole time.

Ray was also reprimanded by the general for aiding in the dysfunction of the unit. Plainly said, Ray got in trouble for telling Drew everything Ranagan and Lois said. Whaley told the XO that while Ranagan had been unreasonable and unprofessional, none of the wives would've found out what had been said behind their backs if Ray had just kept his mouth shut. Still, Ranagan was relieved of command and reassigned to a desk job in Okinawa.

The women were pleased their voices were eventually heard by someone who could make a difference—and there was definitely a difference. When Ranagan came back from his meeting, he and his wife lived a very private life. We all lived and worked in the way we should've always been allowed to do.

On the day that the Ranagans left, the ladies all swore they'd stand in front of their homes and wave at Mrs. Ranagan just the way she'd demanded, but in the end, no one did anything out of the ordinary. To say that day was anti-climactic would be an understatement; it was just like any other day.

Major McCarran asked for orders out of Gitmo and when he left, I took his job. Regina, with the unrelenting support of Audrey, decided that fifteen years with Adulterer Dan had been more than enough and had the movers pack two sets of shipping crates. On the day that Regina had to leave Gitmo, she asked Audrey not to go to the Ferry Landing to say goodbye; she thought it would be too sad. Instead, they said goodbye in our driveway and cried just as hard anyway. Currently, she's thriving in a new job back in the States and is madly in love with a great guy.

Surprisingly, Father Blankenship received orders to leave Gitmo rather hastily about a month before the Ranagans; no one ever knew why or where he ended up. Audrey had serious trust issues with clergy members after that, and it took her several years to attend church again. When she finally did, she told her story to our new pastor and was stunned by his comment. He explained he, too, had been a chaplain and in his thirty year career, he'd come across many chaplains that didn't deserve to be one. One of his duties at the Pentagon, in fact, was to place the "really bad ones" out of the mainstream military. The pastor wasn't surprised two of them had found their way to Gitmo.

Chet Dingle left the island on the same day as McCarran and flew to Florida to pick up his new Harley, purchased at the behest of his good friend Aidan Foster. Aidan convinced Chet—who was a novice—that the two of them needed to be different than every other Marine by riding their new bikes to the gates of the Paris Island, their next duty station. This romantic notion played right into Chet's arrogance, so he bon voyaged with his buddy Aidan.

Aidan arrived solo in South Carolina a week later, telling a harrowing tale. According to Foster, he and Chet experienced severe weather during their journey through the back roads of Georgia and sought shelter in a seedy biker bar. In the darkness and commotion of the room, Aidan lost track of his buddy and was unable to locate his best friend when the bar closed for the night. He got on his Harley and raced to Paris Island, but Chet never arrived. Today his whereabouts are still unknown.

When I first heard that story, I recalled the night I had to pry Aidan off of Chet for the stunt he pulled with Kelly. I remembered the hateful, unforgiving stare Aidan had in his eyes. Could Aidan have been responsible for Chet's disappearance? Absolutely.

The Razors and Sergeant Major Ormond all left Gitmo soon after the Ranagans. The Commandant of the Marine Corps decided Cuba no longer posed a threat to the base and downsized the Barracks from 400 permanently stationed Marines to a rotating force of about 100 reservists. It was sad seeing so many Marine families leave the island all at once; I knew I was witnessing the end of an incredible era in our history. The hospital followed suit and downsized their own staff by sixty percent. For a while, the mass exodus of personnel made Gitmo feel like a ghost town and Audrey and I weren't sure if we should stay behind or leave with our friends.

In July of 1998, Lt Colonel Henry Ray became the Commanding Officer for the Marine Barracks in Guantanamo Bay, much to the Ranagan's chagrin. In the beginning, life was great and Ray was exactly the kind of leader the defense force needed. Unfortunately, his new position alone couldn't influence Drew's return to Gitmo. As time went on, he became a dispirited, lonely person. He'd come over to our house for dinner sometimes, or even spend hours talking to Audrey about his personal life, but nothing seemed to cheer him up. He and Drew had been so close, he wasn't the same man without her and we knew he'd begun to doubt his decision to let her leave alone. However, around Christmas of that year, he showed up to a Christmas party with a skip in his step and a gleam in his eye. We all assumed that he'd heard good news about Drew's return, but we were all wrong. When the Ranagans moved out of their house, the Navy quickly moved the new base XO into it—right next door to Lt Colonel Ray. Her name was Felicia Dahlquist and she was a divorced Navy Commander, disliked for various reasons by most of her naval colleagues. From the moment she saw the attractive Henry Ray, she made a decision to go after him, and did she. Old Henry didn't see it coming and once she got her claws in him, he didn't have a chance. She'd come to his office at the White House and sit on his desk with her uniform skirt hiked way up, laughing flirtatiously and bombarding him with endless compliments. Since every Marine adored Mrs. Ray, respect and admiration for our new CO quickly faded.

At first we all agreed he wasn't doing anything but enjoying the company of a fellow officer, until he began to work-out like a contestant for the Mr. Universe competition. That old guy ran every day, lifted weights, sunbathed and even had his teeth bleached! The trouble didn't start until the new base CO, Captain Elgory, signed an order to allow Drew back. Ray pretended to be happy, but none of us bought into it; the reality of his life hit him and he couldn't hide it. He'd fallen hard for Felicia and was thoroughly enjoying his affair. When Drew arrived, Ray snuck around to see Felicia, but he wasn't very good at it. He drove around in a banana-yellow pick-up truck that could be spotted for miles, and he ordered various Marines to "hide-out" on Friday nights because they were his alibi. None of them ever did. As the weeks passed, the guilt began to consume him and his lies to Drew spun out of control. He became irritable, unreasonable, and a downright bastard to work for.

Not understanding her husband's change, Drew would pick fights with the wives saying, "If only your husband's would do their damn jobs, my husband might not have to work so hard!"

The truth of the matter was that with the decrease in staffing by the Commandant, those of us who stayed in Gitmo were each doing the job of three men. I felt like I never saw Audrey and our heart went out to Drew. She was such a wonderful, classy lady who was being treated like a second class citizen by her own husband. Lt Colonel Ray became the base joke.

Ray could feel he was losing the respect of his men, but the only thing he did about it was act like a bigger ass. It was inevitable that he'd explode and it happened with me. It was 5pm on a Thursday when I picked up my leave papers; Audrey and I had seen so little of each other that we decided to take our cruise after all. As I went to walk out of the White House, the new XO of the Barracks—a squirrelly fellow, hand-picked by Ray who was lower ranked than me—handed me a paper I'd put on his desk two months earlier. I took a look at the paper and saw he'd written "Do Better" across the top—nothing more. As he walked away, he told me the CO wanted the paper re-written before I left on vacation—which was the following morning. I became incensed! The moment I picked up my leave papers, I was legally off-duty, but I've always been an over achiever, so I went back into my office to re-work the document. As I sat there rewriting, the XO stopped by on his way home for the night and gave me another task to complete; the blood in my veins began to simmer.

Sometime after midnight, Lt Colonel Ray walked into my office with the original re-do paper in his hand. He looked like he'd been on an adrenaline high: his eyes were a wild, his speech was quick and disconnected.

"Good Adam...this is very good work...but it still needs to be changed further," he said calmly and professionally. I sat there speechless. I'd been racing to try and complete assignment two before our flight at eight in the morning."

"Sir? I did the best I could, considering I received no feedback from the XO, and I'm barely going to get *this* thing finished," I said, pointing at my current project.

"I don't know what to tell you. This needs to get done before you go." Ray's voice was firmer.

"Sir, I understand and will do my best to get it finished."

"I don't need your best," he said with a patronizing tone, "I need it done."

"Sir, I'm doing the work of two men tonight, and I hesitate to promise you something I may not be able to deliver."

"Get it done. That's all I have to say." The colonel's voice was strong and authoritative. I no longer recognized him.

"Aye, aye, sir, I'll do my best, but in the event that it needs a little more work, who do you want me to turn it over to?"

"No you will not!" he shouted. His face turned bright red and the veins in his head were visible. "I'm sick and tired of everyone in this fucking place slacking off and leaving all the work to me! I'm the God damned colonel here and you will all do as I say!"

"That's bullshit, sir!" I shouted. He'd pushed my stress button and I couldn't hold back my anger anymore. I hated being the victim of his guilt-ridden feelings—we all did. "Every Marine here works his ass off for you!" I pointed at his face. "We work harder and longer for you than any of us has ever worked before! I did this paper two fucking months ago! Yet, here I am, on leave, after midnight busting my ass for you!" I stopped, fully realizing I'd just demonstrated total insubordination to my CO. "It's not my damn fault that your piece of shit XO didn't make the changes until today."

"Let me tell you this!" He got right into my face. "All of you have taken advantage of me and I'm sick and tired of it! This is the thanks I get for being a laid back, easy to get along with CO—I get shit on!"

I immediately thought about the letter he'd asked Audrey and me to write to the general that day. Was this my thanks for putting my career on the line for him? "Sir, the work stoppage is not with me! We're all doing the best we can! Go ask your fucking XO what his problem is!"

"You think you can shit on me?" He threw the paper at me. "Well, let me tell you this! You will finish all your work before you go on leave, or there won't be any leave at all! Am I clear?" He stormed out, shaking with anger. I stood there and should have been trembling, but I wasn't. Though my voice was hoarse and my face flushed, I felt strangely calm. Sitting back down in my chair, I put both assignments in front of me and worked on them until just an hour before my flight. Never in my life would I've ever thought that I could yell at a CO like that and get away with it. Somewhere inside, he must've known I'd considered him a friend and that I was the Marine he thought me to have been.

In turn, I understood his life was upside-down and that he was literally swimming in guilt and desperation. That didn't change the fact that Audrey and I—and the other Marine families—were again living with a CO and wife who were out of control. What was the lesson here? Watch out for what you wish for; you may just get it.

ONE OF THE MOST INTERESTING postscripts of the whole saga arose from a phone call I received a few months after the Ranagans left. Oliver Orcher phoned me from some island and I took a few minutes to fill him in on all the Gitmo excitement. He was pleased to hear what we had done with the money. He was also glad to know Daryl Loring would finally have some peace. Oliver made me promise to look for him or his boat whenever I passed by a marina, and I agreed.

"I'm sure you'll be easy to find," I said happily. "There aren't too many old houseboats named *The Lady John* out there!"

"*The Lady John?*" he paused for a moment then corrected me. "My boat is called *The* Ladies' *John.*"

My expression changed from significantly scrunched up in confusion, to the largest grin you've ever seen. Lam had told me the Gitmo bank had been robbed in the seventies, by a person who he believed wanted to prove something; he also told me that the robber broke into the bank through the ladies rest room. Oliver had been in Gitmo in the seventies and he often used the expression "they all thought I was Private Nobody". With a boat named after a women's toilet, what were the chances? When I inquired about the infamous crime, he chuckled and said, "Well, I don't know much, but if I'd done it, I'd have carried the money out of the bank in my sea bag, hid it in a bunker until the hullabaloo died down, and then taped it to my body when I flew off the island—but what do I know?"

The roll of duct tape and sea bag I'd found in the bunker suddenly made sense, as did Oliver's apprehensive disposition in Key West—the guy pulled a flare gun on me. It seemed strange to me then, but I guess all my questions must've aroused his suspicion. Perhaps he thought I'd been there to investigate the robbery—who knows? In the end, Oliver sailed off to casinos unknown, certain his secret was safe with me.

Epilogue

The second half of our tour was better without the Ranagans, but the turmoil surrounding the Rays made work-life almost as unpleasant. The ladies who had once vowed to stick together became like strangers. All the stress they'd endured eventually drove them apart, and, while they were civil to each other, their cohesiveness never returned. They all wanted their privacy and I can't say I blame them.

Dissention began when a few of the wives began to question their decision to write the letters, their self-doubt grating. The gatherings in the park became fewer and farther between, and, with the Marine families moving on, the housing director filled the homes with a wide variety of personalities and professions outside the Corps. But despite the fact that they'd all begun to drift apart, when those ladies had to say goodbye at the Ferry Landing, there was something in their eyes that I couldn't overlook. Even though it hadn't turned out exactly the way anyone had planned, they knew they had, together, made a difference in the quality of life for themselves, their families and for each other. I'm sure they've not forgotten what their teamwork accomplished.

AUDREY AND I LEFT GUANTANAMO BAY on July 4, 1999—Independence Day. Lt Colonel Ray asked if he could personally drive us down to the Ferry Landing and we agreed. He never told us why he took us that day, but I assumed it was his way of saying we'd meant something to him—without actually having to say it. When I shook his hand for the last time, I'd thought about our war of words that night. He'd been right in one respect; I'd considered him more of a friend than a CO because of everything we had gone through with the Ranagans. I've always felt guilty for not stepping in and letting him know he'd been making a clown of himself with Felicia. I think I owed him that as a friend, but as my CO, I had no place.

When the ferry horn sounded, Audrey and I waved vigorously at all the people who had come to say goodbye to us: Becca and Donny, Lydia Voorhees, the Gellars, the Elgorys and some wonderful new navy friends, the Dakota's. As I looked out at the crowd, I realized for all the bad we had endured, Gitmo had become rooted in us. We'd become apart of something totally unique—something we'd never again experience. We also left knowing Gitmo was in wonderful hands with Captain Elgory and his wife. They brought back the fireworks, the swimming pools and the fun in Guantanamo Bay. They were caring, light hearted, respectful of others, humorous and genuine.

As the ferry cruised through the cobalt waters, my thoughts drifted to our first trip across the bay two years earlier—when Mathew Conway told Audrey Gitmo had been the best and worst military tour of his life. As Windward faded in the distance, we finally knew what he meant. Audrey and I did more learning and growing there than in any other time in our adult lives.

I also thought about Oliver. I'd dismissed his notion about the ghosts of Guantanamo Bay, but now I understood. In the hearts and minds of those who once lived there—and to those who have left a ghost of themselves behind—it is, and will always be, the place we once called home.

Be sure to visit the author's website at:

WWW.KRJONES.NET

for instructions on getting an autographed
copy, and for information on upcoming
novels and events

About the Author

K.R. Jones was born and raised on Long Island, New York. Jones studied political science and international relations at Marymount College of Fordham University, including one year at Humboldt Universitat in East Berlin, and the Universidad de Salamanca, Spain. After graduation, Jones married and spent the next six years at various duty stations with the Marine Corps, before a final two-year tour of duty at U.S. Naval Base Guantanamo Bay, Cuba. K.R. Jones now lives and writes in rural northern Virginia.

Printed in the United States
88499LV00004B/91-198/A